EIGHT STRINGS

Margaret DeRosia

PUBLISHED BY SIMON & SCHUSTER
New York   London   Toronto   Sydney   New Delhi

SIMON &
SCHUSTER
CANADA

Simon & Schuster Canada
A Division of Simon & Schuster, Inc.
166 King Street East, Suite 300
Toronto, Ontario M5A 1J3

This Simon & Schuster Canada edition March 2023

SIMON & SCHUSTER CANADA and colophon are trademarks of Simon & Schuster, Inc.

For information about special discounts for bulk purchases, please contact Simon & Schuster Special Sales at 1-800-268-3216 or CustomerService@simonandschuster.ca.

Interior design by Wendy Blum

Manufactured in the United States of America

10 9 8 7 6 5 4 3 2 1

Library and Archives Canada Cataloguing in Publication

Title: Eight strings / Margaret DeRosia.
Names: DeRosia, Margaret, author.
Description: Simon & Schuster Canada edition.
Identifiers: Canadiana (print) 20210264284 | Canadiana (ebook) 20210264322 | ISBN 9781982174071 (softcover) | ISBN 9781982174088 (ebook)
Classification: LCC PS8607.E745 E48 2022 | DDC C813/.6—dc23

ISBN 978-1-9821-7407-1
ISBN 978-1-9821-7408-8 (ebook)

For Tracey

Let us look at the matter thus: may we not conceive each of us living beings to be a puppet of the Gods, either their plaything only, or created with a purpose—which of the two we cannot certainly know? But we do know that these affections in us are like cords and strings, which pull us different and opposite ways, and to opposite actions; and herein lies the difference between virtue and vice.

Plato, *Laws*

The one entertainment which never fails of drawing and delighting full houses is the theatre of the puppets or the Marionette, and thither I like best to go. The Marionette prevail with me, for I find in the performances of these puppets no new condition demanded of the spectator, but rather a frank admission of unreality that makes every shadow of verisimilitude delightful, and gives a marvellous relish to the immemorial effects and traditionary tricks of the stage.

William Dean Howells, *Venetian Life* (1866)

PLAN OF
VENICE

La Serennissima

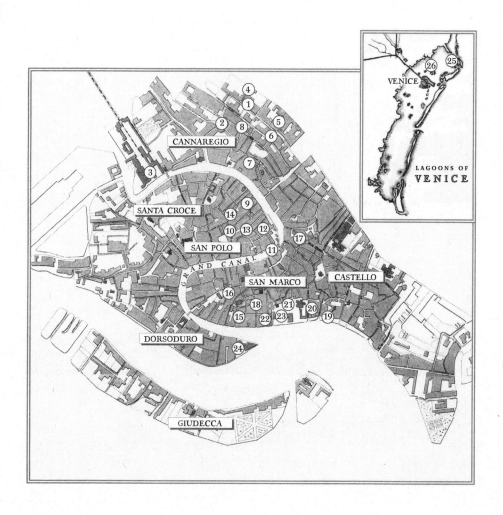

CANNAREGIO

SANTA CROCE

SAN POLO

GRAND CANAL

SAN MARCO

CASTELLO

DORSODURO

GIUDECCA

VENICE

LAGOONS OF
VENICE

EIGHT STRINGS

1

Venice, August 1895

I lifted up my newsboy cap, squinting at the stage door in the dark. It was much too early for anyone to arrive at the Minerva Theater, but I had no place left and no chance at sleep. I tried crouching against the wall, but my heart raced too fast to sit. So I paced and waited for dawn, sweating in the fog along narrow Calle Traghetto Vecchio, clutching my satchel in one hand and a knife in the other.

Indeed, no one did come for hours. It was midmorning when two men approached from the canal. Distracted by desultory talk of bad knees, they ignored me and stopped at the Minerva. One of them I recognized from the newspapers. The theater's director, Pietro Radillo.

All night my mind had spun with how I might plead my case. Now, I froze as the director unlocked the heavy iron door. My mouth went dry. Speech fled. Radillo pulled the door with some force, a bracing screech after hours of silence, and the men disappeared inside.

I had no choice. I couldn't go back home. So, summoning my courage, I strode over to the theater with more confidence than I felt.

At my knock, the man who'd accompanied Radillo peered out. Tawny and lean, he greeted me with only an arched eyebrow.

"I am here to see the director, Signor Radillo," I said, trying to kill the quaver in my voice. "To audition."

He shook his head no and started to close the door.

"Wait!" I protested, withdrawing my grandfather's letter from my jacket. "I have a recommendation from my teacher, famed in Verona. This is what I have trained for, to join the Minerva Theater of Marionettes as Signor Radillo's apprentice. Please."

After a moment, the man took it and tore the seal. I fidgeted as his owlish eyes darted across the page. Then, without a word, he left the door open for me to follow.

Soon we were winding through a labyrinth of dark smoky wings, the floor fresh with sawdust. The burnt smell of last night's gas lamps and limes hung in the clammy air as we traveled fast to a worn oak door at the back.

At the man's knock, a voice replied, "Come in."

We entered an office, where Radillo sat reading on a pale green divan. He glanced over his scuffed spectacles, first at me and then at the man who'd brought me in. "Who's this, Leo?"

"The boy wishes to audition," Leo replied. "He has a letter you might want to read."

Radillo took the letter. Up close, he was older than I expected but spry, in his late sixties, I guessed. His skin was tanned and lined like leather, but his blue eyes were clear and intent on the words my grandfather had hastily scrawled last night. Feigning that he was a famous but itinerant Veronese puppeteer and I his protégé, my grandfather had written that I was a diamond in the rough, primed to shine on Radillo's artistic fare. It wasn't true, but as I gripped my trembling hands behind my back, I hoped it was enough.

Radillo folded up the letter and tucked his spectacles in his pocket. "Well? Don't just stand there. Let's see what you can do."

"Here? Not onstage?" I asked. I'd envisioned a great height from which to drop a marionette down. To climb into the Minerva's rafters would also conceal me. In this cramped office, I felt too seen.

"I can gauge well enough from here whether your esteemed teacher inflates his claims." Radillo spoke with the derision of a man who knew the outcome long before a situation unfolded. "Besides, I need to see your hands on a holder and how you move. Leo"—he signaled to the other man—"fetch him something."

"No, thank you, sir. I have brought my own." I withdrew my grandfather's elfin Carlita from the satchel. Rapidly, I unwound the strings encircling her walnut holder's pegs, then I steadied her stance and held my breath to start.

When I lifted my left index finger and right thumb on the holder, Carlita's hand extended toward Radillo in greeting. He moved to grasp her hand, but I withdrew it, making her skip in a turn and pace with her back to him, uncertain but proud. He laughed and I tilted her head back to mimic him, too nervous to make eye contact with Radillo myself.

Next, I began to make Carlita dance, shuffling her feet as if debating whether to let Radillo see her face—and veering from his gaze at every turn. When Radillo cajoled her to come forward, I felt his interest deepening. So I stepped her into profile, angling her head in imitation of his curiosity. I lifted her modified eyebrow string and made her curtsey, an action more daring than deferential.

"No voice?" Radillo said. "How can I know this flirtatious girl if she does not speak?"

In response, I made Carlita swoon, hands near her chest. "Oh, but for one dance with my beloved Scaramuccia!" I cried in a false girlish voice and swept up her long black hair as if preening at a mirror. "I would sooner die than live without his eyes upon me. Why, look—here he comes!" I threw the last words to appear as if they came from farther back.

Before I could do more, Radillo stood up. "Have you ever worked a proper stage?" he asked me.

"No, sir." I nodded at the letter still in his hand. "My teacher handled marionettes and more at the Malibran just down the street." Part of that was true, I thought. My grandfather changed lights for the Malibran's shows.

"Ah, the 'People's Theater,'" Radillo said. "Modern-day gladiators, I suppose, given how often the censors shut them down. Not much puppetry there now, but it's where I had my start many years ago. How long were you training with him?"

"Since I was a child. He saw something in me."

"He saw well. Your voice, too. Odd, like it's neither you nor her." He glanced at Carlita and then scanned the letter. "What's your name again?"

"Franco Collegario." I bowed. "I wish to train with you, sir, as an apprentice here at the Minerva."

He drew closer. This time, I forced myself to meet his eyes. "How old are you?" he asked.

"Eighteen."

"Any family?"

"No—dead," I lied.

"Your accent," he said with hesitation. "Pure Cannaregio."

"That is where I grew up."

Radillo folded his arms. "An orphan foundling lands on my doorstep, straight from the Ghetto Nuovo. The city is teeming with your kind, desperate and poor. Why should I give you a chance?"

"I trained on eight-stringed marionettes alone. They are all I wish to perform. Whole and serious performances like yours, not cheap glove puppet stalls in the street or mere comic sideshows to actors. Most places still only use two-stringed marionettes. You're the master, the one who invented the art. Who *made* marionettes art." I lifted Carlita up to make the point. "That's what I want to do. I learn fast and am strong. I will work hard, sir—you'll see."

"You are bold to show up on my doorstep," he said. "But I like that. You read or write?"

"Both." The image of my grandfather, tracing the words of a book for me, flickered, but I banished it.

"Really?" Radillo leafed through the thick, yellowing tome he had been reading when I came in. It was Boccaccio's early Renaissance classic, *The Decameron*. He held it open in front of me and tapped the page. "Show me. Read.'"

"'Dear friends in the grove,'" I began. "'Behold how history marches forward to forget the past. Rarely can we see what truths have been buried by time.'"

Radillo snapped his fingers, halting my reading. He gestured to Leo. "Take him to Carmine. We're down a man these days, thanks to that ingrate Stefano running off. Auditions take too long, and we'll need help for the fall." Radillo turned back to me. "Don't even think about stealing. Leo, our stage manager here, will know. As an apprentice, you'll come to the theater every day but Monday. Watch the shows every night. Same spot, back of the pit. Good thing you're tall. You're not ready for our stage—not yet. For now, you will learn repertoire and technique from Carmine, one of our head men." He paused. "Of course, we'll see if you last the week, Franco. Being an apprentice is harder than you think. But take heart. There's no cleaning. We have women for that."

After the horrors of my night prior, I stood stunned. It had worked. I was in. I heard Leo clear his throat.

"Thank you, sir," I said. "Thank you."

I rushed to shake Radillo's hand, but Leo hustled me toward the door. Over my shoulder, I saw that the director was once more buried in his book. Leo led me back through the unlit theater. I struggled to keep up, the satchel clunking at my thigh as I stuffed Carlita back inside, entangling her strings.

"Café Titian's nearby," he called back. "Carmine's there."

I already knew the café. Yesterday morning, my grandfather and I had gone there for practice. We'd hovered at the curled tip of its mahogany bar. I'd watched men come and drink and go, tossing cigarettes into the gutter that beggars darted out for.

Yesterday, we'd thought I had plenty of time. Months, not hours, to prepare. We hadn't known what my father had done, or that the neighborhood mafioso, Tristano, was coming for me that very night. I remembered my grandfather at the café, how he'd drawn close.

It's working. No one looks twice. You're more yourself as a boy, not less. They think you're one of them, Francesca.

For yesterday, I was still a girl. Francesca. Not Franco. Not yet a boy or a man, never mind a puppeteer. Today, my aim was both more and less modest—to survive.

2

Leo and I approached the breezy, unshuttered Café Titian. Men stood enmeshed in loud debate out front but fell silent as we walked by, distrust lining their weathered brows. I knew these looks. Faces like those of my older brother, Marco, and my father, whom I'd fought my whole life. So I did what I knew best—I glared back.

The café, more of a *bacaro* with its wall of bottles, smelled of cigarettes, coffee, and hazelnut liqueur. Leo led me to the bar, where a man was weaving a complicated tale about a dancer to two other men. Tousled leonine curls framed the speaker's hazel eyes, which were lit up with laughter that faded at our arrival. Though only a few years older and not much taller than me, he gave the impression of a greater difference. Only reluctantly did he glance at Leo and then sip his coffee instead of acknowledging me.

"Carmine," Leo said to him. "This is Franco. Your new apprentice, straight from Cannaregio."

I extended my hand, but Carmine looked indignant. "He's Stefano's replacement?"

Leo laughed. "Look out, Carmine; this one's smart. Even reads."

"Wonderful—a schoolboy. Just what I need."

Leo clasped Carmine's shoulder. "You know what to do. Get him started. Send him to me this afternoon."

"Is he any good?" Carmine asked Leo, but Leo was already walking away.

As I faced the three men alone, every muscle in my body bristled until I heard the clink of a cup on the counter. The lone woman in the café had set a coffee down for me. Her thick wavy hair was the color of night, and her heavy-lidded eyes were dulled a sad gray from too many hours at the bar.

"Pay for his coffee," she said to Carmine, nodding at me.

"Michaela, I don't have any more money." Carmine leaned against the bar in a posture that might have seduced another, but she held out her hand, unmoved. When Carmine tried to kiss one of her fingers, she slapped him. Not to hurt, but to make a point. He dug into his pocket and asked me, "Any to spare, schoolboy?"

"Try your other pocket," Michaela said. "When you paid for Andrea and Niccolò?" She gestured to the two men beside him. "What was it for again? To celebrate fooling a girl into a date? Buy this boy's drink, too. He'll need it, working for you."

Defeated, Carmine placed a handful of coins onto the counter. She took them without a smile and disappeared into the back.

I caught the two other men stealing glances at me as Carmine dove back into his story. They looked to be related, maybe brothers. Both were ample in stature with mousy brown hair and shared the same dubious expression under knots of thick eyebrows.

I chanced a peek at my reflection in the mirror lining the back wall. Even I was briefly surprised. A smudged white collar upturned. Knotted red scarf to hide my throat. My brother Marco's worn linen newsboy dug low on my face. I looked down at my moth-nibbled herringbone trousers and Marco's scuffed boots, chafing at the heel. In imitation of Carmine, I leaned against the bar with my full if slight weight and drank my coffee, tasting hints of cinnamon in the pale foam of milk.

Then, without warning, Carmine sprang from the bar. "Might as well work," he said, and the two men beside him straightened as well. "We don't get paid to drink all day."

I gulped down the last of my coffee and followed the three men back to the theater. Once inside the stage door, Carmine motioned for me to wait. I dropped my satchel and hung back as they went on. Several long minutes passed before Carmine returned, holding out a mop and bucket for me. Foul water splashed over the edge.

"Your first job, schoolboy. An honor fitting your skills."

I glanced at the bucket but did not take it.

"Can't figure it out? It's not complicated. You clean the commode. Shouldn't be too hard for a smart boy like you."

"No." I looked straight at him. "Give me a real job."

"Ah, the apprentice who thinks he's too good for our shit!" He set the bucket and mop down.

"I'm here for the trade, not toilets."

Andrea and Niccolò resurfaced, carrying a sizable trunk overflowing with puppets in long black dresses, with faces frozen in macabre smiles for a diabolical scene. One of the men pointed at the bucket. "Good to see you're cleaning up, Carmine. Have another date tonight?"

Carmine ignored them, stepping closer to me. His warm breath hit the bridge of my nose. "You don't say no unless I tell you to."

"You have women for cleaning," I replied, standing my ground.

Carmine shoved me. Instinctively, I threw a punch. He stumbled back in surprise. I'd drawn blood. Then he went at me. Hard.

His fist to my stomach knocked the wind out of me. Marco had often gone for the stomach, though, so I knew some tricks. While bent over, I grabbed the bucket and cut the force of Carmine's second attempt. He swore and shook his hand in pain. That bought me time to throw the filthy water at him and land a hit to his jaw.

My victory didn't last long. Carmine bounced back, his punch sending me to the wet floor. The impact stung the whole side of my face, but I scrambled upright, only to receive another blow close to my eye. Once more, I fell. When Carmine went to kick me, I grabbed his foot and yanked him down. I spotted the discarded mop and crawled toward it. I was on my feet when someone strong hauled me back.

Leo had me. Other men held Carmine. I tasted blood and spat. When I wiped my mouth, I noticed my right palm was bleeding. My nails had jutted into my hand so hard that I'd cut myself. Across from me, Carmine was in similar shape.

The men let go of us, then Carmine began to laugh. Though the pain in my ribs and face was intense, I went to lunge again, but Leo restrained me anew.

"Easy," Leo said, amused.

Then I saw. Laughter meant our fight was over. Loathing had tipped into respect, even if neither of us had exactly won.

"Let's go see Radillo," Leo said, motioning Carmine over. "You two won't work."

"Wait," I said. I didn't want to prove Radillo right before I'd even started. I held out my bleeding hand to Carmine. "Teach me. No toilets."

I tried not to gasp when Carmine shook my hand. "Come on," he said. "You're a mess."

When the others saw Carmine and me hobble off, the day resumed. Perhaps fights were normal. Maybe this world was more like my old home after all.

As Carmine and I rounded a corner by the stage, some movement in the shadows halted us both. "Radillo." Carmine sighed, looking up at the rafters. "I'll be in for it later. Don't worry. He'll blame me, not you."

"That's not fair."

"Fair doesn't matter to him. Money does. Especially these days. Though you must be good."

"Why?"

Carmine held the door open to a room of sinks. "Because he wanted you to work with me."

"Radillo said you're one of the head men. What does that mean?" I asked.

"I'm the lead. Lucky for you, too, as I'm better than Andrea and Niccolò put together. They're the other head men—brothers. We all work the stage with Radillo."

"Any other apprentices?"

"Not anymore. The last one, Stefano, took off last week. Fed up or seeking greener pastures—who knows? Don't mention him around Radillo." Carmine tossed me a cloth. "Now? You're it."

We washed our scrapes. I kept my head down while Carmine tended his swollen jaw.

"Schoolboy," he said, "I haven't had a real fight in ages. Thanks. Though I won't be seeing any girls tonight." He dunked his head under the icy stream of water and the spray hit my face. "You have a girl?"

I shook my head and continued scrubbing. The dingy room had faulty taps. Droplets hit the warped wood floor.

"Why not?" Carmine asked. "Is it boys for you?"

"No!" I bent low to hide my blush.

"Didn't think so. Not staring at Michaela's tits like you were."

I straightened. "She had sad eyes. I noticed those."

"Sure you did," Carmine replied. "Schoolboy, here's your first real lesson. Focus on the trade. Go to the shows. Follow my lead, and I promise—no toilets."

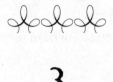

3

Later that afternoon, Leo brought me to a faded canary-colored apartment building a short stroll from the theater on Campiello Barozzi. While he arranged things with the landlord, I bought chestnut fritters from a sullen street vendor by the San Moisè church. I had not eaten in over a day. Only as I wolfed the fritters down did I realize how hungry I was.

Leo waved me to the entrance and passed me an ornate key. "Your new home. The attic. Carmine will fetch you before tonight's show." He frowned and dug in his breast pocket to give me a few coins. "Get more *castagnasso*. You look hungry."

After Leo left, I trudged up three steep, narrow flights. A sour scent of vinegar lingered in the humid alcove. Shabby paint peeled off well-worn banisters, grubby from heat and hands. When I found my room, it was bare, not much larger than my balcony back in Cannaregio, but at least it was all mine.

Only here, alone, could I breathe. I unhinged the shutters, welcoming in the myriad sounds from the crowded San Moisè canal below. Its gondola pitch kept the small square lively with locals haggling for cheaper fares. The stench of filleted anchovies wafted up, ripe from a fishmonger's boat docked in the sun. Few gondoliers sang along this canal. Instead, I heard carcasses of meat being unloaded. Greetings rife with opinions. A baby's throaty wail.

The bed was barely long enough to stretch out on, but I collapsed on it, staring up at the rippling reflections of water flitting across the ceiling. If this morning was any indication, as an apprentice I would not speak much. Hours of work yawned ahead, a new rhythm to my days. My former life and self, gone.

Or was I gone? Already, I could feel something more complex than impersonation stirring. I had always leaned toward being a boy. Too lanky, flat-chested, and strong to seem feminine. Steady eyes dark as coal, like my hair. A mouth I'd learned the hard way to keep shut. Quick to fight and, now that I was older, win.

All my life, my father and Marco had taken a singular view—that I was only a girl, and not even a good one at that. Too much like my mother, Sofia, an actress at the Malibran who'd run off when I was an infant.

I had no memories of her, but she haunted me. My father occasionally relived her betrayal when drunk, an insult compounded by having lost Marco's mother eight years prior in childbirth. Only my grandfather painted a kinder picture of his daughter and her gifts for the stage. He blamed my father for her running away, but I knew I was the real reason. What kind of career could she have had with an infant in the wings?

Perhaps I really was like her. Now I'd run, too.

So far, during my whirlwind morning at the theater, my grandfather had been right. No one looked twice. My new chest binding, padding, hair, and clothes made me fit the part. Yet clothes were no protection. Anyone could reveal me just by removing my shirt—and if they did, I would be attacked or killed. Fantastical plays never told the story I was now living. English Shakespearean comedies may have featured characters who cross-dressed, but they always returned to who they were. As if it were all comedy, merely queer.

For now, though, I was alive. I had scaled the first wall, all because my grandfather had taught me how to divine Carlita's threadlike strings.

Marco had never expressed interest, scoffing at puppets like they were dolls for girls. Only I was drawn to them. At first, it was glove puppets, when I was too small for the dense holder's weight. Then with Carlita, my grandfather had shown me foundations, how to move but not entangle her in ballet or complicated battles.

Feel the marionette as if it were your own body, he would often say in his scratchy wheeze. Too many hours too close to varnish had left him with a persistent cough, spells lengthening in duration as he aged. He'd dangle Carlita over our balcony near Campo Sant'Alvise in Cannaregio, our only audience a small throng of children and the passing black cats. They didn't care that we rarely told a story and rehearsed the same repetitive motions. I could feel their fascination with Carlita. To them she was both real and not, a figure who resembled the girls they knew.

The girl Annella from across the street had been most interested. Before we became friends, she would watch my grandfather and me practice. I'd see her curled at the iron rail of her balcony, level with mine, oblivious to the blazing sun. Her laugh first made me grasp what mystery threaded performers to their audience. In time, she invited me over and we'd play together. Her home was my only reprieve. Until it all ended.

Last night rushed back like a slap. My grandfather shaking me awake.

"You must go to the Minerva, Francesca. Tonight."

Half asleep, I'd sat up slowly, my eyes still closed. I thought he was joking. We had only visited the Titian that morning. The strange idea was months from becoming real, if ever.

"I overheard your father in the kitchen before he went out. He has arranged for you to marry. Sold you, really."

Marriage. What I feared most. I knew my father eventually would scout prospects, but I'd thought I had time. "Who am I being sold to?"

"Daniele Ceresa."

My eyes flew open. Daniele, the dissolute son of Gasparo Ceresa, owner of a glass bead factory in Cannaregio, with ties to massive sulfur-refining plants in the south and headquarters in England. Daniele had a temper, which his arrogance and stupidity did not aid. Recently, he'd been packed off to London after an incident—fighting with a worker who ended up dead.

"He can't sell me," I said. "I won't go."

"Your father knows that. That's why Tristano's coming at midnight to drag you to London. If Tristano gets you there, they both get paid. Your father owes him a great deal." My grandfather hesitated. "You know Tristano's methods of persuasion . . ."

My grandfather handed me his traveling satchel, too polite to say more. Rumors of our neighborhood mafioso's sexual violence were legion. Every mother clutched her daughter's hand tight when Tristano passed.

I rose fast and began to pace. The truth of my predicament—and my father's betrayal—sunk in. By day, my father worked a comfortable, undemanding position handed to him by his father, who had profited from the corrupt Santa Lucia railway station and buildup of the Adriatic Network to Milan. Marco was always at his side, rewarded for his loyalty. Yet by night, my father gambled away his fortune, more often drunk than sober since his father's death. That's when Tristano started showing up, happy to offer funds and bury my father deeper in debt—which only made matters worse at home.

My father was not above hitting me when drunk. Yet I never imagined he would hand me over to two brutal men, one for a husband and another to force himself on me on the long journey to London.

I cursed my naïveté. Hadn't I been taught daily that I didn't matter?

Now, just of age, I had become useful, economical. By marrying me off, my father could get rid of me and pay off Tristano. Two birds, one stone.

My grandfather came close. "There's still time. I'll help you." He pulled out a knife and lifted a section of my long hair, trembling. "Cut it off. I cannot bear to."

The compassion and terror in his eyes jolted me to act. I braided my hair in one long, tight trail and took the knife. Gripping the braid close to my scalp, I pulled the blade straight through the top. After, I felt the evening breeze too cool on my neck.

My grandfather retrieved the crumpled chest binding and padding from the afternoon and gave them to me. "Change into some of Marco's work clothes. He's out with your father, but they will come back at midnight, too. Inside the satchel are some of my old shirts and Marco's coat. Theaters get drafty in winter." He lit a lamp. "Radillo will train you if he sees a boy. I'll write and say I'm your teacher, someone he's heard of but could not know."

I ran into Marco's room and burrowed into his armoire, snagging a clean work vest, morning jacket, and two pairs of trousers, as well as his discarded muddy boots. I stole his favorite black bowler, just for spite. In the dark, I tore off my nightdress, scratchy lace I'd always loathed, trembling as I struggled to wind the chest binding tight around my breasts.

When I returned in my new attire, my grandfather looked up from his pen and paper. "Good," he said. "I knew it. Go to the Ghetto Nuovo tonight. Foundlings sleep in the square. Tristano won't look for you there among the Jews and boys." He finished scrawling his hasty lies, then thrust a purse at me. "Wear it where no thief will go." He pointed to the hook inside the front of my trousers. "It's not much. Your grandmother's wedding ring and my wedding cuff links are inside, which you can sell if desperate."

Either the chest binding or fear was making it hard to breathe.

I stared at the lone photograph of my mother that my grandfather now held out for me to take. Her dark, serious eyes urged me on. She'd loved the theater more than me. What would she think if she saw me now?

I'd never know. She died two years after she ran, a terse telegram our only notice. Staring at her face, I wondered: Would I even live that long?

My grandfather shoved the photograph in my satchel, as if sensing my fears. "You have her blood, and mine, in you. Generations of performers, actors, artists, and, yes, puppeteers, too. Hang on to that when you stand before Radillo. You belong up there. Sofia would never have allowed Sandro's cruelty were she still with us." He looked as if he wanted to say more but turned away, gently placing Carlita in the satchel. "Use her to audition. You know her holder well."

It was nearly eleven thirty, but I couldn't move. The sight of my grandfather's face blurred. That's how I knew I was crying.

He pulled me into an embrace. "You can do this, Francesca. More boy than girl your whole life. Always a struggle, fixing you in a dress." He tucked a curl of my hair in the cap. "Remember, people see what they want, so show no fear. Watch the men around you. Fight with all your strength if you must, but concentrate on the trade. You read and write—that will raise you up. From now on, you are Franco Collegario, my mother's maiden name, and thus unfamiliar in this region."

"Don't stay here." I slung the bag over my shoulder. "My father might harm you."

"He won't dare, not with the neighborhood watching. It's you I've worried about. You're why I stayed all these years. If only I could have protected you more . . ." Sadness lined his brow. "Listen, my dear, don't ever come back. Don't even write."

"Come with me," I said, grasping his hand.

"Francesca, if I went with you, he'd find me, and then you. Imagine what he'd do if he saw you as a boy?" Then he passed me the knife

I'd used to cut my hair. "Keep this close. No one can know you're a girl. They will kill you if they know. Go to the theater. If Radillo or anyone else asks, say your whole family is dead."

Dead. I had managed to say it today. Yet it felt like betrayal. The ink in that letter, still fresh from my grandfather's hand.

Overnight, I had become a foundling, an orphan from the ghetto, one of many scattered throughout the city. No family, friends, or, apart from this springless bed, home.

I didn't care, I told myself. When I saved money, I would go back. I couldn't leave my grandfather with that monster.

But for now, I curled in on my bruised ribs and buried my aching face in the flat, musty feather pillow. It didn't matter that here in this attic I was alone and safe. Inside, I felt like a wild animal, wounded and desperate to hide.

4

An impatient knock rattled me awake. The light had waned. I must have drifted off to sleep. As I scrambled to the unlocked door, Carmine sauntered in.

"Enjoying a nap?" he asked.

"No," I said, smoothing my hair, still so short and strange to me. "Just thinking."

"That won't get you far. Wits serve you better." He noted my bruised face with a frown. "Can't you fix that? It looks like shit."

"Like yours is any better," I said, venturing a smile.

"Yes, but I'm up in the rafters where it's dark. The poor audience must see you."

I rifled through my satchel to pull out Marco's wider-rimmed bowler. "Better?"

"Perfect," he said, pulling it lower over my forehead. "Now I can't see your face at all."

We headed downstairs, passing the mustachioed concierge who propped his balding head on one gloved fist. As Carmine and I left, a portly gondolier ambled in, and we heard a burst of derisive laughter hit our backs.

"Don't mind Sebastian, and don't lose your key, or he'll hate you more," Carmine said, as I hurried to keep up. "On Tuesdays, we get our pay, such as it is. Buy your own food with that. Most of us just go to the Titian for *cicchetti*, or nearby taverns for a date." He eyed me. "Remind me to give you some shirts. They might fit."

"Thanks," I said, adjusting my vest to cover a jagged streak of blood.

An iron sign creaked in the wind above us, and a passing cart over-flowing with garbage spread stench in its wake. Before us, a crowd pulsed in the thoroughfare, a sea of movement, languages, and dialects, with eyes of every shape and color, from alert to elated to fatigued.

"Welcome to your new neighborhood," Carmine said. "San Marco, before curtain. A far cry from Cannaregio, I imagine!"

We plunged into the fray, no room for a wide berth as we snaked among the people who walked with purpose, many heading to the various theaters we passed. A deafening procession of minor-key bells rang out from the nearby great campanile of San Marco. It echoed off brick roofs and stone streets before diminishing. After, voices that had strained to be heard retreated into the tenor of everyday speech.

Our walk to the Minerva was brief, but its crush of people was more than a full day's worth in Cannaregio, a mere half-hour boat ride away. There, time was measured by the clink of a blacksmith's iron or the blue flame of a glassblower's forge, not theater curtains.

Soon enough we reached the Minerva's iron stage door. Inside, I found a backstage full of bodies, including those of puppets, which mingled in the clamor of preshow preparations. The torches for the limelights had all been tested and emitted a fresh scorched scent. Behind the curtain, the set pieces were unfurled for a last-minute touch-up.

Advancing through the maze, smelling the hot gaslights, hearing the discordant cacophony of men volleying demands and musicians practicing difficult bars—it all washed over me like a tonic. Finally,

I was backstage on the cusp of showtime, in a world I had heard so much about but never experienced. I was roused by the thrumming anticipation, wholly distinct from anything I'd felt being in an audience.

Carmine located Leo by the curtained partition next to the stage. "I'll head up now, schoolboy. Leo will show you the lobbies and your spot. No velvet box for you, but you're not dressed for it anyway—enjoy!" He tugged my bowler down a notch and hustled off.

Leo led me through the still-empty theater, until we burst into a display of opulent light. Elegant gentlemen and ladies milled in this small chandelier-laden lobby. Women redolent of perfumed oils fanned themselves. Men drank *aperitivi*. An accordionist played modern popular songs for the indifferent, chattering crowd. Thick cigar smoke hung in the air, despite the lazy lap of ceiling fans above. No one glanced our way, too busy preening for each other. One man stepped on my foot and made no apology.

"This lobby is for the boxes only," Leo said, gliding through it like a dancer. "Don't come in here."

We headed down to the main floor, passing through a purple curtain into a more boisterous space where the scent of Moretti and smoke lingered.

"Come here at intermission if you're hungry or need a drink," Leo told me, before pausing to greet an old friend.

All around me, men downed beer and women sipped water flavored with anise. No fans rotated and the laughter rang louder and coarser, obscenities braided in. Scratchy work trousers revealed hems dingy from mud-splattered boots. Discarded wooden sticks from candied nuts and fruits littered the wooden floor's slats. Peanut and chestnut shells crunched in loud, uneven snaps underfoot as we waded through the crowd.

These were the people I stood with on my one previous sojourn to the Minerva years ago, with my friend Annella on her twelfth birthday. Both she and I had been as enchanted by the faces and voices around us as by the tale of Charlemagne's knights. We were mesmerized by the puppeteers' serene control over every feature, gesture, and mood, whether one or ten characters graced the scene. Each marionette housed a personality all its own, layers of emotion woven by Radillo's techniques in thrilling battles. It was one of my happiest memories.

Her parents must have received dubious looks, though I was too caught up in the drama onstage to notice. Children, and especially girls, never attended Radillo's shows. His fare was strictly adult melodramas and historicals with plenty of ribald commentary. Yet Annella's mother, a Southern Italian Jew in a city not always welcoming to her, knew how to ignore disapproval, and Annella's father knew better than to pick fights with these quicksilver toughs.

Shortly after that trip, however, Annella and her parents disappeared from the neighborhood. Overnight, they were gone. Not even a rumor drifted back. At first, I had been wounded. No goodbye or letter, though I knew Annella could write. Then I feared the worst. My grandfather told me they probably fled south to avoid being caught in the city's wave of influenza. Her father was a teacher in the Ghetto Nuovo, where the outbreak raged at its worst. Their total silence after they disappeared suggested that none of them had survived.

I grieved my beloved friend and, in time, watched a sprawling new family move into her old house. My father befriended them, but I refused. I sensed that to set foot in Annella's old home would betray her.

"Come on," Leo said, cutting through my reverie. The first warning lights were flickering in the lobby as he guided me into the theater, to the far right back, already dense with spectators standing in uneven rows. Above, audiences were also filtering into the three tiers of boxes with tarnished copper Greek scenes that framed the elongated stage. While mine was an obstructed view that even second-class patrons would have balked at, I only felt invigorated to start.

"Excited?" Leo asked. "Here's a lesson for you. The rich step into those boxes for only a few hours. Then it's back to their money. Never forget that we're the people they kick to the gutter everywhere else." He swept an arm wide. "Barkeeps, drunks, shoeblacks, fruit sellers, water carriers, even foundlings like you—here's your real audience, the pit. They'll tell you if you're any good. If they talk at your characters someday, you're doing something right. Make that happen and forget the rest."

Momentarily stunned by Leo's advice, I asked, "Why are you telling me this?"

He hesitated. "Radillo doesn't always understand the pit, despite his start at the Malibran. But from this morning, I think you do." He eyed the top of the curtain. "You want to climb up? Then listen to the people in here. After the show, come to Radillo's office. He'll want to hear what you think. Don't lie. He'll know." Leo straightened his tie. "And if you tell Radillo anything that I just said, I'll make sure you're out the door faster than you came in."

5

The accompanists, a chamber quintet, began tuning a collective A note. Interior gaslights dimmed as stragglers settled. I spotted a beautiful girl around my age scurry into one of the boxes above me and take her seat. Two matronly women lagged after her, but neither resembled the girl they accompanied. While she inched forward in anticipation, they appeared to steel themselves for a night of suffering.

Around me, a volley of whispers among the flower sellers, all in their distinctive dresses, baskets of bouquets at their feet.

"Is that his daughter?"

"The one who just came out in society? Why, see how fine she is!"

"She's in Signor Radillo's box. That's his daughter, Giannina."

I tried to get a better look, but the last houselights fell, ceasing all spectacle beyond the quintet's huddle up front. The violinist steadied his bow near his instrument's taut bridge. Behind and above the bloodred curtain stood puppeteers we could not see, their breath likely already filling the marionettes' strings dropped in place.

The curtain parted on a single shaft of light. Two lovers rested on a park bench, midembrace. Their chests heaved in an almost imperceptible lilt, like the pulsing of nerves. It would be a modern story tonight, I thought, no ancient folktale revived from the past.

See where life starts, my grandfather always said. So I looked up near the curtain's rim. One string near the top hovered in a slight diagonal, off-center, an arresting subtlety.

Then all lights cut. A cry of pain flew overhead, a disembodied shriek. It was Radillo's own voice, thrown. I grew embarrassed by my morning's clumsy attempt.

The violin settled into a plaintive minor-key solo. Bobbing lanterns in the wings cast shadows. The entire audience leaned closer as a policeman emerged onstage, his uniform and posture rigid. He stopped at the empty bench. The female puppet of the pair had stood up and was swaying over her now-prone lover, the thread at the top of her head slack with defeat. As the lights broadened, we saw that her snow-white dress now bore two stark slashes of red ribbon—blood. Her shoulders sloped in grief, and she clutched a knife, which glinted in the spotlight. Her lover's holder lay along the floor, evoking his death.

Morbid silence ensued, more menacing than the scream. When the policeman at last bellowed, "Guilty," the whole audience recoiled.

"No," she cried, and lifted her head unsteadily. "Not my love." The knife fell, clattering. She bent over the body with a shudder of despair.

I peered closer. It appeared as if her expression had changed, but that was impossible. A puppet's painted face cannot change without strings, and I could see her face had none like my Carlita's one eyebrow string. This marionette's face was set in thick, sloping painted lines. Only a change in other strings could give that effect.

More lights flooded the park scene. The sound of heavy footsteps backstage built to suggest an encroaching mob. The audience was alert, commenting on scenes or dipping into smuggled flasks. Only two lovers in the back remained oblivious to all but their own furtive acts. I caught sight of Radillo's daughter, silhouetted in the box above, still as a deer.

Then, a miniature carriage trundled onstage, its gilt of gold eliciting impromptu applause and sardonic remarks. "That murderer is my sister Ophelia," came a shrill falsetto in haughty Italian, not dialect, onstage. "Arrest her."

The speaker then emerged from the carriage, her gold-flecked dress shimmering, and Ophelia gave a mirthless laugh.

"Carmela, you are my blood, but not my sister, after what you did." Ophelia gestured to her lover's body. "You shame our family and will be punished, if only from beyond the grave."

Now the aristocratic Carmela shuddered, but her gesture was riven with disdain. The same physical action as Ophelia's was so distinct in mood that I wanted to watch them side by side. I caught one element of the trick, a simultaneous arch of Carmela's shoulder that raised her chin.

"You speak of blood?" Carmela said. "Look at your own dress. Shame on you."

"I have nothing to be ashamed of. Unlike you," Ophelia replied.

Carmela turned her back on her sister to confer with the police—a sign to the pit that Ophelia was more honorable. As the curtain fell for a change of scene and the quintet struck up a march, the crowd around me jeered at Carmela: "Guilty, to be sure!"

AFTERWARD, I WAITED OUT the applause to wend my way backstage, but Carmine found me first. "We should go," he said, but didn't move. I followed his gaze to Radillo's box.

"Is that Radillo's daughter?" I asked.

"It must be," Carmine said. "She's sitting in the box for his special guests. How did you know?"

I glanced over my shoulder at the departing flower sellers. "I had a little help."

"Giannina. Radillo mentioned she was out in society now, but I've never seen her before."

Up in the box, Giannina was looking down at the pit. I could have sworn she was watching us, but one of her chaperones pinched her arm, impatient to exit, which they did.

Carmine laughed nervously. "Lucky for her, she resembles neither parent. I presume one of those is her mother, to keep her from the likes of you and me."

"Before it started, she was the only one of her consort who seemed excited."

"Radillo's wife never visits—it's true. Apparently, she prefers opera. She comes from wealth. I bet she thinks he's frittering away their daughter's fortune on the Minerva."

Carmine led me backstage, where two lighting technicians were dismantling backdrop cloths, snuffing out lamps, and dampening scorched filters and limes. Wearing thick canvas gloves, they placed the lights on plated shelving that stored what appeared, to me, to be nearly one hundred filters for the electric bulbs. Each shade gave the illusion of night or day, rain or shine, summer's deep greens or winter's drab grays.

Outside Radillo's office, Carmine gave a delicate tap and Leo welcomed us into the gathering. I saw Radillo pouring a brandy, his brow damp from exertion.

"My new apprentice," Radillo said. "Enjoy the show?"

"Very much, sir," I replied. "So did the audience."

"All of them?"

"All but two in the back row. One man favored his companion more."

Radillo laughed. "Did anything capture that man's attention? Onstage, I mean?"

"Carmela's execution at the end."

He eyed me. "You look like you'd enjoy a good violent demise. What captured you?"

There was a right and a wrong answer—I could feel it. So I gambled on honesty. "I liked how, in the opening, you made first Ophelia and then Carmela shudder. No sound. Barely a difference but for you lifting more sharply in the second, perhaps? The same action changed according to the woman. I want to learn that. How to make one gesture express two distinct moods."

As I spoke, Radillo's expression turned melancholic. He addressed Carmine. "You should see the excellent coquette Franco brought. Flirts better than a real woman." Then he plucked my bowler in a swift grab, noting my bruises. "How was his first day?"

Carmine removed his own cap, revealing a mirror image of my scraped face. "Fine," he answered. "Just don't ask him to clean toilets."

"I'll bear that in mind," Radillo said, and tossed my bowler back. "Don't be so quick to brawl, Franco. The Minerva needs artists, not brutes. If you can bend with the winds as they blow, you won't snap in a storm—or learn everything the hard way. In this business, compromise is key to survival."

Flustered, I nodded. Radillo motioned to Carmine, and Leo jutted his chin in the direction of the door. I left the three of them to talk, knowing I'd just been put in my place.

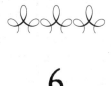

6

Long after my grandfather stopped puppeteering and working lights behind the Malibran's stage, his muscles stayed taut. I'd sit with him on his balcony, and despite his age, he had no trouble remaining agile with a heavy holder for hours. Now I saw why. This work built muscle. It took real strength to hold both yourself and marionettes with skill and ease.

Over those first months, the men of the Minerva never escaped my attention. Nor did my terror of them abate. Fear of discovery coursed through me like blood, day and night. It shaped everything I did and said—or, more often, avoided. I lived each day as if another battle would erupt, but no one tried to fight me after Carmine. Rumors that I was a dangerous foundling fleeing a violent past swirled.

They weren't entirely wrong, and because I said nothing, the stories took on a veneer of truth. So slowly, the Minerva became my true home, far more than my stifling attic or the house in Cannaregio I'd left behind. Ironically, by working in a theater and dressing as a young man, I was hiding in plain sight.

It was a quick sprint south from my pension every morning, down San Marco's sleepy streets to the theater's broad forest green door. The Minerva faced Corte del Teatro San Moisè, a street that marked the theater's former namesake for prior centuries. Before it became the Minerva, Teatro San Moisè had been a popular elite destination, and Italian greats such as Rossini and Vivaldi once graced its petite but illustrious stage. After Giacomo De Col refurbished the theater for marionettes in 1871, Radillo took it over—and made the art form popular shortly before I was born.

On the Minerva's stage, marionettes committed treachery, loved passionately, sought revenge, and mocked the shameless rich. Their mute faces on wooden bodies were no hindrance for Radillo and his head men, who knew how to cast the sense of a smile and speech. Audiences would turn in their worn velvet boxes from a voice thrown close. The men transmuted mood with nothing more than the dip of a left instep or tremble in the line.

For they were always men, and only men, above, holding the strings.

Offstage, I learned that to be a nondescript boy was no simple feat. As the sole apprentice, I mimicked these men as they ate, drank, ran, sweat, laughed, shoved, and yelled. As a girl, I had always been told to keep my back straight, eyes down, and voice soft—or better yet, silent. Now I too strode and slouched or shouted and complained. I recovered an ease of moving unknown since childhood as I elbowed through the Minerva's hectic passages and San Marco's clamorous streets. My chest binding even enabled me to evade the rough sting of the hemp sacks and splintered wood I carried. Because I managed more than the other men, they teased me as being more masculine.

Every day I studied how men moved. Andrea's and Niccolò's loping, bowlegged stride when handling trunks. Carmine's seductive lean toward an autograph seeker when flirting. The light technicians, Bruno and Vincenzo, and their brusque speed in polishing a filter or wiping a bowl of gnocchi clean. But Radillo's confident hands on a holder captivated me most, even if, in the weeks that followed my arrival, he barely spoke to me.

Nearly everyone else did, especially Carmine, who showed me Radillo's techniques. I delivered props and scripts to Andrea and Niccolò, while the taciturn stage manager, Leo, who managed the books and more, kept me running. Even our itinerant accompanists seemed to need me, whether it was for more resin on their violin bows, a clip for their music sheets, or a top-up on pints at intermission.

Radillo had not lied. Shows often ran six days a week, and the daily slog of chores grew backbreaking. Cleaning toilets might have been easier.

Every day started with me helping Bruno and Vincenzo dust the modern electric light filters and check all the brass and translucent reflector filters and old-fashioned limelights lining the wings. They showed me tricks of light and shadow, depending on the source. At times, the lights struck me as a more utilitarian version of Murano glass, filters that could evoke motion on static backdrops, such as the gentle waves of the turquoise Ligurian Sea or tousled olive branches lining golden Tuscan hills. Though much of the theater had converted to electricity, we still employed limes for certain moods, as they were warmer and made the marionettes seem more human—something I began to grasp from the pit. Yet the blast of flame that created limes was tricky, and more than once Bruno needed to dip into the buckets of water that I carried, sloshing from the sinks.

I was also charged with organizing, storing, and repairing all the backdrops—massive sheaths of painted and embroidered set pieces that were housed in the molding, rat-infested basement. Here I learned not to twitch at every tail scuttling over my boots. To reduce my journeys downstairs, I secured an unused dressing room near the stage to keep each week's set pieces and marionettes in rotation.

Above all, I took care of the theater's collection of marionettes. Before every show, I tested each puppet, unknotting their strings, steadying their holders, and positioning them for the head men and Radillo in the rafters, so that they were ready for every performance.

If any puppets were damaged—and nearly every day they were—I would take them to the seamstress a few doors down. Of course, having grown up as a girl and having been expected to do my brother's and father's mending, I already knew how to sew. But I couldn't let Radillo and the other men know. It would've been suspect. Why would a boy from the streets know that skill?

The seamstress was a heavy drinker, so I learned never to arrive before noon. Neither speed nor accuracy was her forte, only rambling conversation, which I had no time for but endured to maintain the lie.

After late September's *villeggiatura*, in which the wealthy decamped from Venice's cloying heat, Radillo reduced our performance schedule to start rehearsing Boccaccio's classic, which I had read from at my audition. *The Decameron* was set to premiere in late October, a first for Venice's stages, marionette or otherwise.

At the initial rehearsal, Carmine took a trunk that I was carrying onstage. "Allow me," he said. "I can't have you turning into a bigger man than me."

"Scared I'll beat you up again?" I asked.

"All the time," he replied. "Keeps me awake at night."

I rifled through the trunk. "Is this it? There must be more marionettes in the basement if we're doing one hundred stories."

"Please, the Minerva could never afford something that grand. We'll just do excerpts, and maybe use some of Radillo's old marionettes. Some have just two strings thicker than rope."

At the base of the trunk, I pulled out a thick manuscript. "Here's the script." I started leafing through it. "Is this production grander than others?"

"Hard to say. Radillo has started courting the rich more as of late. Money is tight."

I had noticed Radillo poring over the books with Leo but didn't mention that now, as Radillo was approaching with Andrea and Niccolò.

Onstage, Radillo sifted through the trunk and distributed marionettes to the head men, then he snapped his fingers at me. "Franco,
glad you found the script. Do the opening for us. Let's see how you
fare as a prompter."

I cleared my throat, but after three words, Radillo halted me with
a frantic wave. "No! Speak to the very back row, not like some timid
beggar in the street. You did better on your first day."

Embarrassed, I began again. "'In this amphitheater,'" I read, "'no
subject is forbidden. Love, both bitter and sweet. Adventures from
centuries past. Dancers and tricksters, wars and journeys. Our ten
brave storytellers did not know whether they had a future left when
they started spinning these tales, given the deadly plague that had
struck down their world.'"

"That's better." Radillo pointed to the script in my hands. "We
have one hundred tales of human error, wish, greed, love, and lust.
Where might we start, given that we can't do them all?"

"Lust?" Carmine suggested.

"Human error," Andrea said to Carmine. "That's more your
style."

"Neither," Radillo said, intervening. "Our first story concerns
greed. A corrupt priest travels to Burgundy. He falls fatally ill at the
home of two brothers. The brothers, anxious that this priest might
die in their home and shame them, get a naïve friar to deliver last
rites. Even on his deathbed, this priest lies, offering protestations of
false piety. The naïve friar believes it all and glorifies him as 'Saint
Ciappelletto' after his death."

Niccolò held a pair of marionettes—two wan, narrow-faced
brothers—joined by one holder. "These seem more petite than our
usual friends."

"They are. Marionettes from the actual era, smaller and lighter
but modified by my own hand for this production. Remember,
these stories remain modern in spirit. Today, we do not suffer from

a plague. But so much disappears from Venice every day—canals paved, theaters demolished, bridges collapsed, burials at sea. That massive railway groans, bringing tourists and releasing thick smoke, even as more locals emigrate to America and never come back." Radillo drew a mottled newspaper out of his back pocket. "People disappear. *Il Gazzettino* reports two foundlings' bodies were located near the palazzo of the opera composer Wagner. No suspects, no motive, no kin. Frankly, no one would have cared, were it not for the famous site where their bodies surfaced."

"Like that man found dead near Ponte delle Tette," Andrea said. "Didn't see that in the papers. Probably a *culattone* propositioned the wrong man."

Andrea was always ready to pounce on a story concerning sex. Yet I thought I should start reading the papers at Café Titian for news of Cannaregio, even if anything concerning my family or Tristano likely would not end up in print.

"My point," Radillo said, redirecting, "is that in *The Decameron*, people tell stories to fight off fear. For death is always howling at the door, whether we tell stories or not."

"Looks like I might have our wicked priest," Andrea said, unwinding his marionette's strings loose at the oak. "How does the script introduce him, Franco?"

I leafed to the start. "Cepparello," I said, "a true 'miracle' of heavenly compassion. A man who gave false testimony at court for any price throughout his life."

Andrea made his portly, red-cheeked marionette appear to admire his own lavish purple and gold robes in an imaginary mirror.

"Behold, our naïve friar," Carmine said. His marionette's eyes were painted heavenward in prayer, delicate hands with an attached rosary, an extension carved into his right hand. Without flourish, Carmine dropped his friar into a devout kneel, arms upraised in ecstasy. I wished he would do it again, so immediately did the marionette transform.

34

"That's the naturalistic movement I want," Radillo said. "Not static types but real people from the street. In the standard story, Cepparello gets away with his deception." Radillo looked at me. "Franco, you're in the pit every night. How would they feel about that ending?"

"They would never stand for that," I said. "A villain must always be punished."

"Correct. We'll right that wrong when we change the ending." He walked by me and patted my shoulder. "Good work. Come to all our rehearsals. Keep an eye on the scripts. Notate changes as we go along, so we have a record."

I swelled with pride and watched as Andrea and Carmine began practicing their opening exchange, their heavy holders seemingly as light and pliable as fabric. I filed away techniques I could rehearse later, while I delivered their dialogue cues from the script.

I was grateful to have gained a voice at the theater, but that night when the four men headed to the cheap nearby *bacaro*, the Britannia, to drink, I wasn't invited. I understood I was still on the bottom rung of the hierarchy. They formed a tight quartet, a world above me. Instead, I headed back to my cramped accommodations alone. Sometimes I opened the trunk where I stowed what wages I could in the hopes of one day collecting my grandfather. There, nestled under my brother's coat, was Carlita. I gently unwound her strings, hearing my grandfather's voice.

Here is the key. Never think what you maneuver below is all you. The ones who think they're more important than what they hold? They'll never get the audience in hand.

I lifted the scratched holder, imitating Carmine's friar falling to his knees in prayer. When I let Carlita lead me, I saw the same gesture transform from devout prayer to devilish defiance.

Don't fear the other person you dance into life. Spirits travel down this horsehair, apart from your will alone. Only be their guide, nothing more.

What spirits lay trapped in Carlita's flaxen, spindly lines? I could sense them aching to be set free at my touch, like voices muffled behind a curtain. Strangely, my grandfather never cared about mundane concerns like a puppeteer's sex, or that girls never apprenticed. For him, there were worlds to unlock, hands to alight, and mysteries to respect—and I had the gift for transmutation.

7

After *The Decameron*'s premiere, I was in my usual spot at the back of the pit when a petite brunette up in the boxes near me caught my attention. Something in her manner, as she bent in whispers to her friend, a lithe blonde, seemed familiar. The brunette's hair was pinned back in a profusion of curls, but the veiled brim of her straw hat shaded her face from my view.

The finery of their dress suggested a station far above mine, and behind them stood two burly, disgruntled men. Together, they formed an odd group, the men more like sepulchral undertakers than theater aficionados.

Then I overheard the blonde say, "Arturo will do whatever you ask. Let's ditch the guards, Annella."

I peered closer. Annella was an unusual name, not heard in the north. It couldn't be my old friend, for this Annella seemed too shrewd, arch, and rich. Not the playful girl I once knew, too shy to leave her parents' side.

Still, it had been five years since she disappeared, so I found myself edging toward the pair of friends as they exited the box. I slipped into the boxes' lobby behind them, weaving through the crowd to follow the train of this Annella's pale rose dress.

Her friend had called the men guards. That fit. The heft of their shoulders and ponderous steps were daunting enough that other audience members parted without a word.

Once out front, the foursome paused at the base of the theater steps. I stayed back, leaning beside the door as if I were an usher having a smoke.

"Arturo," I heard the girl, Annella, say to one of the men, "leave us. Come to the dock at the end of Calle Ridotto at midnight. Signora Cappello won't mind."

If the guard had an opinion about this order, he did not share it. Instead, he dropped a curt nod and both men lumbered toward the water.

"You get whatever you want these days," noted her friend. "Not even Constanza says no to you."

"It's the least she can do after that wretched holiday in Piedmont. I was bored to tears without you, Rossana."

This Annella glanced at the theater, and I saw her face clearly for the first time. My breath caught. It was my old friend—I was sure of it now. Same olive skin, same set of her jaw and full, if now painted, lips. I couldn't look away, thrilled to see her again.

Rossana lit a cigarette. "Next time, ask Constanza if I can come with you. Wouldn't you rather drink wine under parasols with me on the beach? Your predecessor didn't travel nearly as much, I hear."

"Lucky me." Annella sniffed. "It's only to places with boring pastoral scenes."

"Places without theater, you mean? Would you climb up and man those marionettes yourself? I would think you had enough of vaudeville halls, dancing for drunks reaching under your skirts."

"Even if I wanted to, Pietro Radillo would never let a woman up, no matter how ridiculous their falsettos sound." Annella's expression clouded. "As a girl, I had a friend who practiced with a marionette of her grandfather's, a beautiful one with dark hair and saucy eyes. They would dangle her right over their balcony."

That dispelled any last doubts. But still, I could not reconcile the girl I once knew with this sophisticated young woman. What had happened in the last five years? How had she reemerged so transformed? I sensed a thread of sadness under her imperious airs, which made me wonder who her benefactor was. Had I been a girl in a dress, I would have rushed over. Now? I didn't dare.

"Don't worry," Annella was saying. "With Constanza, I've made sure you and I will never fend off rats in a rooming house again."

"Plenty of rats in Venice. At least we make money off them. Your greatest trial, it seems, is boredom." Rossana traced one side of Annella's décolletage, a chain of roses lining a stiff collar. "What a change since July. This new weight suits you."

Annella gave a brief twirl. "Look at those poor tourists," she said, pointing at a group exiting the theater. "So buried in their golden Baedekers that they don't see anything at all."

Then she caught me looking at her and bounded over. "Excuse me," she called, stopping me before I could retreat. Annella had always been shorter than me. Now, she peered up at my face under the cap's rim. "I've seen you before. Are you an usher?"

"An apprentice," I mumbled, pretending to study my feet.

Then I felt something small brush between us. Instinctively, I seized the arm of a boy. "What are you doing?" I shouted at him, feeling for my purse. Intact.

"Nothing," said the boy, fighting my grip.

"You have your purse?" I asked Annella. Her eyes dipped down the front of her shirtwaist and she nodded. A familiar locket encircled her neck, the same one, I recalled, that her mother had never been without.

"I didn't steal!" the boy protested. "But have you any food, sir? Even spoilt scraps?"

I noted his distended belly and dropped a few coins in his hand, then gently shoved him along. "Try La Fenice. Deeper pockets there."

"That was generous," Annella said. Our eyes met, and hers were exactly as I remembered them. That rare deep green. Beautiful without any trace of kohl. I shoved my hands in my suit jacket to hide my nerves.

"What's your name?" she asked.

"Franco," I said.

"I'm Annella. That's Rossana." She pointed to her friend, who offered me a flick of her cigarette's ash. Then Annella smiled. "So, Franco the apprentice, might you give me a tour of the Minerva?"

"Now?" I asked, and we both flushed.

"No. During the day sometime? I'd love to see the marionettes up close."

"Perhaps, but I must go now." I tipped my hat and turned. "Good night."

"I'll return!" she called after me, but I didn't look back. I just ran inside, bumping headlong into Carmine.

"Slow down, schoolboy," Carmine said, as he noticed Annella lingering outside. "Busy flirting? That's a first."

"No," I replied, too flustered to say more, full of dread from the encounter.

"Nice choice, but a little ambitious."

"Wait." I stopped. "What are you doing out here?"

Now it was Carmine's turn to blush. "Hoping to see someone," he replied, scanning the room before shrugging in defeat. "Guess we're both empty-handed tonight."

We started backstage, and I dove into striking the set. I hadn't expected to see anyone I knew at the Minerva, and certainly not Annella. She did not recognize me, but any joy I felt at seeing her alive was tempered by the memory of my grandfather's frantic parting words.

No one can know you're a girl. They will kill you if they know.

40

8

The Decameron turned into a great success, and more shows, excerpts, and hasty rehearsals were added to our schedule as we sped from late October through the busy Christmas season. Every night, I looked for Annella in the boxes, but to my relief, she didn't show up again. As the weeks went by, I focused on the money I was saving for my grandfather, to spur me past fatigue.

I was up in the rafters depositing three repaired paladins one chilly December afternoon when I heard a woman talking onstage below.

"Signor Radillo, my companion speaks highly of your theater," I heard the lady say in measured, moneyed Italian. "I thought I should come see it for myself."

I peered down to see Radillo greet the woman with a chaste kiss on her cheek. "You are most welcome, Signora Cappello. Anytime."

"I believe we have a mutual acquaintance in Count De Rossi?"

"Yes, he has sponsored the theater in the past."

"He tells me your productions entertain Venice's finest families, including our esteemed mayor, Lord Grimani." She gestured to the boxes, then gazed into the pit. "I hear the place is always teeming from front to back with character."

"A bit too much character," Radillo replied. "That's why I seek to better its fare. The Minerva was once home to Vivaldi and Rossini, Albinoni and Monteverdi. It even premiered Goldoni's opera buffa sensation *Il mondo della luna*. The Minerva was the jewel of our city's theaters before La Fenice emerged. The future I have in mind now requires those who appreciate its unique and glorious past."

I crept down the ladder for a better view. The woman was robust in stature, slightly younger than Radillo, and she donned a sharp-cornered bow tie tight at her throat. Her violet waistcoat and skirt were quasi-masculine in cut with silver embroidered threads that echoed her graying blonde hair, whorled tight into a chignon under a man's Borsalino.

Without warning, she looked straight at me. "Perhaps that boy could give my companion the tour she's been pestering me about?"

Embarrassed, I burrowed into the filters. Radillo murmured apologies, and then I heard him summon someone in the pit. A few moments later, the curtain parted near me. Annella stepped into the wings. Upon seeing me, she smiled warmly.

I bowed, averting my face.

"Don't lag, Franco," Radillo said. "Bring her out. Let her see the marionettes' view."

I gestured for Annella to go first, and we joined the woman and Radillo onstage.

"Franco is a recent addition to our troupe," Radillo was saying. "Our sole apprentice."

I bowed again, but Annella's benefactor ignored me, attuned only to her charge.

"Why, look at this view!" Annella said. "You can feel its history underfoot."

"Sawdust, more likely, to soften the patter of wood," Radillo replied.

"Signor Radillo," the woman started, "tell me more of the Minerva's past. My enterprises are expanding, and I am keen to know more of Venetian theater, if you are so inclined?"

"Wonderful!" Radillo said. "Our new spring production of commedia dell'arte will delight you. I'll make sure you receive tickets and join me in my box. With more support, Signora Cappello, I could restore the Minerva as one of Venice's grandest theaters."

"Let's not stand on ceremony. Call me Constanza." She linked her arm in his, then addressed Annella. "Take a tour with the boy while Signor Radillo and I talk."

Radillo guided Signora Cappello offstage, leaving Annella and me alone in the quiet, empty theater. While I had been able to mumble out of my last encounter, there was no chance of that now.

"How small the stage is," Annella said. "Yet the rafters reach high. The top curtain conceals their great height when you're in the audience."

"A smaller stage and great height make the marionettes appear more lifelike to the audience," I replied. "The rafters need to be tall for group scenes, like ballets and battles."

She craned her neck up. "It looks too cramped for men to move at all."

"The hard part is not entangling, or so I'm told." I inched away. "I do not perform myself."

"Really? But you must wish . . ." She trailed off when I looked at the floor. Then she added, "I used to dance in venues not far from here myself." As if to demonstrate, she pointed a toe, revealing polished chocolate brown boots.

"You dance?" I remembered how she'd twirled around her bedroom as a girl in Cannaregio.

"Vaudeville preshows only. Once even the French cancan, but with clothes on, of course. We aren't that modern in Italy, compared to France. I stopped when Constanza hired me as her companion in July."

So Annella had become a stage dancer and was now a paid companion to a wealthy woman. My childhood friend seemed another woman entirely, but her fascination with the theater remained.

"What a hot, burnt smell hangs in the air," she said, strolling about the stage. "Limes always scorch when they shine, but I see you have modern electric ones, too."

I pointed to the filters. "One hundred shades for twice that many moods."

"How I sweltered under the limes every night," she said, but now only watched me.

"Come this way," I said, gesturing for her to head offstage.

I shifted toward the wings and Annella followed, but her dress snagged on a low stage light, throwing her off-balance. Instinctively I reached for her. Close as we were, I caught the lilac scent of her perfumed hair, and I held her waist too long, even after she had righted herself.

"Thank you," she said. "More proof that dancers are surprisingly clumsy. Pirouettes, apparently, are easier than walking."

That made me laugh, but I stopped when I saw Annella's eyes widen.

"Why, look at me!" she said. Her hands were greased with the grime of chalk from where she'd grabbed the ladder for balance. "What's this?"

"All the men chalk their hands before they climb up," I said, but noticed the back of her waist, where I'd caught her. "I'm afraid I marked your dress, too. Let me get you a cloth."

I ran down to the sinks, eager for the reprieve. While I waited for the water to fill the pipes, I peered at my face. Dark circles from too many restive nights. No makeup or powder papered over the blemishes. My rough-hewn hair had grown out, the wavy locks dropping almost rakishly over my eyebrows.

Good enough, I thought. It seemed the face of a real boy. The only visible trace of a girl was that my face stayed smooth against my calloused fingers. That had worked in my favor, for to Carmine and the others, I was a youth playing at manhood by shaving too much. But I couldn't let Annella see me too closely.

As I approached her again, I marveled at Annella standing in the wings, a world typically devoid of women. I gave her the cloth and she scrubbed her hands, but she strained to see her own back.

"Could you help me?" she asked, fretting. "Constanza will be angry."

"If you like." I felt her intake of breath as I gently patted off the chalk with the cloth. "What soft silk," I said, forgetting that men would not comment on fabric.

"France's finest, not Venice's. Tailored from scratch. Constanza must put her imprint on everything."

"Well," I said, "at least my imprint's gone." I paused, unnerved as she turned around and our eyes met. "We'll skip the head men's dressing rooms," I added, rushing away. "Not the cleanest, and we've already had one mishap."

"Head men?"

"The three puppeteers." I guided her down the hall. "Along with Radillo, of course. He stages everything."

I saw her want to speak, but then she heard the murmur of Constanza's and Radillo's voices behind his closed door. She urged us on.

"What do you do, besides give tours?" she asked.

"Read the scripts in rehearsals, call out stage direction and lines, and get everything set before and after shows. Mostly these days I take the broken marionettes for repairs to the drunken seamstress down the street. She takes too much time, but she's all we can afford."

"I used to repair all my own costumes and shoes when I was a dancer."

"Now you work for Signora Cappello?" I asked tentatively. "Do you like it?"

Annella fixed a wayward strand of hair. "She's good to me, I suppose, but I won't go back to the stage. Constanza would forbid that." She pointed at the stage door. "Where does that go?"

"Into our beautiful garbage-strewn alley."

"Can I see?"

I obliged and gave the door a hard shove. Outside, I found Carmine, Vincenzo, and Bruno smoking on the step.

"Giving a tour, Franco?" Carmine asked, looking from Annella to me.

"This is Annella," I said. "The companion of Signora Constanza Cappello, with whom Radillo is meeting inside." To Annella, I added, "This is Carmine, our lead puppeteer, and Vincenzo and Bruno, our technicians."

Carmine gave her a jaunty bow. "I can't imagine why you'd like a tour. The Minerva is hardly as glamorous as you. Mostly it's just dirty."

"So I noticed." Annella glanced at me. "Franco had to clean chalk off my dress."

"How helpful you are, Franco!" Carmine beamed with delight as I cut him a look.

"What magic you all conjure nightly," Annella said to us. "Even more impressive with such modest resources."

Carmine bowed. "We mustn't keep you. Franco. Give her the full tour."

As I ushered Annella back in, the sound of their whistles outside followed us.

"Ignore them, and ignore those steps, too." I pointed to the cobwebbed archway that led into the basement storage. "Too many rats down there for a lady."

"They say there are more rats than locals in Venice." She paused. "You're from Cannaregio, aren't you? Your accent's like mine. I grew up there. Campo Sant'Alvise has the worst rats when the markets depart, doesn't it?"

I nodded nervously and drew her to my makeshift storage room. "You want to see the marionettes?"

"Oh, yes!" she exclaimed, and I illuminated the expansive but cluttered storeroom. One whole wall shelved the marionettes in current productions, their holders tucked on stands in three rows.

"May I see her?" she asked, gravitating to one.

"That's Lauretta," I said, taking her holder. "One of *The Decameron*'s narrators. She prefers stories of reversals of fortune."

Annella smiled. "Don't we all?"

I handed the marionette to her. In this close room, Annella's floral perfume once more wafted over me.

"I forgot how heavy these holders are. They seem like they should be light, given the size of the marionettes." She handed it to me. "Show me something?"

"If you like." I took the holder and unwound just enough to dangle Lauretta between us. I gestured Lauretta's arms wide to Annella, then had her do a brief, delicate ballet.

"There's a pirouette," I said. "Less graceful than yours were."

"Bravo!" Annella applauded.

I felt like we were back in her bedroom in Cannaregio, practicing, until Annella rushed close and touched my wrist, her gloved fingers warm and soft.

"I lived across the street from you in Cannaregio years ago," she whispered. "We were friends before I needed to leave so suddenly years back. Don't you remember me? Annella?"

I froze. Then I heard her benefactor calling for her in the distance.

"I'm in here," Annella cried, to alert them.

"You're mistaken," I said, my voice thick. "I don't know you."

"But surely you must?" Annella stepped closer and I moved back, steadying myself behind the worktable.

"Here you are, my dear," Signora Cappello said, breezing in and registering the wall of marionettes. "Why, look at this conglomerate of faces. How garish they are."

"Franco was just telling me that he has many repairs every week," Annella said. "I could be of assistance?" She turned to Radillo. "I mend well, and there is no need to pay me."

"How generous," Radillo replied, "but we wouldn't impose."

"Believe me," Signora Cappello said to him, "Annella only ever says what she means. Part of her charm." She peered at Annella. "While I'm certain he could use the instruction, I need you more."

"But I wish to ease his duties," Annella protested.

"You're kind to offer," Radillo said, "but the seamstress is fine."

Annella tried to say goodbye to me, but Radillo ushered them out. I followed at a distance, watching them from the wings.

As they admired the frescos in the pit below, a man dipped out of the shadows, motioning Signora Cappello over.

"Pardon me," she said to Radillo apologetically. "I will only be a moment."

The man brought her back near the stage, where I hid. I heard Radillo telling Annella snippets about the frescoes on display, but my stomach twisted in knots. Annella recognized me. Would she reveal me? How did she know it was me? And where had she disappeared to all those years ago? My thoughts swirled until part of Signora Cappello's conversation floated up from below.

"You have news of the girl?" she was asking the man.

"Yes. Found her in the ghetto this morning. A sad one, she is."

Signora Cappello looked relieved. "Once she's cleaned up, bring her to the palazzo. I need to keep a closer eye on her."

"Leave it to me," he replied.

Signora Cappello said no more but rejoined Radillo and Annella.

"All is well?" Radillo asked.

"The problem of the foundlings worsens daily," she replied. "How I wish there were more I could do."

"You do so much," Radillo said, reassuring her. "It must grow taxing."

"At least today's problem is only a small wrinkle. Easily remedied."

They all left the theater and my chest tightened. Annella worked for a wealthy woman whom Radillo was courting for money. One word from Annella and everything could collapse.

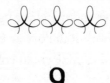

9

I hurried toward the boundary of the old Ghetto Nuovo, my first time back in Cannaregio since the horrible night I fled months ago. As I walked near the periphery, I shivered in the shadows of the square's imposing walls.

Three days had passed since Annella's revelation. If she spoke up, I would need to escape the city fast, but I wanted to say goodbye to my grandfather first.

I entered the main square, eyeing it for threats or a familiar face. But nothing seemed amiss along these stalwart walls and quiet stone streets. Still, the morning's silence unnerved me after San Marco's daily throng. I wondered who, if anyone, might be watching me from behind a tipped shutter.

Given its history, the square should have been a busy tourist landmark, but it never was. Until thirty years ago, when Venice joined the then-new nation of Italy and achieved independence from the Austrians, the Ghetto Nuovo had been the only place in the city open to Jews, and it was still an enclave of sorts. When Annella's parents came to Venice, they settled near it so that her mother could feel safer.

Yet the square remained a vexed place. As children, Annella and I knew not to come here alone. We overheard her parents' distress about the increase of orphans and foundlings in the city. Venice's prior history of abandonment laws initially had been designed to discourage infanticide by enabling parents to legally deposit their infants at orphanages. But as Venice's postindependence poverty swelled, parents abandoned not only infants, but older children at nearby orphanages because they could no longer afford them. These places could house grueling, disease-ridden slums or cheap workhouses from which children ran, landing in this square. As my grandfather explained to me, for those runaways, the imposing walls, sprinkled with ancient Hebraic inscriptions, did not imprison but protect, sheltering them in a city that elsewhere saw them as a mere blight.

Today, the broad, windswept plaza was quiet but for a smattering of religious reformers who had just arrived. Foundlings huddled under a portico. I kept an eye out for Signora Cappello, uncertain whether she might visit here herself.

I could not knock on the door of my old home, not if my father or brother were inside, so I'd come here to find a boy who could tell a convincing lie. It did not take long for a gaggle of prospects to appear at my side, peppering me with requests for candy, money, food. Dressed in my brother's coat and bowler, I looked like someone worth begging. Small hands tugged at my scratchy wool, but when I spotted an older boy with lank hair and sour eyes, I shooed the rest away.

"I seek an old man by Sant'Alvise," I told him. "You'd go to the door, deliver a message, and, depending on who answers, bring him outside to me. I'll pay."

The boy seemed eager, but then I glimpsed a wound at his right temple. I waved him off. "Never mind. You're hurt."

"No, I can do it," he said. "Better if I get out now." He gestured to a pair of priests in the distance. "Rumor has it they're not really priests but men snatching boys for factories in France. Can't I go with you instead?"

Annella's parents had warned us that devotional garb concealed those who would gather up anonymous children to fling them across Europe, sometimes into trades or, for girls, prostitution. False promises of education belied the pittance these children received, in what amounted to indentured servitude. Only their handlers, her parents said, ever truly grew rich.

I dropped three lire in the boy's open palm. "There's more when you bring me the old man. What's your name?"

"Rico."

We walked in silence and soon entered a broad Christmas market in Campo Sant'Alvise. Candles twinkled around a shop's nativity scene. Ladies dressed in ermine and saturated shades of velvet also illuminated the dull streets. With it being days before the holiday, delivery boys with arms akimbo scurried by with gold leaf–wrapped parcels.

Then I heard the Church of Sant'Alvise's bell ring ten times. Its echo flattened me. Despite today's icy wind, it threw me back into the muggy summer night when I'd sought protection from Tristano near here.

How terrified I'd been. I'd tripped over the splayed leg of a man so drunk he did not even cease snoring. Another had veered toward me with an open flask. I'd raised my knife and shouted, but too high, like a girl, just as a group of noisy men entered the square, careening more sideways than forward.

That night, I'd had no place to hide, so I'd slunk down at a door, imitating the passed-out drunk and hoping they wouldn't spot me in the fog. I heard them stumbling closer, tossing empty beer bottles at walls while they walked. One broke above my head, as if thrown at me. They'd lingered near me, with several shouting.

Fucking ghetto scum. Dirty Jews. Disgusting rats. You dare sleep in our *streets?*

I braced myself, sensing a kick, but a man toppled, too unsteady from drink. That prompted frenetic laughter from the others until one cold, deep voice cut through: Tristano.

Too worn out from that last boy, Tomi? He won't wake up after what you did to his face.

Rico's hand on my shoulder jarred me back into the present. "Are you all right, sir?"

I blinked. I was bracing myself against a wall. "Yes," I muttered, my breath visible in the cold. "Let's keep going."

As I led Rico out of the square, though, the rest of Tristano's words rang in my ears.

The girl's been warned, but she can't have gone far. Find her. If we lose her, boys, we don't get paid.

Months had passed since that night, but it all felt too fresh as we reached the makeshift Sant'Alvise dock near my old home. The water's familiar pungent scent hit me. High residential walls faced a dead end of bleached brick, broken only by a locked iron grille.

I pointed down the short stretch of my former street, Calle Larga Legname. "Take this letter. Keep it in your pocket." I handed Rico the sealed parchment. "Last house on the left. Ring the bell and press hard, so it can be heard above. If an old man named Alfonso answers, give him this letter and bring him to me. If anyone else opens the door, say you're the grandson of the old man's theater friend, looking for him." I tapped the letter in Rico's hands. "Only the old man sees this, and only if he's alone. No one else."

Rico nodded. "What if no one answers?"

"Ask the neighbors. I must find him today." I hesitated. "Whatever you do, don't lead anyone else to me. If you do, I'll run and you'll get nothing."

Rico took off. I could not see who answered the door but saw that he was invited in.

As I waited, I paced Sant'Alvise's dock, the gray-green waters upwelling from a passing trawler plumbing the channel's depths.

53

Its horn's lonely blare mingled with the north winds that swept this stretch untrammeled. I pulled my bowler over my reddening ears and yanked up the collar to burrow within. My frozen fingers wouldn't warm, even in my pockets.

I was starting to wonder whether I should try the kitchen side door myself when Rico emerged. He gave me a furtive signal and took a circuitous way over.

Soon I saw why. My father stepped out. Instinctively, I moved back. He peered after Rico, then disappeared again inside. After so long, the brief glimpse of his sandy hair and fastidious dress was jarring. Yet while I felt a lash of rage, he struck me as somewhat shrunken, not quite the tyrant I'd held in my head.

Rico came up beside the dock, glancing around. We were alone. "Your grandfather can't come down. Too weak from a sore throat, he says. But he wrote this letter and sent your own back, for safety." He handed them to me.

"Who was there?"

"A man named Sandro answered. Skittish, like I was a robber bold enough to ring the bell. He brought me to your old man."

"Keep an eye out. Tell me if anyone approaches." I leaned against the stone arch. Then I began to read:

My dearest,

I cannot chance seeing you. Sandro and Marco are oddly not at the station today. Yet how relieved am I that you survived and found Annella! I understand your fear but cannot see a benefit to her revealing you. Once, you were close. Talk to her. Maybe you can help one another.

I am safe—the neighbors would shun Sandro if he cast me out—but Tristano continues to search for you in brothels. I said you fled to America, but Sandro claims you could never afford passage and has spun a lie of your absence as a turn at finishing school. Appearances, as you know, are everything to him. Your happiness is immaterial, compared to what fortune you, married, could bring him still. And his debts are only mounting. Tristano has even enlisted Marco into his gang as payment.

It's too dangerous for you to visit like this. Please stay away. I could not bear knowing you came to harm because of me.

I remain with you in spirit and love, always.
Your grandfather, Alfonso

Rico cleared his throat in warning. I looked up to see my brother, Marco, approaching. From his stance, Marco appeared drunk. I passed by Rico, discreetly squeezing a small purse into his hand behind my back. "Go," I whispered. "Run. Now." Then I lowered the rim of my bowler and continued walking as Rico took off.

But Marco was not deterred. "Where is she? Where is my sister?" he shouted after Rico. He caught up to the boy and lunged, dragging him down as they both fell to the ground.

"Leave the boy alone!" I said, sprinting back to kick Marco from behind. That freed Rico, who scrambled to his feet and scampered away without a glance back. I kicked Marco's stomach twice more and he curled up like a snail, covering his head with his hands. Then I ran, too.

Only when I was far from Cannaregio did I slow my step. I took a different route back to my attic, looking over my shoulder often, rattled by my grandfather's warning that Tristano was still on the hunt. Any man on the street could be one of his hired fists, and any shred of safety I felt being outside of Cannaregio had just evaporated.

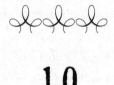

10

In the month that followed, I stayed busy in the theater, touching up set pieces and shadowing Carmine, but my mind lingered on my grandfather's words as I did my best to shake my fears of discovery. A theater of marionettes, run exclusively by men, was the last place Sandro or Tristano would look for me. If they did, would they recognize me? Marco hadn't. But he'd been drunk and focused on Rico.

Still, I kept reliving the elation of besting Marco. How many times had I pined for strength as a girl when on the receiving end of his or my father's blows? Since my arrival at the Minerva, my body had been transforming by time and labor. Having worked past fatigue for months, I bled less now. My forearms and bicep muscles had grown from so much heavy lifting, and now my shoulders had broadened, too, slimming my waist by default and making my already-small breasts even smaller. No one would guess my chest was a woman's now.

Yet it was more than that. I had begun to feel more myself among these men, not less. Stronger physically, but something more intrinsic was taking hold, too.

It was as if my grandfather had known. No one at the Minerva doubted my sex. Older men at the Titian sometimes teased me as youthful, but they did so with every man under thirty. I looked down at my scuffed boots, faded black trousers, and frayed red flannel shirt, castoffs of Carmine's. I did look the part, more so now.

And because there were no women in this world, no one considered that I might be one.

Carmine joined me onstage and he started sifting through the trunk to locate his marionette for *The Decameron*. Today, they were rehearsing a new story, in which a girl from the Amalfi Coast nurses a greedy, shipwrecked merchant back to health, and to repay her kindness, he reforms and leaves her the treasure chest.

"I have almost an entire sea in need of repair and only this much azure." I pointed at the dwindling tub of oily light-blue, more cracked than wet. "Why do so many of our backdrops depict the sea? At least canals I could muck up with green for algae. Radillo made it clear we have no more money for paint."

"Try some fish or a swan?" Carmine suggested, noting the larger tubs of yellow and white. He nabbed a brush. "You look tired. Is that pretty Annella keeping you out late?"

"Hardly," I said, dotting in kelp. I hadn't seen her since her tour. "Though you've been rushing out after shows."

"Very observant."

"As your apprentice, it's my duty to follow your lead. Who's the girl?"

"Trade secret," he said, painting in a misshapen goldfish. "All I will reveal is that she's from Dorsoduro."

"Is she rich?"

"Indeed, and a gorgeous redhead."

"How did you meet?"

Carmine spotted Radillo arriving with Andrea and Niccolò. "You're not ready for that lesson. Besides, duty calls," he said, joining the others.

I watched the four men practice a pirate fight before returning to my canvas. I lost myself in dotting in swans until I heard Radillo and Carmine arguing. Then Carmine called me over.

He tapped the script, which sat propped open on a wobbly tall stool. "Franco, read the notes on this character's voice."

"The notes aren't the point, Carmine," Radillo said, sighing.

"They are *your* notes," Carmine shot back, "and I think Franco should read them aloud."

"Fine." Radillo rubbed his forehead. "Go ahead, Franco."

I bent over the script and, after a quick search, started. "'The girl's dialogue should blend Italian with Venetian dialect when she discovers the shipwrecked merchant's body on the beach.'"

Radillo began to protest, but Carmine just handed his marionette to me. "Do the girl's role," Carmine demanded. "No falsetto, just as yourself, but with those notes in mind."

I adjusted the marionette, eyeing both men before I began in dialect. "At first I thought he was a demon risen from the sea." I tilted the marionette's head back in fear. "But then I saw it was no demon, only a man, near-drowned on the rocky shore. I could not bear to see him suffer, and now worried he had washed up dead."

I shifted into Italian proper for the narration of the group. "Together, we aided this man as a village to become a gentleman. We wanted to bring him back to breathe on our shore, but only together could we help this stranger live."

"Enough." Radillo took the marionette's holder from me. "What is your point, Carmine?"

"Franco's from here. He understands the cadence. Private speech in dialect flows easily into Italian with strangers. Back and forth, depending on the address."

"I know how Franco speaks. He handles dialect against Italian perfectly. But the whole story takes place on the Amalfi Coast. It's more authentic to speak Italian."

"The pit wants—and expects—to hear their own voices," Carmine pressed. "These stories transform when they travel. Dialect makes them ours."

"True," Radillo said. "But the pit doesn't deliver enough money. Only the boxes, who prefer Italian, do. That's why I'm meeting with Count De Rossi and Signora Cappello next week."

I tensed at those names. If Radillo was meeting Signora Cappello, then Annella could be present. Might my secret come out?

"More dialect-based theaters still survive in Venice than Italian ones," Carmine persisted, "even though it's been more than thirty years since the Risorgimento told us we were part of one nation, with one way to speak. If Italian was going to take hold, it would have by now. You say we must adapt? Most of our audience cannot even read. They'll stop coming, and they're more consistent. Then we'll really lose money."

Radillo appeared to be wavering. I knew Carmine was right. Unlike many other theaters in Venice owned by generations-old wealthy families like the Grimanis, the Minerva had remained independent of patronage under Radillo's tenure. It needed audiences to exist. *The Decameron's* recent success only left Radillo restless for more changes.

"We cannot adapt by catering exclusively to the rich," Carmine continued. "Even the rich think dialect is more authentic. They like the grit and grime of being in here, albeit at a remove in their velvet perches. Don't you see? They all want to be in the same room."

Radillo's eyebrows knit together in frustration. "After decades, I know this room better than you. Remember, I made marionettes popular on this stage. I moved us past primitive one-act stalls in the street with their two strings and buttons for eyes, limp bodies stuffed with straw. In this theater, puppetry has become art." He gestured to the stage. "We could transcend mere lowbrow laughs to *succeed*, Carmine, not just survive."

Carmine folded his arms. "But we can't speak to only one side when we're stuck in the middle. It's almost the twentieth century. Don't go back to antiquated patronage by the elite. That will close us down, I swear." Then he faced me. "Franco, the pit returns, night after night, right?"

"Yes," I replied. "They come back to the exact same shows."

"What do they usually say if they hear Italian?"

"They jeer." I cut a nervous glance at Radillo. "That's how they know it's the villain."

"I know that," Radillo said, tossing Carmine's marionette at him. "We don't have time for endless debate. We'll rehearse in dialect for now," he conceded. "But we need different tactics." He fixed on me. "Get back to the set, Franco. The paint must be dry by tonight. I, not Carmine, will let you know if you're needed again."

I hurried back to my painting. The head men resumed their rehearsal. Yet tension hung in the air. I sensed that my one place of refuge, the theater, was in jeopardy.

11

Carmine sat tapping his leg nervously against the bar of Café Titian until Michaela's glare stilled him. "Schoolboy," he said. "I'm bored. Let's go to Riva degli Schiavoni."

"Great!" I tossed my copy of *Il Gazzettino* aside and jumped up.

"Guess I'm not the only one who's bored. You've been there?"

I tugged on my coat. "I go every Monday to get ideas."

"Ideas? You're not ready for those." Carmine drank the dregs of his coffee. "Or maybe you are. Your technique's improving. I've told Radillo, and I'm working on getting you up there."

"Thanks," I said, stilling at this news, but Carmine just strode out, motioning me to follow.

The brisk day shone as we headed over to the ramshackle stalls of raucous showmen lining the Basin near San Marco. Riva degli Schiavoni was a waterfront market that amassed the most glove puppet stalls in Venice and more, all in one spot. Unlike the Minerva, it offered blunter and bloodier fare, short bursts of scenes by itinerant, eager glove puppeteers.

When we arrived, the wintry waters glistened. Shrill sounds of performers lured us to a stall, where we found a Pulcinella bashing a cowering servant.

"That's what we need," Carmine said, applauding. "More lurid, less lofty. Think of the decapitations!" He pointed to one of the glove puppeteers who had several heads secured to a wide cowhide belt, ready for quick changes.

"Something tells me Radillo wouldn't approve," I said.

Carmine frowned. "For so long, Radillo catered to the people. Lately, I worry we'll lose that." He eyed the water. "Perhaps it's just a shrewd move for the moment, given that his daughter's marked for marriage to De Rossi's ugly youngest."

The sounds of the Pulcinella's rage faded into a mélange of dialects as we strolled among the loosely hammered pine stalls of the saline-scented thoroughfare.

"This is what true 'Italian' theater is," Carmine said, pointing. "Not the fine fare of La Fenice."

I nodded. "As a young man, my grandfather traveled with showmen all over the Veneto, and even went as far as Bologna, before settling down in Venice at the Malibran."

"Bologna?" Carmine stopped. "Wait—you're not a foundling?"

"Not exactly," I added quickly. "My father was a gambler and a drunk. My mother ran off when I was born. Her father—my grandfather—raised me. He taught me technique, but Radillo would never have let me in the door if I hadn't claimed I'd had a real teacher."

"I get it," Carmine said, surprising me. He started walking again. "Respectability, status—that's what counts with Radillo. All those scripts and notes he makes you read? He wants art with a capital *A*, just for the elite. That's who he favors first and last, probably because he's one of them."

I hurried to catch up. "So if he's rich, why is he so worried about money?"

"His wealth and status come from his wife. And the Minerva is up and down. These days, more down, given his move to bigger shows.

So he's been courting the De Rossis for his daughter . . ." Carmine trailed off, as the stalls began to crowd tighter. "You ever see your family?"

"No. They're all dead." I pressed on, unable to say more.

"I'm impressed that your grandfather worked the Malibran," Carmine mused. "Twice the size of the Minerva but a cut below in class. Its doors always shut for indecency."

"He used to say, 'Stage shows with actors get censored, but plays on the street with puppets? No fuss.' For him, censorship was being chased out of town after stealing a meal."

Carmine laughed, pulling me toward a dirty scarlet curtain concealing a makeshift stage of hammered crates. A tattered violinist drowned out nearby players as two glove puppets, male figures in top hats, towered over a veiled maiden in white.

I knew this tale. Its quick-witted hero gets his rival committed to the madhouse, so he can woo the maiden unencumbered. Carmine and I watched the trio alternate dialogue in rapid dialect and then use the *pivetta* to whistle scene changes.

"We did this at the Minerva last year," Carmine said. "Big hit with the pit."

Before we moved on, I tossed a coin in the red flannel cap. Ahead, a scrum of loutish boys no more than ten years old begged some fishermen for food or work.

"You'd think in a city of water, they'd bathe," Carmine said with a grimace.

"Would you jump in that?" I pointed to a foamy cluster of half-frozen algae and fish heads. "In February?"

"Fine. I see you're a reformer now, like the widow?" he replied.

We paused at a more elaborate stall. A huddle of children sat cross-legged before a tiny, glittering ice queen puppet wielding a wand. Beside her lounged a real fluffy white cat, a grand otherworldly beast next to its miniature monarch. When the queen bowed for the audience's applause, the cat lolled, reaching a paw out to dab a child's head in the front.

"Behold, our future audience," Carmine said, "if only Radillo would let those kids in the door instead of hand-wringing over the boxes."

"It's not like they go to school."

Then a scream rang out. The foundlings and fishermen fanned out fast as a group of men appeared to drag something from a heap of trash near the entrance to the Giardinetti Reali. Rats sprinted off in irritation.

We edged closer to the public garden, and my heart caught in my throat. It was Rico, the boy who'd helped me on Sant'Alvise.

A broad spread of browned blood covered the boy's lifeless chest. His small, bare feet were calloused, caked with dirt and ice. It pierced me to see his head wound had healed—only for him to now be here, dead.

A few men knelt in front of him, but most of the crowd slunk back in horror. Nauseous, I tore my gaze from his body, panicking. Only then, to my surprise, did I spot Annella. She rushed over, clutching her velvet wrap, Rossana at her side.

"What are you doing here?" Annella asked me quickly.

"I could ask you the same thing," I replied.

"I always drag Rossana past the stalls." She eyed the street. "Get out of here. You don't want to be near when the authorities arrive. They round up young men, and you don't have papers . . ."

"She's right," Carmine said, grabbing me. "The police will assume the worst of us. They'll beat you until you confess, even if you're innocent. Let's go."

"Wait," I said to him, then whispered to Annella, "I need to see you—alone."

She leaned in as if kissing my cheek goodbye. "Tonight. Wait for me by the stage door after the show. But please, go now!"

Carmine gripped my arm and dragged me away as the first policemen approached.

Veiled by the thick crowd, Carmine and I evaded the police. Still, when we safely could, we broke into a run, cutting through the private gardens. We did not stop until we reached the Hotel Monaco. Here I doubled over, struggling to catch my breath. When I stood back up, my head spun.

"Don't faint on me, schoolboy," Carmine said as he hauled me into the hotel and through its ornate lobby, ignoring two concierges' feeble protests until we were in the empty outdoor café on the other side. Then he grabbed two chairs by the door.

"That's enough inspiration for today," he said. "Sit." He snapped his fingers at a waiter and ordered us beer.

I ran my hands through my hair as I heard the imposing Basilica of Santa Maria della Salute's bells, heavy but distant. All I saw was Rico, blank eyes fixed in death, and felt like I was hearing the Church of Sant'Alvise's bell that night.

The crash of bottles. *Fucking ghetto scum.* Tristano's snarl.

I wanted to cry, recalling Rico. He'd asked me if I was all right.

Carmine reached across the table to pat my hand. "Franco, what's wrong?"

His voice stilled my racing heart. "That boy. I knew him. I. . . It could've been me."

"What? No. Those kids are killing each other. Probably robbery. It had nothing to do with you."

"I was one of them. It's why I ran."

Carmine went quiet. The waiter arrived with our drinks, refusing to set them down until Carmine threw payment on the plate. A beer landed on the table hard in front of me, foam pooling at the base. I wrapped my shaking hands around the icy glass to steady them.

Carmine waited until the waiter left. "What made you run?"

"These drunks were chasing me that night. I thought they were going to kill me, but their ringleader made them take off. They were after some girl. I'd been planning to audition at the Minerva, so I ran there. Waited all night until Radillo and Leo showed up."

Carmine motioned me to drink. "This explains why you were so quick to fight that day."

"Sorry about that," I said, drinking too fast.

We drank in silence for a beat, then Carmine spoke. "The Minerva was my refuge, too."

"How?"

"I'm from Bologna. Hence this fair hair." He raked a hand through his curls. "My father, the great nobody, drove me out." Carmine stared at the water. "Always drunk."

"Sounds like he'd have been friends with mine."

"Mine used to kick the shit out of me all the time, but my mother had it worse. I tried to defend her once. I was thirteen, thought I was a big man. That didn't go well. He certainly gave it his all." Carmine sipped his beer. "When I came to, he kicked me out. Told me he'd kill me if he ever saw me again. I knew he meant it. I can still see my mother, hiding behind the door with her black eye, mouthing for me to return after midnight when he'd be dead to the world. I did, but only to get what I needed. Tried to get her to come with me, but she was too scared. I stowed away on a coal train that dumped me here." He threw his arms wide. "In paradise."

"Nobody's going to kick you now." I tapped his foot under the table with mine. "Except me."

"Dream on, schoolboy. I won that round." He clinked our half-empty glasses, but his usual bluster had diminished.

"So why the Minerva?" I asked.

"Radillo found me working the docks like those grimy ruffians. Watched me handling the ropes and levies and pulled me aside. I'll take marionettes any day over chilblains." He fidgeted with his hands.

"Does he still look for apprentices at the docks?"

"No. He had a point of pride after your predecessor, this kid named Stefano, took off. 'No more foundlings,' he told me, as if Stefano and I hadn't been worth the trouble. He gave up on apprentices—unless they're bold enough to knock on his door, I guess. Radillo liked you right away. You talked about making marionettes art, not just cheap thrills." Carmine exhaled. "But me? Radillo only ever sees me as a dirty boy pretending to be a man. Worthless, never enough."

I frowned in sympathy.

Carmine stood up to stretch. "Ready to head back, schoolboy? I'm not exactly on Radillo's good side these days. Don't want you in trouble, too."

We walked back in a companionable silence. As we neared the theater, Carmine said, "Tell me something your grandfather taught you. You teach me for a change."

I kicked a loose stone as I walked. "He always said that eight strings are more complicated than those of the past. You can make puppets come to life with two or three, but that's old-fashioned. With eight strings, people forget they're watching wood. They're seeing someone they know—or if you're really good, someone they'd want to know. 'Eight strings,' he'd say, 'and you have a soul.'" I shoved my hands in my pockets. "That's why I came here."

Carmine stopped. "Is that what you see up there?"

"Yes," I replied. "From you especially."

"At least we're alone in paradise together," he said. "Though if I need to convey a whole soul, I am going to need a lot more rehearsal."

12

After everyone left for the night, I waited for Annella by the stage door, jittery at every intermittent sound. Three men sauntered by, and I patted the knife in my front vest for comfort. I would not be lulled into imagining I was safe—not after this afternoon.

Then I noticed Annella coming up from the water.

"Are we alone?" she asked when she arrived at the door.

"Yes. It's just us." I glanced behind her. "Are you alone?"

"One of the guards brought me. He's waiting in the boat." Seeing my face, she added, "Don't worry; Arturo's a friend. He won't follow."

Once inside, I lit a lantern and led her through the gloom to my storeroom. I stood waiting as she sat down at the table.

"Such a gentleman," she said with a faint smile in the dim light.

"My life depends on these customs," I said, taking a stool far from her, by the door.

"Of course," she replied, softer.

"When did you recognize me?" I asked her.

"I felt drawn to you but didn't know why at first. Later, your laugh gave you away."

My laugh sounded like a girl. I was in more danger than I thought. I stood up and paced.

Annella registered my dread and stood, too. "Don't worry. No one but me would notice, someone who spent time with you as a child. Even I did not know you that first night after the show." She paused. "The truth is, you seem more yourself now. The dresses and long hair of before? They were awkward, false. This is who you are, isn't it? No disguise. The truth."

I paused my pacing. I wanted to believe her but kept fearing the worst. Blackmail. An angry knock on the door. Threats. But not once had she called me Francesca.

"Can I trust you?" I asked her.

She came closer. "I, of all people, know you could never be at the Minerva as a girl, or any of these theaters. There are so few options for women. Dressed as you are, you can become a puppeteer. I am the last person who would destroy that or expose you to harm."

Her cheekbones were brushed with a trace of powder. She had grown up to be more beautiful than any other woman I'd seen— which is saying something in Venice.

"I did not recognize you either at first," I said. "Your dresses and jewels, your place in the boxes, the company you keep? You may have changed more than me. Remember when your parents brought us here all those years ago?"

Even in the poor light, I felt the air shift. Then I knew. For all her money and confidence, her story had taken turns far worse than mine.

"I can't get warm these days," she said. I saw that she was trembling.

I unwound my scarf and wrapped it over her shoulders. This time, I pulled our two stools close. "Here, sit," I said, and sat beside her.

In time, she spoke slowly. "My parents are dead. Five years ago. That's why we disappeared."

Although I'd suspected their deaths, learning the truth was a shock. I could still see them in such vibrant detail, could hear her mother's laughter and her father's infectious singing. "I'm very sorry," I said. "What happened?"

"They tried to leave for Padua, where my father's friend lived, during that influenza outbreak that ravaged the ghetto. But they were too late. At the station, a doctor refused to let them board. He separated me immediately, as I was not yet ill. My mother barely had time to press this into my hands." She traced the locket, loose at her throat. "They died the next day," she added quietly. "By then I'd fallen sick, too, and was quarantined at that new hospital for infectious ailments over on Sacca Sessola. I nearly died, so I was only told of their deaths weeks later. My father's sister, Maria, his lone relation, had already buried them at sea. She said it was their wish, but I knew: it was cheaper. There wasn't even a grave to visit."

I offered her my handkerchief so she could dab her eyes.

"I don't know why I am this upset after all this time," she said. "I thought it was behind me. I moved on, made the best of my life that I could."

"Grief tends to surprise us," I said, recalling my mother. "Time passes and you're fine, but then some small thing shifts, and it's like it was yesterday. Maybe the dead try to speak to us, but we're stuck over here, clumsy and unknowing."

Annella nodded. "I had to forget so much to survive. Some days I don't even recognize myself. You knew me, from before. But now? No one does. Now, I am only this." She smoothed her dress.

"Clothes cannot change everything. You always made me laugh, and you did on that tour, which gave me away." When Annella smiled, I eased on. "Where did you go?"

"My father's sister lived in the poorest stretch of Castello. She made no secret that I was a burden, like her five other children. She hated her brother for having been favored by their parents, and then for marrying my mother, a Jew from the south. She even suggested I had sickened them."

"I'm sure that wasn't true. Your father worked where the outbreak was at its worst."

"That was the least of her cruelties. I sent you two letters . . ."

"Nothing came. Everyone told me you had died or moved south. I couldn't imagine you never saying goodbye, though. When I saw you alive, I was overjoyed, but I couldn't take the risk."

Annella looked at me sympathetically. "I knew she never sent my letters. I planned to find you when I was well. Before I could, though, her husband, Giuseppe . . ." She faltered. "He cornered me in the bedroom one day. My aunt was out, the other children at school. I was still so weak."

A heavy beat of silence stretched between us.

"Oh, Annella. No."

Her silence confirmed the worst.

She would have been so small then, barely thirteen. My hands clenched at the thought of a man hurting her like that.

Eventually, she went on. "He said he would kill me if I told anyone, and I was numb. My whole world was gone. I wished I had died, too. He kept coming after me—until my aunt found out. She blamed me, of course. Said I'd tempted him."

Her stoic expression made my heart break. "I wish I had been there," I added quietly.

"There's nothing you could have done, and I was too ashamed to see you," she replied gently. "That's when I learned my aunt's true motives. She was biding her time for the courts to finish. Guardianship gave her my parents' house and money."

I recalled the family who moved into her house. Slowly, it dawned on me. My father had befriended that man. They drank at the bar, visiting every week.

"After the papers were signed," Annella continued, "my aunt dragged me to the Catholic orphanage. Gave them a false name, told lies about me needing a firmer hand and a trade. She could do all that with impunity, given that I was under fourteen, the age limit for admittance, and my parents were dead. It isn't only infants dropped at the turnstiles, and I wasn't legally old enough to marry off for a price." Annella straightened. "I suppose I'm lucky she didn't know about the agents who show up to take children abroad for factory work as indentured servants. Contracts can stretch for years. That way she'd have made even more money from me. As it was, by getting rid of me, she gained the house, their money—everything. They slept in my parents' bed while I sweated in a laundry for days on end. Of course, the nuns tried to convert me, and when I resisted, they punished me. That's why I ran. Besides, I feared staying. I couldn't let that disgusting man find me again."

All this time, she'd been right here in the same city, and so terribly alone. "I'm so sorry. You've endured far too much," I said quietly.

"Not unlike you." She twisted my kerchief in her hands. "I remember the bruises you hid and why you kept me from your father. I know why I never came into your house, and why my father made a show of walking you home. You know what it's like not being safe in your own house, don't you? Is that why you ran to the Minerva?"

I rose to adjust the lantern's wick. "In a way. It was my grandfather's idea. I left suddenly because my father planned to recoup his gambling debts by marrying me off to Daniele Ceresa."

"Even before I left, I heard talk of him. The fights . . ."

"My father knew I wouldn't go willingly," I said, "so he sent Tristano." She glanced up sharply. Like every Cannaregio girl, she knew the mafioso. "That's why I escaped," I continued. "But my father still hopes to find me and marry me to another. Fortunately, Tristano is only looking for me in brothels, so I'm safe." I attempted a laugh. "I ran to the right place. Only men."

"Right where I would find you," Annella said, taking my hand. "I have not told anyone about you, nor will I. I promise—you're safe."

I looked at our hands. Her tenderness reminded me of my grandfather's parting embrace.

After a moment, Annella let go and handed me back my scarf. "Constanza may be angry if she realizes I've slipped away this late. But before I leave, tell me—what name would you like me to call you when we're alone?"

For months I had acted out of necessity to survive. To be asked what I wanted felt incomprehensible. Yet my answer was as clear as it was swift.

"Franco," I said. "It's who I am now. I think it's who I was before."

"It suits you," Annella said, standing. "How glad I am that we found each other, Franco."

"Me, too." I walked her to the stage door.

"Remember those sewing lessons I mentioned?" she asked, as I locked up the theater behind us. "Constanza wishes to support Radillo's theater more. She might be more amenable now. Let me see what I can do, and then we could see each other, because you already know how to sew. Maybe we could try to meet in two weeks?"

"Your benefactor won't be concerned about you being alone with a man?"

"Constanza saw you as a timid boy. Let her—it's safer." A gust of wind picked up, and she adjusted her cloak. "I'll go to the dock alone, so Arturo doesn't see us."

On the solitary street, the gas lamps shone thin in the icy fog.

"I'll listen for you from here," I said, pulling my own coat tighter around myself, "and thank you, Annella. Truly."

"There's no need to thank me," she said. "Just get ready for your first sewing lesson."

13

Two weeks later, I sat in the same room where Annella and I had talked in the dark. Once more, I awaited her arrival, for I'd learned she had convinced Radillo and her benefactor to begin my sewing lessons—and save the theater money by completing our repairs in-house.

In daylight, the room overlooked a brick-walled alley at the back, its large window testifying to a once-larger thoroughfare, which now permitted only a narrow shaft of sky. I lit some lamps and continued working my way through a hefty stack of scripts that Radillo had dropped off.

Like the fingerprints of many puppeteers on a holder, each script was a palimpsest of notes. I wasn't sure why Radillo wanted me to read them, but they revealed Greek myths, Venetian folktales, and even Italian operas. I read tales of men who became horses, women who became trees, gods lured into mortality—all for a glimpse of their beloved disguised as a witch. Each showed the hand of history haunting our myths, where even the dead could return to life.

At first, the notations baffled me. Marks for specific gestures, stage direction, and tableaus limned the margins beside rivulets of candle wax and red wine. Rushed flourishes covered pages riddled with older dialect-specific or Latin symbols at which I could only guess. My grandfather had always disdained scripts, preferring impromptu stories in the open air, standard when few puppeteers could read. Yet with practice, I began to grasp patterns.

The additions inscribed in a graceful, dark slope intrigued me most, for these were Radillo's notes. In his asides, I glimpsed adroit reversals, where even the thrill of a truly improbable deus ex machina made sense. The Minerva's cast of characters could morph into comic slapstick or turn tragic—sometimes in the same night. Love's labors were lost to murder, cheats, and fate but always beamed with a last-minute rescue. His notes on the myth of Cupid and Psyche dramatically changed the ending, with Psyche voicing her anger at being a puppet of the gods. In the end, she accepted Cupid but rejected becoming a goddess, jettisoning immortality for a more finite human life.

It struck me that these notes were in contrast with Radillo's contemporary desire to appease the boxes. Radillo once favored a more irreverent, freewheeling spirit to the classics, focusing on ordinary men and women, real people who contained worlds of desire, rage, and woe worthy of the ancients. I wondered what changed his approach. Perhaps it really was just to abet his daughter's hand in marriage to secure that wealth.

That day I was so lost in my study that I did not notice Signora Cappello and Radillo enter the room. At Radillo's cough, however, I jumped to my feet. Annella hung back by the door.

"So this is his work space?" Signora Cappello said. "Dark, but functional, I suppose."

"I've taken to calling it 'Restoration,'" Radillo said, "a new department at the Minerva. Are you prepared, Franco?"

"Yes," I said, looking past them to Annella. "If there is anything you need, I can fetch it."

"I'm sure you could," Signora Cappello said. She brushed the table's edge with a finger as if checking for dust. The faint aroma of lemon oil still hung in the air from my earlier attempt at cleaning. "Restoration," she echoed. "To restore, from the Latin *restaurare*. To renew, rebuild, or alter and return to a state of original beauty." She motioned to Annella. "Come see for yourself."

Annella stepped forward, and Radillo aided her in removing her cloak. A tangle of iridescent rubies clung to her ears. She wore the same silken rose ensemble from the night of *The Decameron*'s premiere, but the bustle had been removed. Now, it gored tight to her hips, the sleeves tautened with a soft bell of lace at her forearms. While her benefactor gazed at her in admiration, Annella assessed the marionettes in need of repairs.

"You've done such good work, Franco," Annella said. "Whatever you lack in equipment, I may have here."

She placed a small patent leather suitcase on the table and snapped it open to reveal needles neatly lined in a row of glass cases, three pairs of scissors, thread in a spectrum of colors and widths, and even a fresh set of paintbrushes, oil paints, and a clean pine palette.

Annella nudged the case to me. "This is for you to keep."

"How generous," I replied.

"Shall we leave them?" Radillo asked, motioning to Signora Cappello.

She nodded at Annella. "Franco can see you home safely, but I expect you for dinner. Don't be late. I have guests coming. Change into what I've laid out for you. Not this modest daywear." She traced Annella's cheek with her fan. "More color. You're peaked."

"Of course," Annella said, stepping back to let them pass.

"Franco," Radillo said, "get Lauretta fixed for tonight. The pirate story's on." He tapped the page of the script I'd been studying. "Ancient stuff up next. Commedia dell'arte, including Venice's favorite fool, Facanapa."

Annella and I waited until they left. Then she whispered, "Can we be heard beyond the door?"

"Only if we fight," I whispered back.

"Let's avoid that. We'll have plenty of time, given that you already know how to sew—if anyone comes, pretend to learn." She pulled the case over. "Your friend Carmine won't join us?"

"I wanted you all for myself. Besides, you'd need to fight him off."

"He has enough girls swooning over him, I'm sure."

I laughed. "Not lately. He doesn't even go to Goldoni's Alley like the others."

That was a narrow stretch I had navigated uncomfortably before. Nicknamed after our city's most famous playwright, it was not exactly a reverent tribute, given the prostitutes who worked it at night.

"Do they try to drag you there?" she asked.

"No!" I blushed. "I do admire the women's inventive propositions when I walk by, but that might be awkward."

"You might be surprised. They've likely seen it all before."

"Maybe I should visit and ask," I joked.

But Annella didn't laugh. "That's exactly where Tristano might look for you."

"I wouldn't," I said. "I was joking."

"Oh, of course." She brightened. "Show me our first repair. We should do at least one."

I picked up the Lauretta marionette and lifted the frill of torn lace at the bottom of her royal blue velvet gown. "This lace hits too close to her feet. It's torn in three spots and worsens every week from the knifelike edge of her boot. Watch." I began to demonstrate how easy it was to damage, maneuvering Lauretta in a minuet. Twice more it caught.

When I stopped, though, Annella stared at me, not Lauretta.

"What's wrong?" I asked.

"Nothing. It's just all too strange and wonderful. Here we are, you making another dark-haired girl dance. It's as if we've never been apart—except for how skilled you've become."

"I am slightly altered." I modeled my morning coat's lapel. "As are you."

"Yet now you match your attire, no longer concealed in skirts. And your face." She came closer and pushed a lock of my hair back. "No longer hiding. What kind eyes you have, dark brown with a spark near the iris."

I felt shy at being seen. As girls, Annella and I had often sat cross-legged, knees touching, hands on the same holder of Carlita in the corner of her bedroom. Yet now when I looked at her, she was a woman standing in front of me, and I, a kind of man.

"You wore this dress that first night I saw you," I said. "Only a few months and it's already tailored, isn't it?"

"A few months means three seasons in Milan. Constanza often has my clothes replaced. I must not be seen in anything old, even if the changes render it harder to walk, move, or sit." Annella pointed to her sleeves. "These are too tight now, like the hips."

"Does she always select what you wear and tell you how to dress?"

"I suppose. That's what a companion is for, right? To illuminate the dowagers we serve and mark their status. They take us in, but we keep them safe, too. You see, one woman, alone and powerful in public among men, is suspect. With a companion, however, she seems more amiable to the men with whom she must deal to survive."

Since our last conversation, I had been wondering more about who Annella's benefactor really was, so now I asked.

Annella looked bored, her words rote, as if practiced. "Constanza is a wealthy widow who engages in social reform with the foundlings, literacy campaigns—that sort of thing. Her late husband was quite affluent, but she's had to shore up her place in society since he died ten years ago. I think this is part of her new interest in the Minerva: patronage in the arts."

"How did you meet her?"

Annella meandered over to the wall of marionettes. "After one of my shows. She came backstage, said she could help me. She was my way out, I suppose. Rossana's, too, for I insisted she take us both in." Annella faced me abruptly. "Do I look peaked to you?"

"Is she blind?" I laughed. "You could wear no powder at all and be beautiful."

"Beautiful?" Annella stilled. "Is that how you see me?"

"It's how you are."

She blushed, then pointed at Lauretta. "What if we just cut off that lace at the hem?"

"And reveal Lauretta's ankles? What will the censors say?"

"That she's a shameless harlot? Or worse—an American Gibson Girl riding a bicycle?"

"A bicycle would be a challenge to puppeteer, especially with a bustle."

"Good thing they've gone out of style." Annella grabbed the scissors and snipped them close to Lauretta's heels. "Shall we?"

"Do it," I said, pinching out the lacy hem. "Scandals draw a crowd."

My time with Annella passed fast. After she shut the sewing case, I picked up her plush velvet cloak and held it open for her. How petite she was when we stood close. My chin could have rested in her hair.

"Let's walk," she said, tying the ribbon of her hood loosely at her throat. "More time with you. How I wish we could have started on Saturday, your birthday, but I was stuck at one of Constanza's soirees."

"You remembered."

"Of course!"

"We'll do something special in November for yours," I said, throwing on my coat. "To make up for all the birthdays we've missed. Not that I could top Constanza's gifts, of course."

"Ah, but she does not have these," Annella said, surveying the marionettes. At the sound of Carmine's voice in the hall, she lifted her eyebrow. "Come, let's make sure your friend sees you with a girl."

We stepped into the hall as Carmine strolled by. He stopped and bowed.

"Annella's just given me my first sewing lesson," I said.

"Is he an impossible student?" Carmine asked her.

"He did very well," she replied. "Only time will tell if he becomes a proper tailor."

"I need to see her home," I told Carmine. "Don't wait for me for dinner."

"Turns out I also have a date," he replied, "so you're on your own."

"The gorgeous redhead?" I asked, but Carmine shushed me, refusing to reply in front of Annella. "If you have any repairs tomorrow," I added, "leave them here. Radillo's christened our workroom 'Restoration.'"

"Appearances are everything with that man." Carmine looked at Annella. "How often will you be instructing our Franco?"

"Every Thursday, I hope. Learning to sew takes a long time."

"If he causes you trouble, I would be happy to assist."

"I'm sure you would," she said, "if you're not busy with a gorgeous redhead."

He chuckled. "You brighten the Minerva considerably. Take your time coming back, Franco. Andrea and Niccolò can handle their own props for once." Then he waltzed off, whistling.

Annella and I ventured outside and started toward the Grand Canal, but after a few blocks, she touched my arm. "Don't rush. You're wearing trousers, but I'm not and have nearly tripped twice."

"Sorry; I have forgotten what it's like to walk in a dress."

We passed a group of men who gawked at Annella.

"I wouldn't mind forgetting," she said with a sniff.

We waded through crowds and dodged photographers over the Rialto Bridge. I hardly ever visited San Polo, where we passed back-to-back *trattorie* lining San Silvestro. February's chill kept diners inside, their foreheads pressed to steamed-up windows for a glimpse of the elite gliding into their palazzi across the broad Grand Canal.

Gold threads of sunlight streaked the sky above as we continued along the cavernous stretch of Calle dei Sbianchesini. More residential than San Marco, the homes here in San Polo stretched into the sky, narrowing passages, blinding out light, and blackening placid waters.

"I can go from here," Annella said. "It's just on the other side."

"I wouldn't be a very good chaperone if I left you alone in a dark alley."

"I suppose," she said, looking around warily.

"Or are you ashamed of me?" I teased.

"No, it's just . . . the guards can be cruel."

"I can take care of myself."

Annella led me down Sotoportego del Tamossi, into Calle Stretta, an alley that was slimmer than almost any other in San Marco. Even walking single file, dust from the limed brick flaked onto our shoulders.

When we emerged, I gazed upon a massive palazzo. It occupied half of the sprawling stone square, having annexed equally elegant homes on either side. Torches blazed beside the forest green front doors of the marble-lined first floor, and most of the shuttered windows sat dark. Above, a corner of the rooftop garden stood unused under icy winds, the only signs of life a forlorn stand of forgotten sheets flapping in the wind.

"This is your home?" I asked.

"Hardly mine. It is, however, where I live."

Unlike most public squares, this one held no people. No workers or tourists or old men huddled over games of chess. No cafés or shops or even a shivering flower seller. No neighbors stretching out of windows to feed lines of washing. Even the sky and rooftops were devoid of pigeons, as if an unspoken rule had decreed this was all private. The only people were four men framing the doors, looking like somnolent gargoyles resting on their bayonets.

"Why does she have guards?" I asked. "She's just a widow."

"As a woman alone, she worries." Annella scanned the second-story balcony. "Bear with me at the door. I will need to seem officious."

"I understand. See you next week?"

"I can't wait," she replied, but fell silent as the guards saw us approach. Annella offered only faint acknowledgment before they parted to let her inside.

After she disappeared, one of the guards faced me. "You've done your duty; go on. This is no place for the likes of you."

I stepped away, feeling a familiar braid of anger, fear, and concern. It echoed my old desire to protect Annella from my temperamental father. But I brushed it off. Annella didn't need my protection now. Clearly, her benefactor fed her every whim. But as I left the square, I couldn't help but wonder why Signora Constanza Cappello kept such a menacing presence at her door. Were those guards meant to keep people out—or trap them in?

14

My weeks were full over the next months as winter turned into spring. Carmine and I visited the stalls at Riva degli Schiavoni on Mondays for inspiration, and Annella and I worked on the marionettes every Thursday, trading stories over cones of nuts that I spirited from the Minerva's stash—and sometimes returning to the stalls ourselves. I learned that her benefactor Constanza had rescued other girls like Annella, getting most of them work as cleaners in factories. But she had taken Annella under her wing, which enabled Annella to secure Rossana a place as a companion to one of Constanza's cousins in the same home. In exchange, they were often kept busy attending events—of which there were many—but Annella didn't elaborate beyond that.

I had trusted Annella with my secret and hoped that if she ever needed to confide in me, she would. Most days, she breezed into Restoration in high spirits, as did I. We began to extend our afternoons together, as time went on. After every session, I walked her right to her door, despite her protestations. Then I began to count down the days until her next visit.

Today, however, she was late. I distracted myself with one of Radillo's special puppets—the ruddy Venetian *contadino* with only four strings. After I finished restringing and polishing the holder, I stared into his face, waiting for his voice to surface. Each marionette's character always came if I waited, and he was no exception.

Here was a pleasure-seeking old Veneto farmer, distinct from my gruff but refined grandfather. The *contadino*'s ruddy cheeks made me decide this old man had tilled the soil all day and oiled himself with liquor all night. I began to practice a jig. Perhaps he sought to amuse a lady and blow foam off a beer stein in a drunken toast. Despite having only four strings, the *contadino* felt nimble in my hands. Even his face seemed to change expression from the slightest shift in his chin, swerving into a sidelong lascivious glance.

At the creak of the floorboards, I looked up. Radillo had been watching me practice.

"All is well?" he asked, entering.

Unsure if he meant the puppet or me, I nodded yes.

How long had he been there? I held his prize, who only made rare appearances onstage, certainly none as robust as what I had been staging. I held out the holder and he checked the repair that had sent the puppet into my care.

"Good work," he said, and handed the *contadino* back. "I came to say that you start weekdays as Carmine's partner in two weeks. It's our new show, commedia dell'arte, for today's audiences. Puppets, wearing masks." He took in the cramped room. "If a change in environment suits you?"

"Very much, sir," I said, riveted. "Thank you."

"Thank Carmine. He's been telling me of your skills. I wanted to see for myself. Franco, *The Decameron* and commedia are just the beginning of a new slate of more ambitious works for the Minerva. Reimagined classics and folktales that once put Venice on the map. That's why I gave you these to read." He patted the stack of scripts stacked on the worktable. "Learn this history, of a time when Venice suffered wars and imperial isolation. It will help you to depict it. Which have you read so far?"

"All of them."

He tapped his forehead, and his blue eyes sparkled. "I thought so, from your observations during rehearsals." He stared at me. "It's odd. Your style reminds me of someone, but I can't quite place who."

"Thank you for this chance, sir."

"You earned it, though I'm afraid I'll need you in Restoration, too. It will be busy, but I have confidence in you." He looked at the *contadino* in my hands. "A drunken farmer, dancing and failing at giving a toast. I just may work that in."

After he left, I felt stunned. The puppet seemed to eye me, gratified.

After months surviving and laboring behind the scenes, I was climbing up. This is what had drawn me to the Minerva. It was not merely to hide, carry props, and paint sets. I had run here to perform.

Then I heard Carmine out in the hallway.

"Look who I found on my way back from Dorsoduro," he said, ushering a flushed Annella into the room.

Annella didn't give a reason for her delay, just settled beside me and picked up a repair. "Carmine, what do you do to these poor creatures every night?" she asked.

"Between shipwrecks, heartbreak, pirates, gods, and war, they suffer greatly," he replied. "Thanks to you, at least they don't suffer from the drunken seamstress, too." Carmine picked up his Angelica, which he used in the weekend preambles. "Start with this one, if you don't mind. The holder feels off."

"Radillo was just here," I said, taking the marionette from him. "He's bringing me on for commedia in two weeks."

"What?" Annella squealed. "You'll finally be working the stage!"

"I've been telling him to do it for weeks," Carmine said. "Congratulations!"

"Thanks," I said, grinning as I tested the holder of Angelica, practicing her dance sequence with one hand.

Carmine watched me. "You should be up there tonight, not me. Your hands are steadier. Just arc here more when she faints," he said, pointing to my right wrist. "Make her fall with more dignity." I adjusted accordingly and he nodded. "There you go."

"Now if only I can avoid ruining opening night," I said.

Annella was beaming. "Franco, I could watch you all day. You would need to work hard to make a mistake."

"Unlike me with Radillo," Carmine said. "Lately, he and I have only been able to agree on one thing—you."

I set Angelica aside. "What's wrong?"

"Is it that girl?" Annella asked him. "Is that why you were in Dorsoduro just now?"

Carmine hung his head and sighed.

"Definitely the girl," I said to Annella. "The frequent clothing changes, the shaving, and the rushing out after shows. Then he's busy daydreaming." I paused. "Come on—tell us about her."

Carmine shook his head. "No stories, schoolboy. This one's different."

"Afraid I'll steal her?" I teased, but caught Annella's blush.

"I am in real trouble," Carmine said. "Not that it matters. She won't choose me."

"Does she like you?" Annella asked, as she began threading a needle.

"I think so."

Annella stopped. "You think so, or you know so?"

"I know so." Carmine grew serious. "We both do. Only, I should step away."

"Why?" Annella asked. "You can't be all that bad. Is there someone else?"

"No," Carmine said. "But there are other consequences—things I can't ask of her."

Annella pointed at him. "There also are consequences if you don't take the chance. Think what you both would regret. Don't make up her mind for her. We're nearly in a new century. Stop acting like the self-sacrificial medieval knights you puppeteer. Just talk to her and it will fall into place."

"Perhaps, though I can't imagine what she sees in my face." He picked up the Angelica marionette and peered at it as if it were a mirror, then set it down. "Enough about me. We only have two weeks to get you ready for your big debut, Franco. It's a minor character, of course, but there are tricky bits to navigate. Let's start tomorrow." He gave Annella a formal bow and smiled at me. "Today, you have more important matters to attend to."

When he left, Annella went to ensure the door was fully shut, then she rushed back and flung her arms around me.

"Franco, I'm so thrilled!" She clung to me. "To see you perform on a proper stage? It's too wonderful for words! I wanted to do this before, upon hearing your good news, only Carmine was here."

"It is wonderful." Tentatively, I held her, breathing in her hair. We didn't move apart.

It should have been ordinary, to embrace. But it wasn't, especially as the embrace lasted. Only when we heard Leo's and Andrea's voices beyond the door did we separate, and even then, reluctantly.

"Come." Annella drew me back to the table. "It looks like you repaired half of *The Decameron*'s cast already, given how late I am." She noted the script half-open on the table. "Is Radillo staging this Shakespeare play, *Romeo and Juliet*?"

"We couldn't afford a production like that, judging from the notes. Commedia's as elaborate as we'll get."

"Unless Constanza funds it. Her money could grow the Minerva."

"Is she offering? Usually reformers prefer to shut down theaters, not keep them open."

"Believe me, Constanza is no nun preaching decency. In the music halls, I saw plenty of priests. They'd stay for the whole show and only after they'd had their fill, issue a closure." Annella leafed through the pages. "From how she talks lately, Constanza may be as taken with the Minerva as I am."

"Keep reading," I said, getting a pair of damaged Saracens. "I know you love the scripts. I can take care of these last two—just a few scuffs to buff out."

She shook her head. "Give me one of those brave soldiers. We'll finish faster together."

"Brave? The pit thrills when the virtuous paladins strike the Saracens down."

"History," Annella said, concentrating on her Saracen's face, "is only ever told by those who conquer. The Saracens die without fanfare in Italy, but what might their own version of the tale be? To them, the paladins are far from virtuous." She made the Saracen take a few steps.

"You remember the technique," I said. "Your fingers are even in the right position. Just press more firmly with your thumb, like this." I rested my hand atop hers, but then Annella quickly passed the marionette back.

"The base feels crooked," she said.

I took it and examined the front crossbar, which attached to the head's strings. Every night, the deaths of the Saracens were shown by the puppeteers throwing their holders onstage. It's why the Saracens landed here for repair so often. Casting them down was a simple but brutal technique. It seemed like it should break the illusion and expose that someone was managing the marionette, but it never did. Night after night, the audience responded as if the marionette's life really did end, gasping at the sight of mere wood in shock.

Still, what would the pit do if a Saracen ever triumphed? Annella had a point. A whole world of shadows haunts history. So many stories, untold on any stage or page.

After we finished, Annella said she needed to return, so we walked to Constanza's in a restive silence, threading our way through the Carampane District, and still it felt like we reached the now-familiar alley too soon.

As we were about to enter the square, a burst of noise broke through Constanza's front doors.

Annella hung back. "Wait."

Five Frenchmen in top hats spilled out of the palazzo, loud and indecorous. Even from afar, they emitted a scent of scotch and opium.

"Why are they here?" I asked. "They will accost you, and I'm no good against five."

"They've already tried—believe me."

"Have you told Constanza? She'll protect you."

"The guards will. There are certain benefits to being Constanza's companion."

"But, Annella . . ."

Then lamplights flared on the second-story balcony above the guarded door, and Constanza stepped out with a group of men smoking cigars. Servants hovered behind, heads bent.

"I'm supposed to be up there. She will be vexed," Annella added quickly. "I must go. Now, and alone. If she sees you, she'll know I lied."

"Lied? But you come to the Minerva every Thursday."

"Yes, but today I wasn't supposed to."

"Why not?" I gestured at the men on the balcony. "What exactly must you do for her?"

Annella squeezed my hand. "Don't worry, Franco. It's fine. I'll see you next week."

Then she left me—fled, really. As soon as the guards spotted her, they shooed the drunk foreigners out of the square.

Above, I watched Constanza turn from her guests midlaugh and stare down at Annella. Even from here I could sense her disapproval flare. Then, strangely, Constanza looked to the alcove where I hid.

There was no way she could see me, but I slunk into the shadows nevertheless.

What was it Annella had said? That it was safer for Constanza to see me as a timid boy? Now I couldn't help but wonder if she meant it was safer for me—or Annella.

15

Carmine's shout of "Ten minutes!" echoed through the rafters as I disentangled a knight and maiden that he needed for a second-act lovers' scene. Crouched on my right was Vincenzo, whose ragu-stained shirt meant mine now was too, for he was leaning against me in a corner to insert a new filter.

Tonight was my first show handling a minor, and I was unsure how this chaos could morph into order. I heard the lute tuning, our sole accompaniment, and the audience rustling beyond the curtain. Radillo was also out there to watch my debut, a fact I couldn't think about without feeling queasy.

Our commedia was a puppet version featuring the popular local hero and fool, Facanapa. The mainstays of this theater were familiar to Venetians, but our novelty was masked puppets—a return to commedia's cinquecento origins. Puppets had come first in the fifteenth century, traveling actors after. But coordinating the mask-string attachments with lighting and voice to evoke illusory changes of expression for the genre's frequent double entendres was a challenge in itself.

Over the past two weeks, I'd been struggling with keeping the mask in place during a key dance sequence. Just yesterday in rehearsal,

Carmine had said, "Schoolboy, when you're up there, there are no second chances. So whatever happens, keep going."

Now I tried to recall my character's first words and could not. There was a tear in the first scene's backdrop, so we all needed to adjust positions—no small feat. Usually, I was out front by now, so maybe this chaos was normal.

"Go fetch that extra beaked mask in Restoration," Carmine said to me. "We might need it for act two."

Grateful to move, I scrambled down. On my way back, I peeked at the audience and spotted Annella and Rossana with two guards in a box—and without Constanza. It was my first time seeing Annella, who had not been back to work with me in Restoration since our rushed goodbye two weeks ago. I hoped she might see me, but her eyes were fixed on her program, and both she and Rossana seemed subdued.

The call of "Five minutes!" got me running again, but up in the rafters, my fingers now felt dipped in glue as I tried to secure the leg strings of my puppet, the cuckolded buffoon, Pedrolino.

Carmine saw my trouble and stilled my hand. "Breathe," he said. "And *merde*. It's French for 'shit.'"

"I know, but why say it?"

"Dancers say *merde* before a show."

"Why not just wish good—"

He covered my mouth. "Never say that! That's bad. Usually just before we start, Radillo says, 'In the mouth of the wolf.' Then we respond with, 'Death to the wolf.'"

"That makes no sense."

"Precisely!" He laughed. "Takes your mind off how nothing is working."

When there was another problem with the lights a moment later, Carmine gave me a wild, broad smile. "You're up here, schoolboy. Enjoy it."

More than anything, that helped. My knees still shook as I leaned against the *appoggio*, glad the bar was steady, but now my heart began to race in anticipation, not panic. I was finally running the strings. Not from a balcony or in Restoration. Here, at the Minerva.

Without thinking—indeed, only if I did *not* think—I knew my lines. Carmine was handling Venice's beloved Facanapa and the lover Flavio tonight, and Andrea, the maiden Isabella. Facanapa was a sharp-tongued braggart in the guise of a doctor. He lied, but kept the audience in on all his lusty antics, comic dances, and witty asides. My Pedrolino had few words. His tendency to sputter worked in my favor, too. Pedrolino sighed often and loudly. I could manage that.

Then I noticed Andrea and Carmine conversing with some urgency. "Two minutes!" came Vincenzo's cry. This time I was absolutely fine, until Carmine motioned me to the center.

"Don't panic," he said, "but you're doing Facanapa and Flavio now."

"What?"

"I'll do Isabella," he continued, "and Colombina in the second half. Andrea has a bad cold. No falsetto. He can't voice a girl or the lead. So he'll do Pedrolino. I'm the only one here with a believable falsetto, so I'll do Isabella. That makes you the two men."

"Let me do Isabella. She barely says anything!"

Carmine passed my puppet to Andrea. "Don't be silly! A falsetto takes practice. You'll overdo it. It'll be a disaster."

"I can't, Carmine!"

"Of course you can. I've seen you run these scripts a thousand times down there. What's the difference?"

I nodded in the direction of the audience. "Them."

"Aren't they the point?" He set Facanapa in front of me. "They don't care about you—only him. Give them the voice that comes to you." He paused. "Look, you're better than most of us—even me. Trust me for once?"

Everything was slowing. I heard my grandfather: *Never think what you maneuver below is all you.*

Carmine whispered to Vincenzo, "Cue now. Lights down."

"Carmine," I called out, "what about the lines?"

"Forget the script, schoolboy. It's commedia. It's meant to be fresh. I'll cue you—but I doubt you'll need it." He dropped Isabella in position in the wings. "You can't study forever. Give it a try. See what happens next."

The lights softened as the lute began its overture. I could no longer see Carmine's face. I lowered Facanapa and planted his boots in a cocky stance.

An alchemy commenced. My terrible fear began to guide me. It did not disappear but urged me on. A sense of my own body dissipated, trailing into Facanapa's forward-thrusting chin. In the hush, I became both immaterial and Facanapa below—a true medium, dancing in the pull of the line.

The curtains parted. Light flared onto a pastoral road to Venice.

"Good day, fair lady of the north!" I cried. "Most beautiful are you."

I confused Facanapa's gaze from Isabella's chest to her face, and the audience applauded with "A fine day, indeed!" and "It's looking much better now!"

"Good day, kind sir," cried Carmine in a timid falsetto, swishing Isabella's skirt.

"Dear girl, do not step a delicate toe in this street's vulgar mud. You are so wise and beautiful; please tell me—what is the time of day?" My Facanapa fell to one knee, caressing the hem of her dress amid the crowd's various catcalls.

"I do not know the time," Carmine's Isabella replied demurely.

The pit mocked Isabella's reticence with suggestions for how she and Facanapa might spend the time. When a woman urged Isabella to teach Facanapa manners, another shouted, "How much more proper can he be? He's only asking her the time."

Facanapa attempted to dance. While Carmine and I twirled the pair, I leaned Facanapa in for a kiss. Isabella delivered a smack of a slap, and Facanapa reeled back to the crowd's delight. Above, Carmine and I shared a smile.

"How dare you!" Carmine shouted as Isabella. "You are not my one true love!"

On cue, Andrea shuffled Pedrolino onstage, and I moved Facanapa downstage to confer with the audience in an aside. "*That* is my rival? Why, he is nothing more than a buffoon!" I called to Isabella, "Sweet lady, which of us steals your heart?"

Carmine made Isabella swoon. "My sweet, my most handsome . . . Flavio."

Both Andrea and I gasped. "Flavio?"

As Isabella waltzed about the stage, Carmine began describing Flavio's winsome virtues, ending with, "But why has he stayed in Padua and left me on this treacherous road?"

"Padua?" I tilted Facanapa's mask to the audience as if sharing a secret. "He is far, so I have a chance. No maiden can resist my artful dance, and besides, both her men are no better than dogs." The crowd egged me on, and some concurred by barking.

I moved Facanapa to approach Isabella in a comedic shuffle, but she leapt back in fear. "How you sneak! You are a robber come to steal my gold!"

"My dear lady, I am no robber, but that bandit you travel with is. I shall protect you."

I drew Facanapa's sword and leveled it at Pedrolino. The pit cheered with cries to fight.

We had them. More precisely, I did. The crowd divided between mocking Isabella, hating Pedrolino, and, above all, loving Facanapa.

It was my first taste. Not of losing myself in a puppet, for that had occurred in Sant'Alvise. Rather, it amplified the sensations of that first makeshift audience tenfold. I recalled the music of my grandfather's and

Annella's laughter, now undulating in the mirth of one hundred more. Performing was better than any opium, ineffable yet real, a glimpse of the divine on earth. It made me wish my grandfather could see how far I'd come from that first frayed glove puppet so many years ago.

After the final curtain was closed, I climbed down to Carmine's hearty slap on my back.

"Come, let's celebrate," he said. "Go get Annella and her friend. I saw them in the audience."

"In a moment," I said as Radillo strode up.

"Franco," Radillo said, hands planted on his hips. "Playing Facanapa on your first night out? I don't even know where to begin."

"I'm sorry, sir. Andrea was ill . . ." I faltered, glancing at Carmine for help.

Instead, Carmine nodded. "Sir, he insisted he play the lead. The arrogance was astonishing. He left me no choice, for the show must go on, no?"

"What?" I shouted, but then both Radillo and Carmine broke into laughter.

"Your face, Franco," Radillo said, pointing. "Such an open book. We're teasing! You did very well, stepping in at the last minute. Andrea would've been a terrible Isabella, and Carmine was right." He patted my back. "You were ready."

Giddy with relief, I could only shake my head.

"Let Bruno and Vincenzo clean up. Let's all go enjoy a drink at the Britannia."

It was the first time I'd been invited to join them, but I'd wanted to see Annella. "Let me just put these masks away so they don't get damaged."

"So devoted!" Radillo said. "All right, but hurry up."

By the time I had dropped the masks off in Restoration and run back to the curtain's edge, however, the box in which Annella had sat was empty. I slipped in with the crowds to scan the lobbies and street, but she was gone.

16

My success as Facanapa led Radillo to put me on all shows but the Sunday historicals. On commedia, I started alternating between Flavio and Facanapa with Carmine, as new and glowing reviews surfaced of us both. One even referred to me as "a man to watch."

I wanted to share a laugh with Annella over that, but she had not returned to the theater. When I asked Leo why, he only said, "She's been doing us a favor. Signora Cappello needs her now."

"For what?" I fished.

"Charity work, I suppose."

"Could I send Annella a note?"

Leo shook his head. "Better to not. It's delicate with Radillo courting the widow as a patron." He smiled. "Though if it's not sewing you seek, you'll see Annella at Saturday night's party."

Over beer at the Britannia, Radillo had told us about an upcoming soiree hosted by one of his old friends, Count De Rossi, to celebrate our new production. All the head men were invited. Leo had handed me a small but hefty purse for Carmine and me to get new suits from Leo's cheap tailor in Santa Croce.

"She will attend?" I asked Leo now.

"I assume so. The late Signor Cappello had ties to Count De Rossi's shipping routes. Signora Cappello maintains the relationship to stay in the count's graces."

I nodded, feigning interest. All I cared about was seeing Annella.

The intervening days passed in a blur of performances and repairs. Finally, the night of the party arrived. After our show, I donned my first real suit, marveling at the feel of the freshly starched linen dress shirt and black silks, a grand step up from the boyish attire I'd long outgrown. The suit fit perfectly, despite the more delicate sartorial fitting I'd refused, complementing the ivory cummerbund and matching tie, while my grandfather's silver cuff links glimmered at my wrists. I'd received a proper trim at the barber, and an hour of polishing my new dress shoes made them, and me, look the part—a man I had not imagined I might ever be.

Outside the theater, I joined Leo, Andrea, and Niccolò, decked out in their finery. Andrea was impatient to depart, but Carmine was lagging. We needed Leo to vouch for us all, or we would not be admitted.

When Carmine at last strolled up, everyone stopped. His skin glowed against his fitted suit, and his normally languid gait had morphed into that of an aristocrat's.

"Not bad," I said, standing back. "Trying to impress someone? Might she be there?"

Carmine ignored me. "How can a boy so agile with the strings be so clumsy with a tie?" As he adjusted it, he whispered, "Turn heads tonight, schoolboy. Especially rich ones."

"You're in a good mood."

"And why not? Tonight is our night!" Carmine moved on to Leo, flourishing his arm like the captain of a ship. "A thousand apologies, Leo. Am I suitable enough?"

"You'll do," Leo said, and started us on the path to Count De Rossi's palazzo, housed in a neighborhood of diplomats.

After a lengthy walk, we arrived at the marble gate. Sounds of a dulcet string quartet and glasses meeting in toasts emanated from inside. Butlers guided us in and through a small courtyard up to the grand foyer. Here, an imposing English grandfather clock chimed eleven so loudly that I felt its echo in my feet. In the spacious adjoining ballroom, elegant guests milled, including Radillo, conversing with a sophisticated couple in bone-white garb.

"Ah, look at the old chums," said Carmine, popping a canapé in his mouth. "Our hosts, the Count and Countess De Rossi. Every time they show up at the Minerva, the poor cleaners are taxed beyond belief."

"Why? I didn't think the Minerva had a patron."

"Not officially," clarified Leo. "Emergencies only—and we've had a few. It's a delicate art," he added, scanning the room, "asking for financial support while seeming successful enough not to need it. Speaking of, there are the Grimanis, Radillo's first investors."

Even I knew the name. Venice's mayor, Lord Filippo Grimani, and Lady Teresa Grimani were one of Venice's oldest aristocratic families. Unlike most of the people in this room, even the most affluent, the Grimanis' wealth began with Venice's first empire. Their name allowed them to exist outside of history's vagaries. Instead, they made history.

We watched their entrance. Lady Grimani's sweeping azure gown matched the shade of the lord's shirt, collar upturned to elongate his neck. They were the very picture of aristocrats, with refined features to transfix any painter: his high cheekbones and finely arched nose, her deep-set eyes and a creamy complexion tinged with hints of gold—the pair gleamed in silks beneath the chandelier.

"They have been instrumental in Venetian theater from the start," Leo explained as he passed us flutes of champagne. "And at last year's international glass exhibition, they helped finance the revival of Murano glass, which you're holding."

I'd heard of Murano glass—every Venetian had. After centuries of decline, it was once more flourishing in decorative forms and as San Marco's restored mosaics. Its admixture of crystal, enamel, and flecks of fired metal and semiprecious stones fell in resplendent colors rarely seen outside nature. But I'd never touched it. Now, when I held the featherlight flute to a candle in the wall sconce, an opalescent green light sparkled as I twirled its base.

"The manufacture of Murano glass is a closely guarded secret," Leo continued. "Its rarity makes it a valuable commodity, protected on its namesake island and drawing substantial tariffs when traded abroad. Why, with the recent revival, Italy's getting richer at France's expense. And why shouldn't we? Murano glass is nothing like those cheap French champagne bottles—though what's inside them is fine." He gave me a nudge. "Enjoying your first taste?"

I toasted Leo, but Carmine was only half listening. He tapped his glass to create a melodic ring. "Do the Grimanis know the secret formulas?" he asked Leo, who only frowned.

"Please remember where you are," he said, scolding Carmine, and then moved off.

I watched Leo join Radillo, approaching the Grimanis. They were offering a bow when the Count and Countess De Rossi strolled up with Constanza, sharing introductions, it appeared. I had missed Constanza's arrival entirely but now strained to see the rest of her retinue. First, I spotted Rossana, but then my breath caught as Annella came into view.

Annella's black evening gown glistened with a train of embroidered white gemstones in the pattern of a ghostly butterfly, wings spread wide, with diaphanous tulle loose at her shoulders. The transparent rim of her dress hooked at the back, with tight stitching to accentuate her waist. Her hair had been loosely gathered up, two tendrils curling on either side to reveal teardrop diamonds glinting in her ears, and three delicate bracelets encircled her wrist.

"Cat got your tongue, Franco?" Carmine said.

I couldn't reply, unable to look away.

"I see why you're at a loss for words. Strangely, so is she. Not her usual chatty self."

Indeed, as we listened in, everyone in the consort but Annella grew lively. Snippets of their talk drifted over. Trade routes to the French port city of Marseille. The Bandol vineyards in the Riviera. Someone's estate renovations. Plans for a luncheon near La Fenice.

"Sometimes I'm glad I'm not rich." Carmine sighed. "What insufferable conversations."

Then Annella saw me. In her haste to come over, she nearly tripped on her gown.

Carmine tipped my glass toward my mouth. "Drink, before she gets here."

I'd never drunk champagne but drained the glass. Everything instantly warmed too fast, which left me swaying.

"Franco, how handsome you look!" she said. "And your debut! Why, I was there; did you know?"

Up close, she was even more beautiful. She touched my arm and I felt a jolt of heat.

Confused by my silence, she continued. "You were even mentioned in the papers. Think how far you've come . . ."

"He's not just a decent tailor, then?" Carmine asked, rescuing me.

"Hardly," said Rossana, who had followed Annella. "Franco, even I enjoyed your debut. We wanted to come backstage after, but the guards made us leave. Annella was so upset."

"I saw you were there," I said, weighing my words too carefully. "But I haven't seen you in Restoration since."

"Oh," Annella replied, fidgeting with her bracelets. "Constanza has kept me engaged—that's all. Never mind her. What was it like performing? I almost didn't recognize your voice."

"It's true," Rossana said. "You simply transformed." She stepped back. "And again tonight."

"Transformation is never simple," Carmine said. "When you're up in the rafters, you're not yourself."

"Sounds like my work," Rossana replied offhandedly.

"In our illustrious past as dancers," Annella added quickly, and glanced back at Constanza. "There are days when I felt more myself dancing, not just a polished ornament."

"Oh, you're more than that," Rossana said, but she quieted at Annella's pointed look.

"We all must work—it's true," Carmine opined. "But if you're lucky, you meet someone who reminds you who you really are."

Annella brightened. "Anyone in particular?"

"Most definitely." He snapped for a passing waiter to bring a fresh round.

"I think we know which way his conversation went," Annella said to me with a wry smile.

Carmine wrapped an arm around me. "Why so quiet, Franco? We should be celebrating!"

"I agree," Annella said. "Think of all you may do next."

"Like dance with her?" Rossana nodded at a girl tittering with her friends in the corner. "She's staring at you. Guess you really are 'a man to watch.'"

I peered at the blonde, who hid behind her curls. How strange, to be admired by the kind of girl who once would have loathed me. Now? Standing here in a suit? Everything had changed.

"Go on; ask her to dance," Rossana said. "Facanapa would not hesitate to act."

"I am no Facanapa," I said, downing more champagne too fast.

Annella raised her glass. "I'll drink to that."

Just then, Count De Rossi clapped his hands lightly. "Everyone, it's time to meet our special guests this evening: the puppeteers from the Minerva Theater of Marionettes."

"That's our cue," Carmine said, and Annella nodded encouragingly.

When Carmine and I moved away, he whispered, "What is wrong with you? She practically runs over, calls you handsome, and you just stand there, mute?"

Silence fell for the formal presentation, saving me from a response. Radillo began to describe the Minerva as a haven for fantastical tales of epic battles, last-minute rescues, swooning romances, and other gems of Italy's great past. I gazed at the finery lining the room. The world beyond these grand doors seemed more haphazard—which the pit understood. Yet tonight, I was evidence that with some grit and will, we could make our own fates, too.

As the butler announced each puppeteer by name, we were to greet the De Rossis and their two sons, then the Grimanis, and Radillo's family. As the newest puppeteer, I went last.

"So this is our celebrated Facanapa," Count De Rossi said, once my name was called.

"Indeed," Radillo said. "Franco showed up on my doorstep and I couldn't turn such a talent away, even an orphan from the ghetto."

"A foundling," the count's wife mused. "Signora Cappello has told us all about her rescue efforts. Tell us, were you born in an alley? Or dodge rats as a baby?"

"Franco rarely speaks from whence he came," Radillo replied for me.

I felt too visible under their intrusive gaze, so I deflected. "The opulence of this room calls for a better topic than my origins."

The countess clapped her hands. "He speaks! What a charming accent. Like one of our old tailors in Castello. We must attend the show tomorrow and see Venice's famous foundling in action."

"Nothing would make me happier," Radillo said, and moved me along. "Lord and Lady Grimani, may I present Franco Collegario." Radillo turned to me. "Lord Grimani's tremendous collection is one that he has been most generous to share with the Minerva."

I bowed. "A great pleasure to meet you."

Radillo continued. "Franco has a gift for restoration. He completed some of our most delicate repairs on your Venetian *contadino*."

"Really?" Lord Grimani replied warmly. "One of my favorites. My family has been supporting theater in Venice for generations. We even have a theater in our palazzo for private shows. How I admire Radillo's collection of marionettes. Why, I remember my first visit to his airy studio strung with swaths of colorful fabric, vials of paint, smudged cups full of brushes and wood stain, and lined shelves of marionettes both ancient and wily, some with only two or three strings. The array of expressions emits all the noise and color of human personalities."

"Let the boy pass," Lady Grimani said, teasing her husband. "So, you are Franco Collegario? Quite a namesake to live up to—freedom. It seems you have brought something fresh to the Minerva, according to the press. We look forward to seeing you perform."

"We would be most honored," Radillo said, clearly pleased that I'd gained the approval of his inner circle. Titters from the crowd revealed they were growing restless, however, so Radillo quickly stepped me over to his wife, Esmeralda.

She was not at all whom I expected, much younger than Radillo, with a severe, high forehead and watery eyes that held little interest in me. His daughter, Giannina, however, was a bright strawberry blonde with dewy skin. About my age and delicate in stature, she was not without will, like a determined ballerina. When I bent to kiss her hand, I felt calluses on Giannina's index finger and thumb, much like my own. So she, too, had spent time with her father's collection.

She gave me a winsome smile. "I heard you were to be Pedrolino on opening night but stepped in for Facanapa at the last moment?"

Before I could respond, Radillo did. "Indeed." Then he clapped his hands to recommence the music, concluding introductions. Around me, trays of food and champagne sallied forth, and I rejoined Carmine, who held out a glass of champagne for me.

"You look like you need this," he said, then scanned the crowd.

"Looking for someone?" I asked.

"I see a maiden who needs me to dance with her."

"But you don't know these dances, do you?"

"A minor obstacle," he said, handing me his glass. "Wish me luck."

I watched him approach, of all ladies, Giannina, clumsily intercepting—and disappointing—one of Count De Rossi's sons. Esmeralda sought to thwart him, but Carmine swept Giannina away as if oblivious to her mother's efforts. Unwittingly, I caught Esmeralda's eye, so she strode up to me, lips pursed at the effort of more unwanted business.

"Don't think you can dance with my daughter," she stated.

I wavered, thrown by her sudden hostility.

"My husband may have taken you under his wing and deluded you with his grand plans for that derelict theater," she said. "But make no mistake. You're just a puppeteer, and the Minerva, a relic of his former passions. But given that you're here, by all means—please do enjoy the party. We're all here for you." Then she turned on her heel.

On the dance floor, Carmine was managing well enough. He had positioned himself between two men to imitate their movements. As he spun Giannina, I saw how, under the warm glow of the chandelier, her hair shone, as did Carmine's eyes.

Then I knew. Giannina was the redhead.

Someone was standing in their way. Radillo. That's why Carmine never talked about her. Was that also why Radillo had been fighting with him more?

Still, seeing Carmine and Giannina entranced me. They radiated such ease. I could not help but hope for his success, cheering him on as the dance ended and he led Giannina to a lonelier stretch of the terrace.

When I looked back, I spotted Annella dancing stiffly in the arms of an older, dour man. I felt a pang of jealousy at seeing her in that inept partner's arms. Rossana was nearby and looked uncharacteristically forlorn herself, as Lord Grimani had just excused himself from their conversation.

"Who is that with Annella?" I asked, joining Rossana.

"Oh, don't worry; she's just working."

"What do you mean, 'working'?"

Rossana inched closer. "You know she's not merely an ornament, right? In Constanza's dealings, Annella serves as a powerful distraction. But her duties are becoming more extensive."

"Like dancing with that oaf? Is he one of Constanza's relations?"

"Hardly." Rossana seemed to sadden. "Annella made sure I wasn't left behind when Constanza took her on. You have no idea what a struggle it was for us before Constanza, and how often we went hungry. But now I worry. Constanza has started controlling Annella's every move, look, and choice." She paused to face me. "Except her choice of you. Annella likes you. You saw her face when I mentioned that pretty blonde, right? That's when I knew."

Privately, something leapt in me at Rossana's words. Yet my anger deepened as I glimpsed Annella trying to inch away from her partner, his hand splayed at her back.

Then Rossana laughed. "Oh, Franco, I guess it's mutual. Now you're the one who's furious and blushing."

"Well." I drained my champagne. "I think it's time I cut in."

"By all means," Rossana replied, stepping aside.

I circled the dance floor, full of swirling bodies with wafts of cigar smoke, the tang of too much alcohol thickening the air, then took advantage of a break in the crowd to capture Annella's hand and steal her from her partner.

"I came to rescue you," I said as her disappointed partner sulked off.

"How gallant," she said, repositioning my hand at her back, to mimic the man in front of us.

Couples twirled, and I did my best to follow suit. "I'm afraid only my marionettes dance well," I said, catching her waist a beat too late.

"Puppeteers must be agile and trust their instincts. Dancing is similar." She deftly curled into the crook of my left arm, then lifted my right to hold her hand. "Don't slouch. Look up."

"But I'm trained to look down."

"Watch my eyes," she added with a soft smile. "Otherwise, your partner might back-lead you—which is exactly what I plan to do." She initiated a simple box step, and then I stepped back, like the men around me. "There you have it," Annella said as we walked side by side, holding hands. "You're much better than my last partner. He hung on to me as if I were keeping him afloat."

"Have you been fighting them off all night?" The music's end made us face each other as she curtseyed. But I stared at her, forgetting to bow. "Because you look . . . exquisite."

She flushed. "I've seen girls staring at you all night, too. If they could ask for a dance, you'd have no peace, either."

"I hadn't noticed."

"Not even one girl?" Her gaze stayed steady on me.

The air stilled. Neither of us moved. Couples began to leave and enter the dance floor all around us. Yet it felt as if all sounds were fading—until a familiar voice rang too close.

"A party is no place to discuss the tedium of sewing, is it?" Constanza said, handing us each a drink before linking arms with Annella.

I stepped back, bowing.

"Congratulations, Franco. What an impression you made. The

Grimanis seem quite enthralled with you, despite your dodging rats as a baby."

"Thank you," I said. "I was just saying that I have some difficult repairs this week on which I could use Annella's expertise."

"Surely you must know how to sew by now," Constanza stated. "Or has Annella's instruction been wanting?"

"No, she has been most helpful," I hastened to say. "Only I have less time to spare."

"So does Annella." Constanza waved to someone in the distance. "Right now, I require her talents. But I gather I soon will see yours."

I moved to let them pass, and Annella cut me an apologetic look.

Troubled, I decided to stay close. I fell in with a pair of inebriated gentlemen walking closely behind Constanza. All I could think about now was getting Annella alone, drinking too quickly as I walked.

Then I heard Constanza say to her, "Why did you let that boy cut your dance short? Did our friend Vittorio attempt at a tête-à-tête?"

Annella nodded.

Constanza continued. "This palazzo has private rooms. Perhaps he'd share more about his dealings in Marseille if you were in a more intimate setting."

"I won't go that far—"

"Don't think that you set the terms with me, like the men in this room do," Constanza snapped. "You and I both know your gifts lie more in a bedroom than a ballroom. I've enjoyed keeping you for myself, but make no mistake: you'll go as far as I tell you." She gestured to the ballroom. "After all, isn't this better than Goldoni's Alley?"

Trembling, I dropped the flute still in my hand. Glass shattered, drawing attention.

I apologized and bent to pick up the shards, despite the waiters' protestations. When I stood, I caught Annella's eye and she blanched. Silently, I implored her to join me, but Constanza drew her to a waiting group of men. All I could do was stand aside, helplessly watching.

17

The image of Constanza's tight grip on Annella burned into my mind as I lay in bed. Unable to sleep, I left my pension early the next morning to walk and think. The streets were devoid of people, except for drunks and guards waiting for the day's start. Even the rats seemed asleep when I entered the great gray Piazza San Marco.

Caffè Florian's chairs sat upturned on tables salted with dew. Our famous winged lion and San Teodoro sat atop their columns, gazing blandly away from the empty port. The loudest sounds at that hour emanated not from tourists, bells, or freighters, but from complacent pigeons and cleaners' birch brooms, pressing the birds into flight.

Restless, I kept traveling along the familiar path to Constanza's, as if my body were leading the way. When I reached the palazzo, I found it dead quiet, every window shuttered. No guards manned their usual post. For a moment, I considered how I might send a message to Annella, but instead I slumped against a wall in defeat.

Who did I think I was? Why had I come here? As if I could just walk in there.

At that hour, I was reminded of the time I'd spent pacing in the shadow of the Minerva's door that first night, wondering if I'd survive. Despite everything, I had.

Until last night, I'd thought Annella was safe, too. Yet while Constanza had rescued her from poverty, those veiled threats and that snide mention of Goldoni's Alley revealed that Annella's salvation had come at a price. What exactly, I did not know, but one thing was certain: Annella was no mere companion. Rossana had tried to warn me, too. Constanza clearly expected something in return for her charity.

I wished I could talk to Carmine. I had searched for him at the party to no avail. Though perhaps it was for the best. I did not want to reveal Annella's secrets, and he had his own predicament. If he and Giannina loved each other, Radillo would never let those two worlds fold into one.

Just then, the doors of the palazzo swung open and I froze. My brother, Marco, strode out. Then he froze, too.

"Who are you?" he shouted at me. Fearful my voice might give me away, I scampered away, praying that he was drunk. But he caught up to me fast in the alley.

"I know you," he shouted, yanking the sleeve of my coat. I spun around and managed to land a punch, but he slammed me against the wall, eyes wild with confusion. In this close space, his breath was sour in my face. "Francesca?"

I struggled to shove him off, but his grip tightened. "Did you think you could fool your own brother?" he asked, gawking at me.

I cursed myself, panicking. Was this why Annella never wanted me in the square? Had she been protecting me all this time?

"So, you're the one dropping Constanza's girl off," Marco went on. "Radillo's apprentice that everyone's so fond of. Makes sense— the puppets, the Minerva, Annella."

I grabbed his lapel and managed to switch our positions. I reeled my fist back, but then he added, "What would Constanza do to Annella if she knew who you really are?"

That made me waver. Marco shook himself free, dusting limestone off his shoulder. "We need to talk."

I had no choice. When he lit a cigarette, I noted jagged scars slashed his right hand. Why was he here?

His gaze drifted lazily down to my chest. "What's your name now? Constanza just calls you 'Radillo's boy.'"

"Franco," I said, the square beyond eerily silent.

"Sandro might like you more as a son, but clearly he's willing to exploit us both."

"What are you talking about?"

"After you left, our dear father couldn't make good on his debt. So he forced me to start working for Tristano." A shadow passed over his face. "When Sandro couldn't sell you, he used me. Only, dear old Alfonso didn't bother to warn me, like he did you."

This was what my grandfather had written of in his letter. Marco had taken my place and was bound to Tristano, a man far worse than Daniele Ceresa.

"I heard Annella was teaching you how to sew," Marco went on. "Ironic, after all the shirts and socks of mine that Sandro made you darn, though I see why you'd pretend."

I rushed close. "Leave Annella alone. She doesn't know who I am," I lied.

"Really? She might like you more if she did."

"What?"

"Constanza doesn't spend her evenings with Annella reading sentimental novels. She's more modern than you think."

I stopped. Was that what Constanza meant by "keeping Annella to herself"? The idea of two women together was something I had never imagined. Both Rossana and Carmine presumed that Annella and I were more than friends. Might she, too? I couldn't think of that now.

"How do you know about Constanza if you work for Tristano?" I asked.

"My duties extend here, not that Constanza ever notices, since usually I'm forced to take the back door. I work like a dog, doing things I'm not proud of." He paused to smoke. "Because of you, I lost Paola."

His fiancée. Paola had been kind to me, which had eased things at home. A flash of her warm brown eyes and carefully plumped auburn curls resurfaced. Last summer, Marco had asked her to marry him.

"I'm sorry," I muttered.

"I need money. Help me run to Croatia."

"I don't have money. I'm just 'Radillo's boy,' remember?" I turned out one of my morning coat's pockets, glad he wasn't seeing me in last night's suit.

"Yes, I recognize that jacket. Looks better on you."

I pointed at his own expensive suit. "Besides, you clearly have more than I do."

"Tristano keeps me in silks, but I never see what I earn. It all goes to Sandro's debt, which, as you know, will never be paid. His salary might as well be water, given how it slides out of his hands at bars every night. Eventually, everyone falls out of favor with Tristano, unless they keep making him rich, like Sandro. If I run, Sandro will be screwed." He inhaled. "I want that more than you know."

I had never heard Marco speak of our father with such spite. He'd always emulated him. So I had a hard time believing his words. I had the money I'd saved for my grandfather. It might cover Marco's escape, if only just, but I couldn't offer it. My grandfather was my family. He'd saved me. Marco, as usual, only wanted to tear me down.

Marco observed me closely. "Don't make me, please."

"Make you do what?"

"Spell it out," Marco said. He waited a beat, but I said nothing, so he went on. "If you don't get me money, I'll tell Sandro. If he doesn't kill you, he'll shove you back in skirts and ship you off to ports unknown as some new brute's wife. Tristano will see to it personally. Believe me—you don't want to know the payment that man will extract when he sees you dressed like this." Marco tossed his cigarette. "Or what about Annella? Constanza gets jealous. Annella will suffer, if Constanza learns the truth."

I stepped back, sick at hearing all my darkest fears aloud. Now I had endangered Annella, too. But I couldn't let Marco see me scared. I learned never to make that mistake years ago.

"You're worse than our father," I spat. "Quite an achievement. No surprise whom you take after."

"Don't compare me to him!" Marco shouted. "You'd do the same if our spots were reversed."

"No, I wouldn't." I grabbed his wrist and he gasped, not expecting my strength. "I'd leave you be. I did, remember? I didn't come here looking for you."

"There's the problem, isn't it? I wouldn't be here if you hadn't run. You owe me, Francesca."

"Don't call me that!" I shoved him against the wall hard.

We stared each other down, but he knew he had the upper hand.

"Fine," I breathed. "I'll get your money, but not one word of me to anyone. If I hear even a whisper, I will find you and slit your throat while you're asleep—I swear."

I felt Marco's fear ripple in his terse assent. He rubbed his wrist. "Listen, since we're talking, there's something else."

At my glare, he held up his hands in mock surrender. "It's your grandfather. Alfonso hasn't been himself. Sleeping more, not eating; that cough's worse in the night. Something's wrong."

Was this a double cross? Maybe, but Marco's eyes seemed genuine, his bluster gone. A heavy weight settled in my heart.

"Help me to see him," I demanded.

"Bring the money next Monday at two. I'll make sure Sandro is out."

That left me a week. I had no choice but to trust him if my grandfather really was ill.

Marco started to leave but stopped. "I know you don't believe me, but I'm glad you lived."

"Of course you are," I said bitterly. "I'm your train ticket."

He shook his head. "You always were the smart one, 'Franco.' This time, Sandro went too far. With both of us."

I glared at him. "Then why blackmail me?"

"Because I want a better life, too." Marco glanced in the direction of Constanza's. "Get me my money, and I promise—we'll never see each other again."

18

I left Constanza's with a new and more urgent problem. Now that I was wide-awake, the thought of returning to my cramped pension only intensified my fears. So I dragged myself to the Minerva, looking for a distraction. The repairs had piled up in Annella's absence, and once inside Restoration, I sunk on a stool, holding my pounding head.

"Everything all right?" Leo said, startling me.

I looked up fast. "Just too much champagne."

"Well, it was quite good," he said, eyeing me carefully. "You turned a few heads at the party. Is one of your admirers to blame for your disheveled state?"

"Nothing as exciting as that."

"On the bright side, at least you didn't follow in Carmine's footsteps." Leo shifted his ledger from one hand to another. "He's out."

"Out?" My thoughts raced to him and Giannina. "You don't mean permanently?"

Leo shrugged. "Not clear. He must have offended Radillo, which he has a knack for. They've been fighting for weeks now." Leo paused. "Tonight, Radillo wants you up there with him, just the two of you. You're Facanapa and Flavio. He'll handle the rest."

"Why not the other men?"

"Franco, Radillo respects you." Leo quieted for a moment. "Take your chance. The others, Carmine included, put their own interests first. So tonight? You do the same. Make it a good show."

THE REST OF THE day passed largely with me drinking too much of Michaela's coffee to stay awake and trying to find Carmine on breaks, but without success. My concerns from the morning receded as my apprehension about the evening show with Radillo grew.

That night, just before curtain, I was onstage with Vincenzo checking filters. The theater sparkled from an intensive cleaning. Even the sawdust felt fresh.

"Does the blue look good for the dusk sword fight?" Vincenzo asked me. "I want to replay it in the ghost visitation."

Distracted, I nodded, pacing to quell my nerves. Beyond the doors, I heard a thrum of voices intensifying, the scent of beer wafting in, ushers with one eye on the clock nearing eight.

"Why so nervous?" Vincenzo laughed. "Every night, another happy ending."

"Not always," Radillo replied for me, stepping out of the wings. He warmed up his hands, balling them in and out of fists.

"I brought some tools," I said, pointing above us, "for any last-minute surprises. Pedrolino's elbow string has been dislodging."

"No surprises tonight, not with our special guests, including my daughter."

At the mention of Giannina, I didn't dare ask about Carmine.

"Others, too, from the party will be attending. The count and his family, Lord and Lady Grimani, Signora Cappello."

I perked up. Maybe I'd see Annella again.

"Her companion is unwell, apparently," he added, as if reading my thoughts. "Perhaps too much champagne like you? Leo said you were a bit rough this morning."

I tried to laugh it off but knew Annella would not miss a show unless Constanza forbade it. Was Annella being punished for not going upstairs with that dolt? Or worse, had she?

Radillo motioned me to the ladders first. After we climbed up, Vincenzo pinned the curtain shut. Soon after, the sounds of the audience's entry intensified.

I realized that Carmine had been beside me every night until now. Was he safe?

"You'll have a tougher time with my Isabella," Radillo said. "Carmine goes too easy on you."

"Facanapa and Flavio work hard when the reward is sweet."

"You, a romantic? Isabella may take advantage. She needs one bolder than the rest."

I lowered Facanapa onstage, testing his T-bar. "Facanapa is nothing if not bold."

"That's why the crowd loves him," Radillo said, unwinding Isabella's strings. It was a mechanism he did by heart.

On the other side of the curtain, the pit shuffled in. A hum of whispers suggested Radillo's guests had arrived. Constanza had no reason to suspect me or Annella, I reassured myself. Marco would keep his promise, at least this week.

"Facanapa does what he pleases," Radillo was saying as he dropped Isabella in the wings. "Damn the consequences, like all lovers, right?"

"I wouldn't know," I said, steadying Facanapa's strings for the start.

"No Isabella of your own at the party?"

When I shook my head, I saw Radillo watching me, almost sadly, but he brightened. "No matter. In the mouth of the wolf, Franco!"

"Death to the wolf," I replied half-heartedly.

Radillo cued Vincenzo. The lutist finished tuning. Bruno lit the first scene's lamps for the pastoral road. A scrap of Carmine's advice resurfaced. *You're up here, schoolboy. Enjoy it.*

Then, something magical unfolded. With Radillo, I thought I would be more tentative, given my nerves. Yet as my Facanapa and later Flavio attempted to woo Isabella, I felt the balance of power shift. I could make Facanapa's red-cheeked jowls provoke laughter straight to the back row. The audience's reactions and commentary emboldened me, and I drew scenes out, speaking extemporaneously to enhance the script.

So did Radillo. The two of us built an interplay that, I had to admit, had never transpired as easily with Carmine. In Radillo's hands, Isabella grew subtler and smarter. That made the reward of her affection more desirable, for the crowd had much to share with us from start to finish.

After we climbed down, I handed Radillo a cloth to wipe the chalk off.

"Your nerves got to you at times," he said. "But I liked your revisions on the spot, and I'm sure Constanza was as impressed as the pit." He tossed the cloth back to me. "Tonight was really *our* audition for her."

"Is she becoming the theater's patron?" I asked, uneasy at the thought of her in these wings—and piqued by Radillo's remark on my nerves.

"I hope so. We can't always rely on the De Rossis to rescue us."

I remembered Carmine's words about the De Rossis' son, his impending marriage to Giannina, the look on Carmine's face as we'd strolled along Riva degli Schiavoni. It all prompted me to speak up. "The wealthy may keep our doors open, sir, but from what I've seen every night, the pit is more loyal. You've been savvy enough to court both and disappoint neither, a skill that is its own art."

Radillo placed his hand on my shoulder. "Leave the business to me, Franco. Focus on your craft. You have more than what you gave tonight. I caught a hint of it up there."

"It felt easier," I acknowledged. "Like I knew what to do without thinking."

"Yes, that's good. Feel your way more. You're the lead all week. Let's see how you fare when you're not stuck in anyone's shadow, including mine."

LONG PAST MIDNIGHT, THERE came a soft tap at my door, like a mouse's scuttling, followed by Carmine's whisper of "Franco, let me in."

Instinctively I felt for my chest padding but, exhausted, I'd fallen asleep in my work clothes.

"How'd you get past Sebastian?" I asked, opening the door.

"Snuck up." Carmine grabbed at my sleeve. "You sleep in this?"

I shrugged. "Where have you been?"

"In love," he replied, and flopped on the bed in bliss.

"I suspect I know with whom. A certain theater owner's daughter?"

Carmine jolted upright. "You know?"

"Even I could see it last night, watching you two dance. And her red hair?"

He relaxed. "It's completely different with her, schoolboy, since Radillo introduced us last winter. I've wanted to tell you, but everything was complicated. I tried to get Radillo's blessing at the party, for her sake, but he fired me from the theater, ranting that I would never be good enough for her." Carmine hesitated. "So Giannina and I are leaving tonight. We're running to Milan to elope. If we don't, Radillo will marry her off to the De Rossis' youngest." Carmine frowned. "You saw that man. I can't let her see that ugly face on the pillow every night. She'd die of boredom."

"How noble of you to step in." I sat beside him on the bed.

"I do what I can." The moonlight shone on his profile. "I was with her last night, Franco. She is luminous."

"I am happy for you, truly, but what about Radillo?"

"Our plan is to not get caught." He tapped the side of his forehead. "Foolproof, right?"

I remembered the sight of them dancing, how effortless it looked in that stifling room. "You must love each other to go this far."

He jumped up. "Come see us off properly. She's waiting at the back dock."

Carmine and I slunk downstairs, skirting Sebastian, who was dozing with his head on the desk. Outside, a cool breeze echoed my morning's predawn sojourn. When I saw Giannina hurry over to Carmine on the dock, it hit me. Carmine was leaving. I felt bewildered by all that had transpired in just one day.

He wrapped an arm around her. "I believe you two already met?"

Giannina greeted me warmly. "Carmine has spoken of you so much that I feel like I know you. My father, too . . ." She faltered.

"Steady now," Carmine said. "He'll come around—after he starts missing you more than hating me." He turned to me. "It'll be good for you to work with him, Franco, though it won't be easy. Now that I've stolen Radillo's only daughter, he can't secure the De Rossis' money. Andrea's quick to envy, too."

"Don't worry." I shrugged. "I can take care of myself."

"Speaking of," Carmine said, "great show tonight. I snuck in the pit. Wanted to see you one last time."

"It was brilliant from the box, too," Giannina said. "Such charming interplay. Facanapa is a fool, but you make us love him, with those ridiculous mannerisms and how honest he seems when he tilts aside the mask."

"She's an excellent puppeteer, you know," Carmine boasted.

"With Radillo as your father, I'm not surprised." I pointed at her hand. "I felt the calluses at the party."

Giannina spread her fingers before her. "Hands of a laborer, dressed up like a lady. The De Rossis' son complains about it whenever we're forced to dance. I think he'd prefer a doll to any real woman. He only dances to ensure everyone sees he's with me."

"It's a shame you aren't onstage with us," I said.

"I've tried to persuade my father to let me join. The Minerva could benefit from the novelty of a father-daughter pair, and its finances are not as robust as he wishes, but all he ever says is"—she paused to lower her voice to imitate Radillo's—"'The Minerva is no place for a woman, and only I know how to grow the theater.'"

"You sound just like him," I said, both Carmine and I laughing.

"I won't miss the endless etiquette lessons and always being shushed," Giannina added. "It's only this man," she said, beaming at Carmine, "who wants to hear everything I have to say, no matter how banal. I've tricked him into running away with me, the fool."

"She uses magic—I swear," Carmine teased. "Some sweet elixir I cannot get enough of."

As I looked at them, I couldn't imagine the ease of loving someone without question or fear. "What will you do in Milan?" I asked.

"Rent our own theater," Carmine replied. "The stage is changing. The kids at Riva degli Schiavoni every week? They're our future. Children's shows—I can sense it."

Giannina smiled. "One of my more romantic aunts settled in Milan with *her* once-inappropriate paramour turned husband. She will aid us until it's too late for my father to thwart our marriage."

I glanced at Carmine. "Can I tell Annella? She can keep a secret."

"Oh, what secrets does she keep?" He raised an eyebrow. When I shook my head, he added, "Sure. Last night it was clear where her interests are, and it's not with the Cappellos."

Standing there, I had to admit it: I hoped he was right.

Then, in the distance, we heard the campanile chime three times.

"We barely had time in the rafters," Carmine said fast. "I'll miss you, and not just up there. Performing these past weeks, going to the stalls, killing time in Restoration, drinking too much? We had fun, didn't we?"

I swallowed hard. "More than that. I wouldn't be here without you."

Carmine cleared his throat. "Radillo knows what he has in you. Before the party, he told me so, and clearly the crowds love you. He thinks you—unlike me—won't throw away your chance. I just hope he treats you better." Carmine stepped closer. "The Minerva will change, Franco. Don't let it change you. Trust your instincts. You're really good, but don't be afraid to become better. And if things ever get hard, we'll have a spot for you in Milan."

"We should go," Giannina said, fidgeting. "My father always rises early when he's happy, and after Constanza's comments last night, he's *very* happy. At least that might bode well for you, Franco. May we meet again under better circumstances."

"Maybe even perform together?" I moved to kiss her hand as a goodbye. "Keep working on those calluses."

"Now, now," Carmine joked, separating us. "Get your own girl. Too bad I won't be here for that lesson, schoolboy."

"Too bad." I looked from Giannina to him. "You clearly know what you're doing."

Carmine hugged me and we clung to each other.

When we finally pulled apart, he said, "Sebastian loses mail, so I'll write you at the Titian after we settle. Tell Michaela. She likes you more than me, so she'll help if you ask. If you ever leave, give her your address. Then we can find each other again."

"I hope you both make it," I said. "I'll just wish you a dancer's *merde* for now, as you're already in the mouth of the wolf."

"Thanks, partner," he said, and assisted Giannina into the boat. I unwound the rope anchoring them to the pile as Carmine settled in with the oars. "Who knows? Maybe it'll all work out. Trust me for once."

With that, he pushed off into the glossy black waters.

19

When I appeared at the Minerva on Tuesday morning, a pall had fallen over the theater. Leo said that Radillo had left town quickly on "family matters" and placed me in charge. I didn't mention Carmine and retreated to Restoration to avoid Andrea's bitter looks.

I passed the week by diving into my mountain of repairs, performing in the evening with Andrea and Niccolò, and keeping an eye out for Annella in the crowd. But as my return to Cannaregio neared, my thoughts shifted to family matters of my own. Was I trusting a brother who'd hand me to our father? Even if it was not an ambush, I was about to give Marco my savings—what if he demanded more?

So spun my thoughts by Sunday morning, the day before my rendezvous with Marco. I headed to the Minerva early, the air thick with rain itching to burst. In Restoration, I stared at the recently repaired marionettes perched in rows on stands. Angelina, Arlecchino, Guinevere, and several more. My deep kinship with Radillo's marionettes had unfolded through these months of repairs. By closing my eyes, I could register flaws in their movement by touch, not sight, and hear their voices conjured from stage and scripts.

If only solving my own struggles right now were as easy as

repainting Colombina's worn smile with cinnamon or trimming the rose sateen of Lauretta's hem.

I heard the stage door open and presumed it was Leo, bound for his ledger. Only moments later, though, Annella appeared, hovering in the archway and twisting a parasol in her hands.

Something kept me from rushing to her. All week I had been desperate to see her. Now I had no idea what to say.

"I saw you come in," she said, and smiled weakly. Her long hair was loosely tucked up. Dark circles lined her eyes like bruises. "Has Carmine been helping you in my absence?"

I went to the doorway and glanced down the hall. No one else was there.

"Carmine is gone," I whispered anyway, closing the door. "He eloped with his rich redhead. It's Giannina, Radillo's daughter."

Her eyes flashed in surprise. "That's why Carmine couldn't talk to us. What did Radillo do?"

"He's gone after them. Don't tell anyone, but they're heading to Milan, with plans to start a children's theater."

"Puppets for children," Annella said, as she wiped a smudge off one of the newly repaired Saracens' cheeks. "Are they happy?"

"Deliriously so," I said, wistful at the memory.

We both seemed unsure what more to say, so I reverted to our old ways. I gestured to the Saracen. "Want to try this brave soldier out?"

She nodded and I unwound the puppet's strings enough to dangle it on the table. Tentatively, I guided her hand into position. When I let go, the Saracen slumped.

"It's hopeless," she said.

"Just slow down." I put my hands over hers on the holder. "Adjust your left hand here. Now, arc this wrist more to lift his left foot."

"How do you do this every night? In my hands, he just looks drunk."

"I've had more practice. Come, let's make him walk together."

I kept my hands on hers to complete the motion, she and I shuffling side by side until she managed it better. I stepped away and she experimented, lifting and dropping him in spots. Soon he appeared to amble along the table with his own unique stride.

"That's it." I applauded. "Soon you'll have calluses like Giannina's."

"Giannina?" She stilled.

"I guessed Giannina was a puppeteer when I kissed her hand at the party." I stopped when I saw Annella's green eyes dull as if defeated.

"The party." Annella focused on the puppet. "You heard Constanza, didn't you? That's why you dropped the glass."

"Yes," I admitted. "Are you all right?"

"Not exactly," she said. I waited as she settled on a stool. "I'm sorry I kept secrets, Franco. I never lied to you, but I was afraid you'd think less of me if I told you the truth." She looked up at me. "I couldn't bear losing you again so soon."

The thought of me rejecting her seemed so absurd I laughed. At her confusion, I added, "You can tell me anything, Annella. I would be the last person to judge you."

She set the Saracen on the table. "You know that Rossana and I worked at dance halls for years, but she and I couldn't always survive as dancers alone. When there was nothing to eat and shows were closed by the clergy, we took turns." Annella inhaled. "One of us would work in Goldoni's Alley. We'd share what we made to get by."

I sat beside her. "I am sorry for having spoken so flippantly before."

"My story is hardly unique. Most girls in the theater, dancers or actresses, try to capture the eye of someone wealthy, usually a married man. Hunger can be a great motivator. When Constanza came backstage for me, I saw a rich widow and a mark, an opportunity that did not involve a man and, frankly, one that provided greater sums than any other route." She straightened. "Rossana is like my older sister. I was lucky to meet her when I first ran away. She took me under her wing and kept me safe when I had no idea what to do. I'll never abandon Rossana, so I went with Constanza for her sake as much as my own."

I thought of Constanza's casual cruelty at the party. Was it an easier burden to endure than the men in Goldoni's Alley?

"Who is Constanza, really?" I asked.

Annella smoothed the lapel on the Saracen's coat. "The rare widow who increased her husband's holdings after he died. Other widows would have relied on their husband's families for charity, but Constanza's in-laws now depend on her. The palazzo, his wealth, all his enterprises—all willed to her alone. But she is beset by men who would steal her fortune if they could. That's where Rossana and I come in. In society's eyes, we're just pretty faces at parties. To Constanza, we're more valuable. We later reveal what men say to impress us." She hesitated. "Among elites and wealthy foreign tourists, it's an open secret that Constanza runs a high-end bordello in the guise of a salon—for men only, of course. For Rossana, that means more than just dancing and flirting, but she finds that work easier than I do, especially with all Constanza's protections. I have been spared that because of Constanza's investment in me."

"Investment?" Our eyes met.

She wavered. "Constanza is not so different from those married men."

I felt myself blush. "This salon . . . What about the city's ban on bordellos?"

"The authorities turn a blind eye because the men at the top are invited in for favors, and the ones below won't challenge those whom they work for. Why would they? They hope to be invited in themselves one day."

"So the police know but do nothing?"

"For the right price, a great deal of nothing can be done."

I picked at the Saracen's threads. "Are you in love with Constanza?"

Now Annella laughed. "No, but it has been easier for me to bear a woman." She paused. "Until now."

"What's changed?"

Annella searched my face, then stood up and paced away. "Constanza sees me as too entitled and has begun threatening me, as you heard, to sleep with men. But it's an idle threat. She is far too jealous. That's what people like her do. I let her think she's in charge to get what I want."

"Do you, though? Get what you want?"

"She'll give me anything if I play the part. I slipped up that day when I snuck out to see you. She needed me at the palazzo for a business engagement and I thought I could escape unnoticed, but she was upset. Since then, she's grown stricter."

"From where I stand, it seems like she holds the strings." I paused. "Annella, you don't really believe your gifts only 'lie in the bedroom,' do you?"

"Franco, this is about surviving—something I have done longer than you, and in dresses the whole time." She came close and placed her hand on mine. "Are you . . . jealous?"

"Of course not!" I rose abruptly, winding the strings of the Saracen fast as I returned it to the stands. Strangely, Annella's story made me think of my mother. She had only lived two years on her own. Annella had been on the streets for more than five. I pictured Constanza touching Annella and had to stop myself from wincing. Why was I so angry?

"I'm sorry," I said, my back still to Annella. "I see why you were afraid to talk to me. I just wish . . ."

"Wish for what?" Annella began. "Might you want . . . ?"

As she trailed off, my heart raced. I faced away from her, out of my depth with all I felt.

"I don't like how she belittles you," I said, turning around. "You deserve better. You're my friend."

Briefly, disappointment flickered in her eyes, but then she said, "Don't worry. I have a plan to get out."

"Out?"

"Always have an exit ready, right?" she said lightly. "One day, probably after a year, someone new will catch Constanza's eye and she'll kick me out. The other girls tell me that's been her pattern. So I've been stealing small amounts of money where I can, if I'm sent out to purchase a dress or Rossana and I are handed fare for the theater. When she is done with me, I'll use that money to live and find work as a seamstress." Annella gestured to the table. "Or maybe paint and design sets. Working with you gave me the idea. I bide my time now to live as well as a spinster-seamstress can later."

The isolation of this scenario pierced me. "Those aren't your only choices," I urged. "You could love someone. You're intelligent, beautiful. I've seen how men look at you. One man could take you away from her."

"Beauty fades, Franco, and intelligence is more often a liability in men's eyes. They would lord it over me that I was a 'fallen woman.' None would marry me for that reason, either. With no family name or wealth, I have no worth or place. I bear with Constanza so I can amass what I need for my future. The deeper truth is that I prize my independence too highly to hand it to any man—something you'd understand."

I did, all too well. I had run rather than face a marriage of my own. I couldn't argue with Annella's course. Yet why did I want to?

"What's wrong?" she asked. "You're angry—I can tell."

"It's not you." I looked down. "I went to Constanza's to see you the morning after the party, but then my brother, Marco, walked out of her doors."

She gasped. "Why didn't you say so earlier?"

"I thought you knew. I thought you'd been protecting me, and that was why you never wanted me to be seen."

"No, I would have warned you! What happened? Did he recognize you?"

"Yes." I outlined the situation. "Have you ever seen Tristano at Constanza's? Marco suggested they were connected."

She grew more worried. "Neither Tristano nor Marco have been among the guests Rossana and I entertain. But many men come and go whom I don't meet," Annella went on. "Priests helping with her work with the foundlings, businessmen with her late husband's affairs, visiting merchants. Still, I can't imagine Constanza connected to Tristano."

"If Tristano is there, then perhaps you should leave sooner."

Annella shook her head. "I will have enough to make my new start later this summer. But if Tristano is involved with Constanza, you also should keep your distance."

"There's something else. Marco threatened to tell Constanza about me. He implied it would endanger you. If I pay him tomorrow, he'll run."

"That sounds like a trap. Let me go instead. I can give him the money I've saved."

"No, absolutely not. Keep yours. I have some money saved, too. Besides, Sandro and Marco are unpredictable. That man who hurt you lives right there." I hated them in a rush.

"Then let's go together."

I ran my fingers through my hair. "Too risky."

But she cut me off, adamant. "I am going with you. I'll vouch for you as my husband if anyone questions or ambushes you. Believe me—wealthy dress intimidates people." She paused. "We just found each other again, Franco. I can help you."

There was no point in arguing. I saw that her mind was set. And if her monstrous uncle dared show, I'd deal with him.

"All right," I said, conceding. "Meet me at the Sant'Alvise dock just before two tomorrow afternoon. Come alone."

"Good." She drew out a pocket watch. "I must go." She forced a smile. "Until then, my new husband. What was I saying about never marrying?"

I moved to her side and lifted her hand to my lips. "Until tomorrow."

I'd meant the gesture as a quick joke. But when I inhaled the scent of salty air in her skin, I lingered. Nor did she let go of me.

Then the door swung open. We separated instantly as Andrea entered.

"Hard at work, I see." He shook water off his cap and his shoulders. "Here's one more." He placed his Pedrolino on the table.

Annella glanced at the marionette. "Can you take care of this one alone?"

I nodded to her. "Shall I fetch you a boat? It's raining now."

She pointed to her parasol. "No, thank you. Good day."

Without looking at me, she moved to leave. Andrea, however, didn't step aside, forcing her to brush past him too closely.

"She's here early," he said, gazing after her.

"This was the only time she could come."

"So she spent last night with you." He stated it casually.

"No, it's not what you think."

"Isn't it?" He drew up to his full height. "How ambitious you are, ingratiating yourself with Radillo and now her? With Carmine mysteriously gone, you're left as lead and I'm stuck with this buffoon." He regarded Pedrolino, then me. "I see how you look at her. I watched that girl at the party, saw who she flirted with. Don't get your hopes up. She's too expensive."

I stiffened. "She's not for sale."

"Maybe, maybe not." He started to leave. "But be careful. If I can walk in on you, anyone could."

20

Later that same afternoon, Andrea and I were testing a scene onstage with the repaired Pedrolino when Radillo barged into the pit and bounded up the steps with a heavy, impatient tread.

"Franco," he called up, his olive skin ashen in the glaring stage lights. "Come down."

As I descended the ladder, I caught Andrea rolling his eyes.

"Welcome back, sir," I said, slapping chalk from my hands.

"Let's go to the Titian. We need to talk."

I followed Radillo out of the theater, wary. Had he found Carmine and Giannina? Had they made it to Milan? He moved rapidly but was stiff with tension, and reminded me of those modern steel beams that gird sinking palazzi. Without them, the best marble disintegrates, even in canals less than two meters deep.

When we reached the Titian, he pointed to one of the outside tables. "Wait here."

He entered the café and snapped his fingers at Michaela. Despite his efforts, she moved languidly, making him wait.

Radillo soon joined me to stand at the rusty wrought-iron table.

Across from us, a group of children still in their church attire fecklessly chased pigeons, their voices shrill with play.

After a few moments, Michaela sauntered over with two cups. She glanced at me in sympathy before going back inside. Radillo sipped his coffee, then drew out a cigarette. He offered me one, but I shook my head.

"Franco," he asked, lighting the cigarette, "will you marry?"

Thrown, I recalled Annella's speech. "No."

"I admire how you concentrate on your trade. Sales are up these past weeks, just as I anticipated. Leo said you carried us well in my absence. And you're in early every day."

"Thank you," I began, sipping my coffee. "But is this about Carmine?"

"I suppose."

"Are he and Giannina all right?"

He tilted his head and I realized my mistake. "So you know," he stated.

"I suspected as much at the party. Are they married?"

Radillo nodded, grim. "The beauty of Venice is that should I wish Carmine dead, no man would punish me for his betrayal and theft of her virtue." He studied me. "Carmine was your friend, not Andrea's. Where have they gone?"

Relief. He hadn't found them. "I cannot say."

"Tell me! I could save her."

Some of the nearby children stilled at his shout.

I took a deep breath. "They spoke to me in confidence. I will not betray that. But I will say that they love each other. It is not my choice, or yours, to thwart their course."

He pointed at me with his cigarette. "You don't have a daughter, obviously."

I met his eyes. "If I did and she was a puppeteer, I'd want her by my side, not stuck in the De Rossis' drawing room."

"She told you that?"

"Why not allow her in the Minerva? She's probably better than all of us, with you as her father." I thought I'd gone too far, but Radillo just laughed.

"Oh, Franco, you're still young. You haven't the faintest idea what damage a woman can do. Believe me—we're better off in the Minerva without them." He gazed into his cup as if it held answers. "Once, I was like you. I thought customs of distinct worlds for men and women were foolish. Italy had just become a new nation. It was time to cast off the shackles of our old-world ways, eliminate all that we had outgrown to embrace the new!"

"What changed your mind?" I asked, curious.

"When I worked at Venice's other theaters, there were women I taught, and one with whom I—" He caught himself. "I learned the hard way never to make that mistake again. You'll learn that women have their place in a home or with children, of course, but beyond that? No. And while I can understand your loyalty to Carmine, that must be to the Minerva from now on, am I clear?"

I nodded. "Yet you admit one woman—Constanza."

"A patron is different. A patron is not a distraction. They don't mysteriously disappear." He shook his head bitterly. Then he pulled a few coins out and held one up. "Now that Giannina will not marry De Rossi's son, their interest in supporting the Minerva, and me, will cool. The Minerva could not have gone on much longer without Constanza stepping in."

I straightened up. "So, she has officially taken us on?"

"Yes, so there is some good news, at least. Now we can refurbish the theater and offer higher quality, more artistic fare, which, frankly, you understand better than Carmine anyway. That's why I brought you here. It is to be a new time. I had a hunch about you the day you arrived. That you weren't a typical foundling. You read from *The Decameron* like you knew it, but Leo says you also know the pit, and obviously, you reach them well. You, like me, see more than cheap thrills in marionettes. You see how they can deeply move us, too." He stared at the children chasing pigeons. "You've proven yourself well, Franco—and proven my instincts correct. I want you for this next stage of the Minerva's life. By working with me, you will become much more than a man to watch. Mark my words."

I had expected a fight over Carmine but found myself flattered by his speech. He had done so much for the art form and here he was, asking me to work at his side and grow the theater. Despite my doubts about Constanza, at least her patronage would keep Annella in my world.

"Thank you. The Minerva holds a special place in my heart, sir."

"Had you come to it before?" he asked, drinking his coffee.

"Only once, when I was twelve."

"You probably snuck in the pit like other foundlings," he teased. "Maybe I should dock your wages."

I smiled. "Half the time I watched the strings, trying to imagine what you were doing to make the marionettes seem so real. That's when I knew I would try out one day."

"Now it's your home. I certainly spend more time there than my own. My wife does not understand the theater." He sighed. "But Giannina did, I'll admit."

"She could come back to you, sir, if you wish."

He stiffened. "There's no point. She's lost. Besides, we have work to do, you and me. From now on, Andrea, Niccolò, you, and I will meet more to prepare. Our repertoire will broaden, with grander productions ahead. You will manage all shows with me, and I will hold auditions for two new apprentices," Radillo went on. "Andrea and Niccolò will oversee them. For a time, you'll continue in Restoration, but that will change." He stilled. "Congratulations. You're Carmine's replacement. Head man and lead."

I caught up to what he was offering me, the magnitude of his words. "Thank you, sir," I said again. I couldn't wait to tell my grand-father. How proud he'd be—if I saw him at all.

Radillo looked off into the distance. "Andrea won't be pleased when I break the news. He and Niccolò are solid players, but you have a sense of mystery. You make people stop and laugh until they cry. Andrea and Niccolò are great technicians, reliable with a range of parts, but they are not like you or, much as it pains me to admit it, Carmine." Radillo refocused. "You're too gifted to stay in minor parts. Show them"—he gestured to the children playing, as if they were our audience—"more."

I tried to take in all that he was saying. Had I been holding back? Perhaps, but now I had a chance to see what I could do.

"Still, running a theater takes more of you than you know. And if anyone asks, say that I fired Carmine and he fled—alone. Do not mention his marriage to my daughter. If I learn you told anyone the truth, you'll be out, too. Understand?"

"Perfectly," I replied, but I knew it was an idle threat. News would spread. Radillo just needed this reassurance. Besides, I was too over-joyed to argue. As we started back to the theater, I dared to glimpse this fortuitous new world opening up to me.

Yet I also saw what held me back. Marco, Sandro, Tristano—all in the wings, ready to strike. My grandfather could not save me now, and might be ill. Nor could Radillo help, for all his encouragement. When I thought of Annella, I saw only Constanza's shadow. Or was Constanza the Minerva's—and my—saving grace?

Cannaregio, which I thought I had left behind, crowded back in. Murky and shrunken, miserly and mean, it had one intent—to drag me back to that person I no longer was.

21

I paced near the Sant'Alvise gondola dock, waiting for Annella's boat, which was late. As the sun beat down, the air filled with the uneven slaps of gulls' steep dives. I grew dizzy, my nerves too pitched for food. Once more, I felt for my grandfather's knife, tucked in with two envelopes of money in my brother's stolen jacket.

All around me, Cannaregio appeared unaltered. The mild waters spread wide and green, with Murano's and San Michele's shorelines glittering in the distance. Elderly men had settled on well-creased elbows to fish and grumble at the massive vaporetti lumbering past Sant'Alvise's unsteady dock, while bored dockworkers cast dice and groaned and cheered.

I spotted a gondola drawing near, then Annella came into view. She was wearing a sea green dress and hat, which, from a distance, blurred her with the horizon.

When she arrived, she gave a half twirl. "Do I look like a respectable married lady?"

"Always respectable," I said, admiring the sapphires that dotted her ears and throat, and glad for her veiled face. "I fear I am underdressed as your husband, though." I smiled wanly to mask my rising dread and jutted my chin in the direction of her boat. "He will wait?"

Her gondolier had joined the dockworkers' game. "Yes. I paid him well." Then she added, "I'll go to San Polo after. Constanza expects me in two hours, so plenty of time." She edged nearer. "What's our plan?"

"If anyone asks, say you are Elena Lazzaro." I eyed the earrings. "A jeweler's daughter. I'll be Giorgio, grandson of Alfonso's theater friend from the Malibran."

She nodded, but then I caught her furrowed brow at the sight of her former home.

"You don't need to do this," I said. "You can wait here."

"No. Give me your arm." I felt her clutch me. "Let's go."

We started walking, heads bent to conceal our faces. "We'll go to the side door," I said, "and I'll keep my bowler low. Marco should answer. Then we'll go up the servants' spiral staircase near the kitchen, which leads up to my grandfather's room. If Sandro or, worse, Tristano answers, just run. Don't you dare stay to help me."

"We'll see," Annella said, briefly glancing at her childhood home when I knocked purposefully.

As I'd hoped, Marco alone ushered us into the kitchen.

"Is anyone else here?" I asked him quickly as he shut the door.

"Just us and Alfonso upstairs." Marco gestured to Annella. "I thought she wasn't involved?"

"She deserved to know, given that you threatened her, too."

Marco looked embarrassed, and Annella stepped forward. "I came to help Franco," she said. "If you set him up, it will be my word against yours. Remember, I have Constanza to back me up."

Marco smirked at me. "I see why you like her. What about my money?"

I reached into my jacket and gave him an envelope. "Here's half. I'll give you the rest after I see my grandfather safely. Otherwise, no more."

"Sounds like you've thought it all through," he said, taking the envelope. Then his gaze drifted from me to Annella. "Must be nice to have someone who cares."

I recalled what Marco had said about his fiancée—*I lost Paola*—but I couldn't afford to be distracted right now.

I started toward the servants' stairs.

"Wait," Marco said, lifting his eyes to the ceiling. "He's worse."

For the first time since I arrived, I noticed the kitchen's decline. Plates and cups were piled precariously in the sink. Two wine bottles lay in shards by the door, as if thrown in rage. A stale, yeasty stench emanated from discarded beer bottles. Despite the bright day, the kitchen felt as dank and dark as when I'd torn through it last, at midnight.

"What does the doctor say?" I asked, as Marco started to ascend in front of me.

"To make him comfortable." Marco paused to look back. "He has a fever, and the cough, you see—his lungs are giving out . . ."

"Wait." I stopped. "He's dying?"

Marco's pity confirmed my fears. "It's good you're here. He's been calling for you."

Now Annella took my hand and guided me up the stairs. Nausea lined my empty stomach. I had been so intent on preparing for a battle with Marco that I had not fully believed my grandfather was sick, never mind dying. In my mind, he remained strong and vital, and we would be reunited in time—but not like this.

At the landing, Marco pressed a spent candleholder into my hands, beeswax spilling onto its wick. "He likes it better with the shade drawn."

We entered the room. With the weather warming, I might have expected to find my grandfather sitting in his rocking chair by the open window or out on the balcony, but as my eyes adjusted to the dark, I saw him lying prone on the bed, wheezing. It was not the soft breath of sleep but an unwinnable struggle. His lips were parched, his long cheeks sunk in the hollows of his face, and when I came to touch his hand, it felt cold as ice.

My knees buckled and Annella took the candle, her arm about my waist.

"Get a chair," she commanded Marco.

Marco rushed to bring one in. "At least his cough subsided," he said. "Last night, before I had to go out, I thought his ribs might crack."

"Don't ever leave him alone!" I cried.

"I always get one of the neighbors to come if Tristano needs me." Marco stepped toward the door. "I'll stay by the landing in case anyone drops by."

"I'm right here, too," Annella whispered to me, lifting her veil. "At the door, to listen for any trouble."

I bent close to my grandfather's face and kissed the top of his forehead, salty from fever. "It's me," I said, "Francesca." My former name garbled in my throat, so long unsaid.

"You?" he asked, so faint it might have been an exhalation.

"Yes, I'm here." I fumbled for the wet cloth in the basin of water by his bed. "I'm here."

As I dabbed at his parched lips, his eyes opened. "Safe?"

"Very." I managed to smile. "I am to be the lead puppeteer now at the Minerva, with Radillo. You taught me so well." I glanced behind me. "Annella is here, too. We are friends again."

"Good, good." He paused. "Your mother would be proud. She was a natural, and you have her talent." He tried to take a deep breath. "Poor Sofia. She never wanted to leave."

"Yes." I knew the story. Her love for the stage had been stronger than any love for me. Still, I inched closer, desperate to be close to him. "A shame I got in the way," I said.

"No," he protested. "Sofia loved you. Sandro made her go." He reached for my hand, his grip strangely sharp for how weak he was.

"Sofia only married him to give you a father . . ." A coughing fit silenced him.

He had to be rambling, delirious with fever. I dabbed his forehead again. "Don't strain yourself."

But he began shaking his head, his eyes widening. "Listen—you must know. Sandro is not your father."

"What?" I faltered. Another extended cough shook the bed.

"Franco," Annella said from the door, her tone urgent. "Someone is downstairs. Marco went to check."

I could hear voices below rising in argument but turned back to my grandfather. "Who is my father?"

"She wouldn't say. She protected the man so that Sandro couldn't abandon you in a scandal. But Sandro would have killed her if she'd stayed."

My grandfather was gasping for air but seemed lucid. A tear traced a path down his cheek. "I made her go, to save her. She made me promise never to tell you, but I can't . . ."

Now I couldn't breathe. Annella rushed over. "We need to go. Now."

"I can't leave him alone!" I cried, bewildered.

My grandfather squeezed my hand. "You must go. Be safe. She couldn't have what she loved, but you can. Goodbye, my dearest."

I gulped back tears. He was dying, but here he was reassuring me.

"I love you," I said, shaking as I leaned over him, smoothing his brow.

"I love you, too."

I held on to his cheek. "You saved me and I won't let you down. Rest now." I lost my voice, unable to say more, as Annella hurried us to the door.

Below, I heard the pop of a cork, a fresh bottle of beer being opened and then poured. It broke when someone tossed it. Marco was shouting louder now.

I glanced back at my grandfather one last time as we left the room. When Annella shut the door, it felt like I vanished, not him.

Gingerly, Annella inched me toward the spiral staircase, but we halted at a loud thud. The arguing ceased. We tensed in the ominous silence that ensued.

Then Sandro called from the base of the main stairs. "Francesca!"

"No," Annella called out before I could speak. "It is I, a friend of your father-in-law's."

She gestured for me to use the servants' stairs and hurried toward the main staircase, up which Sandro was already bounding.

"I didn't mean to startle you," she said, stepping noisily down the stairs to cover the sounds of my descent. "I was just visiting Alfonso. He's an old family friend, and I heard he was ill."

There was a pause before Sandro recovered. "Yes, my good friend Giuseppe across the street told me Marco brought a young woman in—I thought it might be my daughter, from finishing school."

"Giuseppe?" Annella's voice quavered.

"You know him? A fine family indeed, much better than the Jews from before."

I clenched the rail.

"Where has Marco gone?" Annella asked. I could hear her moving toward the foyer. "Alfonso needs him."

"Off to work. How sad we are for Alfonso's turn, the latest of my sufferings."

"You look well enough," Annella said stiffly.

Once in the kitchen, I found Marco. He'd been struck and lay flat on the floor, his cheek bleeding. I checked his pulse, which still beat strong, and gently shook him. As he grew alert, I shushed him before he could speak and we went near the alcove. Sandro was blocking Annella's exit.

"You are a friend of my daughter's?" Sandro asked.

"No," Annella replied. "Alfonso is a friend of my husband's family, from their days at the Malibran."

"You are married? A pity." Sandro rested a thick stein of beer by the banister. "Join me for a drink before you go."

"No, thank you. I must return to my husband."

"I insist."

Years with Sandro made me know when he'd turned. Marco did, too. We looked at each other.

"You're no theater man's wife," Sandro began, "not with sapphires like that. You're the Jewish girl from across the street. You know where Francesca is and you're going to tell me."

"You're mistaken," Annella said, but sounded shaky. "I must go now."

Then Sandro grabbed her arm and I lurched forward, but Marco stopped me. Running in, he scooped up the beer glass from the banister and slammed it hard on Sandro's head. Sandro staggered a few steps before he slumped to the floor.

Marco looked at me. "Run," he urged. "I'll find you later!"

Annella rushed to me and we tore out the front door, racing to the dock.

"Are you all right?" I asked, aiding her into the boat.

She nodded, but her breath was almost as shallow as my grandfather's. Our laconic gondolier grasped the urgent need to depart, and took broad, swooping rows out. The vista of Sant'Alvise's dock soon shrank and blurred.

"He knew who I was, Franco," Annella said. "What if he tells Giuseppe?"

"It's all right," I said, helping her settle. "Sandro's drunk, and they're not wealthy enough to mingle with Constanza. Even if he did know where to look, he'd never get past her guards."

Annella started trembling violently as I sat beside her. "I'm sorry," she said. "This happens when I get scared. Ever since . . ."

I put an arm around her. "You're safe now. I won't let anything happen to you."

We huddled together, muddy water sloshing at our feet. Under

the sheltering *felze*, no one could see us, so I left the cabin's lou-
vered shutters open for air. I gazed at the receding shore. The old
men fished off the pier and the dockworkers stood immersed in their
game. It was the same tableau of an hour prior, but everything had
changed—the past I once knew had been rewritten with my grandfather's last words.

22

Annella and I drifted in silence down Rio di Noale, the rhythmic rowing a balm. By the time we crossed the teeming Grand Canal onto the more sedentary green Rio de San Cassan, we were both steadier. At the church where I thought we would part, Annella surprised me by disembarking, too.

She pointed to a small *bacaro* at the base of the bridge. "Let's have a quick drink. We won't be spotted in there."

"Do you have time?" I looked up at the cathedral's clock. It was getting close to four.

"I'll manage." She spoke to the gondolier, then turned back to me. "He'll take me to her private dock," she added. "Come."

All of the *bacaro*'s windows were open to capture the gathering breeze, strong enough now to churn boats docked next door. An elderly couple plunked out a half-hearted duet at the piano, with a bored accordionist chiming in while he nursed his beer. After ordering, Annella and I stood at a damp stand near a flapping awning that offered respite from the heat, and soon a waiter delivered our drinks.

"To your grandfather," she said, lifting her glass of grappa.

We clinked glasses and downed our drinks in one gulp. An instant heat filled my chest.

"You were right," I said. "I never could have done that alone. How brave you were."

"We make each other brave, don't we?"

"I am sorry to have put you through that—all because of Marco."

"Well, in the end, he saved us both. Who knows what he'll face for that?"

It was true. Marco had stopped me to take on Sandro himself. Maybe he had changed. My grandfather's revelation left me doubting everything, including why my mother had really fled. I'd always assumed it was my fault, and while I wanted to believe my grandfather, I couldn't imagine that my mother ever loved me as he'd described— even on his deathbed.

Annella guessed at my thoughts. "Your mother was pregnant, unmarried, and had to settle with that monster to save you both. I shudder to think what Sandro did to her when they were alone. One thing is certain: You are nothing like Sandro. Not even one feature."

"Everyone always said I looked like my mother." I toyed with my empty glass. "But I wonder: Who is my father?" I couldn't voice my other fear to Annella, that my mother had been forced. But if she had, then why protect the man?

"Maybe you could ask Marco? He would have been old enough to remember, right?"

Marco had almost eight years on me. He would have known my mother better than his own, given that his died in childbirth. A flush of envy startled me, thinking that he'd shared time with her, time I'd never had. I patted the remaining money in my pocket for when I saw Marco next.

The man at the bar caught my eye, so I motioned for the bill. "You should go," I said half-heartedly. "We must keep Constanza happy if she is to let you come back to Restoration."

146

Annella's face fell. "I did not want to mention it earlier, but Constanza has forbidden me from giving any more sewing lessons. She says it's too 'demeaning' now that she is the Minerva's patron. I sense it's more of her way to control me."

"You told me she'd give you anything you want if you played the part. But that's getting harder, isn't it?"

"My mistake was revealing my love for the Minerva, so now she withholds it. I can't let her question my loyalty, so I've played up my indifference to you. At least she believes that, for I've never shown an interest in men."

I took a chance and reached for her hand. "Will I still see you? At shows?"

"Of course, but always with a chaperone." Annella pulled her hand away. "Now that you are the lead, as I heard you tell your grandfather, you're hardly just 'Radillo's boy' anymore. That will make it harder for us to meet." She tried to smile. "Congratulations."

I had been hoping for Annella to rejoin me every week, but no. Once more I felt her slipping away. It weighted the moment, which felt too final. When could we be alone again?

"I'm sure you'll be so busy in the coming months," she said, "you won't even miss me."

"Of course I'll miss you." I felt my heart sinking. Days or weeks were bad enough, but months?

The waiter arrived. "One last round?" he said, setting down two more drinks. "You look like you need it."

"Thanks," I said, dropping a generous handful of coins in his hand. Wearily, I lifted my glass to Annella. "To braving your absence ahead."

She replied, "May we not always need to be brave."

We downed our drinks and reluctantly headed out. In the distance, her waiting gondolier began to ready the ropes. I looked around the empty square and saw that Annella would not meet my eye.

I missed her already and she was standing right next to me.

Then I knew. My grandfather's last words about my mother: *She couldn't have what she loved, but you can.* I couldn't let Annella just walk away, not without knowing the truth.

We were near a narrow passage beside the bar, so I pulled Annella down the secluded slip. A pair of seabirds were carved whimsically into a gate at the end, where I stopped. Annella studied me, confused, but I didn't speak. I could only act.

I kissed her. Then I pulled away fast, ready to apologize.

Before I could, though, she drew me back. We kissed again. This time, we did not rush. I grasped the small of her back, feeling the prick of eyelets and lace. Her lips and tongue were delicate, and I savored the taste of her, warm like cinnamon from the grappa. All I wanted was to wrap her closer to me, and so did she, it seemed, as she slid a hand around the nape of my neck. The longer we kissed, the more the pain of the day evaporated.

We only wrenched apart when two women struck up a conversation a few stories above. Ropes screeched as they stretched lines of washing, but they ignored us.

"Yesterday in Restoration," Annella whispered breathlessly, "the way you talked, I didn't think you were interested . . ."

"I did not lack interest, Annella. I lacked the courage to tell you how I really felt."

She smiled. "Today, you did not lack courage. Today, we only lack time."

We had already taken a risk with the drinks, the clock rounding on four. Still, I wanted nothing more than to press her against the wall and kiss her again.

"I must go now," she said, squeezing my hand. "Let some time pass for me to make things right with Constanza—though waiting will go much too slowly after this." She kissed the back of my hand.

"Until we find each other again, imagine me in your audience when you perform. Isn't that where I have always been?"

With that, Annella hurried out of the alley toward her waiting gondola. I followed to watch her get in, then round the bend where the canal narrowed under a bridge. All I could think about was that kiss and what I would give up for even just one more.

23

In the weeks that followed, I took refuge in that kiss, amazed that something so fleeting could persist so vividly in memory. Buoyed by her, I dared to imagine us together, even if the shape of any future remained restlessly uncertain. Still, that brief kiss revealed that Annella and I shared the same sense of wanting something *more*, which glowed hazily on the horizon.

My thoughts often drifted to her during sleepy mornings at the Titian before the day commenced, or when I strolled along the stalls of Riva degli Schiavoni for respite and inspiration on Mondays. While I relished what Radillo had given me—every night, thriving in the rafters—the Minerva, once a place of solace and delight, felt hollow with neither Annella nor Carmine beside me, more so in the wake of my grandfather's steep decline.

As I'd been warned, Andrea smoldered over my promotion at the theater. Niccolò shared his brother's heated resentment. That left rehearsals chilly until our two new players, Paolo and Eduardo, an eager, bulky pair from Trieste who became Andrea and Niccolò's apprentices, relieved me of my former duties.

Radillo also hired a tailor to free me, as he put it, from "being stuck in the gloom of sewing." I'd tried to smile as he'd described the tailor, Lorenzo: "A medieval friar, with the clumsy gait of boys who grow too tall too fast." When I asked if we could afford him, holding a last, slim hope for Annella's return, Radillo added that, thanks to Constanza, money was no obstacle.

During this unsettled time, I was leafing through the morning paper at the Titian when I saw what I'd expected and dreaded. A beloved name in print. The notice that my grandfather had died.

A thick noise swarmed in my ears at the cold, black type, which described how Sandro was orchestrating an elaborate funeral procession. Much as it pierced me, I could not attend. I could only make peace with my private, truncated goodbye, and read about my grandfather like he was a stranger.

Never again would he give me a taste of his coffee. No more would he rest his wrinkled hands on Carlita's holder, nor would he laugh as he told me a story. Now, riddled with new questions, I had no one to answer them. The one person I'd loved my whole life was gone.

I stared at the spot where he and I had come to the Titian that first and only time together. The rush of lessons in one single afternoon had been the ground for the man I'd become.

Now he never would teach me anything again.

"Are you all right?" asked Michaela, pausing in front of me, midpour. Normally she had little to say.

"Just tired," I muttered. "Coffee will help."

"Perhaps these will, too." She set an unrequested plate of biscotti down. "Eat."

It was a small gesture, but with all that had gone on, I had to hold back tears.

"Thank you," I said, staring at the biscotti.

Michaela cleaned the counter. "You're too young to read obituaries. Usually that's what old men do, looking for their friends."

"My friend was ill . . ." I stopped, fearing my voice would break.

"My condolences," she said. "Want something stronger?" She pointed to the well-stocked bar.

I shook my head, but then remembered Carmine. "There is something. Carmine left town and mentioned he might send a letter here?"

She lifted an eyebrow. "So I am your post office now, too?"

"I'm sorry—it was my idea," I fibbed.

"Franco, it's fine. I rarely get letters, so it will be exciting. Congratulations, by the way. I overheard about your new role. That's a bright spot," she said, tapping the newspaper before she turned, "even if your old friend has moved on."

I watched her move away, and then caught Marco's reflection in the mirror behind the bar. A fresh bruise framed his right cheek, visible even from afar. We had parted so fast that we hadn't settled on a time to meet. I'd taken to keeping the money in my jacket, expecting him.

He joined me. "At the Minerva, they said I'd find you here."

I gestured to his face. "Sandro's artwork?"

He shrugged and noted the newspaper. "So you know."

"Thanks for letting me say goodbye," I said, "and for rescuing Annella."

"Don't thank me yet. I tried to throw Sandro off and said Annella was just a stranger, but he doubts me. No surprise, he hopes this big funeral will draw you out. It's costing Sandro. He's digging his own grave with Tristano—or mine."

"Maybe this will help you," I said, fishing the envelope out. I set it on the bar but kept my hand atop it. "First, I need to know about my real father."

Marco took a deep breath. "Alfonso told you?"

I gripped the money. So it hadn't been delirium. "When did you know?"

"I've suspected, but Alfonso confirmed it when I was taking care of him. He was desperate to tell you. I guess it's time to make good on a promise I made long ago but never kept." Marco paused. "To look after you."

I laughed bitterly. "What fool did you make that promise to?"

"Your mother."

I sat back, too stunned to speak.

Marco went on. "I made it the night she ran."

He paused as Michaela arrived to pour him a coffee and give me a dubious look. I waited, holding my breath until Michaela walked away.

"Hard to believe it now," Marco began, "but Sandro used to be decent. When he first saw your mother, Sofia, onstage, he was mesmerized and fell in love fast. I guess I did, too, after they married. I'd never known my own mother, obviously, and Sofia was so kind and attentive. Sandro let her have anything. He was in heaven that she'd chosen him and then got pregnant so quickly. We were happy."

I pictured the blissful trio. "Let me guess. Everything changed when I was born."

Marco nodded. "You were born too early. That sparked Sandro's jealousy and he accused your mother of betraying him. She denied it, but he knew. Sofia had planned to return to the stage, but he forbade it. Then he refused to let her leave the house. One night I found him beating her. It was clearly not the first time." Marco gazed into the distance. "But it was my first time seeing him like that. When she tried to protect me, he hit me, too, just to taunt her, I now see." Marco looked over at me. "Later that same night, when she came to check on me, I lashed out. I parroted Sandro's words back, that she had ruined our lives and I hated her, too."

He would have just been eight years old. Instantly I recalled how terrified I was the first time Sandro hit me.

"The next morning, she was gone," Marco continued. "But before she left my room that night, she made me promise to look out for you. I didn't think she would really disappear, so after she did, I hated her and blamed you. So did Sandro. You were the proof, every single day, that I'd lost two mothers, and for Sandro, that another man had Sofia's heart. Hating you won me his favor, but I see now that was no prize."

I thought about the taunts and bruises I'd endured when my grandfather wasn't around. Studying Marco's face, I saw how Sandro had betrayed him, too. No loving father would have beaten his children or put them in Tristano's hands. To Sandro, we were both pawns, whether flesh and blood like Marco, or me.

"Do you know who my real father is?" I asked.

"Sorry, no. Nor did Sandro, I think. Your mother was a great beauty, and you have her eyes, you know? I can't believe a man wouldn't do right by her—unless he was already married."

"All my life, I thought I was the reason she left. That she'd never wanted me. That I'd ruined her career, and then she died . . ." I couldn't finish.

"No, Sandro drove her away. Sofia ran from him, not you. She adored you in the brief months you were together. I saw it. I can't imagine how it must have hurt her, leaving you with that ruin of a man. But it was the only way for you, as a girl, to have a chance—with his money and name and, sadly, without her."

I stared at the counter. Marco's words cracked something open in me. My grandfather had been telling the truth all these years. My mother had loved me. She hadn't wanted to abandon me, but Sandro had left her no choice. I knew well the desperation of a midnight flight into the unknown and now I ached for her, as well as myself.

"Only," I said, trying to piece it together, "why didn't Sandro just get rid of me after?"

Marco laughed bitterly. "And lose face? Not a chance. When Sofia ran, Sandro became the pitied hero, not the villain. She was the selfish *puttana* who abandoned her family. Sandro still had money then. He couldn't raise suspicions by dumping you at the turnstile. Only poor families did that, and besides, he probably calculated he could make money off you in marriage. Your grandfather remained to protect you." Marco looked down. "Clearly I didn't."

We sat together in silence. I took in this new picture. Annella had said actresses, like dancers, only survived on a rich man's purse. My mother must have gotten pregnant from one of them at the theater. I could see my grandfather promising my mother he'd stay for me. That's also how he'd known what to do when I had to run, eighteen years later.

Had my grandfather concocted his plan for me when he first sensed he was dying? He knew that, as a man, I could become more myself, not less. He'd helped both his daughter and then me run to the theater. That flight took her down, but it was raising me up.

"Go." I slid the envelope over to Marco. "Force Sandro to pay his own way for once."

Marco took it with a quick nod. "Sorry I never kept that promise."

I finished my coffee. "Good luck in Croatia."

"Thanks, but you'll need more luck than me. A piece of advice? If you care for Annella, and I can tell that you do, Constanza shouldn't be trifled with."

I wanted to ask him more, but he stood up fast and tucked the money inside his suit. "Don't take it the wrong way, 'Franco,' but I hope I never see you again."

Then, with a tip of his cap, he ambled out past men hunched over drinks, faces down.

I watched him go and thought of all I had lost. My real father, a mystery I'd never solve. Marco and my grandfather, gone. Their last words had unwound a tight knot in me. Its weight was only becoming apparent now, in that unwinding.

All of my life, I'd envisioned myself as my mother's burden. That I was not worth her love, not worth staying for. At times, to avert the pain of being so thoroughly cast aside, I'd resented her, too. But I'd been too quick to embrace Sandro's story. He'd beaten it into me, after all. Sofia, mere ghost and cipher, contained in a single photograph I had taken with me when I ran but kept locked in my armoire.

Now her eyes would no longer taunt me. Now they urged me to remember and to *see* her in full, for the first time, really.

Marco's money had been a meager price to give me back my mother and liberate me from Sandro. Both acts nudged me toward the new life I'd begun at the Minerva. It pleased me to know that while my pain was easing, Sandro's soon would begin. Marco would get out. His disappearance would land Sandro in a morass entirely of his own making—a just and fitting end, even if it arrived nearly two decades too late.

24

Several weeks after seeing Marco, I arrived at the theater one morning to find Constanza and Radillo deep in conversation with three unfamiliar men. I couldn't help but wonder if they might have visited her secret bordello. After hearing Annella's story, I saw Constanza in a new light, in which she directed the worlds she moved through as if they were her own private theater.

"Ah, Franco, there you are!" Radillo said. "Come see who Constanza has brought us for a show at the Minerva."

I greeted Constanza and cast a glance around for Annella.

"My companion is home entertaining our guests' wives," she said to me, clearly reading my intentions. "If you're wondering."

"Not at all," I lied.

Constanza wrinkled her nose. "Tired, Franco? Out late with an autograph seeker, perhaps?"

Radillo chuckled. "That's unlikely. His head's always down in a cloud of thoughts, and he never brags of any conquests. Come to think of it, I've yet to see him with a girl."

"You were going to introduce us?" I said quickly, removing my cap with a bow to the strangers—and eager to move the conversation along.

"Yes," she said. "Franco Collegario, meet the Lumière brothers, Auguste and Louis. Inventors from France who've been making news across Italy on a grand tour of their exciting portable device, something they call the Cinématographe."

Radillo addressed the third man, a lithe Roman who I gathered was the brothers' translator. "Tell them that Franco is a rising star here at the theater."

"Pleased to meet you," I said as the brothers took in the translator's words.

The Frenchmen did not look like scientists or showmen. Stocky like bricklayers, they sported full beards with gruff, graying sideburns and unruly eyebrows set in perpetual frowns. Though both appeared to be in their thirties, they bore the veneer of grandfathers.

Auguste transformed, however, when he unpacked their unassuming technological wonder. His eyes glittered as he unhooked the case's velvet straps and set the Cinématographe on a table. It appeared to be a familiar, larger version of a common camera perched atop an ordinary tripod. Once assembled, it stood no taller than an alert cat.

"Apparently," Constanza said, "this device takes and develops photographs and then stitches them together in succession to project pictures on a wall or tapestry. It gives the illusion of one mere minute of seeming life, what they call *actualités*."

"Photographs that move?" I said. "Like shadow play? When puppeteers play with light to cast silhouettes on a cloth?"

The translator cut in. "The Lumière projections are not silhouettes. They are indeed photographs. Scenes straight from life."

Sensing our confusion, Louis began to explain how the Cinématographe worked, and the translator condensed his descriptions into what us laymen could follow. As Louis gestured to the different parts on the device, we were told that the photographic images would pass in front of a protruding bulb to splay onto a large canvas cloth that we would string across the midline of the stage.

Louis then encouraged each of us to take a turn examining the device. When I lifted it, I was astonished. It felt lighter than a marionette. How could it project at the scale and speed they described? Photographs were compact and grainy to view in hand. How could the back of the pit see anything at all?

Constanza cleared her throat, interrupting the translator. "Apparently the device was inspired by the rhythm of modern mechanical sewing machines, such as my girls use in our French textile factories. I know it is hard to imagine moving photographs when you have not seen them, but I caught a demonstration when I was traveling in France last fall. That's what sparked my desire to bring the brothers to share their *actualités*. I think it might be perfect for our new audiences."

"New audiences?" I tried to smile. "Is something wrong with the ones we have?"

"Not wrong," Constanza replied evenly, "but with the Lumières, we have a chance to expand, to let Venice peek at the century ahead."

"Precisely," Radillo said, animated. "The brothers are in town for three more days. We'll hold their show two nights from now, but start advertising it immediately as a grand mystery. Let's double the price of admission. When people expect more, they pay more."

"But the pit won't be able to afford that." I stared at the device, hopeful no one would glimpse it in the dark and fear they had been duped.

Constanza sighed. "Keep their fare as is, then. We want crowds in droves." She eyed me closely. "Come sit with me during the show, Franco." She gestured to Radillo. "Ensure the Grimanis have a box, too."

Radillo nodded to me. "You'll find it's a far better view than your usual back row."

"I'll even bring Annella," Constanza said to me. "She'll be curious to see this marvel."

My heart leapt at seeing Annella, more than I could conceal, for I caught Radillo and Constanza sharing a furtive smile.

OVER THE NEXT DAY, word spread fast of our intriguing mystery event. Tickets, even at premium prices, flew out the door. Queues of those seeking last-minute rush spots began forming by midafternoon.

On any other night, I would have been in the rafters, hands and trousers dusted with chalk. Tonight, however, I stood in Radillo's box in my suit, waiting for Constanza and Annella. From here, I watched the masses stream into the pit below, bewildering ushers.

All noise of the crowds around me faded, however, when Annella hurried into the box alone. After so many weeks apart, she and I both stopped, struck into silence, and me, awash with relief at how well she looked. Annella stood bright against the drab back curtain, a splash of light in a canary yellow dress. A glint of diamonds flared at her wrists when she brushed back her hair and they caught the light. Above the fray as we were, I felt upon seeing her as if I were suspended in midair, floating more than standing.

"Annella," I said, taking her hand to kiss it. This time, as I did, we did not let go of each other, her fingers warm in mine as I gave them a gentle squeeze.

"You're blushing," she said a little shyly.

"So are you," I teased. "Or maybe it's just how close we are to the stage lights."

"I'm sure that's all it is, tricks of light." Then she cast a glance over her shoulder. "Constanza and Rossana are behind me in the lobby with the Grimanis. Constanza's talking their ears off about her charity work. How are you?"

I looked her up and down. "Once more without words, it seems. How have things been with Constanza?"

"Better, I think, given that I'm here. As curious a spectacle as it sounds, I am a touch sad there are no marionettes you'll be handling. Though if you were, I wouldn't be talking to you. You'd be up there." She jutted her chin toward the rafters. "Tell me quickly, did you see Marco?"

"Yes." I smiled. "I'll likely never know who my father is, but it changed me, to learn my grandfather had been right about my mother after all."

"I can see it. You do look different somehow," Annella said. "And not just the suit."

I looked over her shoulder to glimpse Radillo with Constanza and the Grimanis. "I heard from Carmine, too. He sent a letter through Michaela. He and Giannina are wed."

"How wonderful," she said, growing wistful.

Happy as I was for Carmine, a pang of jealousy pierced me. He had spirited away with his forbidden love and was now free. Yet Annella and I had been forced apart for weeks. Nor did I divulge to Annella that Carmine had asked me about her. *Have you kissed her yet? Spark any fires of your own, schoolboy?*

I hurried on. "They rented a theater called the Gerolamo and are planning a run of matinees for children."

"Children's matinees?" Constanza had just entered the booth with Rossana and a pair of guards, one of whom I recognized as the implacable Arturo. "Radillo never mentioned that."

"No," I fumbled, offering the women a bow. "I was referring to a colleague."

"I see," she said. "Do you like the view here, Franco?" A glint in her eye suggested she'd observed me with Annella. Before I could answer, she traced my arm with her fan. "How smart you look, as if you've been up here in the boxes all along."

When Constanza turned to wave to one of the other boxes' inhabitants, Rossana gave Annella a knowing look and then flecked the shoulder of my suit like a valet might.

"They are about to start," Annella said, mildly flustered. The last warning lights in the lobby flickered.

"Sit here, Franco," Constanza said, tapping the seat directly behind Annella. I waited for the women to sit in front of us, then complied dutifully, finding a guard squeezing in on either side of me. "It's a bit close," Constanza added. "I had hoped the Grimanis would invite Rossana to sit with them, but their entourage is rather large tonight, apparently."

Below, Radillo paraded the Lumières and their translator onstage to introduce the night's entertainment. After a few words, darkness fell. I forced myself to focus on the stage, not the back of Annella's bare neck, although the trace of her lilac perfume made it hard to concentrate. Still, Constanza's two bored, gruff guards beside me kept me in check.

The only sounds now were the crowd's soft shuffling and muttering, until the device creaked to life. A single large bulb flashed, illuminating the white canvas backdrop. What unfolded next, however, silenced everyone.

Up on the larger-than-life canvas we saw a man, real as the sunlight in which he stood, surveying his rose garden. He frowned at his watering hose, oblivious to the boy who had stepped on it to stop its flow. Only when the confused gardener held the spout close did the prankster release his foot—and water gushed straight into the gardener's face.

Laughter broke the awe. In under one minute, we had witnessed an entire story in vivid, flickering life.

More photographic vistas followed. Workers exiting a factory at closing time. A child's face big as a moon, breaking into a toothless grin. Two boys' rough-and-tumble game of tag. An enormous locomotive, bathed in rolling folds of steam, gliding into an airy Parisian station to discharge its passengers, tiny as scattering mice.

The final *actualité* took place in Venice and featured several passengers boarding a *traghetto* on the familiar Grand Canal, where Annella and I had traveled back from my grandfather's just weeks ago. I stared down at Annella and recalled my reply to Carmine. *Yes, I kissed her. That fire has sparked. But with Constanza ever present, there is no way for me to tend it.*

I focused on the strange black-and-white moving picture, a scene both familiar and not. Even on the foggiest mornings, the real Grand Canal burst with color. Threads of green and blue in the spray, the scarlet of gondoliers' emblazoned coats, the fashionable hues of ladies' skirts. But on the canvas, the waters ran black. It could have been dusk or noon or even a moonlit midnight, judging from the ambiguous tint. Gone, too, were the sounds of seabirds' cries, gondoliers' hearty tenors, waves lapping at docks. All that visceral texture had evaporated in these photographic images, which, for all their vigor and novelty, lacked the real quality of light on water that one might have seen in a luminescent Murano vase.

Still, it was all mysterious and marvelous. When the bulb in the projection device at last went dark and the houselights rose, the applause cracked. Enthusiastic cheers from the pit and the boxes forced Radillo to chaperone the brothers back onstage for questions that discomfited their slender translator, barely able to navigate the cacophony or dialect.

With the houselights up, I stole another glimpse of Annella, but there was no time to ask her what she thought. Constanza ushered us into the main lobby, where the Lumières were buffeted by a throng of men seeking, but being denied, purchase agreements for the device. Leo parted the crowd to introduce the Grimanis to the brothers, as Radillo stepped into our circle.

Constanza beamed at the crowds. "Look at them all, so happy from one mere night. There's no debating the Cinématographe's appeal."

"I wish they were selling them. We could incorporate projections into our shows," Radillo said. "What did you think, Franco?"

"They were mesmerizing, to be sure," I replied, "but the Grand Canal streamed quieter than a museum painting. It felt odd, seeing life move only in black and white, with no color or sound."

Constanza nudged me. "Whatever you may think, we secured a much larger return on the box office than the marionettes alone ever could. As we've seen tonight, Venice and Italy are changing. So must the theater keep up."

Surely she was not suggesting we do away with marionettes, I thought. Radillo had told me to verse myself in the art of compromise, but I couldn't stay silent. "I would not want to see the marionettes displaced, and not just for my own self-interest as their handler."

Radillo put his arm on my shoulder. "Franco, we would do well to listen to our new patron, who has brought us this technological phenomenon to profit our theater." He softened. "Not to worry—the Minerva will always be a marionette theater, first and foremost. Even if tonight's gimmick lasts, your talent will ensure we do not go out of business."

"Indeed," Constanza said with a thin smile. "We must keep you happy or you may run off to do children's matinees."

"Children's matinees?" Radillo asked, bemused.

"I am honored to be here, and very happy," I said, eager to smooth things over and change the subject. "And inspired by wonders like tonight's."

Radillo nodded approvingly as Leo brought the Lumière brothers to us. "Let's all celebrate our triumph at the overpriced Caffè Florian."

"Will the Grimanis accompany us?" Constanza asked.

"It appears they have already departed," Leo answered.

Disappointment flashed in Constanza's eyes, but she recovered. Still, I wondered whether her interest in our theater had anything to do with art, marionettes, or, now, *actualités*. Perhaps it was more about how she would be seen and by whom.

As we set off toward Piazza San Marco, I looked at the brothers, who appeared to be mere ordinary tourists carrying their suitcases, hard-shelled and scratched from many travels. Yet those suitcases cradled an extraordinary device, which conjured a kaleidoscopic new future. I sensed that the twentieth century would be no mere continuation of the past, but a sharp break from it. What would that mean for the Minerva?

I wanted to ask Annella her thoughts, but she was back to playing the role of the amenable companion under Constanza's watchful eye. So I retreated into my own musings about the night, imagining how to preserve the past while incorporating new forms as the next century beckoned.

25

Wе had just climbed down from the rafters when Leo pulled a copy of *Il Gazzettino* from his ledger and said to me, "Have you seen your latest commendation?" Then his gaze encircled the other men. "Franco is in this week's Ladies' Column."

I froze, worried, and Radillo saw it. "You don't know the column?" he asked. "It is penned by 'Lady Margherita Umberto,' which is an irreverent pseudonym that pays homage to the cult of our Turinese Queen Margherita and King Umberto in Rome. Yet this columnist is no passive angel. She has a knack for unearthing scandals. Her caustic pen spares no one." He nudged me. "What trouble have you been up to, I wonder, to make an appearance there?"

I had never read that column in the Titian, so now my nerves got the better of me—what would a women's scandal sheet have to say about me? When might she have even *seen* me?

I reached for the paper, but Leo swept it back and wagged a finger.

"Read it aloud, Leo," demanded Radillo. "All of us should hear this."

"Must we?" Andrea groaned, but Leo cleared his throat:

"Ever since spring's commedia dell'arte with marionettes, I have noticed an increase in heady excitement among us ladies when attending Pietro Radillo's mechanical theater of marionettes at the refurbished Minerva—home, too, to the recent and delightful 'moving pictures' of our neighbors in France, sharing their mechanical device.

"If La Fenice is Venice's glorious theatrical crown, then the Minerva is surely its princess and sparkling jewel. Even when full of sorrows, we know the play will resolve into union by its end, no matter how improbable. The Minerva has always been a treat, but now we see much more than marionettes in a fresh light. We ladies may not love the insistent fool, Facanapa, but we have grown quite curious about Facanapa's handsome handler and Radillo's new lead puppeteer, a one Franco Collegario. If you have not paid a visit to the Minerva lately, don't miss your chance to spy Collegario's fine skills onstage, or his fine masculine form after."

By its close, the men were all laughing, mocking my "form." I released the breath I'd been holding. Lady Margherita Umberto had not cast aspersions on me or linked me to a scandal. Rather, she had sung my praises alongside the Minerva. It made me wonder who she was. She must have been at the Lumière brothers' show. Had she seen me with Annella?

Andrea tried to go along with the joke but looked at me as if I'd paid for the publicity to be planted myself. Radillo, however, was giddy. "Bravo to our own bon vivant. All the more reason for us to revel in the delights of Festa del Redentore tonight."

Venice typically bewildered and enchanted its tourists, but the Festa del Redentore, the city's annual celebration of a sixteenth-century plague's end, subjected even the most jaded Venetian to spectacle and intrigue after somber morning masses and afternoon picnics. Every boat and terrace was strung in garlands, and masked revelers inundated San Marco and the Grand Canal. Just this evening, as I had made my way to the Minerva, I'd threaded through the crowds gathered for the hallmark fireworks that would illuminate every strand of sky and sea at dusk's close.

By evening, many had dusted off opulent and now-unused *carnevale* attire, dressing to masquerade. Some women clustered in male garb or masculine Bauta masks beaded with jewels. Men, too, appeared with their chests trapped in tight dresses, lined with lip pencil to suggest breasts. Enormous peacock-feathered plumage obscured identities. Others disappeared in shapeless black robes, memento mori staring in withering silence. Even the pit had been in full form, many in makeshift costumes, which seemed to encourage them to be even more raucous than usual.

Now, instead of our usual trip to the Britannia, it appeared that Radillo had other ideas for our night.

"We must take in the city!" he was saying, and tossed dresses in a variety of pastel shades to us. "Here are your costumes, 'ladies.'"

All I could do was stare at the creamy rose confection Radillo had thrust at me. Then I saw everyone but me had leapt into the game with enthusiasm.

I held out my dress. "Sir, I cannot wear this. I will not."

"Oh, I insist. You especially must, for your new feminine fans." He passed me a wig and a small makeup case, then gave me a gentle push toward the dressing room, where Andrea and Niccolò were heading. "Don't make us wait."

I had no choice. I stumbled off, slipping into Restoration instead for privacy.

There was little time to think. I shed my trousers and work shirt but left my masculine undergarments on and, of course, my chest binding before pulling on the offending dress, which was both too tight and too loose in various spots. Desperate to hide, I rifled through our lost-and-found box, which I used to replace props, and found a shawl to wear instead of the red-checked scarf I usually knotted around my throat to hide a missing Adam's apple. With shaky fingers, I applied the bare minimum of color to my lips and my cheeks in a smudged mirror, dabbing kohl over my eyes. I affixed the wig, pulling its long, coarse black hair to hide as much of my face as I could. Then I took a breath to steady my nerves before facing the mirror.

I stilled as a terrible disgust overcame me. *Always a struggle, fixing you in a dress*, my grandfather had said. Now I saw why.

My reflection revealed the woman I might have become. I had left home a lanky tomboy of a girl but now saw, and more painfully *felt*, how garish I looked as a woman, so entirely separate from myself that it made me want to rend the garments in shreds. The artifice was exaggerated, of course, but no more tasteful, tailored version would have fit. On me, femininity would branch like a crack in a windowpane—and I felt like I might shatter. My refusal of this attire had come to transcend survival, circumstance, or necessity. As a woman, I was all wrong.

This pale pink dress showed me exactly the man I had become.

Then Radillo barged in, wearing a flamboyant outfit of silks and looking the part of a dandy. I jumped at his interruption.

"You'll do," he said, looking me over and gripping my elbow.

"No—" I started, but he just dragged me to join Leo and the other puppeteers, similarly attired but far more jovial. Outside the theater, motley bands of horns, violins, and accordions crescendoed in the cloying heat.

"Why, 'Lady Francesca,'" Leo said, now dressed as a Napoleonic wonder himself. "Truly, a vision."

I winced at my former name and Leo tugged me aside. "Take a mask. I thought you might like one when I heard of Radillo's plan."

"Thank you," I said, grateful to obscure my face. "Where are we going?"

"You'll see," Leo said, as we wound up Corte del Teatro San Moisè toward Piazza San Marco.

I told myself I just had to bear this hideous dress until the fireworks, then I would be free, so I tried to concentrate on the revelry around me. No stretch lacked masks, music, dancers, acrobats, jugglers, and drunks—as if Riva degli Schiavoni's stalls had burst into living tableaus. It reminded me of the stories my grandfather told me about the final days of Napoleon's reign, when people threw elaborate street parties at all hours, believing the city would crumble any moment in a siege. Under the specter of death, work was forgotten while decadence flourished.

So it was again tonight, but already I was exhausted by the pretense. I lagged behind the other men, trying to get lost in the crowd. But Radillo wouldn't have it.

"Take hold of him," he directed Andrea and Niccolò. "We have something special for you," he said to me.

I shook as Andrea grabbed me, shoving me so hard that I nearly tripped over the hem of my dress, all while Niccolò guffawed in my ear.

As we fought our way upstream over the bridge at Rio dei Scoacamini against a sea of inebriated crowds, it dawned on me that we were heading out of San Marco, not toward it.

"Where are we going?" I shouted.

Radillo kept directing us. "To see what kind of lady you really are."

He ferried us across the crowded Grand Canal, over the Rialto Bridge toward San Polo. It couldn't be, I thought, when we squeezed single file down the same narrow alley that Annella and I had so often traversed.

We were going to Constanza's, but why? Dread pooled in my stomach.

The familiar square now throbbed with people. A band of horns stood atop a makeshift stage where men were singing full-throated, off-key. Everyone leered as I knocked over a pile of empty prosecco bottles, tossed in a heap.

Radillo leaned close. "Tonight will be an education."

I tore off my mask. "Sir, I—"

But Radillo was already guiding me to the entrance.

The guards moved aside, the thick doors screeched open, and with a final push, I entered. Radillo paid no mind to the four guards with rifles stationed in the atrium. "This lady is ready for her adventure," he announced.

Then I saw Constanza emerge from the shadows wearing a gold Bauta. She was my inverse, sheathed in a tailored masculine suit threaded with peacock feathers and leather riding boots cropped at the knees of her trousers.

"No mask?" she said. "Showing us who you really are?"

My heart caught in my throat. Did she know? Did Radillo? Was the Ladies' Column revealing more to some inner circle to which I was oblivious? I contemplated running, but the four guards with rifles now blocked the door.

Constanza set her mask on the mantle. "I'll remove mine, too. If only Lady Margherita, whoever she is, could see your 'fine masculine form' now."

Radillo, along with the guards, heartily laughed. Why was I here? Why was Constanza now beginning to lead me through her grand house while Radillo smirked by the door?

My whole body tensed as we moved down a long, candlelit hall and deeper into her palatial home. Briefly, it occurred to me that this was a hall Annella would traverse daily. Where was she now? She couldn't help me. If I tried, I'd endanger her, too.

"I know of your tale," Constanza began. "Few foundlings would ever think to audition at the Minerva, but Radillo tells me you appeared on his doorstep last summer, all hungry and eager. He underestimated you and what you are capable of." She looked toward the palatial staircase we were approaching. "But there are some secrets you've failed to conceal. That's why you're here."

As we passed a dining room, I heard men drinking and saw a butler handling cloaks and revolvers.

"Where are you taking me?" I demanded, stopping in my tracks.

She turned to me with a serene smile but said nothing and urged me to keep walking. I had never been so close to her, and I noticed that her eyes were an icy, penetrating blue. I felt pinned by her gaze.

"People have underestimated me, too," she said. "As if a woman is incapable of dictating the rules. But like you, I play the game to win. What might you win tonight if you trust me?"

She hooked her arm in mine. Up this winding maze of staircases and high-ceilinged halls we went, passing several rooms guarded by enigmatic men donned in butlers' attire. Behind one hall's doors came intermittent sounds of pleasure, a woman's moan followed by a stinging slap. At another room with an open door, I spotted a small arsenal of weaponry tacked to a wall.

So this was her salon, the bordello. I tried to slow down, but Constanza urged me on.

"I don't need to tell you that men can turn into brutes," she said, nodding at the wall of weapons we'd just passed. "My girls need protection."

"Your girls?"

"Foundlings like pretty little Annella land in my salon for respite. Some from your neighborhood, perhaps even an old friend or two?"

I arched an eyebrow at a man exiting a door, drunk and dishabille. "A salon? Really?"

"There are many ways to exchange . . . ideas." She smiled wryly. "You might frown upon it, but we both know that women are commodities, like glass and silk, to be paid for and traded. By the time these girls come to me, they are not exactly innocent, but I take care of them. I give them a way out of poverty and the streets that would have driven them gaunt or left them pregnant, syphilitic, or mad. I ensure they're well paid, fed, dressed, cared for, and that the men who pay for them behave enough. Believe me—the man who'd replace me in here would be far worse." She paused. "I wonder: What might you be willing to do, or bargain for, under the right circumstances?"

"For what might I be dealing?"

"We shall see, won't we? Until then, come. You can't put this off forever."

We had reached the last landing. I was trying not to tremble. Constanza tightened her hold on my arm.

"You would not get far if you ran, my dear 'lady,' and it's much too late to try."

Lady? It was dark up here. No one was on this floor, and no one would hear a sound, given the raucous noises below. What was ahead? Tristano? I stiffened, ready to fight and die rather than succumb. Yet a part of me wanted to cry, remembering my grandfather's efforts to save me. Was it now for nothing? Everyone whom I'd ever cared for flashed before me. Carmine, with his wild smile on the night of my debut. Radillo, with whom I'd performed. Annella. Would I never get more than that one kiss?

Constanza stopped at a large, enameled door. Beyond it, only silence. To my surprise, she gently kissed my forehead.

"Curious," she said, stepping back in surprise. "What soft skin you have . . ." She paused. "Trust me—tonight is only the beginning of what I can offer you. If you're smart and support me with Radillo, I can reward you handsomely. Loyalty will get you far indeed—but its absence will send you back to the gutter you came from so fast that your head will spin."

She unlocked the door. My eyes struggled to adjust to the darkness into which we waded. I glimpsed one blue lantern by a bed, barely illuminating what seemed to be a large, dim attic.

Then I saw Annella. She was perched on the edge of the bed, eyes downcast, wearing nothing more than deep-purple lace lingerie. Her hair tumbled loose over her shoulders, and her hands crossed her bare thighs as if to cover herself. Once more, the diamond bracelets encircled her wrists. Now, a matching necklace displaced her mother's locket.

My heart was beating so loudly that I was sure they both could hear it.

"Franco," Constanza began, drawing me toward Annella, "you have grown to be Radillo's prize, a jewel of the Minerva. So here's a jewel of a girl. Tonight, she's yours, all night. A gift from me, as a reward for your successes. I've seen how you look at her, so now? Do what you want. She won't deny you, even—or maybe especially—in that dress." She bent to caress Annella's cheek, and Annella flinched. "Only don't scar her face. I'm too attached to it."

Constanza handed me an ornate key and left. When the door closed, I caught up to the words she'd said.

A gift. My reward. A jewel of a girl. All night.

I hurried to lock the door, then returned to Annella's side. I held out my shawl for her to cover herself. "Here," I said, averting my gaze. "Are you all right?"

"Yes," she said, rising. "You?"

"What is this? What's happening here?"

She pulled the shawl over her shoulders. "You're my punishment, Franco."

"Punishment? For what?"

"For stealing. She caught me, a few days after that Lumière brothers' show. She confiscated the savings I'd gathered. It's all gone. So is my chance at getting out. Constanza was furious and threatened to make me work like this to pay it back. Until now, her jealousy has prevented her from following through. But I crossed a line. That's why I'm here, as a 'gift' for you."

"Is this some kind of a game?"

"It's Constanza's to play." She gave a heavy sigh. "Don't you see? She's using me to make you indebted to her. That way, she can get you on her side for the theater. She brought in the Lumières but saw how Radillo values your judgment, and now the Ladies' Column? If you dissuade him from her course, you're a threat to her plans, plans not even I am privy to."

Everything Constanza had said took on new meaning. What in panic I'd read as threats had been her cajoling and negotiating. *Loyalty will get you far indeed.*

"So she does not know?" I asked, my stomach finally uncoiling. "About me or . . ." I hesitated. "Us?"

For the first time, Annella smiled. "Can you believe it? To punish me, Constanza brought you, the only person I want." Then pity shone in her eyes as she reached over to touch my sleeve. "How miserable you must be in this dress."

I flooded with embarrassment and tore off the wig. Annella pointed to a basin by the window, so I went to scrub off the makeup until my face was once more my own. As I dried my hands, I heard the low boom of the first fireworks.

Below, the square was brimming with motion and color as a flare lit up the sky. Festa del Redentore, the endless night of light.

"It feels like our own private show," Annella said, joining me at the window. Even with my shawl, I could see the lace of her negligee. My breath caught.

"Annella, we don't need to do anything . . ." I trailed off.

She gazed into the night sky. "But we could. I've been dreaming of when I would see you next. After all, when might we ever get a whole night together?" She faced me. "I thought the way you kissed me that you might want to?"

I lifted her chin. "I kissed you because I couldn't find the words to tell you how much more I want."

"Then let's have more," she said. "Stay with me. All night."

For a moment we stared at each other. Then I kissed her, just as another round of fireworks went off. My senses were awash in the sweet taste of her lips, the warmth of her skin, the scent of lilac threaded in her neck and hair. Beyond us, the thunderous flash of blue and gold raced over rooftops across the night sky.

"Take this awful dress off," she demanded, and I gladly obeyed, kicking the offending garment aside once free.

"And you," I said, nodding at the shawl. She let it fall to the floor. "No need for these chains, either." I unhooked her bracelets and kissed the inside of her wrist as we edged toward the bed. I undid the necklace and then traced the décolletage of the negligee. "Though maybe keep this on for now?"

"These, too?" Annella ran her hands along the thin linen under-garments that I wore every day but only I had ever seen. "How hand-some you are, Franco," she murmured. "So strong. More than I've imagined. And I have been imagining you every night since that kiss."

"As have I."

We tumbled onto the bed and I bent over her, fanning out her hair on the pillow.

"Tonight, I need your instruction in something besides sewing," I said.

"We have all night to practice."

She snuffed out the bedside lantern, then pulled me to her, as the kaleidoscope of fireworks brightened our wide, soft bed.

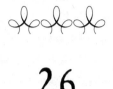

26

In the blue dawn, I awoke with a start. A spacious, shadowy attic. My arm wrapped around Annella, her back folded into me. Both of us naked, and she, fast asleep.

The night unfurled back in all its intensity. Her body. I had not let myself feel how completely I had wanted her, until I did. Nor had I known my own body at all. Now I felt content, as if I'd been floating in the water.

Last night, I had been too focused on Annella to see anything else, but now I saw my surroundings more clearly, including an adjacent sitting room and shelves piled with books beside a charred hearth. Outside, the bells of a nearby church summoned people for dawn mass.

I traced a strawberry-shaped birthmark on Annella's right shoulder. "I should dress," I whispered near her neck.

"Not yet," she murmured. "Constanza won't rise for hours, and besides, you have the key." She turned over and opened her eyes, which were sleepy in this thin light. "Isn't there something more that you want, which I can't deny you?"

"There will always be more that I want from you after last night."

I trailed my fingers along the outside of her thigh, but a creak on the floor below made me stop. I began digging for my chest binding and undergarments that were tangled in the sheets.

She sat up and stilled my search. "This can't be our only night."

"It won't be," I replied. "This is only the beginning."

We stared at each other in the bed, disheveled yet happy, until all my concerns from last night edged back. Constanza had followed through on her threat. She'd willingly given Annella to me. What would stop her from doing so again with another man? I voiced my fears to Annella.

"I know," Annella replied, "but I do not think that will happen. She gets jealous. And she gave me to you, someone she's trying to bring over to her side at the Minerva, and perhaps as another favor to Radillo, too. If I had truly fallen, her punishment would have been harsher. I once saw a girl who tried to escape working at the bordello. She had been beaten. The next day, Rossana heard rumors she'd been sent abroad."

"That is exactly why I'm worried," I pressed. "Why couldn't that girl just leave?"

"Perhaps because she made Constanza money, or . . ." Annella hesitated. "She knew too much. Besides, where would she go? No money, clothes, family, home, and all alone?"

"Wait—when was this? The girl who tried to escape?"

"A while ago, last winter, when I first visited the Minerva with Constanza. Why?"

I remembered Constanza's whispered conversation with that man, whom I now guessed to be a guard. "She spoke of 'cleaning a girl up' whom a guard had found after a search. Something about needing 'to keep a closer eye on her.' I thought it was her charity work." I looked at Annella. "Now you have no money. Mine went to Marco. So you said you can't leave, either."

"Not yet, it's true, but I have a plan," she said. "Let me tell Constanza that you are excited to work with her and Radillo, not to mention grateful for this gift." She gestured to the bed. "She will be pleased with me for bringing you around and relieved to find you so easily amenable, with me to 'manipulate' you in the future, if needed." Annella inched closer. "I'll let her think that last night was indeed torture for me and that I'm contrite—that I've come around, too. She'll forgive me and expect you, as a man, to be easily swayed. Her ego will blind her to us both, and we can find ways to see each other in secret. Over time, we can save money to find a place of our own for when she eventually tires of me."

I leaned back in the bed. "So what role must I play, exactly?"

"The lovestruck puppeteer, of course." She smiled but then turned serious. "And for the next while, be agreeable. Go along with her at the Minerva. Let her think she's winning, and in time, so might we."

"Though if I'm not agreeable," I said, tracing her arm, "might she placate me with another 'gift'?"

"If you raise her ire, she might suspect me. It's a fine line I must walk. She knows I love the theater, but I'll pretend that being around you, after last night, is a burden. She'll enjoy that, too, putting me in situations where we see each other, to discomfort and test me. It'll make her think she still has me, and now you, too, under her thumb."

"I can manage that, but your acting skills will need to rival the great Eleonora Duse."

Annella pulled a blanket over her shoulders. "I've done it before, when I first met her. Constanza thought she was molding me into a Sapphist. Yet I knew who I was long before she ever looked my way."

A picture of Constanza arose unbidden. Constanza, touching Annella as I had last night. The swell of rage caught me off guard.

Annella seemed to sense it and took my hand. "Franco, Constanza is always one step ahead, but not this time. We are. If we play this right and bide our time, we could be together when she loses interest in me—which I'm certain she will. She is too fickle not to, and there was a string of companions before me. The very fact she gave me to you suggests she already cares for me less. In the meantime, if she acts as I expect, in a few weeks I can start sneaking out on Monday afternoons. We'll pick a café for you to wait at, and if I show, we can find a hotel? Your pension is too risky for me to be seen at, but maybe somewhere in Cannaregio, where she never travels, but of course, not Sant'Alvise. Her interest in me will wane—I know it. When it does, we shall be ready."

The possibility of having everything I ever wanted began to sink in. Perhaps, like Carmine, I could one day have both Annella and my life at the Minerva. Radillo would bear the brunt of negotiating with Constanza. All I'd need to do was play along with this charade.

"You're willing to take this chance?" I paused.

"You are who *I* want." She looked closely at me. "I've never had or felt that before last night. You know me. You *see* me. For me, you are the best of two worlds in one body. I am wary of her, but I am far more scared of losing you."

Staring into Annella's eyes, I knew I would steal any hour, go up against any enemy, so long as I could be with her again. Hours to talk and touch. Hours like last night, in which I felt most myself, too.

I skimmed the edge of Annella's collarbone. "All right. Let her caprices run their course. We'll wait, and while we do, we'll find bedrooms of our own on Monday afternoons."

Annella slipped her fingers around my neck. "It's still early. No one stirs, nor will they for at least one more hour. Come. Let's say a proper goodbye."

It was a mystery how something so tender and simple as touch could make me brave enough to fight. The world denied Annella and me words, names, and even a place beyond this stolen bed, but here we were, alive and together in spite of everything.

The sun wasn't fully up. The stairs were dead silent but for the scuttle of mice. No one could enter this room because she was right—I had the key.

AN HOUR LATER, I left Annella's room dressed in a dusty policeman costume she had saved from her theater days. The trousers were too short, but I was grateful for anything that kept me out of that horrendous dress.

The sun had fully risen, but many were sleeping off the night's festivities. Other than a few hushed women's voices emanating from behind closed doors, the house was quiet as I retraced my rambling path downstairs.

On the ground floor, I found no guards inside or out, only a charwoman who had opened the windows and doors to encourage a cross breeze. At the door, I adjusted my official-looking *Carabineri* hat and was about to leave, when I heard a man in the courtyard, a voice from the refrain that haunted me.

If we lose her, boys, we don't get paid.

Tristano was out there.

Gingerly, I peeked outside. There he stood, wearing a fine navy blue suit that accentuated his broad shoulders. More menacing than his body, however, was his bristling stillness when enraged— as he clearly was right now. Sandro's rage had been chaotic and hard to predict, but Tristano, with his slick dark hair and piercing blue eyes, was like a panther contemplating its prey. Right now, that prey was the man he towered over and whom he'd backed against the alley wall.

"You thought you could just disappear?" Tristano said to the cowering man. "That I'd stand for that?"

Tristano stepped aside and my stomach dropped. Marco was the prey. He had not escaped. Now he lay there, battered, with one eye swollen half-shut. Instinctively, I started to step out, but Marco saw me and shook his head almost imperceptibly.

"You were seen at the station buying tickets with that old flame of yours, Paola," Tristano was saying. "She's a pretty one, isn't she?"

Paola. Marco's fiancée. That's why he'd needed money.

"Your spies are mistaken," Marco sputtered. "Paola left me long ago when I started working for you. All the neighborhood girls are scared of you—and for good reason."

Tristano crouched down and gripped Marco's lapel. "How did you even get the money? As I recall, you have your father's debt to work off. If I find you've been stealing from me, you'll pay in more ways than one."

Then Tristano stood up and, without warning, began kicking Marco, over and over.

I couldn't stand by any longer, so I threw my voice. "Shut up out there!" I cried, and it echoed against the stone. I saw the sleeve of my costume. "The *Carabinieri* are coming!"

Tristano halted. He looked around wildly, disoriented. "Who's there?"

I froze behind the door. A long beat passed, the silence punctuated only by Marco's wheezing. Then I looked out to see Tristano hauling Marco to his feet.

"You're lucky your father's a friend. Anyone else would be dead after what you tried. Betray me again, and you will die. I'll see to it myself, with pleasure." Tristano stepped back, smoothing his hair as he surveyed the palazzo once more. "Get me a new girl. That's who Constanza needs for Marseille." Then he buttoned his suit jacket and strode out of the square.

I waited for Tristano's footsteps to fade before rushing to Marco. I took his handkerchief out of his suit and dabbed his face wounds.

"What are you doing here?" he asked, bracing himself against the wall.

"It's a long story. You need a doctor."

"No," Marco replied between wheezes. He eyed me. "At least if Tristano returns, your costume might keep him at bay."

I looked around the square, listening for any sound of footsteps. "Don't worry. He's gone."

"As you can see, I didn't get far. Paola . . . it was for her, your money . . ."

"I gathered." I checked his forehead; it was warm. "Marco, you need help."

"I have an apothecary, by the Bridge of Sighs. Just help me to the vaporetto," he muttered, clutching his stomach. I wrapped an arm around him and as we set out, I began putting the pieces together.

"Tell me the truth," I said. "Does Tristano provide Constanza with girls? Is that what you do for him?" When he feigned confusion, I added, "Annella told me about the bordello in Constanza's, then I saw it for myself last night."

Marco tried to smile but recoiled. "That must have been a little awkward."

"I got by."

Marco sighed. "I get prospects from Cannaregio. Only girls. The more desperate and hungry, the better. Tristano told me they'd trust me because I talk like them. I spin a lie about factory work, training, wages, and then I bring them to Constanza's. That's why I was here the day I met you. Some are sent to work in factories, but they are indentured servants, as Constanza takes a percentage of their earnings in exchange for taking care of them. Those with a certain look stay and are lavished with clothes and lodging in exchange for 'entertaining' men; they're paid and fed well enough not to complain. But they can't just leave. If they talk to the wrong people, they could shut Constanza down."

I knew better than to ask why the police might look the other way. Even if they did not take bribes, they were powerless against the mafia, if Tristano was involved. Besides, Constanza's reform work was lauded by many in power. I'd overheard conversations at parties and in the Minerva. She was reducing the swell of impoverished children, seeming to improve their well-being. No one asked questions because they didn't want to know the truth.

We were through the narrow passageway now. The ferry was just up ahead. A boat dipped in the waters, sparse with sleepy partiers.

"I'm not proud of what I've done, but I didn't have a choice," Marco said. "At first with the girls, I thought, *Better them than me*. But then Tristano started hounding Paola . . ."

"For himself or Constanza?" I asked.

"Himself. Paola's no foundling. Like every girl on our street, she knew Tristano's ways, so she left me. Went to her aunt's on the edge of Dorsoduro, started working in a *bacaro*. After I got the money from you and some others I shook down, I convinced her we could make a fresh start in Croatia. We'd bought tickets and were going to meet yesterday, when I thought Tristano would be distracted by the festival. But he was onto my plan. I threw him off enough to give Paola time to escape, so she went alone." Marco grasped my shoulder for balance as we staggered to the vaporetto. "She knew to leave if I didn't show. At least now he can't touch her."

"What about you?" I held on to him. "I can't leave you like this—"

"Don't worry about me. I got Paola out. That's what matters."

"What was Tristano saying about Marseille?" I asked.

Marco sighed. "Constanza has textile factories in France from her late husband. Italian labor is cheaper, so she fired the French workers and has been sending Venice's foundling girls to Marseille, using the De Rossis' rails to Genoa and shipping from there. I hear it's brutal, those factories. Seven days a week, all day into the night. And the local French hate the Italians for taking their jobs. There have been violent protests. The girls are attacked in barracks where they sleep with rats." He paused. "None of those girls will ever afford passage back—and despised as they are, they will want to run home. Once there, they are trapped. Paid nothing and worked to death, alone and unable to speak the language."

"So Constanza's been playing the part of a benevolent reformer," I said. "Cleaning up streets, reducing crime, 'saving' foundlings, helping girls, building foreign trade. But why become a patron of the arts? She must have some larger aim."

"If so, I am in the dark. I can't figure out why she wants the Minerva." The boat's engines rattled, beginning to churn the waters and drown him out. Marco gripped me in a quick hug and hung on. "I told you before, Constanza is dangerous. Stay out of her business. If Annella can get out, she should try. I've said too much already, so maybe it's safer if you stay away from me, too." Then he lurched onto the deck and ducked out of my sight.

27

The truth about Constanza's work with the foundlings haunted me, and I worried for Annella. She might have Constanza's protection now, but what would happen when her interest waned, as Annella predicted? Could she be sent off to France? For now, all I could do was follow our plan and wait for our next rendezvous, hoping she was right that we still had time.

After we wrapped up commedia's run two weeks later, Leo gathered Andre; Niccolò; the new apprentices, Paolo and Eduardo; and me together on the stage for a surprise announcement. Radillo was bobbing on his toes with excitement, one eye at the doors as he spoke.

"Today, we start preparations for our most ambitious production to date: a full-length adaptation of William Shakespeare's Veronese-set *Romeo and Juliet*. Four full acts, a first for our Minerva, and possibly even Italy—Shakespeare with marionettes." He opened the trunk and handed me the script. "Look familiar, Franco?"

I thumbed the heavy text he had me read months ago, trying to imagine how we would translate the play's antiquated dialogue.

Radillo paced across the stage, as if sensing my thoughts. "Our version will be acted without as much dialogue. Our beloved pit could not concentrate on that many lines. We'll keep key scenes, of course. Add more ballets to convey Romeo and Juliet's burgeoning love, family fights, and tragic separation. Our lovers' silences and gestures will need to be as eloquent as Shakespeare's words." He retrieved two youthful puppets, one male and female, from the trunk, and I was surprised when he held the female one out for me. "Franco, you're our Juliet."

I set the script aside and took the marionette. Familiar with the play as I was, I knew Juliet was a true dramatic lead. Radillo was giving me a great honor, but as my first falsetto role, there was no denying this was also a test of my abilities.

"So Franco knows his way around a woman now?" Andrea said. Although he was smiling, his voice hinted at a snub. "When are you going to tell us which lady you conquered that night?"

I rolled my eyes as the others joined in the teasing. It had been like this since the Ladies' Column and my night with Annella. Constanza's bordello, I learned, was more an open secret among Radillo's circles and now, because of my "gift," these men, too. Only in a letter to Carmine had I revealed the truth—or the parts that I could.

Irritated, Radillo waved his hand to silence them. "Enough. The play is what matters. As for the other major roles, Andrea, you will be Franco's Romeo."

"Ha!" Andrea sneered. "Sorry, Franco, but you're not my first choice."

"Clearly not mine either," I replied.

Radillo continued. "I shall play the narrator, the Montague and Capulet parents, and Friar Laurence. Niccolò, you are Romeo's best friend, Mercutio." He gave the more minor marionettes to Paolo and Eduardo. "Take some time on your own to know them, referencing the script with Franco as needed, and we'll get started shortly."

The others began investigating their new marionettes, but I drew

Radillo aside. "How will you end this play, sir?" I asked. "It is bleak. Not typical Minerva fare."

"Death will shock them most of all," he replied. "I've always wanted to stage this at the Minerva, and now is the time. For you, it's a serious lead and a step forward. Depending on how you do, you might get your own full shows handling male and female speaking parts after."

I nodded hopefully and began practicing dropping my Juliet in a swoon. She was a rosy-cheeked marionette with ginger hair, and her elaborately embroidered dress was brand new, not from any of our other productions. I glanced back at the thick script. The Minerva had never done a play on this scale. How was Radillo paying for it?

That soon became clear, when Constanza entered with Annella. A rush of jealousy nearly overcame me at the sight of her at Constanza's side. I had to look away.

As I did, I caught Niccolò eyeing me suspiciously. I moved upstage, pretending to master one of Juliet's balcony-scene gestures. Yet even with my back to Annella, my memories of that night and her body drifted back.

Then Radillo clapped his hands to get our attention. A smile lit up his face.

"Gentlemen, please welcome our patron, Signora Cappello, whom I invited to take in our first rehearsal. She'd like to say a few words to start."

Onstage, we bowed. Briefly, I caught Annella staring at me as Constanza stepped forward.

"In this new era for the Minerva," Constanza began, "which I am pleased to generously fund, our aim will be to cater to much more than illiterate fishmongers. Now is the time to keep, and please, the boxes with lavish productions and dramatic, artistic spectacles such as this one. Our goal is to do them exceptionally well. So, you will have extended time to rehearse. I'm closing the theater for an entire month to prepare for our September premiere."

A new era for the boxes? Closing the theater for a month? Sneering at the pit full of "illiterate fishmongers"? These were ominous harbingers, but judging from everyone else's hearty cheers, I stood alone in my misgivings.

Then Radillo snapped his fingers. "Franco, find the balcony scene. Let's have you and Andrea start there with a quick run-through."

I ruffled through the yellowing script, grateful to focus on the page, then elevated my Juliet atop the trunk of marionettes onstage, reducing the give in her strings to evoke the balcony's height.

I heard Radillo say to Constanza, "Juliet is fresh in love here. You'll recognize this dialogue."

Then I began to read in falsetto, gesturing my Juliet to Andrea's Romeo beside me:

> *Wherefore art thou Romeo?*
> *Deny thy father and refuse thy name.*
> *Or if thou wilt not, be but sworn my love*
> *And I'll no longer be a Capulet.*
> *'Tis but thy name that is my enemy:*
> *Thou art thyself, though not a Montague.*
> *What's Montague? It is nor hand nor foot*
> *Nor arm nor face nor any other part*
> *Belonging to a man. O be some other name.*

When I finished, Andrea did not continue the dialogue. He and Niccolò stared at me, unable to suppress their laughter.

Radillo stood perplexed in a frown. "Franco, your falsetto sounds too comic to be believable, let alone a woman bound for a tragic end."

"Perhaps he is too much a man now," Niccolò said to Radillo. "Should Andrea and Franco switch roles?"

I flushed with embarrassment but couldn't respond. I had failed at the falsetto, only to be held in greater esteem as a man. Annella blushed and did not join in Constanza's tittering.

Radillo nodded to me. "I'll coach you on techniques for producing a higher and more feminine tone. It's only a matter of practice, elongating a muscle at the back of your throat. We have time to make it right and we will. Everything must be perfect for this premiere."

Constanza motioned to Radillo. "Something else didn't ring true. Franco spoke in dialect. The play concerns two aristocratic families. They would speak Italian."

"You are correct," Radillo concurred. "I have been wanting to experiment with Italian since *The Decameron* but was persuaded . . ." He trailed off, likely thinking of Carmine.

"Sir, how will the pit partake without dialect?" I asked. "They are more than half of our audience."

"Though sizable and loud, they pay very little," Constanza reminded Radillo.

Annella shot me a look of warning, but I pressed on. "Yet they are more consistent. Over time, that's more lucrative, is it not?"

"We are all mandated to speak Italian these days," Constanza said. "Here is a chance for us to take pride in what links us, instead of sowing division. The pit can step up and join us in the twentieth century, or not."

Before I could reply, Annella intervened. "That's true. I think we all want unity after decades of division postindependence. However, the pit can't speak a language that aristocrats have the time and means to learn. A mix of Italian and dialect onstage allows them to *infer* meaning in Italian. If anything, that might aid their instruction— if indeed literacy in a national language is the aim."

I saw how carefully Annella was appealing to Constanza as a reformer to smooth tensions. "Perhaps," I chimed in, "we can use Italian for the antagonists, since it signals villainy on our stage. Italian alone might confuse the audience if it's all that our two doomed lovers speak."

A haughty smile spread on Constanza's face. "I'm afraid your falsetto would not aid anyone's understanding. It would turn the tragedy into comedy and only confuse the pit more."

Andrea and the other men snickered, but Radillo shushed them.

"Let's hope," Constanza continued, her eyes fixed on me, "that with additional rehearsals, everyone can at least seem aristocratic."

Privately, I seethed but kept silent for Annella's sake.

Radillo must have seen, though, for he added, "Andrea, let's show Constanza the fight scene between Romeo and Mercutio instead."

"I hope Juliet's not in it," Andrea said to Niccolò loud enough for all to hear. "Otherwise, she might join in the fight, considering how manly 'she' is."

Then Constanza called to me. "Franco, given that Juliet is not in this scene, why don't you take Annella on another tour?" Constanza cut Annella a sharp look. "She has trouble holding her tongue, so perhaps you can learn something from hearing her voice. I gather she's yielded to yours before."

"As you wish," I said with a light bow, and headed offstage. But near the edge, Andrea caught my arm.

"Wait—were you with *her* that night?" he whispered, eyes glittering.

"Don't you have a scene to do?" I shook him loose and did my best to hide how flustered I felt.

Annella met me in the wings, her face implacable in front of the other men, who were staring at us offstage. "Want to go to Restoration?"

"Lorenzo, the new tailor, is working in there."

"Right, of course." She fretted with her locket.

"Why don't we go out back for some air, take a walk?" I suggested.

We didn't speak until we were outside and alone.

"Sorry," I began. "I didn't have a good start, not with the falsetto or in being agreeable. Hopefully she will think that I was distracted by your presence." I smiled. "Which isn't untrue."

"I couldn't even look at you, not without remembering your hands . . ."

The air between us shifted. I quietly took her arm, feeling her edge closer to me as we began to walk away from the theater, toward the quieter slip of Calle Traghetto Vecchio. I knew exactly where I was going: to a hidden archway of an abandoned apartment.

When I found it, we both looked around. I took my chance, or perhaps she did, as we kissed.

"What are we doing?" she whispered.

"Taking a tour?" I murmured, kissing her neck. I resisted loosening her hair, wanting to run my fingers through it, but she did not bother to hold back with mine, and my cap fell to the ground.

After a moment, we broke apart, and I studied Annella's face. "How have you been?"

"Miserable. At least I can be openly so, even if she misreads the reason. Constanza has interpreted my low spirits as a sign of my contrition, so she seems appeased. She told me she regrets her decision to 'punish' me in that manner. That suggests she won't do it again. I think she might even be a little jealous of you."

"Now, why would she be jealous, I wonder," I said, holding her waist.

"I can't imagine." Annella drew me closer. "But clearly I've been sent out alone with you to fish."

"Tell her I see the error of my ways much more clearly now, or almost have," I added, sliding a hand up near her breasts.

"We'll discuss that on Monday." Annella gently pressed me to stand back. "Promise me you'll be more amenable on this show, despite how misguided her approach is. For my sake?"

"Only if you promise you'll join me on Monday." I tried to kiss her again, but she playfully sidestepped me to switch positions. "Not fair," I added, "to use your dancing skills to thwart me."

"Like it's fair of you to corner me in a dark alley?" she teased.

"I'm not sure who is cornering who here."

"I can't help it," she said. "Nor am I certain who's yielding to whose voice."

I gave her hand a quick squeeze. She hung on to it and pulled me back onto the walk.

"But we must return," she said, "lest they come looking for us."

So we each smoothed our clothes and hair and began meandering back to the theater. "There's something I must tell you," I said. "I saw Marco when I was leaving Constanza's after Festa del Redentore. He didn't escape." I explained about his fiancée and his revelations about Constanza's factories in Marseille.

"That's where the girl who was beaten must have gone." Annella's face set as the truth sunk in of how vulnerable she was. "I suppose I should be grateful that Constanza had other plans for me," she said with a hollow laugh, as we neared the stage door.

Leo opened it, startling all three of us equally. I was relieved that it was not Constanza and I caught Leo eyeing me approvingly.

"A tour of the alley?" he asked me. "Not much to see out there."

"We were just taking in some air, to escape the heat," Annella replied. "Does Constanza need me?"

"Yes. She wishes to leave." Leo held the door open. "Franco, Radillo wants to see you, too."

As we entered the wings, Annella left me without a look back, joining Constanza as they departed. I found Radillo, and he launched into a breathless speech about our new rehearsal schedule, plans for the production, and enthusiasm for Constanza's suggestions. Dutifully, I listened and tried to sound encouraging, even against my own judgment.

Thanks to Constanza, the Minerva was being handed an opportunity too good to be true. Her money would enable weeks of rehearsals for our grandest show yet, by one of the greatest playwrights of the world.

But what was Constanza's real use for the Minerva? Something didn't fit. Did she really want to become a patron of the arts, and if so, why now? She could have done so decades ago, but didn't. Was the Minerva, like her "charity work" with the foundlings, masking a separate purpose? As I stood in the wings, all I could think was that now, my life, too, was in Constanza's hands. In trying to be more agreeable, what exactly was I agreeing to do?

28

The morning of my reunion with Annella, I hurried to our agreed-upon spot of Café Zancani in Campo dei Mori, damp from the thin rain. I sat at the window, worrying two false gold bands, bracelets I'd stolen from the theater and winnowed into rings so Annella and I could pose as married tourists seeking a room at a nearby pension I'd found.

Nearly two hours passed, but frustration pushed me to linger. The waiter and I struck up a conversation to pass the time.

"You look out the window often," the waiter eventually hinted. "Waiting for someone?"

"I was, but she may not join me today," I replied.

"I hope she's worth the wait," he said, moving to take care of a few regulars who came in, shaking off the wet of their umbrellas.

When I looked back, I spotted Annella approaching. She scanned the street, then entered. Briefly she stilled when she caught sight of me, but then hurried over. As I took her hand for a kiss, I slid the false band into the curve of her palm.

"Constanza left late for business in Padua," she explained. "I'm so glad you waited."

"You're here. That's all that matters." I paused. "And the hotel near the Madonna dell'Orto has rooms. Their sign was out when I passed to check."

"Let's go."

We made a fast tear to the canal and within a few minutes arrived at the pension with its faded ROOMS TO LET shutter swaying in the wind.

Inside, the tiny lobby was infused with the scent of strong coffee. Behind an iron grate, a distracted but patient woman was assisting some guests lamenting their icy water. When they left, I approached the desk alone and spoke to her in dialect.

"My wife and I would like a room, just until late afternoon."

"Not the whole night?" she asked, visibly relieved to be dealing with locals. "Venice has many charms after dark."

"We must join her family this evening." I leaned close, like Carmine once had with his autograph seekers. "That will inhibit our time alone. . . to rest?"

She smiled, then skimmed the board behind her. "I see. In that case, I'll even give you a discount since you'll leave it before nightfall." She affixed a copper key in my palm. "Top floor, back from the stairs. No one below you, and not even the maid until four. You won't be disturbed."

Annella and I restrained ourselves on the long climb, but once the door was locked, we kissed with abandon. Her perfume of lilacs was so fragrant it startled me. I unpinned her hat, tossing it on the bed. She wore a deep-red dress, the skirt full with a slip and layer of tulle. I ran my hands over the curve of her waist, pressing her hips into mine as she tore off my bowler and unbuttoned my vest.

"This is what I wanted to do that day in the alley," I said, and turned her roughly against the wall to rapidly unhook the eyelets of her dress, loosening it off her shoulders. As I did that, she was unknotting the tight bun so that her hair fell free as she pivoted back to face me. I couldn't speak, only bury my face between her breasts as she rested her hand on the back of my head.

"Practice makes perfect, I see," she said.

"One can never practice too much."

I knelt before her and moved my hands up under her dress and the tulle, pulling down her silken undergarments. With her eyes on mine, she stepped out of them gingerly, then I lifted her dress, kissing her bare inner thighs and parting them, inching upward as I slipped first one, then two fingers inside her. When I pressed my mouth onto her, she gasped. The pressure of her hand on my head was steady as I heard her tell me not to stop. As if I would.

AFTER, WE LAY ON the bed half-dressed in each other's arms, gazing at the sloped canopy of our ceiling, plaster crumbling from earlier rain damage. I smudged away a trace of the scarlet lip pencil she'd worn earlier. It surprised me, the alchemy of contentment and excitement she made me feel.

Outside, the rain had slowed. We watched the sun slip in and spread across the bed. The rhythm of a blacksmith's intermittent hammer struck tough stone over and over, as a throng of women and children began to shout their wares from a nearby market. Yet all in my heart felt quiet.

Annella looked over at me. "How have things been at the Minerva?"

"Apart from heavy-handed lectures on the importance of compromise, good enough."

"I told Constanza you would just need some time to come around, which, sooner or later, it seems, we all must." She sat up. "Constanza insists that I attend an important luncheon of hers this Friday when she returns from Padua. She wants me to report what these men say and do when she steps out. She says I must let their interest in me 'flourish.'"

"Flourish?"

"Merely flirting, she reassures. But I doubt much will flourish with those anti-Semites. I don't relish being alone with them."

"Here's a trick if someone tries to hurt you." I shifted in the bed. "If a man raises an arm, dodge under. Twist his arm back, like so." I demonstrated gently, not wanting to hurt her. "Then kick the back of their knees, while you have leverage."

She laughed. "Franco, I cannot use these techniques."

"Keep them in reserve." I paused. "Is there anyone at Constanza's you trust besides Rossana? Someone who could be nearby?"

"The guard, Arturo. He's always been kind for some reason."

I folded my arms. "I can think of a reason."

"It's not like that. Once, he confessed that I reminded him of his daughter." She nudged me. "Now you're jealous? I suppose I was, of that desk clerk flirting downstairs."

I gestured at the space, which was more modest than Annella's attic but all our own. "She gave us the best room. The end justified the means."

"Then so does my kindness to Arturo. He helps me slip out un-detected, like today." She glanced at the open window. "For now, though, I should head back, so that we can take our time."

As we began to gather up our clothes, Annella gestured to the back of her dress. "Help me."

When I started to tighten the lacing at the back, she just laughed. "You're much better at undoing it."

"Tighter? That makes my chest binding seem loose."

"Welcome to femininity. Nothing can be comfortable." She adjusted her sleeves. "Otherwise, women might run in reckless abandon."

"We can't have that." I separated strands of her thick hair to braid it. So neat at her arrival, it tumbled wavy and uneven down her back. I kissed the side of her neck when finished. "Done."

Annella twirled her braid into a neat chignon and pinned it at the nape of her neck. She located a small vial in a hand-sewn pocket hidden in the folds of her dress. After dabbing some of her familiar perfume behind her ears and on the insides of her thighs, she relined her lips.

"Presentable again?" she asked, smoothing her waist.

"You'll do," I said, teasing her as I buttoned up my trousers. She gave me a playful shove that knocked me off-balance. Then I reached over, drawing her back. "I prefer you undressed, bare shoulders, lips unlined from being kissed."

"Perhaps that is how I will be 'presentable' again next Monday, just for you," she replied, reaching to the bed and handing me my bowler.

After I returned the room key and paid our bill, Annella and I strolled west from Campo dei Mori along Fondamenta de la Sensa. Our time together was almost over, and a melancholy settled over us.

"A long time ago, I lost everything, even you," Annella said while we walked. "For years I barely survived. Over time, I stopped asking myself what I might want. I thought only about how to not get hurt. Once, I thought Constanza would keep me safe. But now it's like I'm being slowly strangled there. Standing in those rooms, pretending every day—I am forced to watch how her and these men around her get to live—while I feel like I am slowly disappearing."

I took her arm and folded it in mine. "I won't let you disappear. Because you're much more than a 'jewel' or distraction. You are beautiful, there's no question, but you are also intelligent. Remember the day you told me about the Saracens? How you said history is only ever told by its winners? You see things that others don't. I admire that."

She blinked back tears. "You see the parts of me that never get to be in the world. It's only with you that I feel really myself. Like now in the open air, strolling along as if we were nothing more than an ordinary pair of lovers."

"And who's to say we aren't?" I asked. To emphasize my point, I waved over a flower seller and bought a posy of carnations for Annella's wrist.

"I can't wear these after we part," she said.

"So? Enjoy them now. A more tangible gift than stolen hours in a rented bed or half a dance in a crowded room."

She plucked one of the carnations and tucked it into my vest pocket. "We may get another dance soon. Constanza told me she wants to have a party to celebrate the success of *Romeo and Juliet*. She hopes to entice the Grimanis to attend."

"I hope we can celebrate its success. I'm still having trouble finding Juliet's voice," I admitted. "Even with Radillo's techniques, something doesn't feel right."

"You will figure it out. It is in love scenes that Juliet mostly speaks, and you are a fast learner there."

"Now you're making me blush."

The heady scent of garlic wafted toward us from canal-side *trattorie*. Annella and I approached a bridge, lingering on it to stare down at the green waters rippling below us. Then, nearby we saw a gaggle of small children in rags and bare feet cluster around a photographer. His elaborate camera teetered on its triangular stand, as the children besieged him with requests. After he assembled them in a group shot, he presented each one with payment of tiny, wrapped candies.

"Foreign photographers," Annella said. "So fascinated by foundlings. You know they aren't from here because they hand out sweets instead of chasing the children out of a square with a broom."

I thought of Rico, the young boy who'd helped me but died far too young. How many of those other boys that day had succumbed, or been lured away, also never to be seen again, just like the girls Constanza sent to France?

Annella slipped her arm in mine, rousing me from my thoughts. "Come; let's find a boat for these sleepy back channels before we part."

She pointed to the dark, narrow slip on the other side of the bridge, devoid of passersby, and we found a weathered man napping in his gondola along Campo della Maddalena. I handed Annella a teal parasol for ladies to shade them from the sun, as the cabin was a modern one, all open air with no *felze* to sit beneath. As we glided along slim tributaries, we admired freshly painted rows and shade-lined cafés. Ribbons of dripping men's white shirts crisscrossed above us like ceremonial flags. Open shutters released the clank of dishes and conversation and one child's tenacious but poor piano scales.

As we drifted up to the uninhabited dock where I would leave her, I remembered Annella's comment about the Grimanis. Constanza had made a concerted effort to befriend them, I noted, thinking back to the Lumières' show. But to what end? She already had power and prestige, which even her illegal activity, her so-called salon, only consolidated.

Then a half-formed thought crossed my mind: What would the Grimanis think if they knew the truth of the foundling workers trapped in France? Or did they already know and not care, happy to rid the city of its destitute? Perhaps whether the poor ended up in bordellos, factories, or France didn't matter. Besides, who would believe me, a foundling turned puppeteer, anyway?

The risk was too great. If I was to keep Annella safe and eventually have her to myself, then I had to keep Constanza happy. All I needed to focus on right now was perfecting Juliet.

I reached for Annella's hand and held it in my own. "For saints have hands that pilgrims' hands do touch," I began tentatively, "and palm to palm is holy palmers' kiss."

"Have not saints lips, and holy palmers too?" she asked, voicing Romeo's line.

I smiled. "Then have my lips the sin that they have took?"

"O trespass sweetly urged!" she replied. "Give me my sin again."

We snuck a quick kiss goodbye under her parasol as the gondolier slung a thick, wet rope to dock. I stepped out and then gazed after that teal umbrella as it drifted away.

Like Juliet, Annella was trying to shape her own fate. Her words sung in my head on my walk home, and through this refrain, it happened. I heard and spoke aloud the timbre of my Juliet's voice. In rehearsals among only men, I'd been trying too hard, for fear of sounding too feminine. Perhaps, though, our voices were not so distinct by sex, at least when expressing desire, fear, or love. Juliet's voice should be infused not just with romance, but also longing and intelligence, aware of the impossible demands of her situation. With the echo of Annella's voice and body still fresh, I began to practice speaking quietly to myself as I strolled home, occasionally touching the carnation in my vest for company.

29

The night of the premiere, all six of us crowded into the rafters—Radillo, Andrea, Niccolò, Paolo, Eduardo, and me. None spoke. I kept near the right edge, my Juliet suspended in the wings. Not since my commedia debut were my nerves so pitched. This late September night, however, there was no Carmine to reassure me.

Our rehearsals had been beset by tensions and plenty of Constanza's unhelpful suggestions, given the frequency with which she dropped in unannounced. Radillo and the others made every effort to placate her, but the best I could do was stay silent, holding on to the promise of Annella's eventual freedom—and our Monday afternoons together. Still, I couldn't help but imagine how I might correct Constanza's errors in judgment as we drew closer to the premiere.

Now that the night had arrived, a half-hearted chorus of "In the mouth of the wolf" went around. Out front, the quintet with Renaissance instruments finished tuning. Constanza had insisted the musicians share a spotlight with the pit to become part of the show, oblivious to how they loomed too large and would disorient the scale for the audiences once the marionettes were dropped down.

At last, the curtain parted on the lute's solo, and I steadied my gaze atop Juliet's head as Radillo began his opening prologue. I had held back some in rehearsals but knew my Juliet's voice would not be naïve like commedia's Isabella. Radillo had called Juliet one of the drama's lead roles, not secondary to Romeo. She had a say in this tale, a role to play in her own life. The denial of her voice was the key to this tragedy.

Under cover of darkness, I brought Juliet onstage to hang mute as Lady Capulet and the Nurse discussed Juliet's impending marriage to Paris. When Radillo voiced Lady Capulet's command that "younger than you, here in Verona, ladies of esteem, are made already mothers," I heard his vocal technique well.

Yet as the production unfolded and we transitioned to the glittering banquet hall, the pit stayed too quiet. As I'd feared, they had not understood the lines of action and characters we'd built up in Italian. Only when Romeo and Mercutio emerged illicitly, their faces concealed with repurposed commedia masks, did the audience respond, applauding Andrea's skillful handling of Romeo's dance and the physical altercation with Paolo's Tybalt.

After Tybalt's exit, Romeo and Juliet remained bathed in limelight. Andrea and I kept our lovers alert to each other, drawing out the moment. It was as if their first sustained look spun a fine gold thread. No words or touch occurred, but the audience already intuited the essential wordlessness of love, as we brought Radillo's narration to life: "But passion lends them power, time means, to meet tempering extremities with extreme sweet."

The other marionettes of the ball began levitating up, as Vincenzo gradually extinguished all but a few limelights, which stayed on Juliet and Romeo. The effect was applauded, evoking without words how everyone but the beloved disappears at that first knowing glimpse. Andrea and I made the lovers glide toward each other, then skitter nervously away. Two lutes and a single hand on a tambourine commenced a tender dance sequence.

After the sequence ended, I elevated Juliet to her bedroom's balcony. Andrea's Romeo cried out from below: "But, soft! What light through yonder window breaks? It is the east, and Juliet is the sun!"

I hesitated before speaking my first lines, capturing Juliet's bind. I felt the audience's palpable annoyance at Andrea's Italian. We had just begun to hold the pit's interest in our wordless dance; something needed to shift to keep them engaged. So when I spoke, I made the impromptu decision to use dialect:

What's in a name? That which we call a rose
By any other name would smell as sweet;
So Romeo would, were he not Romeo called,
Retain that dear perfection which he owes
Without that title. Romeo, doff thy name,
And for that name, which is no part of thee,
Take all myself.

I felt Radillo turn sharply in the rafters, but I ignored him. Down below, the pit breathed a sigh of relief. Juliet was now their own.

Andrea responded dutifully in Italian, and the rift in voices worked on another plane—to capture the lovers' two opposing worlds in language. When Andrea said his lines—"Love goes toward love as schoolboys from their books, but love from love, toward school with heavy looks"—the crowd intimated a variation on what he meant, which my replies amplified.

The second act continued, now with more enthusiasm from the pit in spots. After the curtain closed, Radillo looked at me but didn't say anything, only descended for intermission. Andrea, Niccolò, and the apprentices followed him down. For a moment, I lingered in the rafters alone, with Juliet resting at my side, surprised to hear a long-buried female voice in myself again.

AFTER INTERMISSION, WE COMMENCED a series of thrilling battles, during which I kept Juliet still but trembling in the balcony tower, even in scenes in which she did not have lines. That transformed her into a discomforting surrogate for the audience. Though she did not speak for much of the second half's battles, she appeared alive, not static. Each struggle, banishment, or death in the second half held more weight. Despite the strain, not once did I let go of her strings.

As the fourth act unfolded, we offered hope that the tragic lovers might circumvent their fate, something I could tell the pit eagerly expected from previous stories on the Minerva's stage. They protested, and some even joked, when I eventually delivered my character's somber toast—"Romeo, I come! This do I drink to thee"—and consumed the sleeping potion that would give a false impression of death. Then, their cries of disbelief resounded at the lovers' actual suicides, Romeo's by poison and Juliet's by blade. When I released the red ribbon that suggesting Juliet's mortal wound, Andrea and I threw our wooden holders on the stage at the same time—to audible gasps.

There was no denying it now. After cries of protest, the theater went silent. This time, the lovers really were dead.

An unsettled silence ensued as the surviving characters assembled onstage for Radillo's concluding sober monologue, which, to my surprise, he delivered in dialect, too:

> A glooming peace this morning with it brings;
> The sun, for sorrow, will not show his head:
> Go hence, to have more talk of these sad things;
> Some shall be pardon'd, and some punished:
> For never was a story of more woe
> Than this of Juliet and her Romeo.

Then the lights extinguished. The curtain fell. I heard our quintet out front lower their instruments, the papers from their sheet music faintly rustling. Bruno stealthily passed the two holders back up to Andrea and me.

When the curtains parted for the closing bows, the applause from the pit was more muted than from the boxes. It did not last as long, nor had the pit offered up their usual colorful commentary. Only when Andrea and I brought our leads forward did we hear some genuine enthusiasm at seeing the lovers revived.

Frustrated by the tepid response, and after weeks of labor on a scale we'd never done before, Radillo gestured for the curtain fast. It had barely closed when he was already down, exiting the stage more hastily than our own impatient audience. Out front, few lingered as they usually did to debate and discuss. It felt too quiet beyond the curtain.

If Constanza had attended, then she, too, had departed, as I did not see her or Annella after I climbed down. I went out back with the other men to leave and encountered fewer autograph seekers than normal, though one woman blushed when I signed her program.

Andrea elbowed me. "Juliet, how dare you gaze upon another when we are still fresh in our tomb?"

"Romeo, you are dead. It is time for another. Try to avoid poison on your way home."

"Are you two 'lovers' fighting? You just revived," Leo teased, but went quiet when Radillo joined us.

Radillo took my arm and moved us off to the side. "You went against Constanza's and my direction."

"Respectfully, the direction made no sense. Surely you could feel us losing the audience. Even you spoke in dialect at the end."

His voice pitched in frustration. "You may have saved us from getting pelted with boos, but you angered our patron, who paid for this entirely. Tell me, will the audience even matter when we have no money to keep our doors open?"

"And what is a theater without an audience?" I asked, emboldened. "Constanza wouldn't be pleased if they left in droves, either."

Radillo rubbed his forehead, and when he looked at me again, I saw how bloodshot his eyes were. "I did my best to explain that to her now, but the damage was done."

Damage. Would Annella suffer for my actions?

"Sir, please, I didn't mean—"

"Good night, Franco," Radillo said, interrupting me. "We'll discuss this later. Coming, Leo?"

Leo stepped back toward the door. "Go on without me. Just need to finish up."

Radillo offered him a curt nod, then left with Andrea and the others. No one was in any mood to celebrate. Only Leo surprised me by suggesting we walk together.

We headed briskly toward Campiello Barozzi for several minutes before Leo said anything.

"Franco," he began, "be smarter. Radillo wants you with him, but he needs Constanza's money. Play nice and you might take over the Minerva someday."

I stopped. "Is Radillo retiring?"

"Not yet, but he will need to leave the Minerva to someone eventually. Carmine's gone. Giannina's elopement has left him ruminating on his legacy—and the theater. Who will run it when he stops but you?"

Carmine and Giannina. So far away and alone and struggling financially from what I read in Carmine's letters. Despite their happiness, I knew they both should have been here, too.

I heard the distant hum of a vaporetto rounding a bend. "I know Radillo had high hopes for *Romeo and Juliet*," I said, "but tonight, with Constanza at the helm? All did not go well. It went exactly as I feared."

Leo moved closer. "Maybe failure will hasten their partnership's end. My advice? Let their association run its course. Constanza is fickle, and the Minerva clearly a diversion. I believe she will turn to something new soon, so let's store up her money now, to carry us over when she abandons ship."

"Perhaps."

We resumed walking. My silence with Leo was as much of a concession as I could allow. I had not imagined Radillo ever leaving the Minerva—let alone bestowing it to me—but I wondered if there would be a theater left after Constanza. That was Constanza's way, after all—to exploit. *Women are commodities*, she had said, *like glass and silk, to be paid for and traded*. Was that true of the theater no less?

I had intended the role of Juliet to be a private homage to Annella, but I'd just broken my promise to her. I felt as downtrodden as the pit after Romeo's and Juliet's deaths. Unlike so many fables that advocated only for blessings of life after death, Shakespeare's play offered no hope for either realm. The lovers' deaths restored nothing. There was no justice achieved, only a terrible sorrow crossed by loss—too close to modern life, which the pit came to the Minerva to escape from, not relive.

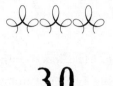

30

Our grand production of *Romeo and Juliet* proved less lucrative for the Minerva as the month unfolded. Reviews were middling beyond a noted preference for Juliet. That spared me the worst of Constanza's complaints, and she gradually conceded we should all employ dialect. Still, the play's bleak ending was never embraced, and the boxes proved fickler than the pit. Perhaps at the Minerva, part of the appeal for them had been the pit's banter. With the pit less vocal, the boxes must have found the whole experience wanting, too.

After the premiere, Radillo had gone on about how ambitious shifts take time to take root. How Constanza brought us vision, a sense of the future—and the means to achieve it.

"But at what cost?" I'd asked, tiring of his enthusiasm and the efforts of my own compromises. That, and Annella had not shown up on a single Monday for weeks.

"Cost is no concern for Constanza," he'd replied.

"Why?" I'd persisted. "Where does her money come from? With whom does she do business? Wouldn't her wealth be better spent helping the foundlings she professes to save?"

But Radillo just waved off my worries. "You've spent too much time anticipating threats, Franco, even when, like now, there are none at hand. Try having some faith. When you perform, you let the moment take you, and where it takes you is magical. That's why you're here."

I'd gone along with him, but in my heart, I knew there was more than one way for something to cost too much.

Rather than admit she'd been unsuccessful, Constanza insisted that the poor state of the theater was diminishing attendance. She initiated a campaign to polish the Minerva's interior every morning. After my days in Restoration, I led the effort, but given how little anyone else did, I sensed I was being targeted for punishment.

So ran my thoughts as I perched on scaffolding, touching up brass on Radillo's family box. When Radillo entered the box, he startled me, making the scaffolding teeter.

"Sorry," he said. "Almost finished?"

"Yours is the last."

He eyed me with a frown. "Hit the sinks. Constanza and I have a proposition for you."

Intrigued, I headed back to slather on the earthy scent of fresh olive oil in a new French L'Amande soap, one of Constanza's literal face-saving efforts. At the sinks, I scrubbed off the dust with an old towel hanging on the rusty hooks, but I had no clean shirt. All I could do was slap cologne on and smooth my unruly hair, hoping my jacket and cologne would cover the worst.

Outside, I found them and, to my delight, Annella, too. I had not seen her since the show began, and now I stood, openly distracted, for she wore the same memorable scarlet dress of our first rendezvous.

"Franco," Constanza said. "Join us for lunch and drinks."

"I fear I'm underdressed," I replied.

"You'll do. Would you accompany Annella? Radillo and I need to discuss some matters on the walk over."

I offered my arm to Annella, as Constanza and Radillo moved ahead. Then I whispered, "Nice dress."

"I knew I would be seeing you."

"So there's hope for me to draw you over to the world of men?"

She wrinkled her nose. "Not when you're doused in cologne."

"Had I known you were coming, I'd have made myself more presentable."

Constanza glanced back, and Annella made a show of sweetly acknowledging her, but Annella's smile did not reach her eyes.

"Acting again?" I asked quietly, but Annella said nothing. I slowed to let Constanza and Radillo move ahead. "Why are we here?" I ventured.

"She hasn't said. She remains angry after your stunt on opening night and that the reviews only favored you. It didn't go well for me, either."

"What happened?"

"Oh, I understand why you did it. Your Juliet was wonderful, the highlight of the show."

"When were you there? I haven't seen you . . ."

She sidestepped my query. "When you disobeyed Constanza's directions, she came at me with questions. Accusations, really. She suggested that I lied to her about you and intimated that I was still scheming behind her back." Annella kept her eyes fixed on Constanza ahead. "Franco, I thought she'd be losing interest in me by now, but her jealousy only seems to deepen. The more time passes, the less willing she is to kick me out. I keep thinking of the stories about those girls in France . . ."

"We won't let that happen to you," I said quickly.

"That's why I can't give her any reason to doubt me. We can't. She's smart. Constanza is always one step ahead."

"You're worrying me. You haven't been back on a single Monday."

She bit her lip. "That's because she had me followed. By Tristano."

I stopped in my tracks, heart racing. "Are you—"

"Here we are," Constanza sang brightly.

I looked up to see that we had arrived at a *ristorante* near Teatro La Fenice.

Just as Annella looked up, I squeezed her arm, but Annella shook herself loose. This time, I wasn't sure whether she really was acting or was genuinely frustrated with me.

Tristano? Did he follow her at Constanza's order, or had he spotted Annella for himself? Either way, it made my mind race with worry. Was Constanza onto us?

A maître d' materialized under a bright red awning to match its door and showed us past the tourists swarming the lower-floor tables, up a set of creaking stairs to a secluded, private dining room in the back. We had barely settled in our seats when a cascade of waiters whisked in *sarde in saor* and cinnamon-scented Bandol from the South of France. No one spoke until the last waiter distributed artichokes nestled in polenta and then closed the curtain by the door.

The mélange of sauces being prepared downstairs wafted up, but I had little appetite after my conversation with Annella.

"Not hungry, Franco?" Constanza said, spearing an artichoke heart. "I doubt you have ever seen a spread like this one, have you? You would never even get to clear tables here."

I ignored the snub. Supporting Annella was all that mattered now that Tristano was involved. "That's true. Thank you for the invitation."

Radillo tipped his glass at me. "Get used to it, now that you've risen through the ranks."

Constanza studied me. "Indeed, what a distance you have traveled from your first embarrassing rehearsal to that genuinely lovestruck girl who alone spoke to the critics. I found your voice as a woman oddly authentic, compared to most falsettos."

What was she intimating? Or was I merely rattled by the news of Tristano? Carefully, I searched for the most diplomatic words.

"It's true that Juliet's voice eluded me at first, but I drew upon Radillo's techniques and then did what any good performer does."

Constanza tapped my wrist lightly. "Find your muse?"

"No," I replied. "Used my imagination." I glanced at Radillo. "A wise man once reminded me that a good performer trusts his instincts. He responds to the audience in the moment. *They* led me to the right voice."

"The audience?" Her eyes narrowed. "What role might they play? You alone hold the strings. You're the marionette's voice. You make it come to life, not the people who watch."

"Taking control involves listening and responding, more than any simple imposition of will."

She laughed. "And do you enjoy taking control?"

"Of the strings?"

"That is what we're discussing, isn't it?"

Constanza nudged Annella. "He can be a handful, can't he?" Annella's cheeks burned, but I focused on Constanza, her eyes coolly assessing. "Even if you have not sought other companions," she went on, "you might. Your second mention in the Ladies' Column last week indicates at least one of Venice's wealthier women has her eye on you."

I feigned a smile. "That does not concern me."

Constanza laughed. "It should. My late husband gave me my great wealth, and Radillo's family money helped bring the Minerva to life. Still, we did not come here to discuss your marriage prospects."

"Indeed." Radillo swallowed some wine. "While *Romeo and Juliet* did not do as well as expected, we must forge on. Now the Minerva needs sales to recoup its losses. We will remount older classic fare, guaranteed crowd-pleasers, in the short term, but Constanza had an idea for a new production, which you're uniquely suited to."

"Oh?" I said, leaning forward.

Constanza took the lead. "It was after that rehearsal, when Annella mentioned the role of the theater in promoting literacy. That spoke to me as a reformer. I thought the Minerva might do a contemporary piece, reprinted as a children's book in 1883 and distributed in local literacy campaigns—Carlo Collodi's popular Florentine serial, *The Adventures of Pinocchio*. It has become a book traveling outside of Italy. Do you know it?"

"I read the serial as a child. A curious story of a puppet come to life."

Radillo added to Annella, "The mischievous wooden puppet, Pinocchio, tries to reunite with the father figure, Geppetto, who carved him. Pinocchio wishes to become a schoolboy so that he may learn how to read, write, and speak in proper Italian."

"After violent travails," Constanza continued, "the enchanted Fairy with the Turquoise Hair turns Pinocchio into a real boy, all because he masters Italian and obedience. Perfect light fare with the requisite happy ending for your beloved pit, to move them past their primitive regionalisms."

"Those regionalisms," I said, measuring my words, "enliven the city and the Minerva, that rare place where Venice's rich and poor converge." I addressed Radillo. "In *The Decameron*, you mixed dialect and Italian. That could work in *Pinocchio*, too."

"Maybe confine dialect to the comic elements," Radillo replied. "Ultimately, we want you to celebrate Italy and the Italian language par excellence. That is what draws us together and what *Pinocchio* is all about."

More likely they wanted me to learn, like Pinocchio, obedience.

"*Pinocchio* is all yours, Franco," Constanza said. "You want control? Take it."

My own show, at last. "Thank you," I said. Even though she was offering this opportunity, I still felt a genuine thrill. It made me wish I could share the production with Carmine, who was already producing children's fare. What might he and I have staged together? My mind began to turn over ideas, including how I could work in shadow play.

"I'll model it along *The Decameron*," I said to Radillo, "selecting vignettes—not the full comprehensive—to keep children's attention. We could add matinees to bring in more women with children. They are likely the ones most familiar with it."

"Exactly," Constanza said, and then added casually, "In fact, I'll sponsor a special performance for the foundlings, a gala for the Minerva on December sixth's Festa di San Nicola. We'll time it to start a bit later, so the show ends just as the Festa's fireworks begin at dusk."

Apprehension coiled in me at the mention of foundlings. Despite Leo's warnings, I still knew Constanza was a master at playing games. She'd just given me exactly what I wanted—again—but I knew any gift of hers came with hidden costs.

I forced a smile. "A play for foundlings and a gala? How marvelous."

"Then it's settled," Constanza said. "We'll have *Pinocchio* for matinees and Andrea's *Rigoletto* in the premier slot at night."

I stilled. "Andrea is doing *Rigoletto*, the opera?" It was one of Venice's most fabled stories, an emblem of the city and national independence.

"Yes," Constanza said. "We will be experimenting with a new format for his show as well—seated dining and drinks for an intimate viewing that will ensure the Minerva becomes an international destination for Europeans."

I struggled to keep my voice even. "What about the pit?"

"Your show's for them. After all, sad plebeian crowds eat up cheap stories so long as there's a dancing dog. In such forms, puppetry is but a poor imitation of life, not its enhancement. *Rigoletto* reaches beyond that."

I sat back, stunned by her harsh remarks.

"This format is just one strand of the Minerva," Radillo added reassuringly, "not the whole braid. With these performances, we satisfy both audiences—something you have long valued, Franco. Your *Pinocchio* is a more creative opportunity than *Rigoletto*."

I could read between the lines. Radillo had once called Andrea a good technician, but what he lacked in talent, he made up for in agreeability—and ambition. Of course he would say yes to this absurd format if it advanced him in Constanza's eyes. My "opportunity" clearly lacked the prestige accorded to his *Rigoletto*, but privately I resolved that my *Pinocchio*, and its audiences, would not be so easily dismissed.

Annella raised her glass. "You have garnered the Minerva real profile, Franco. I'm sure you'll do a wonderful *Pinocchio*. Congratulations."

Constanza and Radillo lifted their glasses as well, and we toasted.

"Profile, indeed," Constanza said, after we drank. "How the press loves you. Radillo and I will exploit that at my upcoming soiree to celebrate the launch of both your show and Andrea's. The De Rossis, the Grimanis, all of Venice's best will be there. Pietro, see that Andrea and Franco get new suits. They will be at my events more often in the coming months, helping smooth us past *Romeo and Juliet*. Shouldn't be too much of a challenge for you?" She paused, eyeing my shirt. "Don't disappoint with this tired attire. We must give the ladies what they want."

Radillo and Constanza chuckled, but I grew self-conscious over the fine-grained sand and sawdust woven in my trousers, the stain of brass polish and dirt embedded in my nails.

Constanza tapped the sleeve of my jacket. "What is the old saying—'Better to spend one day a lion than a hundred as a sheep'? Now's your chance, Franco. Won't he look sharp, Annella?"

"Of course," she said, drinking primly.

Constanza rang a small bell to summon the waiters, who streamed in, saving us from further talk. As I watched Constanza and Radillo acknowledge the array of dishes, I thought how Constanza had called puppetry a poor imitation of life for cheap audiences. What she did not understand was that puppetry appealed across eras and nations not by mimicry but allusion. Marionettes showed what it meant to be human; they revealed how there would always be others who hold and pull the strings—like right now.

As Constanza and Radillo grew engrossed in conversation, I took a chance to make peace with Annella. Beneath the table, I stretched my foot to rest near hers, and she did not move away.

Both Annella and I were being held in check to fulfill a specific function. We were like the waiters swirling around this fine table of delicacies. I knew Annella's, but what was my function? Constanza had a different purpose in mind for me than Radillo did, no matter their illusory united front. Close to Annella as I was, and gifted with Constanza's and Radillo's shining promises and congratulatory toasts, I felt that I could do nothing but sit in obedient silence, covered in dust.

Or was that my only role? I had directly disobeyed Constanza. Her snubs indicated serious displeasure. But she hadn't punished me—unless that's what she thought *Pinocchio* was.

That meant she needed me. And that meant she had not yet achieved her hidden goal for the Minerva. So I had some power in my grasp yet.

I took a chance to glance at Annella, who smiled sadly, her eyes heavy with fatigue. I felt a rush of sympathy for her navigating the tumult of Constanza's moods behind closed doors, and I knew—I was done waiting. I would find out what Constanza was really doing at the Minerva and expose her. With Tristano circling, neither Annella nor I could afford to wait anymore.

31

The night of Constanza's party, I took the familiar path to her palazzo as the nondescript sounds of the street echoed around me. I recalled my last trip here, when the Minerva's men dragged me there in a dress. Now, I wore the very antithesis of that horrible pink confection—a coal-colored silk suit made especially for me by Radillo's tailor, Gianni. A man from Milan with sleepy lids and a fluff of white hair like meringue, he had sighed when I tried on his finished product.

"Perfect," Gianni had said. "Dark hair, dark eyes, olive skin, not much ruddy pink in your tones. Excellent line of jaw." He'd taken my chin in hand. "Very good line for the collar. Ladies will enjoy."

There was only one lady I cared about, and her concerns weighed on me, even though we'd managed a few more stolen Mondays. Tonight, like these past weeks, my every move felt fraught with potential peril. Now, with Constanza's gold-sealed invitation tucked in my suit, I couldn't help but feel as if I were walking into a den of lions. I'd worn my grandfather's cuff links to remind myself of his courage, and my own.

Constanza's two private guards greeted me with a detailed inspection of my invitation. It was deemed legitimate from Constanza's handwriting and seal, so they sent me into an antechamber of weighty velvet tapestries for a quick shine from head to shoe. I gazed at a portrait of Constanza and her late husband, who had been considerably older than her. Though she looked like she'd been in her early twenties for the sitting, she bore the same shrewd and serious visage that she'd perfected three decades later.

Up one more floor I then traveled, landing in a chandelier-lit ballroom bustling with Venice's elite. I noted the Count and Countess De Rossi mingling with other lavishly dressed dukes, barons, and notable society. With so much altered in my life, I felt Carmine's absence anew. He'd steadied me at the De Rossis' soiree, which seemed years, not months, ago. Channeling his bravado, I strode up to Radillo and the Grimanis.

"Had I known what a decent suit would do for you," Radillo said, handing me a glass of champagne on arrival, "I would have sent you to Gianni a year ago."

"He is an excellent tailor," I agreed, bowing to greet them. "He suggested I marry his granddaughter. Apparently, she's a fine cook and I'd get fat."

"Hard to imagine," Radillo said.

"Always a pleasure to see you and your puppeteers in such finery," added Lord Grimani. In black silks, the Grimanis were more conservatively attired tonight than they had been at prior outings.

"The pleasure is all ours," Radillo replied.

Then Lady Grimani addressed me. "We have become quite the fans of yours, Franco." She smiled. "Your marionettes shine, and that is not merely their rendering or gas lamps, is it? Your skills are rather like Murano glass—unique to our shores."

"You flatter me," I said, taking a bow. "Thank you."

"Your Juliet was just as a girl in love would be."

"I'm glad to know a woman found her believable," I replied.

"So," Lord Grimani asked, "you are adapting Collodi's *The Adventures of Pinocchio?*"

"Yes," a voice at my side replied smoothly. Constanza had joined us with the De Rossis, Rossana, Annella, and Andrea in tow. Annella had donned an autumnal russet gown that made her slink into the background of the dark burgundy walls. Rossana, more vivacious in violet, seemed intent on being vibrant for the both of them.

After everyone exchanged greetings, Constanza continued. "*Pinocchio* will fetch wayward children from our slums and, in the guise of entertainment, educate them—if Franco succeeds."

"We will certainly attend," Count De Rossi said.

"All of us have been instrumental in helping our city's destitute better themselves," Constanza said. "Why, Lord Grimani is too modest to say, but when I told him about the count's and my apprenticeship program for foundlings at my late husband's factories in Marseille, he used his influence to fund a program closer to home."

I tensed. Apprentices. So that was how Constanza disguised the foundling girls she sent to France. The De Rossis had few scruples, but I was surprised to hear that the Grimanis were involved.

"Where is this new program?" I asked Lord Grimani.

"On the island itself. In our factory, to continue our work of advancing Murano's artisanal revival," he proudly replied.

Lady Grimani added, "It is only fitting. If we don't invest, we will export our best resources away."

"Yes, the glass is most precious," Constanza said.

"I meant our children," Lady Grimani clarified. "If we don't offer them the chance to remain here in Venice and learn a trade, there will be none left but tourists in our city."

Constanza nodded sympathetically but began discussing her upcoming trip to Marseille in mid-November. I dwelled on this new partnership and the whiff of tension between her and Lady Grimani.

Radillo's voice broke through. "For Andrea's adaptation of *Rigoletto*, inspired by the recent remount at La Fenice, I thought Franco would make a strong Duke of Mantua."

"A Casanova who makes short work of ladies' husbands by having them killed?" Andrea observed, then said to me, "When you're not too busy with your little children's piece."

"Or," Constanza said, "given Franco's recent success as Juliet, perhaps he would be better suited to man the tragic Gilda, Rigoletto's doomed daughter?"

Her tone was playful, but the suggestion chilled me. In the final act of the opera, Gilda dresses as a man. She sacrifices herself to protect her lover, the selfish duke, from an assassin. Was this a veiled threat?

I cleared my throat. "I'm sure Andrea will choose wisely."

Constanza turned to him. "Speaking of, Andrea, would you dance with Annella? She loves it so."

Andrea did not wait for Annella's assent but led her onto the floor as Constanza motioned me to dance with Rossana. "You too, Franco. Take Rossana."

I offered Rossana a hasty bow, and at her uncharacteristically demure nod, we departed, Constanza's gaze burning at my back.

Ahead, I saw Andrea stand too close to Annella, who was near a teetering vase with nowhere to step back from him. Her cheeks were bright with frustration.

"Clearly I've fallen out of favor," I said under my breath to Rossana.

"As has Annella. I am here to keep an eye on her, given that Constanza can't very well let Tristano in this fine room. Besides," she said, lifting her eyes, "he'd far prefer upstairs."

"He's here?" I asked.

She nodded grimly. "In the salon. At least this is a short number. Poor Annella. Your friend's been leering at her all night."

"He's not my friend," I said. "I'll apologize in advance if I step on your fine slippers." The musicians did a few quick practice runs of the melody, the strings sharp, then we began to dance.

"You're quiet," she noted as we walked in a circle.

"I'm just thinking about Constanza's partnership with the Grimanis. Something about it doesn't seem quite right."

"Constanza's charities always have another aim," Rossana replied, her hand resting lightly on my shoulder. "She's been after the Grimanis since last winter. She had me proposition Lord Grimani at the De Rossis' reception."

I caught Rossana's waist. "Oh?"

"She was curious if he would be 'friendly'—meaning, someone I could seduce to learn about his business affairs. But he rebuffed me. He rarely leaves his wife's side." She gave me a devilish smile. "Frankly, if I failed, then he's far too honorable for his own good."

"Obviously," I said, but was distracted by Andrea's hand gripping Annella's waist.

"I'm the woman you're dancing with, Franco, remember?" she teased.

"Sorry." I refocused on Rossana. "Did Constanza say what she wanted you to learn about Lord Grimani?"

"No, but she did tell me to pay special attention if he mentioned anything about his glass factory in Murano—and the tariffs between France and Italy—but our conversation didn't last long enough for him to offer any details."

I ran through what I knew about Murano glass, largely what Leo had told me at that same party. He had said France was heavily taxed for importing Murano glass, its formula a guarded secret so that it couldn't be mass produced. Before I could ask Rossana more, the music ended and she went to rescue Annella from Andrea.

Just then the Grimanis themselves approached me. "We are leaving early," Lady Grimani said, "but looking forward to your *Pinocchio*.

We certainly will attend Constanza's gala. I'm sure your adaptation will enlighten many."

"Thank you," I said, sincerely appreciating them as I shook Lord Grimani's hand. "One of my namesakes, Collegario, means 'to connect.' I try to connect our disparate audiences: the pit and the boxes. That is what I wish most for the Minerva: to be open to all."

"Indeed," he said. "For what it's worth, I envy the Minerva's raucous pit. They seem more part of the show, while our plush velvet boxes can feel a touch removed." He reached in his suit pocket. "For you. A standing invitation for you to see our own private marionette theater anytime."

"I am most honored," I said, accepting the freshly sealed parchment.

As they departed, I caught the frustrated look on Andrea's face as Rossana pulled Annella away. I felt a rush of gratitude for all Rossana was doing to protect Annella, since Constanza certainly didn't care. *Women are commodities*, she had said, *like glass and silk, to be paid for and traded.* Meanwhile, Lady Grimani had called the foundlings Venice's best resource. The Grimanis cared about Venice and its people and traditions. That's why they helped revive Murano glass and safeguard the formula.

I stilled. The formula.

As nonchalantly as I could, I headed to the champagne table where Annella and Rossana were standing. To any observer, it looked as though they were talking to each other, and I, merely fetching a drink.

But Annella was watching me through the champagne. "Franco, what is it?"

"I think Constanza may be stealing the formula for Murano glass from the Grimanis."

Annella paled. "That's quite an accusation."

"Think about it." I glanced at Rossana. "Why would she ask you to glean information from Lord Grimani instead of just asking him herself? Why does she have apprentices in the Grimanis' factory? Rossana, as you just said, her charity work always has another aim." I thought of all the ways Constanza had feted the Grimanis at the theater. "Leo was right. The Minerva was never Constanza's priority. It was just to get close to them—the Grimanis."

"If you're right—and that's a big if to prove—what's Constanza's plan for the formula?" Annella asked. "Blackmail? Extortion?"

I looked to Rossana, but she shrugged skeptically.

"I don't know," I said. "But there's someone here who might." My eyes flitted up.

Annella read my thoughts. "No, Franco. Tristano is up there."

"Then so is Marco. How do I get in?"

Rossana and Annella exchanged a look before Rossana replied. "Take the servants' stairs." She gestured to a nearby set of swinging doors. "But you'll have to charm an escort. It's heavily guarded."

"I'll find a way. If anyone asks, tell them I left the party unwell. I won't return, to sell the lie." I drained my glass for courage. "Annella, Constanza will be away in November. Could we meet for your birthday? I haven't forgotten my promise to do something special."

Annella nudged Rossana. "If my chaperone helps me slip out for a whole night?"

Rossana handed her a glass. "Of course. Arturo can throw Tristano off, too."

We made a quick plan to meet at the Hotel Lo Squero on the fifteenth after the evening show, then I turned to go.

"Be careful," Annella said softly, reaching for my hand beneath the table. "I intend to hold you to your promise."

"If Marco comes through, then we'll have many more birthdays to celebrate," I replied. It took everything in me not to kiss her as I turned and headed for the servants' door.

I SNUCK UP THE servants' discreet back stairs to the third floor, where Constanza's bordello was. Just like on the night of Festa del Redentore,

I spotted guards at the entrance. But then I had some luck. Count De Rossi surfaced.

I joined him, noting his glassy eyes.

"Heading inside, sir?" I asked, as we approached the bordello's doors. "I hope you don't mind, as I do admire you so, but might you use your influence to help me—"

"Enter paradise? Why not?" He held a finger to his lips. "Don't tell Constanza."

I drew close with a firm handshake. "Not a word, sir. A gentleman's honor."

"Ah, to be young!" he exclaimed. "I remember my first visit. You shall have your pick."

With his arm around me, two guards wordlessly lifted the velvet rope to let us pass. How little it took, I thought, for men to invest in one another—and at women's expense.

When we entered the salon, a cacophonous wall of voices, horns, and noise enveloped us. I faced a massive, amber-lit marble world, the air thick with the smoke of imported cigars and cloying opium. Men lounged in plush chairs with gorgeous courtesans perched on their laps. Others formed raucous clusters, smoking and drinking. One section was devoted to gaming tables, with exclusively female dealers collecting dice and bets with sharp and glossy nails, their eyes painted into an exaggerated feline arch.

"Welcome to the 'salon,'" Count De Rossi said, stretching as if readying for athletics. "As a theater man, perhaps you'll want one of the aerialists?"

I looked up. Suspended from the ceiling were fans manned by slight, slim girls, their agile bodies an extension of the contraptions they maneuvered. From each corner of the spacious salon, the aerialists vaulted into their routines. The swaths of taut fabric that suspended them in the air seemed to bind, strangle, and snap as they spun in a circle. Men strained ineffectually to caress them as they glided above, just out of reach.

Pretending someone had caught my eye, I abandoned the count and began looking for Marco.

"A man who knows what he likes!" I heard him shout approvingly. "Decisive already!"

Beautiful, bejeweled women casually touched me as I wove through the throng, scanning faces until I spotted Tristano. He was holding court at the gambling tables, a pair of dice in one hand and a brunette under his arm. He rolled and emitted a cheer at the results, gripping the woman tighter. After he pocketed his winnings, he tossed her a coin. Then his eyes alit on me.

I froze. When he squinted, as if trying to recall who I was, I shook myself into flight. Everyone's gaze shifted toward the aerialists concluding their routine. I used the distraction to slip out the nearest door and stumble onto an empty terrace, shivering uncontrollably from having just locked eyes with Tristano.

Annella was right. I shouldn't have come up. If he had recognized me, all would be lost.

Behind me, the French doors swung open. I spun around, ready to fight, but faced only Marco.

"I was looking for you," I said, exhaling in relief.

"Tristano told me there was an interloper, a boy. I told him I'd take care of it, as I saw it was you."

"A boy?" I repeated. "He didn't recognize me?"

"He doesn't see well after indulging in opium but knew you didn't belong." He glanced warily back at the interior. "What the hell are you doing up here?"

"I need your help." I paused. "You told me that the foundlings you get for Constanza are placed in factories as indentured servants. The apprenticeships at the Grimanis' Murano glass factory are different, though, aren't they? It's not just a cut of their wages she wants."

He ran his fingers through his hair. "You're playing a dangerous game."

"Not by choice. You and I were both forced into this world by our father. But we don't need to play by its rules. I have a plan that could help us both. That is, if my hunch about Constanza is correct."

He crossed his arms, waiting.

"Is Constanza after the formula for Murano glass?" I asked.

His eyes widened, then finally, he sighed. "Yes."

"When did you find out?"

"A few months ago. Tristano asked me to find girls to work in the Grimanis' Murano glass factory as cleaners and charge them with stealing information about the formula, but they weren't able to get it. For one, many can't read."

"That's when Constanza started the apprenticeship program."

He nodded. "Unbeknownst to the Grimanis, she's put five of her most trusted girls in the program. They're slowly piecing together the production process. They talk to me," he explained. "I'm less of a threat than Tristano."

"What's Constanza's end?"

He thought for a moment. "I heard Tristano bragging about a big payment after Constanza's trip to Marseille. Maybe she is selling the formula?"

I couldn't believe what Marco was suggesting. No one would be so bold, except maybe Constanza. "Murano glass is a protected, precious part of Venetian culture. That would be a major international criminal offense," I said. "Not even her friends in the police could turn a blind eye."

"Are you sure? She has spies everywhere. Anyone could tip her off."

"But the Grimanis are more powerful." I held up the card. "I can get an audience with them, but I need evidence." Before he could dissuade me, I rushed on. "If you can get me proof, Marco, we could all be free. You, me, Annella."

"Free?" He laughed bitterly.

"Don't you still want to find Paola? You could be with her again."

He fell quiet. So did I, to let him think.

The courtyard far below sat empty but for clusters of rosebushes clipped and covered in burlap. Everything in this palazzo was so perfectly cultivated in its proper place, but it was a palimpsest. This private salon here was the real party, which the more legitimate one unfolding downstairs served to mask.

In time, Marco slowly spoke. "I can't make any promises . . ."

Impulsively, I hugged him.

He inched away, awkwardly patting my back. "Let me find you. Tristano keeps me alive because I make him money. You don't."

I nodded, my heart a tight knot.

Marco moved a few steps past me to open a door, which had been concealed behind deadened ivy. In the dark, I made out a spiral staircase. "The girls use this when they're tired," he said. "It will bring you near the back dock."

"Thank you, Marco," I said. "You be careful, too."

"I'll try, but don't get your hopes up."

After he left, I threaded my way down the pitch-black stairs to a gondola at the back dock. I had begun the evening thinking I was alone. But an unexpected consort of allies was forming. As I drifted home, I thought of how all around me, the damp hands of fog slid unseen over fragile mosaics and stone, eroding and crumbling them, patient with time to kill. For algae-limned canals snaked through this entire city, even beneath bricked-in streets. In Venice, not even the supplest, most expensive marble of the world was ever immune to the deep, green pull of the sea.

32

All I could do now was wait for Marco, so I threw myself into making *Pinocchio* the best it could be, emboldened by the Grimanis' approval. Radillo had not given me much time to prepare, but Paolo and Eduardo became my hidden advantage. The two apprentices were as open to experimental design as they were hungry to prove their skills.

The premiere was on a Sunday afternoon, a celebration of All Souls' Day to honor the dead. Inside, errors and enthusiasm had reigned in equal measure all morning. An inadvertent tear in the ocean scene's backdrop had to be mended with a swath of blue silk. The mechanism that enabled Pinocchio's nose to grow during a lie was stuck from humidity and making a screech. That, at least, could aid the comedy. Two oil lamps designed to simulate sunrise suggested only a miserable rain.

By the time Leo opened the Minerva's doors, the somber morning church services for All Souls' Day had faded. A distinctly different tapestry of faces, bodies, and sounds filled the space, all peanut shells swept. Children flooded the pit. Above, I saw Radillo in his box with the Grimanis. Around them, several wide bonnets housed faces scrubbed of dirt. The pit, however, held no white patent leather or church attire, but rather children in moth-worn woolen caps and scarves. I saw the boys' outgrown trousers and girls' stained dresses, both dingy with muddied, torn hems. Our somber Turkish pianist Utku, a gifted improviser on loan from the conservatory, drew everyone out of the lobbies and into impromptu sing-alongs of our popular medleys, so that we would be ready to start right on time.

I took a moment to look around me in the rafters. Before Facanapa, I'd thought of my grandfather. Before *Romeo and Juliet*, Annella. Today, I pictured my mother. I now was the same age as she had been when she took flight, trying and failing to survive, wondering how her life had forced her to a place of no return.

For you, I thought, lifting the curtain's edge to meet Utku's eye. At my cue, he started a soft tap of the piano's lower registers, evoking the sound of whittling wood. The lights fell and our young audience squealed as if preparing for a scary story—which it was.

"Once upon a time in our beautiful country of Italy," I said, beginning the narration, "guess who lived among you?"

The children began calling out possibilities.

"A king!"

"A beautiful princess!"

Mothers and caretakers shushed at first, but the commentary quieted in one section only to rise again in another like a song sung in rounds.

"A toad!"

"My ugly cousin Luca!"

"All excellent guesses," I said, "but no one has mentioned this fine hunk of wood."

Giggles erupted as I suspended a single ungainly log against the backdrop of a cozy cottage. Paolo maneuvered the Antonio marionette, a stuffy gentleman with a bulbous nose and elaborate ruffled shirt, onstage. Distracted by his shiny pocket watch, he bumped straight into the log and fell.

"Ouch!" I cried as the log.

Speaking as Antonio, Paolo whined in a fussy Italian at the audience. "Children, quiet! This is very serious art!"

Of course, this only made them shrill with glee, so Antonio clamored upright. I lifted the log to strike him harder and the children begged for more blows.

"I am Pinocchio, the finest grain of cedar!" I exclaimed.

"Am I dreaming? Did that log speak?" Antonio queried the crowd, who reassured him that no, he was not dreaming, and yes, the log was speaking.

As the log, I continued. "Carve me into that which I am meant to be."

"A royal throne?" Antonio suggested meekly, rubbing his head.

"I am not to be sat upon! I am a real boy! Make my body match my mind."

"But no one can make cut wood live." I readied the log to hit Antonio, then he cried, "Wait! Do you hear that? My friend the woodcarver approaches. He can make you a real boy. Stay completely quiet or he will carve you into a toad."

I settled the log against a chair with a harrumph, and Eduardo brought onstage a misshapen but spritely old man.

"Geppetto," cried Antonio too warmly. "May I help you?"

"If only I had some wood," Eduardo said as Geppetto. "I wish to ease my lonely heart, by making a friend who dances, sings, runs, and plays."

Paolo elevated the log's strings. Then Antonio held the log like a prize. "Here is the perfect gift!" he exclaimed.

Geppetto ran his hand over it. "Expensive gifts have hidden costs."

"Nonsense. I only wish to make my friend happy."

Geppetto faced the audience. "Tell me, children. Should I accept this gift?" The children discouraged him, but Geppetto pulled the wood close. "Soon he shall spring to life with strings."

"Enjoy!" Antonio said, scurrying offstage.

I dropped down a small knife to hover in the air and Eduardo made Geppetto clasp it. Together, Eduardo and I simulated the carving as Utku played an animated melody and, offstage, Bruno enhanced the sound of striking wood.

"That hurts!" I cried as the log.

Geppetto stopped, confused, then kept carving, and with each slice, I released a piece of wood from the log's side, which looked like a shaving.

When Geppetto stepped back, the Pinocchio puppet, which had been concealed within the log, appeared dressed in a schoolboy's red-and-green uniform. Pinocchio glanced at his hands in awe, and then rage.

"Why, you have made me a puppet, not a boy!"

"You speak?" Geppetto said, fending off Pinocchio's blows, more dangerous now that he possessed arms. "Be still, my child. Mysteries happen all the time, Pinocchio. Earlier today, I was a lonely old man. Now I have you. If you behave, might your other dreams come true?"

"My dream is to become a real boy who learns to read."

"That is a dream from which one does not turn back. Are you sure you are ready?"

"Yes!" said Pinocchio, but I screeched his nose out—a lie. I heard the children gasp and giggle.

"Don't lie," said Geppetto. "Let me help you."

"No! I will do it myself! Dreams lead to adventures, and I want more!" I made Pinocchio scamper in a heavy-footed circle, his first awkward attempt at running. Geppetto strove in vain to follow as Pinocchio ran offstage calling, "Catch me if you can!"

It was time for the first shadow play. Above, Bruno unfurled a transparent drop cloth as Paolo and I hurried down to the stage and joined Eduardo behind the backdrop. Vincenzo brightened the lights for only the top half of the screen, casting a muted ivory sheen, gray like sunlight burning off the morning fog. Paolo and I elevated the large cut-out figures of Pinocchio and a cricket on sticks, and they hovered like ghostly two-dimensional silhouettes.

The audience, even the adults, hushed in awe. Paolo began speaking as the cricket, urging an annoyed Pinocchio to help Geppetto. Eduardo raised a third, quivering stick figure to show the woodcarver being beaten by the police, voiced by Bruno and Vincenzo in the wings.

Frustrated by the cricket imploring him to be good, Pinocchio hurled a rock. When it struck the cricket, none of us made a noise. Paolo lowered the cricket down into the dark to mark its death, then I bent Pinocchio's shadow to weep silently—only to hear the audience make the sounds for me. The shadow play was as enchanting as I'd hoped, and I felt emboldened by the crowd's reactions.

THE CHILDREN WERE A chatty delight to perform for, as Carmine had said, and by intermission, the play was zipping along.

I raised the curtain on Pinocchio surveying a miniature stage.

One petite puppet, an Arlecchino repurposed from commedia as a schoolboy, gestured to Pinocchio to join him. "Come see the greatest marionette theater in all of Italy! Sell your schoolbook for the ticket. There is no man alive as skillful with the strings as the amazing Mangiafuoco. See why he is called the 'Fire Eater'!"

As the pair ran toward the entertainment, I lowered the wild-haired "Fire Eater," Mangiafuoco. Golden backlights illuminated four small two-stringed marionettes on the tiny stage, which Eduardo and Paolo handled. Thin and domineering, Mangiafuoco chased Pinocchio, believing he was a member of his troupe. When he caught his prey, I made it appear as though Mangiafuoco was manipulating Pinocchio—a marionette puppeteering another marionette.

"You are not mine," I bellowed as Mangiafuoco in Italian. "Nor did you pay for your ticket! Wicked foundling, I will teach you!"

"But I did pay!" Pinocchio protested. "I sold my schoolbook for your show!"

"Puppets do not need school, but I need dinner. *You* will be my dinner!" The other puppets sought to rescue Pinocchio but tumbled in a pile. "Stop, or you will be my second course!" Mangiafuoco shouted at them and pointed at the real children in the theater. "Now, dance for the audience!"

Paolo and Eduardo kept the miniature puppets dancing, while Mangiafuoco solicited recipe suggestions from the crowd. When one woman said a disobedient boy would need to be marinated well, I stifled my own laughter by making Mangiafuoco hum with glee. "I know. You will be the firewood over which I cook my meat!"

In the wings, Bruno and Vincenzo cupped their hands over side gas lamps to suggest flickering flames. As Pinocchio, I pleaded, "Please, sir, spare me!"

"But you are only made of wood and I, the 'Fire Eater.'"

"My father will miss me if you burn me as fuel."

"What are you talking about? You have no father."

"I do! The wood-carver Geppetto loves me as his own son. He carved me."

Mangiafuoco leaned closer. "I see that you speak the truth." He released Pinocchio and pulled out two large gold coins. "For your journey home. I cannot separate a father and son. Find him. Go to school. Become a wiser boy and, one day, a man."

Pinocchio gazed at the money. "Might I become real?"

"Who knows? I've seen stranger things inside a theater's walls, Pinocchio."

Once more I crouched behind the transparent screen with Eduardo and Paolo. This time, Eduardo raised the slinky shadows of a cat and fox, who startled my stick figure Pinocchio.

Eduardo spoke as the cat shadow. "Where are you going?"

"To school," I replied as Pinocchio.

"Join us instead," said Eduardo, now as the sharp-eared fox. "Give us your coins. We'll make your gold grow in the Field of Miracles. An entire tree of coins will sprout. You'll be rich in minutes!"

Paolo lifted a fourth shadow, the now ghostly talking cricket. "Lies, Pinocchio! They will hurt you. Go to Geppetto now!"

The children began to cry for Pinocchio to heed the cricket's warning, but Pinocchio sighed. "A tree of coins will make Geppetto prouder of me than reading a book."

Amid the children's protests, Eduardo leaned the cat and fox into each other, shaking in conspiratorial laughter. "After we get the gold, we'll kill him and steal it all," he whispered as the cat.

The fox, cat, and Pinocchio figures merged to form one single, ominous shadow. Then everything went dark to gasps.

Paolo, Eduardo, and I climbed up, and when the lights rose, a slack Pinocchio marionette hung from a tree. Offstage, the wicked fox and cat cackled. This was the only violent encounter I depicted with marionettes, not shadows. I wanted to show Pinocchio near a real death.

It worked, even on me up above. I felt a chill. Some children sniffled or protested. The strings felt slack in my hands, as if what lay below had indeed weakened.

Then, Paolo dropped the luminous Fairy with the Turquoise Hair. Her profusion of diaphanous azure tulle was met with sighs. She tipped her wand to Pinocchio's forehead. "Live, dear Pinocchio, or your father, like your dreams, will soon die."

Pinocchio sputtered, as if waking from a fretful sleep. "Who are you?"

"Remember that tiny cricket you killed? He was me, your conscience. I keep you whole and safe. Can you be brave?"

"Yes." I made Pinocchio stand. The children spurred him on.

"Hurry," Paolo cried as the Fairy. "Save Geppetto from the belly of the whale!"

He twirled her slowly up, as Eduardo sprinkled handfuls of tiny torn paper scraps, a snowstorm's swirl. The lights fell into a deep darkness, and Bruno shoved a large wooden whale with an empty belly onstage for the climax.

It was a new form of mechanical theater we had built; its floor shifted on diagonal angles and rolled as if churning on waves. So, too, did the ocean set pieces tilt with levers to simulate the sea. Between Vincenzo's bursts of lighting and Utku's cascading scales, we depicted a great storm. Geppetto, already in the whale's belly, called out as the lights rose. "Pinocchio? Are you near?"

From offstage, the fox and cat called, "Forget him and save us, Pinocchio! Our money was stolen and our tails have been cut!"

"False friends!" Pinocchio said. "You taught me only that bad wheat makes poor bread."

I lowered Pinocchio into the belly, and he and Geppetto embraced.

"My child, I am so weary," Geppetto said.

"I will save you, Father, for I have changed and learned and nearly died. The Fairy with the Turquoise Hair brought me back. Look, she guides us out!"

Paolo lowered the Fairy, who gestured them toward the whale's open mouth, but the storm made Geppetto and Pinocchio fall back. The children screamed in horror. Undaunted, the pair inched toward liberation, and after one last plunge into darkness, they escaped, to the audience's thrill.

That applause concealed the clatter of our final scene change, a return to the opening cottage. I began to narrate again.

"So, dear friends, like much in life, Pinocchio has discovered what good can come from learning. How should we end his story?"

The children offered plenty of advice as I brought out Pinocchio and Eduardo positioned Geppetto in an elaborate armchair.

The limelights shone brightest on the Fairy, a breath above the stage without weight as Paolo began her final speech. It concluded with, "Dear Pinocchio, you have suffered and grown. Are you ready for your wish?"

"Please make me my father's son."

The Fairy raised her wand. Pinocchio's arms spread wide, as if to embrace the audience, while Utku's anticipatory strike on the lower registers cascaded into a spiral of chords. When the Fairy tapped Pinocchio's head, I began to spin him slowly up and down, before settling center stage. Now, I made his first steps looser as he admired and tested his limbs. "How different I move as a boy!"

Geppetto rose from his chair. "Not so different, but more yourself."

Then the Fairy, Geppetto, and Pinocchio danced, with Pinocchio's steps a more agile imitation of Geppetto's now that both were human. The Fairy gestured to the audience, and Utku's melody enlivened the room. The children began clapping in time, much as they had at the show's start, as the curtain fell.

I could hardly wait to reopen the curtain, the three of us in the rafters exhilarated by the response—and amazed by our success after so many misfortunes and mistakes in the lead-up. Despite the toil of weeks spent practicing for this show, I couldn't imagine being untethered to a theater. No rehearsals and scripts, performers and audiences, magic and grit? Who would I be if I had never held the strings and felt that mystery take hold in my spine?

As I signaled for Bruno and Vincenzo to draw open the curtain and applause billowed up, I felt a swell of love for the Minerva, and what it had been like in the days before Constanza. With Carmine, I'd seen how the Minerva's plays, even in humble and makeshift forms, could, for its audiences, encompass longing and memory, dream and wish, fear and hope. As a theater, it was both of this world and a flight from it. After the awkward silences of *Romeo and Juliet*, now the many children talking back to me had given this place, and me, too, renewed life.

33

I scurried down from the rafters with the Pinocchio marionette still in hand, giddy and glowing, to find Radillo waiting. Without a word, he simply embraced me, hanging on longer than expected.

"Are you all right, sir?" I ventured.

"I suppose you reminded me of myself back there, with that wonder you just created. You took something minor and made it a masterpiece. Such experimentation, taking risks, understanding your audience, shadow play, all done so well." His gaze fell to his feet. "It's something I used to do but haven't for a long time. You reminded me of when I felt more creative and like a real performer, not just an owner fretting over his costs."

"Thank you," I said, humbled. "I learned that from you on *The Decameron*. Those stories were written centuries prior, under the shadow of a plague to spite death. You said they were fresh, as if written yesterday. You transformed them, gave them new life."

"How long ago that feels," he said, as though something had slipped out of his grasp.

"You know, the Minerva has been a refuge to me," I added, "ever since that first day."

"If I recall, Carmine gave you a black eye."

I laughed. "Two, actually."

Radillo grew thoughtful. "You asked me to teach you something that day. Do you remember?"

I nodded. "The shudder. How to make the same gesture express two entirely different moods."

Radillo pointed at the Pinocchio marionette. "Tell me what you were thinking about in the opening run, when Pinocchio becomes a boy."

I unwound the strings once more. "Pinocchio is overly confident as a new puppet. At first, he is too heavy-footed, like an overgrown toddler."

"Here, watch me." Radillo took the marionette and bent its knees deeply, arms extended wide as if shoving items off a shelf, then set Pinocchio in an almost drunken run. "It's a rapid, heavy motion that starts in the wrist. But now look at the difference." This time he gave a slight heave and drop to Pinocchio's shoulders in a more controlled, confident run. The marionette's head faced upright as he accelerated, slipping fleeting glances at his own hands, arms, and feet. "Slow down your right arm. Drag it out. Make each step like breathing when you first awaken."

Radillo handed the marionette back. I did a rougher but some-what successful imitation.

"Better," he said. "If there's one thing I've done right, it's teaching you. You have such a talent, Franco. A natural, from the start." He ran his hand through his disordered curls. Even in the dim light, I saw his weary eyes. "If only I hadn't taken Constanza's money, but now, without her? The Minerva . . ."

"Will close," I said. "I know."

It was the first time he admitted accepting Constanza's patronage was a mistake. I knew how much it cost him to say it.

"Thank you, sir," I added, "for this show." I looked at the Pinocchio marionette. "I guess I still have a few things left to learn."

"Don't we all?" he said. "Puppetry isn't ever you alone up there, is it? Maybe today especially, on All Souls' Day, I find myself thinking of those who left us, with only our own memories in the pull of the line."

I sensed he was remembering Giannina, as I had my grandfather and mother. They were dead, but Giannina was very much alive.

"She might come back, sir, if you asked," I said tentatively.

"Who?"

"Giannina. Were you thinking of her just now? Someone whom you lost?"

"Yes, her," he replied, ambling away. "Among others."

AFTER I CLEANED UP, I headed out front for a barrage of autographs and several amusing conversations with enthusiastic children. Inside, the exhausted ushers groused as they swept a larger-than-normal amount of debris. After the last children peeled off, I saw Marco emerge, smoking in the early twilight shadows. With a glance around to ensure we were alone, I jogged over. His hair was clean and recently trimmed. From his suit, he would have been at home in the boxes.

He snuffed out his cigarette. "I have to admit it was a damn good show. And I don't even like marionettes."

"No." I laughed. "I remember. Once you even threw Carlita off the balcony."

"Alfonso beat me that day, and you probably stitched her up."

I gazed at the street. "Well, thanks for showing up, but I assume it wasn't to see me perform. Did you find something?"

In the distance, we heard a pair of accordions from an open café. Otherwise, the air hung still and soft all around us, a streaked mauve sunset the canvas for mournful early evening bells.

"Constanza's not selling the formula to the French; she's going to make the glass herself."

My elation over *Pinocchio* evaporated. It took a moment before I could speak. "How?"

"She's opening a glass factory in Marseille."

This was what Constanza had been planning all along. Her greed knew no bounds. And we were running out of time. "So she's close to getting the formula."

"I suspect so. But take heart," Marco said, gripping my shoulder. "I'm to go and help her in France while Tristano ties up some final details here. After months of giving me the worst jobs, he's decided I'm ready for redemption. Since Paola left, I've made sure he only ever sees me as broken, obedient to a fault. Because if there's one thing he's trained me to do, it's to spin lies to get what I need. Without Tristano watching my every move, I'll find proof of Constanza's plan."

I took this in, feeling a swell of hope. Maybe we could pull this off. "Guess you really are my big brother now, aren't you? Making good on that promise."

"Better late than never."

"One thing still bothers me. If Constanza does this, the Grimanis will find out. What does she think will happen then?"

Marco shuffled. "Marseille isn't just a city to make a fortune in; it's a place to hide," he said. "If successful, she won't stay in Venice. She will move away, permanently."

I stilled. What would that mean for Annella?

"There's still time. Don't give up. I won't." Marco moved to leave, eyeing the now-empty street.

"See you soon?" I called out to him.

"See you soon," he replied. Then he pointed at the theater's doors. "Glad to know you found your home, a better one than what we shared."

I watched him amble down to the docks. Part of me wanted to run inside and tell Radillo everything. He had seemed so lost and melancholy today. But I could not, not without proof, and that might not come for a few more weeks. But maybe one day soon, I could give Radillo back the Minerva that he, and I, loved.

34

At last, the night of Annella's birthday arrived. After an evening performance as the Duke of Mantua in *Rigoletto*, I climbed down from the rafters, eager to clean up and leave. The new seating format was encouraging more chatter among guests, who didn't pay attention to the story unfolding before them. Each night we found ourselves shouting over the din to be heard. They only quieted if the soloists sang, and lately, not even then.

I handed off my marionette to Lorenzo for a repair, but Leo stopped me at the door. Radillo had gathered Andrea, Niccolò, and the other men. Since Constanza's departure, he had been invigorated, more like his old self, and I hoped his mood would last.

Carmine had written that he and Giannina were planning on visiting in December, when the Gerolamo would close for a month. He was not looking forward to it, but Giannina missed her father. Despite Radillo's initial threats, I sensed he'd be open to reconciliation himself.

"Franco, listen to this one," Radillo said, his eyes twinkling as he opened a newspaper.

"We are comforted to learn that the old Minerva is adapting to these modern times after her uneven *Romeo and Juliet*. The by turns whimsical and dark adaptation of Carlo Collodi's popular serial, *The Adventures of Pinocchio*, reveals the venue transmogrifying in more invigorating directions, with astonishing mechanical theater and Chinese shadows, no less.

"At the helm of this enchanting new 'Pinocchio' is, of course, the Minerva's beguiling lead, Franco Collegario. Formerly Our Fair but Unfortunate Juliet (and one of the few reasons we stayed in our seats), Collegario reveals hidden depths in this sardonic tale of obedience, filial devotion, and the limits of national unity, given Pinocchio's many perilous encounters. Still, Collegario's vision for La Serenissima's most prominent marionette theater refreshes and refashions it. Once more, we see the best of the Minerva's range, from verisimilitude to bloodthirsty antics, in a satire that brings children in but keeps taller audiences just as captivated."

"Shall I go on?" he added, waving the papers in the air. "Because there are more of these reviews. It's been two weeks and they keep popping up. Congratulations to our own 'beguiling' Franco." He clapped his hands, and the others joined in, except for Andrea.

Rigoletto had not been as well received. The press had described it as "stilted" and "fussy," but to Constanza's point, somehow the theater filled with new faces each night even if they didn't pay attention to the convoluted plot.

Radillo addressed him. "Take heart, Andrea. Yours is a much-loved local favorite, but everyone has their own ideas for how it should go. Ticket sales have been strong."

He was being generous. Had I not been suffering Andrea's boasts the month prior—including his commentary on Annella—I, too, might have been generous. Given what I had endured, however, I chose not to be.

I begged off when Radillo suggested we celebrate at the Britannia. "So humble!" he called after me as I rushed to the changerooms, where I quickly donned my favorite chocolate brown suit, thinking ahead to my night with Annella.

When I left the dressing room, I walked right into Andrea, who had been waiting outside. He flicked some imaginary dust off my suit. "Too good for the Britannia? Or do you only celebrate your own shows?"

I drew myself up. "Why would I celebrate yours?"

"Now you're being honest, at least." He glanced over his shoulder. "Bet you loved all that back there. Radillo fawning."

"You never learn, do you?"

He folded his arms. "I've learned you probably planted that press, seduced the authoress of the Ladies' Column . . ."

"Sure; I did all of that—and just to spite you. In fact, I'm off to see her right now." My sarcasm was lost on him. "I don't have time to talk to you," I added, shoving past him, but he yanked me back.

"Why *are* you in such a hurry tonight? You may have deluded Radillo—"

I cut him off. "You're the one who's deluded. Is it really that hard to understand why I get praise?" I paused. "It's because I'm better than you."

Andrea wound his fist, but before he could land the punch, Radillo and Leo rounded the corner and tore us apart, shouting.

Radillo held Andrea, but I shook myself from Leo's grip and rushed toward the door, ignoring the warning expression in Radillo's eyes. I didn't hear what Andrea mumbled at my back, for I was already slamming the stage door shut, more than ready to depart.

The encounter with Andrea rankled me, but I had more important matters ahead. Dorsoduro was swifter by water, so I hurried to the Grand Canal and roused a gondolier. With Constanza out of the city, it felt like my own home again as I drifted over to the Hotel Lo Squero. It was a luxurious establishment near the glorious Basilica of Santa Maria della Salute, and a hotel known for their discretion. They would offer no leads, no matter the price or person asking.

I had a room reserved under my grandfather's name, and after acquiring the key, I waited for Annella at the hotel's terrace bar, decorated in Moroccan turquoise and gold silk.

From my perch, I could see the back of the Salute, for the hotel stood on the canal's western edge. With its basilica and two bell towers, the Salute was a massive spectacle of gratitude that honored the Virgin Mary for delivering the city from the plague in the seventeenth century. The view of the city, bright under the late autumn moon, was dazzling, but not as much as the sight of Annella walking toward me, rosy from the cold when she kissed the side of my cheek.

"No one followed, least of all Tristano. Arturo kept him ensconced in the salon. So we're safe."

"Good," I said, then offered my hand. "Shall we go up?"

She was already leading the way.

The room we stepped into was grand beyond measure. Frayed with age, we faced parrot green velvet drapes and rose-colored pillows. A translucent canopy floated like a cloud above the bed. I had asked the staff to prepare the room, and so our fireplace was well stoked, its mantel topped with strawberries, chocolates, and a chilled bottle of prosecco just opened in fast-melting ice.

The window overlooked the canal, but we were on the third floor, high above an expanse of water that no freighter or vaporetto drove through. No one could peer in. No buildings stood opposite us, only the indifferent fish below. This was no furtive hideout. It felt like a desert oasis.

The fight with Andrea faded. I pictured Marco, returning with something valuable in hand. It felt as if this room were a harbinger of my future with Annella, of how this luxurious stolen night might become, I sensed, simply my life.

"Do you like it?" I said, locking the door.

"You did promise me something special," she said, warming her hands at the fire. In that light and still clad in her amber cloak, she seemed to glow.

I poured the prosecco in crystal glasses and raised mine to toast her. "Happy birthday."

We drank them in one swallow, and I refilled our glasses.

"How did you manage this?" she asked, taking a strawberry.

"Magic," I teased. "It turns out that Marco confirmed my suspicions about Constanza." I filled her in on Marco's plans. "But good news: He's in Marseille with Constanza right now getting us proof. So soon, we will be free."

I expected Annella to be thrilled, but she frowned. "Constanza will not leave evidence out in the open. She's too smart for that. What does Marco hope to find?"

"I'm not sure exactly," I replied. "He knows a deal's being made, and because Tristano is not there, he'll be free to act."

"But it is still a heavy risk, no?"

"Believe me—he has as much will to succeed as we do. He wants to reunite with his fiancée, Paola, in Croatia."

Annella paced away from me. "Constanza's exposure threatens the Minerva, too, though. Without her money, won't it close?"

"Once the Grimanis learn that Constanza tricked them, I suspect they will aid Radillo." I followed her to the window. "Don't worry, we'll find a place for Rossana and Arturo, too. The net is tightening around Constanza. It's only a matter of time."

Annella forced a smile, but her worry had deepened, not abated. I held her shoulders.

"I know things could go wrong," I said, sliding my hands down to her waist. "But tonight, I want you to forget about everyone else. Be with me. Tonight, let's be nothing more than those ordinary lovers, concerned with one another."

"You can be persuasive in this suit." She caressed the lapel.

"Now, what might I persuade you to do?" I reached up to unpin her hair. She shook it loose, and I saw her eyes soften.

"You know," she began, "my mother always hoped that someday I would know the kind of joy she shared with my father, and now I do. It's so easy with you, like breathing. Even when we're far apart in a crowd, I feel you, as if you're right here, this close to me."

"I know. Once I thought I would never feel anything like what Carmine and Giannina shared. But I do."

She touched my cheek. "They have each other and their very own theater. Maybe there's hope for us."

We stood close, in silence, until I spoke.

"I love you, Annella. I have since that first night I saw you at the theater."

She caught her breath. "I love you, too, Franco. Remember when I fell in the wings on that first tour? I didn't want you to let go."

"I have something for you," I said, and reached in my breast pocket.

She gasped, upon seeing what I held.

"This was my grandmother's wedding ring," I said. "My grandfather gave it to me the night I left. He told me to sell it if I ever became desperate, but now? It's yours." I stared at the diamond, nested in a circle of pearls, and how the gem caught the flickering firelight. "You and I don't live in a world where we should exist. But we do. We weren't meant to survive, but here we are. I love you, Annella. I need you with me. There is no future without you. I promise you one day we will build a better life, one we cannot even imagine from where we stand today."

Delicately, I placed it on her finger. Though slightly loose, it would size down well. For a moment, we both admired the tarnished gold band, which had seen many years before either of us had even been born.

"I will keep it in my locket," she said softly.

We kissed, and I felt her sink into me. On her lips I tasted prosecco and strawberries. The oil of lilacs was fresh in her hair, which mixed with the sandalwood on my wrists. The soft silk of her scarlet shirtwaist covered her body, which by now I knew nearly as well as my own.

"Come." I drew her to the bed. She unbuttoned my shirt, and I cast it off, then undid the binding of her shirtwaist. When I reached for her, though, she stopped me.

"I also brought you a gift," she said, unhooking her skirt herself.

"But it is your birthday."

"It is a gift for both of us, really."

"Now I am curious."

Turning away, she stepped out of her faded satin underskirts, and I glimpsed a leather belt fitted tight to her hips. She seemed to be unhooking a clasp, and then faced me.

"Here." She held out a leather harness. Hooked into it was an oblong leather dildo.

I'd heard of dildos from bawdy tales but had never seen or touched one before. I took it and felt this one as strange and firm through the center—lifelike, or so I guessed, having seen plenty of men urinating in alleys.

"Rossana knows a cobbler who does trade on the black market," she explained. "There's more money in these than shoes. Some of Constanza's girls have one for their clients. I told Rossana that I was curious what they were like."

"How clever." I ran a finger lightly across the tip. "Shall I?"

I removed my trousers and Annella helped me lift the harness in position, guiding me to step through each leg. The dildo's flared base held snug as she tightened the straps. Once done, I was surprised by how it felt like an extension of my own body, oddly natural.

"Wear it instead of your usual padding if you like," she said. "Just fold it up beneath your trousers so you don't appear obscene during the day." Then she pulled me toward the bed, unwinding the stays that bound my chest. "You did promise me something special."

"Will it hurt you, though?"

"It won't—not when I've been thinking about you all day."

We climbed onto the bed and I sat against the headboard. She rested her hands atop the dildo, pressing against the base. Then I lifted her hips up so that she could gently lower herself onto the device at her own pace as I touched her, both of us adjusting to how it felt to be so connected. For a moment we said nothing, struck silent by its novel sensation, and for me, the surprising ease of its familiarity. As we began to move together, I pressed deeper into her. Our breaths came faster and I couldn't tell whether the pleasure I felt originated in her or it or me. It heightened every sensation and made us touch each other more, hungrily, as if we were making a study of our bodies and leaving no part unexplored. It felt as if, for once, time stretched to meet us that night, gracing us by prolonging.

When the faint sliver of light at dawn woke us, Annella and I lingered in bed until the last possible moment. Only reluctantly did we rise and dress. Annella deposited the ring into her locket, and we went downstairs.

Before parting on the empty street, we kissed goodbye, neither of us wanting to pull apart. Eventually she did but touched the locket, close to her throat. "You have my heart, Franco. Always."

I watched her drift away into blue folds of fog, then I proceeded to stroll home, blissfully content until I heard a strange noise, like someone cackling. When I stopped to look back, however, it was just a drunk in the distance staggering away. So I continued on, my body humming with life, urgent with renewed purpose, as the Salute's last morning bells resounded at my back.

35

Two weeks later, Constanza returned in high spirits. She was delighted by the strong reviews for *Pinocchio* and ordered a Saturday evening performance in the new format. I bristled, but Leo explained it was a sign of her restored faith in me.

"Franco, this is good news," he said, as we walked down the hall of the theater toward Radillo's office. "For some time, Radillo has wanted to move you up, to make you a partner in the Minerva, and Constanza has finally agreed. I think her interest in the theater is waning. By the sounds of it, her trip to Marseille was productive."

I tried to appear excited, but I had yet to receive word from Marco. If he had found evidence, he would have shown up by now. Had he been found out? Knowing that Constanza's trip had been a success only concerned me more.

Leo rushed on, oblivious to my fears. "I overheard Radillo and Constanza planning a special precurtain meal at Ruffino's this Saturday, before the evening *Pinocchio*. I'm certain it's where they'll make the offer. So try and act surprised."

I nodded. Leo was telling me everything I'd dreamed of. But I would give it all up—including puppeteering—if I could secure Annella's freedom.

For the next week, I spent every morning at Café Titian, annoy-ing Michaela. After shows, I loitered outside the theater, the early December cold seeping into my bones, hoping Marco would surface. But nothing.

Before the Ruffino's dinner, I met Radillo at the theater. On our way over, he chattered on about that night's *Pinocchio* in the new format—a teaser that might entice tourists to return for Sunday's gala.

Once more, I found myself in Dorsoduro, the neighborhood of my recent tryst with Annella. Today, I was much less confident, de-spite Leo's assurances, as Radillo and I entered the restaurant.

Inside, lanterns hung like clusters of rain-wet grapes, casting soft light on faded ivory tablecloths, hiding the stains of salty oyster juice that was Ruffino's trademark. I scanned the room for our party and spotted Annella—who sat between Constanza and, surprisingly, Andrea.

"Why is he here?" I asked Radillo quietly.

He, too, seemed confused. "Constanza must have invited him?"

She beckoned us over. The only available chairs were across from Constanza and Annella, who was wearing a deep-green dress and em-erald earrings that I imagined would set off her eyes if she raised them from her plate. She did not greet me, stifled as Constanza's or-nament tonight. *A jewel of a girl.* But I took heart that it was my ring in the locket at her neck.

Andrea caught me staring at her, then smiled warmly as if we were friends. Puzzled, I nodded, determined to be cordial as I took my seat.

No sooner had we settled when an ancient, amiable waiter ap-peared. Constanza introduced him as the owner, Ruffino. He carried a sense of youth about him as he circled the table, filling our glasses with Valpolicella from the coolest depths of his wine cellar.

Annella would not look at me, so I feigned innocence and asked her, "Will you be at the show tonight?"

"No," Constanza answered for her. "I require Annella at an engagement this evening, to complete the finer details of my meetings in Marseille. But I will attend the children's gala matinee for Festa di San Nicola tomorrow. As your patron, I couldn't miss that."

"How was your recent trip?" I asked her.

"Marvelous," she enthused. "I resolved a deal that had been vexing me for some time."

The first course of oysters, freshly plucked from dark waters, arrived to keep us from conversing. Grilled calamari in briny butter followed, its succulent tendrils wound around whole cloves of garlic, infusing the room, our clothes, and our fingers with its scent.

"Eat," Constanza said to Annella. "We won't enjoy these Italian delicacies in France."

Annella looked up quickly. "Oh, are you returning again?"

Constanza set down her wineglass. "Yes. As Radillo knows, my new business venture requires me to be there in person for several months. But don't worry. This time, you will be joining me."

Annella stiffened. My mouth went dry. Judging from the tremor in Annella's hand as she attempted to take a drink, clearly this was news to her as well.

"When will you depart?" Radillo asked, sounding hopeful.

"Right after tomorrow's gala, in fact." She nudged Annella. "No need to bring anything. We'll get you all new fashions on an excursion to Paris. Won't that be nice?"

"So soon?" Annella said, trying to smile.

I downed more wine. I had to stop this, but how? Without Marco's proof, I had nothing for the Grimanis. My thoughts raced and collided. Time was running out.

"Why, Franco," Constanza said. "You've barely touched your plate."

"I am always a little nervous before a new show. Tonight's new format . . ."

"Of course," Constanza said. "I wouldn't want our darling of the press to fall ill."

Ruffino returned full of apologies for the delay in our next course, and gave us a few plates of Canestrato, fresh with cracked pepper, to tide us over. He described how he had imported peas by steam locomotive up the coast, but I wasn't listening, distracted into our next course's arrival: plates of linguine with artichokes and the out-of-season spring pea risotto caramelized in the pot.

Once Ruffino had left, Radillo cleared his throat. "Constanza and I have a proposition for you, Franco. That's why we're here." He avoided Andrea, who was savoring the linguine. "Constanza has been a generous patron to the Minerva, and we are in her debt. Sadly, with her new business in Marseille, she will not be as involved in the day-to-day operations . . ." Radillo looked at Constanza expectantly.

"While I will continue to fund the theater," she began, "Radillo and I have discussed naming a new partner to help lead the Minerva. He suggested you, Franco."

Radillo was beaming.

"I'm honored," I said, recalling Leo's words.

Constanza surveyed me over her wineglass. "As you should be. Your rise at the Minerva has been quite the tale of its own, hasn't it? From humble foundling to lead puppeteer. I asked you once before what inspires you. Do you remember?"

"Yes. The audience."

"I think that is wrong." She rested a hand atop Annella's on the table, and the possessiveness of this simple gesture tormented me.

"I think I would know my own motives best," I said, attempting a cheerful veneer.

"Do we ever?" she asked. "I think you play these characters so well because you seem to have one face, one that people underestimate: the foundling, the witless virgin, artistic puppeteer, darling of the La-dies' Column. But other faces, whole other worlds, hide under that mask. You're able to man Pinocchio as easily as the Duke of Mantua or even a lovelorn girl." She paused. "Wouldn't you agree, Andrea? You, who have worked so closely at Franco's side?"

"Of course," Andrea replied, dabbing his lips with a napkin. "A puppeteer to emulate." Then, to my horror, Andrea slung an arm on the back of Annella's chair. "I know exactly how I intend to follow in his footsteps."

I had to restrain myself. "What are you implying?" I asked him.

"Merely getting what I'm due," he said.

"Constanza?" Annella interrupted. "Surely you would not make me endure . . ."

Constanza poured herself more wine.

"Endure?" Andrea said to Annella. "Not the word I would use."

"But it would be accurate," I snapped.

Annella turned to Andrea, her face set. "I am not, nor will I ever be, your 'due.'"

"Envy doesn't suit you, Franco," Andrea said, ignoring Annella and dipping into the risotto. "Perhaps, though, I'll get used to it, once you work for me."

I looked to Radillo, who was equally perplexed. "I think what Constanza is trying to say, Franco," Radillo pushed on, "is that you're a versatile puppeteer, which makes you well suited to lead performances and direct."

Constanza cleared her throat. "Radillo has faith in you." She paused. "But I do not."

Radillo straightened up. "Constanza, we discussed—"

"That was before I learned of Franco's rendezvous with Annella while I was away."

A terrible silence fell. Annella blanched. Our eyes met at last.

Just then, the centerpiece of our meal arrived: enormous swordfish. Massive upturned phallic tails pointed at the center, eyes as wide open as their mouths, gasping for water in stifling night air. Ruffino filleted some, a delicate if gruesome grafting of flesh from bone, unaware of the tension hovering over the table.

"How do I know, you wonder?" Constanza continued after Ruffino left, spearing two pieces of fish and placing one on Annella's plate. "Someone loyal told me."

She nodded at Andrea and my stomach dropped.

He leaned on the table, relishing my panic. "That's right. I saw you," he said to me. "I knew something was up because you were in a hurry to leave the theater, despite Leo and everyone fawning all over you, as usual. So I followed you. I saw you go into the Hotel Lo Squero, and then Annella arrived shortly after." Andrea took a sip of wine. "I came back early the next morning, disguised across the street. You came out together." He mock-toasted me with his wine. "A bold move, I'll give you that. You two couldn't wait for Constanza to go. All over each other when you said goodbye. Shameless."

I felt nauseous. We'd worried so much about someone following Annella, but I'd given us away.

"Annella was a rare gift," Constanza said to me, "in exchange for your loyalty, but you betrayed me."

Radillo touched my arm. "Franco, is this true?"

I couldn't deny it. I had let Radillo down, the Minerva, too, and worst of all, I had put Annella in real danger, given that Constanza was taking her to France. All I could do was try to save Annella, but how?

Constanza faced Annella. "And what do you have to say for yourself, since he's speechless?"

I spoke before Annella could. "Annella didn't want to meet me at the hotel. I forced her. I told her I would go along with you at the theater if she continued to see me." I rushed on, eager to deflect Constanza's rage. "You kept putting us together. I knew Annella despised me."

Annella tried to interject. "Franco, don't—"

I kept talking and focused on Constanza. "I threatened to tell you that Annella had been seeing me for money. So you see, Constanza, she remained loyal to you. I alone did not."

For a moment, everyone was silent. Then Annella stood up quickly. Radillo and I did, too. Annella said, "I'll go."

"You'll do no such thing," Constanza said, her manner disconcertingly soothing.

Annella was as bewildered as I. *Leave with me now*, my eyes pleaded, even as I feared the consequences of that flight.

"I am a fair and reasonable woman," Constanza continued. "I wouldn't dream of letting you go. If he preyed on you before, then think what he'd do if I forced you onto the street tonight." Her seeming concern faded when she alit on me. "I do hope it was worth it, Franco. Because tonight is your last night at the Minerva. You're out."

"Constanza, please!" Radillo shouted.

"You'll do what I've said, Pietro, for the Minerva's sake. Andrea is your new partner. Someone I trust. You and Franco may go now. You two have a show to do and, sadly, must skip this delicious main course."

She snapped her fingers and her guards materialized at the door. One was Arturo, whose stony face betrayed no hint of sympathy.

"Come, Franco," Radillo said. "My appetite is gone."

Constanza paused to slice a bite of the swordfish. "A shame to not sample this local delicacy. Bred in the deepest Adriatic. Expensive beyond measure. How I'll miss this in France."

I gripped the table. It took all my strength not to rush to Annella and pull her to me.

"Do not judge her for my mistakes," I pleaded with Constanza but then wilted at Annella's tearful face. Andrea had risen and was helping—or, more accurately, forcing—Annella to settle back into her seat.

Constanza's eyes were cold. "Don't tell me what to think, Franco.

I'll judge as I see fit. I already have. You'll never grace a stage in Venice again. I shall make sure of that." Constanza gestured to Arturo. "Escort this *gentleman* out."

Her words lodged in my chest like ice.

The guards were yanking me back. The barely eaten swordfish sat at the table. Annella looked at me. "Please go, Franco," she said softly. When Constanza kissed the side of her cheek, Annella closed her eyes, and Andrea dug into the fillet with gusto.

36

"Come, Franco," I dimly heard Radillo saying. He had managed to get us onto a vaporetto at the nearby Salute stop after we shook off the guards. Now we were chugging fast across the Grand Canal, back to the theater.

Radillo. He had given me everything and this was how I'd repaid him.

"Sir, I . . ." I trailed off.

"I'll talk to her when she calms down. The press loves you. I can get you reinstated in time, after she's been in France. Clearly, her pride's wounded."

"I can't let you do that. If you defend me, she will withdraw her support, and the Minerva will close."

The gas lamps at Vallaresso, our stop, were coming into view. I spotted the upturned table at Hotel Monaco, where Carmine and I once shared a beer because I hadn't been able to stop shaking, like now.

Radillo gazed out over the waters. "I had a feeling you'd say that. You're the only one who has ever loved the Minerva like me. That's why I said yes on the day you knocked on my door." He turned to me. "I've never regretted it, either."

"Not even now? After what I've done?"

"What have you done that was so wrong? Loved a girl?" Radillo patted my elbow. "I didn't believe your lie back there. I've seen how you look at her. Whenever she entered the room, you'd grow alert. And I've seen how she looks at you, too. She strove to hide it, and now we see why. Leave them be. Things will be clearer in the morning. Annella will leave her and you two can be together."

I'll judge as I see fit. Constanza's rebuke haunted me. What would she do to Annella tonight, once they were alone? How could I stop her from taking Annella to France? Whatever awaited her there would destroy her, but if I went to Constanza's tonight, the guards at the door would beat me back.

"I do love her," I admitted. "And I've failed her."

"It's not so dire. Be grateful you have this rare and precious thing, Franco." His eyes fell. "A long time ago I loved someone like that, a young woman I worked with, so talented and beautiful. I'm ashamed to admit it was an affair—I was married—but I was ready to give up everything for her. Then out of nowhere, she disappeared. I tried to search for her, but all I knew was her stage name. She never returned. It was as if she had died, and a part of me did, too." He paused. "That was the first in a series of losses. Giannina. Carmine. And now you."

The motor cut as we neared the shore.

"Thank you," I said. "For understanding. For taking me in. For giving me a home. For all that you taught me . . ." I felt my voice catch in my throat.

Tears clouded his blue eyes. "I'll join you tonight. Let's make this last show a good one for you."

My last show. And in front of a crowd of inebriated tourists.

We walked into the theater to see the female dancers already stationed in the boxes on either side, as entertainment before the marionettes, while moneyed elites drank at the cloth-lined tables spread throughout the pit. All eyes were on each other and being seen, and, of course, there was not a child in sight.

As I took in the room, I knew these people would never comprehend the satire of *Pinocchio*, as the pit's display of wit and empathy had revealed to me every prior show.

Bracing myself against the cacophony, I climbed up into the rafters to join Paolo, Eduardo, and Radillo. One look at my face silenced the apprentices. Not even a round of "In the mouth of the wolf" was shared, but we wouldn't have heard it. The entire pit reverberated with talk and the clank of dishes and glasses, which only amplified in volume as we drew closer to curtain. Even when the lights fell and Radillo cued Utku's overture, no one ceased chatting. A glass shattered. Cheers and titters. Utku broke off in response, but the jeers forced him to clumsily restart.

I began my opening narration, my voice scratchy from not having warmed up. No matter what unfolded as we started, no one seemed to notice the marionettes or care. We were like itinerant musicians, propped in a restaurant's corner for ambiance alone.

All I could think of was Constanza hurting Annella. I kept fumbling the strings, by turns shaking and stiff. Radillo took over the shadow puppetry, so that I could stay in one place.

The two hours of performing passed like four. I lost my voice more with every vignette. There was no humor, no warmth, no whimsy.

So it was that by the final scene, when Radillo brought the Fairy with the Turquoise Hair onstage, the noise in my head swarmed. I vaguely heard him say in a reassuring falsetto, "Dear Pinocchio, it is time to receive your dearest wish. Become, at last, a real boy."

He raised the Fairy's wand. It was my cue to bow Pinocchio's head.

But everything felt wrong—myself, the audience, Annella's plight, Marco's absence, Radillo's pain, and, above all, Constanza's complete victory. Here was a story of a puppet and foundling, surrounded by violence, menace, and death. Yet all that violence was mere entertainment for this indifferent crowd, consuming French champagne as if titillated by extreme suffering. This spectacle was a mere interlude in their lives.

But this was my whole life, and it was disintegrating.

I gazed down upon the stage. As if the tip of a wand could solve my Pinocchio's problems. As if that's all it took to become a boy.

"No!" I cried, much too loudly. The word choked in a genuine sob. Onstage, I raised Pinocchio's hands in protest.

The audience went quiet for the first time. They sensed something was wrong.

Radillo looked at me with pity. I fell against the *appoggio* to keep from dropping the marionette. He threw his voice even louder but focused on me, weak at the rail.

"Don't be afraid, Pinocchio. You are so close. Let me help you take this last step to achieving your dream."

"No," I said, staring at Radillo. "My adventures have shown me the ugliness of human beings. They are selfish and greedy, crueler than the villainous fox and cat who left me for dead." Now I really was crying. "Why would I ever want to become one?"

A beat stretched between us before he spoke more softly. "The world may be cruel. But only as a boy might you change it. As a puppet, you have no power. Another holds your strings. Think what you might still do in the world," he added, his voice breaking, too, "if not with me."

With my hands on the holder, I felt nothing pulling in Pinocchio's strings. No feeling for the character, no mystery. Yet I couldn't deny them the happy ending. Nor could I imagine any alternative.

So I gave up. I bowed Pinocchio's head.

Radillo exhaled and raised the Fairy's wand. As its tip made contact, I made Pinocchio dance frantically, full of false frenetic cheer, as Radillo rapidly signaled for the curtain.

Applause during the bows suggested that the audience had not registered much, but up in the rafters, Paolo and Eduardo quietly withdrew, leaving Radillo and me alone.

I stood there, unable to move. I didn't have the heart to lift the Pinocchio marionette up and put it away for the last time. Out there, it was as if nothing had changed from the start to the end of the show, only the patter of the audience a slow fade as they departed.

Radillo stayed beside me, then slowly took the holder from me. I couldn't watch as he raised the Pinocchio marionette himself, winding its strings up and then tucking it away.

"Will you promise me something, sir?" I asked, staring at the sawdust below. "Try to keep the Minerva—the real one—going?"

"I'll try," he whispered.

"Tonight was a caricature. Those tourists will forget us before they get home. But add up all the pit's coins and anise waters, all the times they shout us down and buoy us up? They will make the stage last. They are the real Venice."

He gripped my hand on the rail. "I promise I will make this right, Franco. Somehow."

I couldn't linger, and I hastened down the ladder. Leo reached out, but I tore past him toward the stage doors. Only when I was in the alley did I look back.

It was so quiet that I could hear the waters, dark and glimmering beyond. As I stared at the Minerva for the last time, my heart caved in.

All around me, day after day, Venice's foundations cracked in the endless ebb of those tides. Bridges collapsed. Streets sunk. Theaters crumbled. Sooner or later, water wore everything down.

37

Aimlessly I staggered through the streets, pausing near the Bridge of Sighs—the most beautiful, famous bridge in Venice. Fitting that it was one that only prisoners, not tourists, promenaded over, a torture designed to offer one last glimpse of Venice's golden light, before descending into the bowels of jail.

I started back toward the water, contemplating whether to go to the Grimanis, but it was too late to call on them tonight. Besides, I had nothing but unfounded accusations. I skirted the water's edge, past Riva degli Schiavoni's boarded-up stalls, wincing at memories.

I had failed. I had no power over Constanza now. Without Annella, without the theater, without Marco's evidence, I had nothing.

What price might Constanza's jealousy extract? I hoped Radillo was right, that the best course of action was for me to stay away tonight. Maybe Constanza would cast Annella out in the morning, or maybe I could find a way to get inside her palazzo tomorrow morning, when the guards were not such a presence at the door.

I couldn't go back to my pension, never mind sleep. My life had come full circle, or so it would seem. I was once again deep in the night, stumbling past black canals and somnolent drunks curled in hemp sacks.

Then I remembered the Titian. Maybe a drink could steady me. But when I arrived, I found the lights out and windows shuttered, and there was no answer when I knocked. Frustrated, I shook the door, but it was bolted tight. I slumped back, tripping over some empty bottles that clanged and rolled away.

Then the door creaked open. The bright, uneven light of a shaky lantern flooded out.

"Who's there?" Michaela called.

"It's me—Franco." My voice sounded hoarse from hours in the damp fog.

"Franco? What are you doing here so late?"

She was standing in a blue nightdress and black shawl, and her long coal-dark hair tumbled down her shoulders. Hair like Annella's.

My knees buckled and she rushed to me. "Come." She guided me to the bar inside, then bolted the door. "Sit."

I did as she asked, grateful for the warmth. She poured me a drink. Some colorless, fiery liquid. Grappa, like I'd never tasted before. The slow burn seared my throat, but I liked this pain. It was tangible. I could burn myself from the inside out with that poison—or at least kill time and use its fire to clear my head.

"What happened?" she asked, pouring me another and one for herself.

The whole story spilled out. About Annella and Constanza, Radillo and the Minerva, France and Marco and the glass. It was the truth, or at least the parts of the truth I could share.

"I should have just run away with Annella," I said, "when we could. But I thought I could save her *and* the theater." I stood up too fast. My vision clouded and I thought I might faint. "I never should have risked her life."

Michaela came around the bar and gripped my shoulders. "It

doesn't work that way. You couldn't have known it would all go wrong. You love her." Michaela hesitated. "Love never comes in the form you expect."

She pulled me into an embrace and I gave up. I let her hold me as I started crying. If she let go, I felt I would fall and never stop.

"Come," she said, guiding me up the narrow stairs to a small bedroom above the café. "For now, just sleep." My body sank into her bed. She leaned over to caress my brow, her fingers cool and soft on my forehead, and I began to weep anew.

IN THE MORNING, A shaft of sun struck my eyes. Everything flooded back too fast. I was at Café Titian. Downstairs, I could hear the clank of pots and the hiss of a gas jet lighting. Soon, the aroma of coffee wafted in. I sat up and caught my reflection in the mirror of her dressing table. Dark circles. Smudged and puffy bloodshot eyes. My suit's trousers streaked with mud, and a rumpled shirt. I half expected to see stubble bristling at my chin.

A few minutes later, I heard Michaela trudging upstairs. Soon after, she entered and set a thick bowl in my hands. "Drink."

I inhaled the coffee with its tinge of hazelnut liqueur. Then I began to gulp it. "Thank you."

We sat in silence for a time, just drinking together. Then she said, "You know, you look much better as a boy."

I froze.

She went on. "It's good to see. It's always made me happy, over the past year. You are more yourself, how you came into your own and grew up."

"You know?"

"I notice everything in my café, including that first day you came with your grandfather, the long hair tucked up?"

Ever since the night I had run, I'd lived with a certainty that the only reaction to knowing my history would be disgust and, as my grandfather had warned, death. I should have felt afraid, but Michaela was not threatening me. Quite the opposite.

"B-but . . . you've always helped me," I stammered.

"Of course," she said, a little indignant. "Why do you think I gave you all those extra biscotti on difficult days, or a splash of hazelnut liqueur when you were in low spirits? I know that you've had a much harder path than everyone, all alone." She smiled. "Biscotti helps."

"I don't know what to say. Thank you."

"There's nothing to thank me for." She sipped her coffee. "Now, what will you do?"

"I don't know. See if I can get Annella? Leave Venice?" I looked over at her. "Where are you from?"

"Everywhere." Michaela smiled. "Most recently before here? Morocco, but every street became too full of memories. I needed to get out—that's why I came to Venice."

"Does it get better, somewhere else?"

"Yes and no. In a city without memories, forgetting can be your friend. But memories are like ghosts. They come at you when you want them least, then fade when you seek them out. Where might you go?"

"Maybe Milan? Carmine's there."

"Oh, that reminds me," she said. "Something came from him late yesterday." She went downstairs and returned a few minutes later, holding a package tied in twine.

I took it, but the writing was not Carmine's. As I unwrapped the package, a jumble of papers fell out. I leafed through several renderings stamped CONFIDENTIAL. One detailed an intricate, colorful chandelier, complete with measurements—and on stationery with the name and address of the Grimanis' factory in Murano, their seal broken. Handwritten notes, some in French, dotted the margins, with one statement underlined: "Tristano's addition to comprise the full."

The writing was in Constanza's hand. A perfect match to her party's invitation.

On another paper, I found a separate note from Constanza that left my hands shaking:

> *Dear Tristano: My girls delivered the last piece and we have all we need to commence our factory's production in the new year as planned. I have not forgotten my promise to you of a gift. Once we are out of Venice safely, you shall have it. To confirm, we shall meet at the private dock by the theater on Sunday, December 6, after the Festa di San Nicola gala. Then we will head out on the evening train to Marseille via Milan.*

On the bottom, I found Marco's hasty scrawl. He had mailed these papers weeks ago, but they must have been misdelivered.

> *Here you are. Proof. Constanza made me her lowly messenger, so I intercepted this note to Tristano and pilfered the renderings from her private desk here in Marseille. This should be enough for the Grimanis to act. But don't let Annella get on that train. She is the gift that Constanza plans to give Tristano for his loyalty. As for me, I'm taking advantage of his absence to find Paola at last.*
>
> *Yours,*
> *M*

That was why Annella was being taken to Marseille. That was why Constanza wouldn't kick her out last night. Constanza was handing Annella to Tristano. Another gift. Payment for services rendered.

I trembled in rage at Constanza's lies, at how she'd worked everything out, punishing Annella far worse than me.

Except she hadn't counted on, or paid attention to, Marco. He'd done it. Found proof. Or I hoped it would be enough to prove to the Grimanis how dangerous Constanza was, and that she had been using them to smuggle Murano's glassmaking formulas to France.

My pulse was quickening. With Annella's fate now dire, I had to get her out. Now.

"Michaela," I said, rubbing my forehead. "I need your help."

I shoved the papers back in the package except for one document, which I ripped in two, pocketing the bottom with the seal. I scribbled a hasty note to the Grimanis, explaining that the apprenticeships were a lie and asking them for their help today, then gave it to Michaela with Marco's documents.

"If I'm not back by ten," I told her, "take this to the Grimanis. They'll know what to do. Make them stop Constanza at the theater this afternoon, and tell Annella not to get on that train. But be careful—Constanza has friends among the police."

"Franco," Michaela said, holding the papers. "I can't just go to the Grimanis' door!"

"You can with this." I fumbled in my suit pocket and handed her the card Lord Grimani had given me. I'd taken to carrying it with me, so I could go there anytime. "Tell them I sent you. It's urgent."

"And what about you? Where are you going?"

I rushed to the door but paused. "I'm going to save Annella."

38

My plan to blackmail and double-cross Constanza was risky. She could order her guards to take me down, but I trusted that she would exchange Annella for the documents at today's show. With luck, I could free Annella, and the Grimanis could stop Constanza before she left tonight.

After a brief stop at my pension to retrieve my grandfather's knife, I rushed to San Polo. I emerged from the narrow alley that Annella and I had traversed many a Thursday, expecting to see the courtyard empty—and, I hoped, free of guards—as it was still early. Today, however, I found someone much worse—Tristano, smoking casually near the entrance.

I took a breath. "I'm here to see Constanza."

He looked me up and down. "And you are?"

"Franco Collegario, from the Minerva."

Tristano laughed. "The puppeteer? You're bold to show, though it seems you've saved me a trip to your grubby pension in San Moisè." He tossed his cigarette and took a step toward me.

I brandished my knife. "Don't come any closer."

He raised his hands in mock surrender. "Fighting an unarmed man? There's no honor in youth today."

"I don't want to fight you. Just tell Constanza I am here. Tell her I know about your plans for the Murano glass—and I'll go to the Grimanis unless she gives me what I want."

"The Grimanis? You're a foundling from the ghetto. You're nobody. You think they'll listen to you?"

"I have proof." I waved the torn document and the seal caught his eye. "The rest is in safekeeping until today's show—if she wants those papers back."

His eyes narrowed. "And what do you want?"

"Annella. I'll hand over the documents at today's gala for her."

Tristano said nothing, only reached in his jacket. In horror, I watched him withdraw Annella's locket. He casually opened it and fondled my grandmother's wedding ring.

Any words I might have spoken caught and died in my throat.

"Nice, isn't it?" He snapped the ring back in the locket and put it in his suit. "But not as nice as these." He then withdrew the emerald earrings Annella had worn last night. He dangled them in front of me. "A souvenir."

Now I staggered closer. "Did you touch her?"

"No, but Constanza did, and not very nicely. I saw the girl's body myself. Her friend, the blonde, carrying on . . . . It's a pity, but Constanza has promised me another reward."

Her body? I swayed.

A noise swarmed in my head as Tristano circled me. "You have nothing to bargain for. That girl was a Sapphist and whore, a foundling and a Jew. Now she's just rotting in the sea."

I didn't think. I lunged at him.

Rage gave me speed and force and caught him off guard. Without thinking, I slashed his cheek and left shoulder. Blood spread instantly through his suit.

But he recovered, landing a blow near my eye so hard that it knocked the knife out of my hand and I fell on my back.

Tristano straddled me. The heady scent of his cologne caught in my nose as he wrapped his hands around my throat. I tried to grab the knife, but its handle was just out of reach.

"Constanza sent me to kill you," he said, tightening his grip. "So here we are. Too bad your girl died. I'd have let her live—and paid dearly for her. I had such plans for her in France, but now you can join her instead."

I felt all air slipping out of me. My eyes fell back in my head from the searing pain. Then, I heard an eerie frail voice, like mist: "Leave him, or I'll curse you!"

Startled, Tristano wavered. He looked toward the sound—and away from where the knife lay. His grip loosened just enough so I could stretch that extra inch. Without a second thought, I clasped the handle and stabbed him in the chest, aiming for his heart.

He pitched forward in a gasp and collapsed atop me.

I scrambled from underneath him, wrenching the knife out with shaking hands. I roughly shoved him onto his back and reached into his suit.

"This is mine," I said, yanking Annella's stolen locket out. "Tell Constanza to come for me at the theater this afternoon, or I'll talk." I stood up and tossed the slip of paper with the Grimanis' seal near him. "If you live."

Tristano gripped my ankle. "You missed the heart," he sputtered. "Kill me, like a man. I know a killer when I see one."

I stared at him, felt the knife in my hand. Fat, wet snowflakes were drifting down—a rarity in Venice. Now was my chance. But then someone kicked Tristano's hand away and started pulling me back. A familiar voice came gentle at my ear.

"Don't, schoolboy."

"Carmine?" I whispered. He spun me around. Those familiar curls. Kind hazel eyes.

"Are you all right?" he asked.

I felt my bruised throat. "That was you?"

"New technique for macabre shows," he said, taking in Tristano, who'd curled in on himself. "We need to leave. Now."

I spotted a curtain's rustle in Constanza's palazzo. "I know a shortcut."

We sprinted around the back wall toward an open dock, where a gondolier was resting. We hurried across the freshly fallen dust of snow into his boat, and just as we pushed off, I heard men's voices arriving in the square. Our boat quickly became indistinguishable from the wider parade of them migrating into the Grand Canal, readying for the elaborate procession for San Nicola that would take place near Murano in the late afternoon.

My heart began to slow. I noticed Carmine's shirt. "I'm getting blood all over you."

"Just like our first day," Carmine said, dabbing my cheek with his sleeve. "Some things never change."

"At least we're on the same side now. How did you find me?"

Carmine explained that he and Giannina had arrived late yesterday and were staying with a friend of hers in San Marco while she got her courage up to face Radillo today. "I went looking for you at your pension and then the Titian this morning. That's where Michaela told me about your plan. I rushed to help." He chuckled to himself. "Franco, I leave Venice and you rise to the top of the Minerva, knife a mafioso, and steal Annella's heart? What a flair for drama you've developed!"

But I didn't laugh. Hearing her name felt like being struck again.

"What is it?" he asked, sobering.

"Annella. She's dead." Everything went cold in me, saying it aloud.

Her green eyes. The light in them, gone. Like her parents, lost in the sea. Lost to me. Forever.

"Not Annella," Carmine said, shielding his eyes. "Oh, Franco, I'm sorry." He looked at me, full of pity. "I read between the lines of your letters. I know you really loved her."

Loved. Past. Done. I felt nauseous. The horror sunk in, knowing I only had memories of her now. Annella at the hotel. *Maybe there's hope for us.*

I leaned over the edge of the boat and trailed a hand in its icy waters. Maybe I could just fall in. But Carmine must have sensed it and drew me back, steadying me.

"Did that mafioso kill her? Is that why . . ."

"No." I gazed at the boat's floor, melting dirty snow at my boots. "Constanza did."

My purpose disappeared, like a moon's light evaporates behind black clouds. "You should have just let him kill me," I whispered.

"No," Carmine said. "They will pay. You've seen to that with this plan. The Grimanis will ensure they're arrested and tried for the glass."

"But not for Annella's murder. You know as well as I do that no one cares about people like her, or us. That man back there—Tristano? He destroyed girls like Annella every day." I held my head in my hands. "The wicked have power, Carmine. The rest of us are just *fra Marco e Todaro*, caught in the middle, with no good choices. Nothing will bring her back. Cowards like him and Constanza are never punished."

"One punishes cowards by refusing to die. That's what Annella would want. Living on is far braver."

I felt the bloody knife shoved in my pocket. "I don't need to be brave anymore. I only need to punish Constanza. You heard him. You saw me. Maybe I am a killer."

"No!" Carmine grabbed me roughly. "Do not let a man like that decide who you are!"

"But if it were Giannina, would you not act?" I cried. "Would you do nothing? Constanza killed Annella!"

"That's why you mustn't become a killer. Annella deserves justice, not revenge. The Grimanis are the most powerful family in Venice. *They* will get justice, and not only for Annella, but for others who are still alive. Franco, for once, you are not *fra Marco e Todaro*." He softened. "You can't bring her back, but you can change everything, for the others. Annella would want that. She wouldn't want you to throw your life away for her."

I felt the snow mingle with the tears on my face, the wind's sting. I still couldn't breathe, but dimly, Carmine's words flitted in. *You can change everything. Annella would want that.*

"Be brave, Franco," Carmine said. "Don't give up. You're so close."

"But it's my fault that she's dead." Hoarse sobs made me choke. "It's all my fault."

"Oh, schoolboy, it's not your fault." Carmine clung to me as I crumpled, and he kept murmuring, "I'm here. I'll help you. We'll do this together."

39

Hours later, I had cloaked myself in an alley beside the Minerva as children, parents, and clergy chaperoning foundlings made their way to the theater for Constanza's special free gala of *Pinocchio*. I stayed hidden in the shadows like Marco had, but I was waiting for the sponsor herself. Would she come? Did she get Tristano's message? Or had I become a killer after all?

At last, Constanza arrived. I almost expected to see Annella at her side, so grief flooded me anew. *Not now, not yet*, I thought, steeling my resolve. Later, I could let myself feel everything, but I forced myself to focus.

Constanza had come with her requisite two guards. Arturo, who'd often assisted Annella, was not among them. Perhaps it was just my wish, but she seemed agitated. Neither her gaze nor gait were as steady. When she greeted the De Rossis, she looked past them, clearly distracted.

By now, whether Tristano had lived or died, she would know that I had evidence of her scheme. Maybe she had only come out of duty, keeping up appearances, but as long as I remained alive, she was in danger of exposure. She would want to find me.

The Grimanis were a few paces behind her, ahead of some

dockworkers. I scanned the workers closely, noting the red-and-green scarves knotted at their necks. That was the signal. These were the Grimanis' trustworthy members of the Guardia di Finanza, disguised to avoid detection and ready to apprehend Constanza—but only after I'd extracted a confession and she'd taken the documents, claiming they were her own.

This morning when I had presented my case to the Grimanis, they had believed me. My story and the papers that Marco had sent helped to explain an earlier mysterious incident at their factory. An apprentice had been tasked with returning these renderings to the vault, and they thought she had but now saw they'd been swapped. Still, the police needed to connect Constanza to the theft directly, by the papers' transfer. Lord Grimani assured me that I could trust his men, and so, through the fog of my rage and grief, we devised our plan. Yet I kept my knife in hand now, to use if the Grimanis' men failed.

I stole inside, just as the two-minute-warning lights flickered, and blended in with the crowd of foundlings, workers, and families. With Marco's now-tattered old jacket on for luck, I kept my shoulders hunched and cap pulled low to join a faceless throng in the pit's crowded lobby. Here, a wall of sound struck me, men's talk amplified and oiled by drink. All around me were raucous oyster sellers, fishmongers, gondoliers, shoeblacks, and dockworkers, real and disguised. The shuffle and snap of ladies' fans formed a percussive beat against children's giddy screams and the crunching of peanut shells and toothpicks underfoot. Anise water and roasted nuts, sweat and perfume, beer and cigars, the loam of seawater and scarves damp from the day's light snow—a mélange of scents wafted into the theater as I found my old back row.

I enjoyed seeing the ineffectual dinner theater format dismantled. The Minerva had been restored to its original state for this special matinee, and it was a full house, the kind I would have loved to perform for, and the kind Annella would have loved to be a part of.

My apprentice's perch had a clear view of Constanza in her box, where she now sat vigilant with her two guards. It was why I'd been able to see Annella that very first night. I kept my cap low, but Constanza's attention stayed locked on the Grimanis, directly across from her.

Then I spotted Carmine and Giannina with Radillo, a good sign that they were sharing the beginnings of a reconciliation. While I was happy for them, I couldn't help but grieve that my chance at a reunion was gone. I swallowed the lump in my throat and glared up at Constanza, patting the knife. Radillo had no idea of the Grimanis' and my plan, for his own safety. I knew he'd be performing or in the boxes, but either way, he would not be in the pit.

Then the lights faded, the curtain parted, and Andrea spoke the lines that I alone had enunciated for the past month. "Once upon a time in our beautiful country of Italy . . ."

PINOCCHIO BREEZED ALONG. WE had agreed to act after intermission to lull Constanza into a false sense of security. So midway through the second half, I switched to stand beneath the Grimanis' box. Here, two disguised Guardia di Finanza men also stood, ready to eavesdrop and intercept her.

Onstage, Andrea lowered Mangiafuoco, who cowered over the petite marionettes. Around me, children squealed in delight. Then the shadow play of Pinocchio with the cat and fox started, and with the brighter lighting reflected onto the pit, I knew Constanza would be able to see me. I just needed to get her attention.

"Bad wheat makes poor bread, friends," I called out in Italian, loud enough that my voice sailed above the fray of children's concerns for Pinocchio's welfare.

Constanza's head swiveled to the pit. Our eyes locked. I saw her whisper to her guards, who swiftly departed. Then she turned back to me with a thin smile.

Only, the two thugs never burst into the pit, thanks to the Grimanis' guards stationed as ushers at the door. Above me, I watched Constanza tap her program nervously on the banister. That's when I beckoned her down.

Moments later, she appeared in the pit, jostling past a mother who cursed her for pushing her young daughter aside.

Constanza joined me. "I thought I forbade you from returning here, Franco."

"What can I say? I'm not that obedient. How do you like the pit's view?"

Her eyes did not leave mine. "It leaves something to be desired. Tristano lives, but barely. You should hope he survives, or they'll hang you. I'll have you arrested."

"Are you sure you want me talking to the police? He acted on your orders, after all, to kill me." Now I smiled. "Or he tried to."

Her confidence faded. "He told me you've been spreading rumors."

"They aren't rumors if they're true," I replied. "Once, you told me that women were commodities to be bought and traded. I know about your 'apprentices' in the Grimanis' Murano glass factory. You used your work with the foundlings as a cover and planted girls to get you the glass formula."

"Don't be ridiculous," she said. Behind me, I felt one of the disguised dockworkers jostle closer. Utku's piano playing had increased in volume for the wordless shadow play scenes.

"If it's ridiculous, then why would I have detailed sketches of a Murano glass chandelier?" I patted my jacket. "They have notes written in your hand on them. And a letter of yours to Tristano, saying you have the full formula and are planning to start production?"

Her eyes widened. I had her. She knew it. Maybe I could get her to confess to more than the glass.

"How did you get those?" she asked.

"You're not the only one who can bribe people to do your bidding. You've made a lot of enemies. One gave me these documents for free."

"What do you want in exchange? Your job back? Money? Escape from the gallows, if Tristano dies?"

I let the silence stand, as Annella's voice hovered in my memory. *Constanza is always one step ahead.* Staring Constanza down, I thought: *If you're one step ahead, then you know I have nothing to lose.*

"I would have given you everything for Annella," I said. "But she's dead. And it's your fault."

Constanza winced. "That girl betrayed me. I rescued her from Goldoni's Alley. Gave her the best clothes, jewels, holidays—everything. But she threw that all away for you." She narrowed her eyes. "I read Annella's nature when I first saw her. Yet she fell in love with you, a man? Hard to imagine, after the hell men put her through."

"Not just men put her through hell."

Constanza shrugged. "You may have fooled everyone else, Franco, but I know who you really are. I think part of me knew that first night. Your skin—too smooth for any real man's."

She dared to rest a hand on my cheek, and I swatted it away. "Men and women come in many forms. You ought to know that by now."

Two governesses nearby shushed us. I saw that onstage, Pinocchio hung half dead from the tree. Amid muffled tears, the fox's and cat's laughter in Eduardo's voice rang too shrill. Andrea had forgotten or omitted the darkness and blurred the two scenes.

"You're the fool," I went on. "Annella only pretended with you to survive."

"Don't underestimate the importance of survival," she replied. "Annella could have had everything with me. I understood and loved her more."

I gripped her elbow. "You're incapable of love. You imagine it is a battle to be won. Forcing someone in line to obey for your own ends? For money?"

"Ask any woman. Money keeps you safe."

"But that's not love. Annella loved me as I did her. You took her from me, but know this." I wrenched her near. "You never had her."

She was close to my face. "I should have killed you myself—like I did Annella."

I caught a vein throb in her temple. Constanza and I stared at each other with unmitigated hostility. It was our first and only truly honest exchange.

Behind me, I knew the Guardia di Finanza had heard her, for they fell still. Onstage, the tumult of the great mechanical whale ensued.

"Give me the documents," Constanza said, shaking her arm loose from my grip, "and I won't throw you to the wolves for trying to kill Tristano. I'll even make sure Radillo takes you back."

"Fine." I reached into my jacket to withdraw the papers. "These are yours?" I asked, raising my voice for the benefit of the men behind me.

"Of course they're mine," she snapped, grabbing and scanning them.

"There's just one more thing," I said. "Did you really think I'd hand these to you without first showing them to the Grimanis?"

"They wouldn't believe you." But her face faltered when she looked up at the Grimanis and found them watching us, not the action onstage. She faced me again. "Without my money, your beloved theater will crumble. Are you so selfish that you'd sacrifice Radillo's dream? He's right there."

She jutted her chin to the door. Radillo was making his way through the crowd. He must have seen us.

"What would you know of sacrifice, Constanza? It's over."

Behind me, the two dockworkers whistled, signaling the others.

They all began to move in, provoking ripples through the pit. Confusion flickered in Constanza's eyes at their garb.

But then the theater plunged into blinding darkness. Andrea had truncated the scene with the whale and cut the lights too early.

When they flared again, I saw that Constanza had retreated but couldn't pass because of a crowd of foundlings up front. The dockworkers, momentarily confused, spotted her. Utku's swirling scales were quieting, just as Constanza withdrew a gun from her cloak and leveled it at me, her hand shaking.

"Constanza, no!" I shouted. "The children—"

Then I felt myself fall hard to the floor as gunshots rang out, deafening. A blur of motion and panic unfurled. Houselights sprang on and people rushed to the exits with frightened children. But all was quiet except for a vast ringing in my ears. I expected blood but felt nothing, only an ache in my arm from where I'd landed.

Everything slowed. I struggled to sit up. Onstage, I glimpsed the forlorn skeleton of the whale in the wings, marionettes dropped in haste. The pit was nearly empty but for a handful of men who now restrained Constanza. She was clutching her hand, which was bleeding, and her gun lay a few feet away, as a dockworker retrieved it.

Then Giannina's scream broke through.

I turned. Radillo lay on the floor behind me. His eyes were fixed in quizzical shock, all the spark in the blue gone. His legs had caught in an awkward angle from the fall. Blood seeped through his starched white shirt, around the reading glasses perpetually tucked in his vest.

I moaned. Not Radillo. Not like this.

He must have pushed me out of the bullets' path to save my life. I crawled closer and reached for his hand, still warm but now lifeless. I felt the same calluses as those roughening my own fingers and bent over him, heartbroken that the hand I was holding would never infuse life on a stage again.

Giannina fell at his side, and I backed away. Gently, she wiped a trace of blood from his lips and closed his eyes. Carmine sheltered her as he had me earlier, and his eyes met mine. I recalled the three of them in the box before the show. They had just begun again.

It all hurt too much. I stumbled to my feet and lurched out of the theater.

Outside, I landed in a throng of people who'd gathered from the rapidly spreading news of the scandal inside. I doubled over, unable to stop the tears, gesturing away those who tried to aid me.

Then, the Festa di San Nicola's first fireworks burst in the sky. I stared up at the arcing kaleidoscope of fiery colors, like those I'd once enjoyed from Annella's room on our first magical night. Now, the thud of each explosion reverberated low in my aching chest. Everyone on the street around me also fell strangely silent, all of us unnerved at this opulent display, unfolding amid what tragedy had just taken place in the Minerva.

Above us, too much beautiful light, undulating and disappearing. I watched as the last threads descended into thin, shimmering trails and the evening edged toward night's deep indigo, quiet and littered with smoke.

40

"Eat something," Michaela said, nudging the brioche along the counter. "I baked them myself." Carmine went to reach for one, but she lightly slapped his wrist. "You've had two already. I meant Franco."

"Thank you." I forced a bite and then a few more.

Carmine exchanged a look with Michaela. "Eat another, Franco, or I will steal that, too."

Seeing Carmine's bloodshot eyes, I complied. He had been up all night comforting Giannina, who was now resting with her mother this morning. Out of habit, or perhaps for some semblance of the ordinary, Carmine and I had wandered down to the Titian for a cup.

"How is she this morning?" I asked him quietly.

"A little better. She regrets how long they spent apart, but at least they were able to reconcile. He had even promised her a spot in the rafters."

So Radillo had come around in the end.

"The only reason he was against women up there," Carmine added, "was because of an old heartbreak—some affair he had with an actress at the Malibran just before Giannina was born. Apparently, the actress was a great beauty."

I sat up. Radillo's affair. He had not mentioned that it was with an actress at the Malibran. *A great beauty*—how Marco had described my mother, Sofia.

"How do you know this?" I asked.

"Giannina's aunt told us the story when we first arrived in Milan," Carmine said, sampling another pastry. "I think she was trying to make her niece feel better about running away with me. It's no secret that her parents' marriage is a loveless one." He paused. "*Was* loveless. That's why they only had Giannina, I guess—no other children."

"What happened?"

"The actress disappeared. Giannina's aunt suspects that Esmeralda threatened her. Shortly after, Esmeralda gave Radillo the money to purchase the Minerva, a decision I'm sure she regretted later. Anyway, according to his sister, Radillo never truly got over this actress—hence, his rule about barring women in the theater."

"When was this?"

"Almost twenty years ago? Giannina was born less than a year later, around the same time as you."

My thoughts swirled. The timing matched. The theater matched. The "great beauty" matched. I knew Radillo had started fashioning eight-stringed marionettes while at the Malibran—where my mother had been an actress and had begun to puppeteer herself—but I had never considered that she might be the one with whom he'd had that affair.

"What is it, Franco?" Carmine asked, eyeing me with worry.

I cleared my throat. "Just thinking how everything comes full circle. I imagine Giannina and you will run the theater now—if you can find the means. Esmeralda certainly won't want it."

"We'll see what Radillo put in his will." He lay some coins on the counter, enough for my bill and his own. "I should check on her. Want to come back?"

"I need some time to walk and think."

"Don't brood too much." He patted my back as we parted. "Come back for lunch."

I began wandering over to Riva degli Schiavoni for some distraction from the tangle of unanswered questions in my head. How heavy my heart grew, strolling this familiar stretch. Everything looked the same as it had days ago but felt impoverished and gray after the loss of two people whom I'd loved.

I'd never know if Radillo was my real father, but I glimpsed clues in the moments we'd shared. How quickly his warmth had shaded into melancholy when he'd caught me with the *contadino: Your style reminds me of someone, but I can't quite place who*. He and I were of a similar height and build, similar wavy hair, though I had my mother's dark eyes. I remembered how in the rafters, he and I shared qualities harder to trace than gestures or features. A restless curiosity. A passion for how to evoke life through our affinity for the strings. A love for the theater's mercurial mysteries.

A sliver of hope wended its way past my sorrow. Perhaps, in time, I'd find a way to make Annella and Radillo proud. But not today, not when everything was too fresh and sharp. Not when the memory of their faces pierced me with pain, unrelentingly.

When I arrived at the stalls, only a few shows of folktales were starting. To my surprise, I saw a glove puppet version of my very own Pinocchio. These puppeteers decided that their Pinocchio was more of a Pulcinella, teaching the fox and cat a lesson with fists, not docile obedience. Still, I felt grateful for the irreverent homage.

Two deep, mournful blasts of a horn signaled that the tourist boat from Burano had docked, emptying a mere handful of island locals and picking up three times as many day tourists seeking lace. I watched the ferry lumber off, its engines soon fading, replaced by shrill peddlers selling their wares. Of the passengers gathering their belongings, one woman left the dock with no luggage, her face concealed under a widow's veil and cloak. But there was something in her lightness as she scurried through the stalls that made me stop.

What a fool I was. Wishing. The mind plays such heartless tricks. Cruel hope, only delusion.

I knew better but couldn't help watching the widow as she moved along the street. Then she stopped near me, the two of us in front of the now-raucous and crowded *Pinocchio* show.

I felt the air shift. It could not be. Yet when she tore off her veil and dropped it in the mud, I gasped.

Before me, Annella. Alive. Far more vivid and exquisite than I had allowed myself to remember. I could not move or think or speak. Her emerald dress was tarnished and torn beneath the cloak. Her face, like mine, bruised from a fight. That made my heart ache, even as it also soared, because here she was, not just a figment of my phantom longings. Alive. Or was I dreaming?

"Is it really you?" I managed to ask. "Or are you a ghost?"

Then she rushed forward to kiss me, and I knew. The taste of her made me want to sob. I felt her touch my face, and this time, neither of us let go. Having her in my arms brought back all that had unspooled away from me. We were back in the alley of that first impulsive kiss where we began and the imprint of love was already in its ease, in its sense of a world without limit or hindrance or end, of that ineffable *more*.

Yet here in the widening sun, this kiss was entirely new, too. Because for the first time, we did not worry at all about being seen. No more cloaking ourselves in alleys or stolen hours in hotels. No more avoiding each other's eyes in crowded rooms. No more pretending, no labyrinths of secrets.

The freedom, the exquisite bliss in that one kiss. It was as extraordinary as it was simple—to kiss without fear in the open air.

I pulled back to run my hands through her hair. Her beautiful, luscious hair, tangled in my hands again. "They said you were dead . . ."

She touched my cheek as if touch could prove what our minds still doubted. "I would have been if not for Rossana and Arturo. They got me out. But when I read what happened in the morning papers with Constanza, I had to find you. I disguised myself as a widow—because nobody looks past the black lace."

I took in her words. "But how? Tristano said he saw your body."

"He did. Constanza came at me hard in a jealous rage once we were alone. I tried to fight back, but I was no match, and I passed out from the pain. Rossana and Arturo heard the fight, and when Constanza went to get Tristano from the salon, they found me out cold, my pulse weak. They made the plan to fake my death—or so they hoped it would be fake. When Constanza and Tristano returned, Rossana put on quite the show, wailing and claiming I was dead, covering my body with hers to hide that I was still breathing. I almost wish I could have seen it. She'd even put ice on my hands so I felt cold. Constanza then let Arturo take me away himself, mostly to shut a hysterical Rossana up. He spirited me to a midwife in Burano, who nursed me." Annella winced and felt her throat. "I'm so sorry—I lost your grandmother's ring."

"Don't be." I reached in my jacket and withdrew the locket "This belongs to you."

Tenderly she took it, cradling it in her hand. "Oh, Franco. I never thought I'd see these again. Thank you."

From the stalls, the *Pinocchio* players called to us. "Toss your coins in our cap, you two lovers. We'll make your gold grow in the Field of Miracles. You'll be rich in minutes!"

Annella smiled. "Do you know this story?"

"Never heard of it," I said, dropping a few coins in the cap before drawing her close once more. I took the locket back and opened it, then slipped the ring on her finger.

As I helped her fasten the locket around her neck, I pressed my forehead to hers. "No more hiding, Annella. No more fear. No more separation. Never again."

And then we kissed in the sun, unwilling to let go and too enchanted to stop.

EPILOGUE

May 1897

I was in Restoration, mending Carlita, the latest addition to the Minerva collection, when Annella found me.

"I remember her," Annella said, setting her suitcase down. "She was your grandfather's, the one we practiced with."

"I wondered if you'd recognize her. I was just fixing her eyebrow string." I took the holder and lifted Carlita up on the table. "Carlita, meet Annella, your first audience member." I extended Carlita's hand to Annella in greeting.

"Pleased to meet you, Carlita."

"She'll be perfect for the preambles," I said, passing the holder to Annella.

"Oh yes, I feel a kinship with this saucy girl." She began to maneuver the marionette in a sassy dance that ended in an off-kilter arabesque.

"How much more artful you are now," I said. "It's as if I were the one watching you across the way when we were young. She seems so real in your hands."

"Well, I trained with the best, a real 'man to watch,' apparently. I'm glad you're next to me now, not across the street."

"Close enough to touch." I traced a finger over the calluses of her hand, lingering on her ring.

"We'll have plenty of time for that on our holiday in Vernazza," she said, handing Carlita to me. "Let's stop by the Titian to say good-bye to Rossana before we catch the train."

With Constanza gone, Rossana was free of the rats of Venice and Michaela had taken her under her wing as a barmaid at the Titian.

"I'll meet you there shortly," I said. "Leave your bag. I'll bring it."

After Annella left, I sat Carlita back in her new perch with the rest of the collection, then wandered out to the Minerva's stage with mine and Annella's slim suitcases. Before me swept a dim expanse of clean floors and empty boxes. No gas lamps blazed. The din of San Marco hung in the distance. I stared toward the doors, which were propped open to usher in the first hint of summer.

It did not seem as large a room as when I'd first arrived. This modest enclosure had given the impression of a much wider, three-dimensional world. Here was a stage on which many had fought, laughed, flirted, danced, sung, and died.

How many times had I made wood supple since I dropped Facanapa down? Old and young, male and female, from many origins and nations and motives—they had all faced this view. Standing here rather than above, I felt Radillo's presence, along with centuries of people and performers, all suspended with me.

"Shouldn't you be on a train?" Carmine said, joining me onstage.

"Trying to get rid of me?"

"I'd never do that, 'sir.'"

Since finding out that Radillo put my name, along with Giannina's, on the Minerva's title, Carmine had stopped calling me school-boy. I would never know the truth about Radillo and Sofia—the only person who could confirm it was Esmeralda, and I wasn't going to ask someone with whom I still had such frosty relations.

But when I learned of the will, part of me wondered: Had Radillo known my mother was pregnant? Had he suspected that I was her child and possibly his? Perhaps, like me, Radillo sensed we'd shared something that went beyond mentor and apprentice.

I had offered to sign over my rights to Giannina, but she'd insisted I stay. "You belong here, too," she'd said. "We all do." Together, we'd secured the Grimanis' support to resolve the debts from Constanza's days. They were eager to come on board when we told them of a new summer program to train foundlings and orphans in puppetry and stage design.

I turned to Carmine. "I was just thinking how pleasant it is ever since Andrea and Niccolò moved to Milan and took over the Gerolamo."

Carmine beamed. "Far from us and close to his beloved Constanza's cozy cell in San Vittore." He paused. "Strange how Tristano survived, only to die later at his own men's hands, all before Constanza's trial. Guess they were afraid of what he might say. Her days are numbered, too."

I nodded grimly, but then Leo waved to us from the wings. "We'd never manage without him," I added.

"Definitely not." Then Carmine gestured to the Pinocchio marionette peeking out of a trunk. His glossy striped suit was clean, but some paint had chipped off one of his lapis lazuli eyes. "This one's popular with our new apprentices. Who would have thought: foundlings training foundlings?"

"He may have a longer life than our show, I suspect."

Carmine laughed. "My friend Fabrizio from Florence has plans for an experimental version with live actors. He'll be visiting in August. An intellectual. I can just hear him now." Carmine flung his arms wide. "A puppet being cooked for dinner! Masses of workers rallying to save him! Dark and terrible forces against our tiny wooden hero! It is a most excellent Marxist tale of the people rising up against their oppressors. It stirs solidarity, indeed."

I laughed. Then I remembered the Venetian *contadino*, its original strings of horsehair taut, and the holder's T-bar riddled with nicks and grooves. One of my grandfather's favorite expressions came to mind. *The more strings, the greater the nuance, but also, the more difficult to manage.*

"Find us some treasures from Radillo's collection while I'm gone," I told Carmine. "The more garish, the better. Kids love a good villain."

"Who doesn't?" Carmine replied. "Giannina has some ready. You just enjoy your overdue honeymoon in Cinque Terre." He picked up the cases at my feet. "I'll bring these out front."

Once more I stood alone. The voices of the Minerva's gracious and gritty stage were humming. The more I listened, the softer they fell in the empty pit. They, like me, were curious who might land on this sawdust next.

Annella was just finishing her coffee when I reached Café Titian. As we readied to depart, Rossana stepped out from behind the bar and embraced me.

"Enjoy the sun, you lovebirds," she said. "You think by now you'd at least be bickering more like an old married couple."

"We'll try." I gave her a jaunty bow. "My dear Rossana, I will always be grateful to you for protecting Annella. For being there when I couldn't."

"Well, you can't do everything by yourself, Franco. Bon voyage," she said with a playful shove, moving away to shush a table of rowdy men.

Michaela pressed a package of biscotti, panini, and fruit she'd wrapped in parchment into my hands. "Food on the trains is terrible."

I tucked the package in my satchel. "I will miss your coffee."

"It's only a month. You'll live."

I leaned close. "Anything in the mail?"

"Not yet," she said, "but I'll keep an eye out."

I hadn't heard from Marco but hoped he'd found his beloved Paola. He no longer had to worry about Tristano or Sandro. A month ago, I'd strolled over to Sant'Alvise and learned that Sandro had lost our childhood home and landed in a poorhouse.

"Thank you," I said, taking Michaela's hands. "For the extra biscotti last year, and so much more."

"No need to thank me," she replied. "Now, what is it you people say before a show? 'Into the wolf'?"

"In the mouth of the wolf."

"What do you say back?"

"Death to the wolf."

"That makes no sense," she said, the music of it a gift that echoed as Annella and I left.

We joined the great sea departing Venice as tourists ourselves this morning. A circuitous journey awaited. Our modern transportation system did not believe in linear, simple passages. Italian conductors preferred routes not entirely mapped in advance and rife with meandering delays. We would arrive when it worked out to arrive—nothing so restrictive as adhering to a schedule, not for us.

The train was as crowded as the Minerva on a full night. All around us, people spoke languages we could not understand as Annella and I strained to see past Santa Croce's edge.

"How strange it still feels," she said, once we had settled in our velvet seats, "to simply sit with you. To not worry about being seen or where we go."

"It takes time and practice to become, as you once said, 'an ordinary pair of lovers,'" I replied.

"Then that will be time well spent." Annella smoothed her new dress, a vibrant tangerine. "Who knows what else we might do, or where else we might 'practice' together? Perhaps even your namesake in America one day, San Francisco. Can you imagine?"

"With you, I can imagine anything."

Then the train sprang to life. Its engine rumbled and burst in a hiss while plumes of smoke and steam billowed into the air. The first screech of wheels sounded unlike any machine I'd heard before. I recalled the Parisian locomotive's silent arrival on the Minerva's stretched white cloth the night of the Lumière brothers' photographic projections. From inside the train now, however, the whistle blared so loudly it shook the compartment. We lurched in the first belabored push, the wheels energetic with mechanistic intent.

Annella rested her head on my shoulder as I gazed out our window to look back. For my whole life, I had remained in one place, often on the same brick and coal-stained streets. Now, I watched in awe as I saw my city emerge and enlarge, faded by the sheen of fog. Its breadth and beauty came into view as we advanced.

All of Venice's tight alleys disappeared, vistas growing pale orange from an endless salty spray. Annella and I, too, were casting off our past into the Adriatic, bright with boats in the sun. We were venturing into new worlds, this time by choice and desire, not by force of tragedy, betrayal, circumstance, or fear. As much as we sought the reprieve of a holiday, we had our own home to return to, on the Minerva's flourishing stage.

Venice grew grander than I had ever imagined as the last slip of the city merged with and then dipped behind the curtain of the horizon. The train found its pace as we sailed through the floating world of a languid lagoon. Out here, green water met bright skies, broken only by gulls soaring and diving. The windows were flung open and a breeze filled the train, gathering around Annella and me, together and alone at last.

Annella and Carmine. Radillo and my mother. My dear grand-father and Marco. Michaela, with her biscotti. Francesca, the girl I left behind and within. These were the eight strings guiding my life. My dear grandfather was right—with eight strings, you do indeed have a soul.

A NOTE TO READERS

The idea for *Eight Strings* began twelve years ago when I took a writing course with Marnie Woodrow. In "Fact into Fiction," she gave me short story prompts involving historical research to spark character studies. As a historian and educator, I'd always sought out those voices whom history forgot or denied, preferring history's absences over its more prominent faces; "Fact into Fiction" seemed a perfect way to imagine how ordinary people navigated history's big, world-changing moments on a human scale.

Knowing my love of Venice and marionettes, Marnie suggested a prompt based on the Venetian puppeteer Pietro Radillo. My first search result led to this brief Wikipedia entry:

> *Pietro Radillo (1820–1895), the Venetian puppeteer, made significant innovations in the marionette arts. Expanding upon the traditional rod and two strings for control of marionettes, Radillo's puppets worked with up to eight strings, significantly improving the control over the individual body parts.*

Those two sentences piqued my curiosity. I started to research. Soon I found an image of Radillo's Venetian *contadino*, housed at the

Detroit Institute of Arts. But everywhere else, only the same scant bio of Radillo appeared.

As much as history can generate a presence, it can also create absences. Radillo contributed significantly to puppetry, a global art form spanning centuries and cultures. While *Eight Strings* focuses on Italian—especially Venetian—puppetry, artifacts of early puppets have been found in ancient Egyptian, Chinese, Indian, and Greek cultures, and places as distinct as Indonesia, Mexico, Japan, Brazil, Thailand, Argentina, Korea, and many more. Each has developed their own unique traditions and techniques. Radillo's move to employ eight-stringed marionettes, with all their intricacy and effects, seems like a worthy achievement to record with more than two sentences and one marionette.

History has many silences, in part because there is no uniform answer to the question of who *makes* history, both who makes the cut to be documented and who makes (up) the account. *What really happened?* we ask of the past, but the answers are often contradictory, plural, and uncertain. History can hold people to account, or it can make them disappear. Historical fiction, on the other hand, can conjure people, real and imagined, ordinary and extraordinary, from forgotten scenes of history, which is what I sought to do for Pietro Radillo.

So, I started *Eight Strings* as a short story about his life. Yet as I wrote, an entirely fictional person stepped out of the wings: a teenage tomboy fleeing her family to become a puppeteer. Radillo came into view more through Francesca's eyes, and my short story morphed into a novel about that tomboy, running in terror in the night, transforming into the confident, charming, artist-puppeteer Franco.

Typically, stories that feature a woman passing as a man suggest it is a duplicitous masquerade born of circumstances—the *Mulan* or *Yentl* effect. The heroine often chafes at wearing trousers and suits. She is usually a loner, ill at ease among men, with few friends. Any chance at romance gets played for laughs or tragically doomed, and if she manages to survive, the requisite "happy ending" has her cast off her disguise to return to her "true" feminine self.

As a queer lesbian who's spent twenty-five years in communities with masculine-identified butches, non-binary people, and trans men, this narrative didn't reflect the worlds I knew. Not all stories of gender-crossing end tragically. A majority do not return to femininity and are much happier as a result. What of the pleasures of becoming *more*, not less, masculine on the road to self-acceptance? What about discovering the joys of suits, swaggering, short hair, and seduction after one's early-in-life female body and attire didn't fit—or were truly unbearable? Re-embracing one's femininity would be the painful lie, not an authentic truth or a "happy" end.

I wanted to write a different story of changing genders. Franco may be forced by circumstances into male attire at the start, but that leads to a more, not less authentic masculine self. His self-discovery and bodily changes are transformative and enlivening, and his journey is full of grit and verve and pleasure, not steeped in melancholic regret for a lost feminine identity. Becoming more masculine deepens Franco's empathy with women, too, by allowing him to recognize the violent effects on them when rigid gender norms are enforced. While Franco moves forward to a more self-defined future in the novel, he also recasts and gains insight into his past. The adoptive surname of "Collegario," means "to bind or connect," which plays out on several levels in the book.

I'm sometimes asked who Franco "really" is, in terms of her, his, or their identity. Unlike Anne Lister in the TV miniseries *Gentleman Jack*, who is an upper-class butch in 1830s Yorkshire with family wealth and property—and thus protected as she crosses certain boundaries more openly—Franco couldn't really be "out." But today, would Franco transition to living as a man? Adopt the singular *they* as a pronoun and identify as non-binary? Keep female pronouns as a butch lesbian? Some combination of the above, or something altogether different?

All these possibilities derive from our more contemporary un-
derstandings of gender and sexuality, which weren't exactly available in nineteenth-century Venice. Lesbian, queer, and transgender
historians have done brilliant work reframing the past to show how
the "we" of queer subjectivities and desires have been here all along,
but I prefer to leave the door open to my readers to imagine for
themselves how they see Franco's journey unfolding in the afterlife
of this book.

As for Annella, she is an homage to a character named Annella de
Rosa in the book *Artemisia*, written by the Italian writer Lucia Lopresti
under the pseudonym "Anna Banti" in 1947. (This is also why I didn't
use the more typical Southern Italian spelling of *Anella*.) *Artemisia* is
a hybrid of a novel, autofiction, memoir, and biographical account of
the real-life female Renaissance painter Artemisia Gentileschi, who,
in the book, helps Annella de Rosa, a tempestuous beauty and talented young painter seeking refuge from her violent husband. In various passages, it's implied that Artemisia harbors a romantic love for
Annella. Alas, Annella dies tragically at age thirty, a victim of implied
domestic abuse.

It is not easy as a queer woman to spend a lifetime reading and
watching stories in which lesbians suffer and die. If we're allowed
to live by a story's end, then those stories tend to make sure we hate
ourselves along the way. So, with my Annella, I consciously gave her
a rebirth: she survives an attack to experience a reciprocated love, but
her survival is not simply for Franco's benefit—she becomes a working artist herself. This decision was my nod to the Italian female artists from previous eras, like Lucia Lopresti and Artemisia Gentileschi;
it was also my response to the recent rallying cry of "unbury your
gays," which exists because we've been buried all too often—and
sadly, still are.

In the United States today, I see a frightening level of support for
book bans of queer authors' work, defunding and censoring libraries,

even actual book burnings—just as we need these queer voices and stories more, not less. Queer people, especially transgender youth, are statistically more vulnerable to family rejection, trauma, rape, suicide, and murder.

Against this backdrop, I wrote *Eight Strings* to recognize a particular exploration of queer possibility and "complex personhood," a phrase coined by the brilliant critical race theorist Patricia Williams. For me and many others, "being" queer isn't just about suffering, shame, or self-loathing. It is also joyful and playful. We laugh too loud and stand out. We throw shade and fight back. We get hurt and get back up. We reinvent kinship when we're cast out. We create lives, communities, and protests that are noisy, brash, multiracial, multigendered, sexy, smart, and fun. *Eight Strings* is very much Franco and Annella's shared and complementary tale, a butch-femme friendship that blossoms into lust and deepens into love. Despite living in a world intent on their self-negation, this queer couple lives happily ever after and on their own terms, something my communities do time and again, with a defiant sense of delight.

Queer people aren't the only subjects neglected by history: the working-class community, from which my own family hails, has also largely been ignored. I grew up in blue-collar Rust Belt Michigan, and I watched as people's livelihoods disappeared when automotive plants downsized, then closed, which led to recessions, and, in 2008, substantial home foreclosures and evictions. As incomes dropped and crime rose, my hometown's population went from 91,000 in the 1970s to 44,000 in 2020. For those who live in the Rust Belt, this was a moment of painful historic change, but when I went to university (the first of my family to do so), I didn't see the experiences of my community of autoworkers, electricians, waitresses, secretaries, cleaners, and others—everyday people whom I knew and loved— reflected much in sustained historical and academic inquiry.

This was also why it was important to me to depict the working-class audience of "the pit," who echoed my hometown family and friends. Venetian locals—speaking more in dialect, not aristocratic Italian—were workers who crowded sections of the theaters to be with one another as much as to watch the shows, and to enjoy their creative comebacks, biting interplay, and camaraderie inside the theater.

A novel needs its readers to fully bring it to life. So, too, are marionettes brought to life by their audiences, and not simply by performers or patrons, like the real-life Grimani family. Poorer Italians do appear as theater participants in accounts such as Charles Dickens', written during his travels in Italy during the 1840s, but they are often misread as too easily duped and not attentive (read: silent) enough. Yet there is the pleasure of knowing disbelief and talking back, too, which a former editor of *The Atlantic*, William Dean Howells, understood when he narrated his visits to Venetian theaters in 1866. He offered a contrasting account of working-class audiences as a vital part of the theatrical experience, spectators whose wit and wisdom about the "frank admission of unreality" in theatrical display, especially of marionettes, only added to the pleasure of attending.

This is part of why I cast Franco in alliance with them, first as a spectator and then as a performer, enlivened by their insights, laughter, catcalls, and interactions. To be caught up in a scene upon a stage is not to be duped; it is the essence of what theater offers, to carry people away in the emotions it deliberately elicits.

DESPITE THE SILENCES SURROUNDING Radillo, one thing was apparent: Venice was a vibrant center for marionettes from as early as the 1400s to the early 1900s. Even today, one can still find marionettes hanging in San Marco's shop windows.

The Minerva was indeed a real theater in Venice, and active on and off from the 1600s into the early twentieth century. For most of its life, though, it was better known as the San Moisè Theater, a respected (if petite) opera house where Italian greats such as Verdi, Albinoni, and Vivaldi played. In 1871, it was refurbished for marionettes and shortly after renamed the Minerva. While I found no evidence that Radillo ran the real Minerva Theater, the timing of renovations, coupled with Venice's centrality for marionette culture, suggest that he could have, or in my opinion, *should* have been involved in this era. To honor that—and widen his mark beyond that too-short bio—I gave him full ownership of the theater itself and its artistic vision in *Eight Strings*.

I also took a small chronological liberty by extending Radillo's life an extra year so he could help usher in the auspicious 1896 visit by the Lumière brothers. The Minerva really was the site of Venice's first cinematic projection when these French inventors toured Italy and much of Europe that year to showcase, not sell, their magical new projection device. As it happened, the Minerva Theater would span the transition from nineteenth-century live theater to the main mass art form of the twentieth century—film—when it became one of Venice's first movie theaters in the early 1900s. Today, however, the Minerva exists only as a tiny commemorative plaque, for the theater was demolished and converted into a block of apartments.

The Minerva was one of many theaters in Venice at this time. La Fenice, Venice's grandest, remains open today despite a history of multiple fires, closures, and truly damaging restoration attempts over the centuries. So does the Malibran, which presents symphony orchestras and finer concert fare. It likely won't have its stage shut for indecency now, but I like reminding readers that places, just like people, can change.

In Venice and across Italy, puppet shows adapted stories from folktales, myths, paintings, operas, stage plays, literature, poetry, visual arts, and, later, music-hall vaudeville, covering the gamut of human comedy, pathos, tragedy, and thrills. Puppetry held wide appeal in nineteenth-century Italy; performances were generally not confined to any one group, age, or class, and they took place nearly anywhere, from theater stages to street corners to private, wealthy salons. John McCormick, Alfonso Cipolla, and Alessandro Napoli's comprehensive *The Italian Puppet Theater: A History* opened my eyes to the breadth and range of the art form, and even included a seventeenth-century drawing of the Minerva's interior.

Italy was key to puppetry's development, and in the novel, Franco's grandfather describes how marionette shows took place in Italy with less fear of censorship than live theater. By contrast, in the same era in Mexico, Spanish colonizers found the performances of Indigenous puppetry so subversive that they banned the art form outright— even as clandestine shows kept them alive. This schism reveals how puppetry can morph from frivolous, light entertainment into politically subversive storytelling. Perhaps that's because the figure of the puppet illustrates what it means to be vulnerable and thus, paradoxically, human. We like to imagine we act of our own free will, but systems pull our strings. We exist as individuals *in* history, but are also subject *to* history. A "puppet government," after all, leaves its citizens dangling like flimsy marionettes, forced to obey—or else.

Today, puppetry mostly appears in North America in the genre of horror or on children's television. Though very different, both genres traffic in vulnerability. In horror stories, puppets are inanimate objects that gain violent sentience to reveal human frailty. The puppets on *Sesame Street*, meanwhile, help the very young grasp what they don't yet understand. Certainly, my own experience as a child watching warmhearted, fuzzy, felt creatures on television sparked my fascination with puppetry. This programming taught me and generations of children about life's complexities, from tying shoes to managing feelings. By setting *Eight Strings* on the cusp of the twentieth century, however, I could show some of puppetry's longer and more varied history beyond our contemporary understanding of the form's limits.

At the time in which *Eight Strings* is set, Italy had only been a nation for thirty years. Regionalisms, dialects, and stark divisions persisted, particularly in Venice where the late Industrial Revolution contributed to the city's swelling poverty, immigration, and tourism—which foreign photographers, fascinated by Venice, captured, and which can be viewed in Dorothea Ritter's rich *Venice in Old Photographs, 1841–1920*. The crisis of orphans and foundlings, and the broader trafficking of them into European factories, was not fictional, and for girls, this often led to sexual violence, exploitation, and prostitution abroad. The scale of these problems was bad enough that by the early 1900s, Italy enacted a series of laws to combat the trafficking of its youth. In *Italy in the Age of Pinocchio*, historian Carl Ipsen shows how the pre-Disney Pinocchio figure in Carlo Collodi's original story was not just a stand-in for disobedient Italian youth. Ipsen tracks how the figure also evoked the real-world vulnerability of poorer Italian children in this era and the violent, not imaginary, dangers they encountered.

The presence of prostitution in Venice, despite an ongoing ban across centuries, is also a mix of fiction and history. The city repeatedly grappled with prohibiting prostitution, which contributed to its image as a scene of decadence. In the 1400s, the infamous and crudely named Ponte delle Tette in San Polo drew its slang because sex workers could legally display their breasts at night from the windows facing this bridge. The authorities argued that the mere sight of a woman's breasts would reorient male homosexual desire—another perceived social problem at that time: too many gay men. That begs the question of what an acceptable number would have been. Then, in the 1600s, the Carampane District, also in San Polo, was designated to cordon off older sex workers to a specific zone. *Carampane* is less-than-generous slang to describe an aging beauty past her prime, a term that could have described Venice itself, a once-powerful republic in decline.

To capture a whisper of this history—which is its own kind of theater, really—I invented a fictional red-light district of Goldoni's Alley, naming it after the city's most revered playwright. I was also inspired to place Constanza's own palazzo in geographical proximity to the historical "landmarks" of Ponte delle Tette and the Carampane District, with an ironic nod to the surname Cappello, given that Bianca Cappello was known in the sixteenth century as Venice's "Honest Courtesan." (Take a stroll from Calle Bianca Cappello to those other landmarks, and you'll pass Palazzo Albrizzi, my stand-in for Constanza's home.)

If Venice spoke of male homosexuality as a social problem, the same cannot be said of female homosexuality, perhaps because it was unimaginable that women could be sexual outside of contact with men. Yet the figure of the "cross-dressed" masculine woman does make a few appearances in Venetian lore. One I mention in the novel: the plot of Verdi's *Rigoletto*, in which Rigoletto's daughter Gilda dresses as a man solely for safe passage. (Spoiler: it's not so safe; she dies by an assassin's sword.) Casanova describes another instance in his memoirs. During his time in Venice, he had an extended affair with a nun, and one night, he waited for her at Campo Santi Giovanni e Paolo. Yet when he saw a gondola dock, only a man emerged. Casanova worried that he was about to be forced into a duel, but soon saw it was his beloved nun, disguised as a man—again, purely to travel safely. These vignettes make me wonder if Franco's story may be less unusual and modern as it seems at first glance.

In 2007, long before I began writing *Eight Strings*, I visited Venice. One morning, I rose before sunrise to walk to Piazza San Marco. Only the street sweepers and a few locals were out. The infamous Piazza San Marco, typically filled with throngs of people from around the world, was at that hour so quiet I could hear only church bells, coco brooms on stone, and a symphony of pigeons. (Later I handed a version of that hushed, blue hour to Franco.)

In that moment, I glimpsed how contemporary Venice—not unlike its fin de siècle past—exists for its dwindling population of locals more complexly than for wealthy foreign tourists. When later I edited this novel, during the pandemic, I was transfixed by a Venice no longer inundated with hulking, intrusive cruise ships. There was something poignant to me about returning to the cusp of the twentieth century in *Eight Strings*, and to the relatively small, intimate stage of the Minerva, a single theater that had navigated its own historical moments of change several centuries over, but did not survive long into the 1900s. For better and worse, much of the world depicted in *Eight Strings* has disappeared. The edifices of buildings may remain, but most of the city's people have migrated away, and, by their absences, transformed what was left behind. *Eight Strings* is my way of capturing Venice and its voices—onstage and off—in this particular moment before they vanished.

GLOSSARY

appoggio – the bar or rail on which a marionettist leans when operating
   puppets

bacaro – a bar

Bauta – a Carnival mask, typically worn by upper classes

biscotti – cookies, usually for dipping in coffee

Borsalino – a brand of luxury hats that are typically worn by men

calle – a street

campanile – a bell tower

campiello – a small public square

campo – a public square

Carabinieri – a military branch of Italian police

Carnevale – Venetian Carnival, typically held prior to Lent; it was
   outlawed in 1797 but gradually began to reappear in different forms
   during the nineteenth century, and then officially began to be celebrated more regularly in the later twentieth century

castagnasso – Venetian chestnut fritters

cicchetti – small snacks or side dishes, often eaten at a *bacaro*

cinquecento – the style and ethos of the period of fifteenth-century arts
   and culture, in late-Renaissance Italy

contadino – a peasant or farmer from the Veneto region of Italy

felze – the cabin of a gondola, to shelter those it is transporting; began
    disappearing from use in the late 1880s

festa – a festival

fondamenta – the bank along a canal for pedestrians

giardinetti – gardens

Guardia di Finanza – law enforcement for financial crime and smuggling

La Serenissima – Most Serene, a title bestowed on Venice when it was
    a republic in the seventeenth century, and a name that has become
    synonymous with the city ever since

mafioso – a member of the mafia

palazzo – a palace, a mansion

pension – a boardinghouse, guest house

piazza – a public square (in Venice, the only square referred to as *piazza*
    is Piazza San Marco)

pivetta – a throat whistle, to signal scene changes in an open-air show

ponte – a bridge

Pulcinella – a dualistic commedia dell'arte character who can be from
    the upper or lower classes, who acts as an everyman to sort out
    others' affairs; evolved (or devolved) into the more violent British
    puppet character of Punch in "Punch and Judy"

rio – a small canal

sarde in saor – Venetian dish of sardines fried and marinated in onions

sotoportego – an alley or passageway underneath a building

squero – a boatyard where gondolas are repaired and restored

teatro – a theater

traghetto – a gondola with two pilots; a receptacle for crossing the
    Grand Canal while standing

trattorie – bistros

vaporetto – a public ferry

villeggiatura – a residence or villa in the country, used to escape city heat
    in summer holidays especially

SOURCES

The following is a list of works I consulted as I wrote *Eight Strings*. These writers and historians provided inspiration and helped me create my beloved Franco, Annella, and the vibrant, multifaceted world of "complex personhood" that was late-nineteenth-century Venice.

BOOKS

Banti, Anna. *Artemisia.* Translated by Shirley D'Ardia Caracciolo. Lincoln, NB: University of Nebraska Press, 1988.

Blumenthal, Eileen. *Puppetry: A World History.* New York, NY: Harry N. Abrams, 2005.

Boccaccio, Giovanni. *The Decameron.* Translated by Mark Musa and Peter Bondanella. New York, NY: Penguin, 1982.

Castle, Terry. *The Apparitional Lesbian.* New York, NY: Columbia University Press, 1993.

Cestaro, Gary P., ed. *Queer Italia: Same-Sex Desire in Italian Literature and Film.* New York, NY: Palgrave Macmillan, 2004.

Coad, Luman. *Marionette Sourcebook: Theory & Technique.* North Vancouver, BC: Charlemagne Press, 2007.

Collodi, Carlo. *The Adventures of Pinocchio.* Translated by Geoffrey Brock. New York, NY: New York Review of Books Classics, 2009.

Crane, Thomas Frederick. *Italian Popular Tales.* Edited by Jack Zipes. New York, NY: Oxford University Press, 2003.

Currell, David. *Making and Manipulating Marionettes.* Wiltshire, UK: The Crowood Press, 2004.

Dickens, Charles. *The Complete Works of Charles Dickens: Pictures from Italy and American Notes.* New York, NY: Cosimo Classics, 2009.

Fanelli, Giovanni, Marc Walter, and Sabine Arqué, eds. *Italy around 1900: A Portrait in Color.* Köln, Germany: Taschen GmbH, 2018.

Farrell, Joseph, and Paolo Puppa. *A History of Italian Theatre.* Cambridge, UK: Cambridge University Press, 2006.

Gross, Kenneth. *Puppet: An Essay on Uncanny Life.* Chicago, IL: University of Chicago Press, 2011.

Gross, Kenneth, ed. *On Dolls.* London, UK: Notting Hill Editions, 2018.

Howells, William Dean. *Venetian Life.* Chicago, IL: Northwestern University Press, 2001.

Ipsen, Carl. *Italy in the Age of Pinocchio: Children and Danger in the Liberal Era.* New York, NY: Palgrave Macmillan, 2006.

Jonglez, Thomas, and Paola Zoffoli. *Secret Venice.* Versailles, France: Jonglez Publishing, 2018.

Jurkowski, Henryk, and Penny Francis. *A History of European Puppetry: From Its Origins to the End of the 19th Century.* Lewiston, ME: Edwin Mellen Press Ltd., 1996.

Kennard, Joseph Spencer. *Masks and Marionettes.* Port Washington, NY: Kennikat Press, 1967.

Kirkham, Victoria, Michael Sherberg, and Janet Levarie Smarr, eds. *Boccaccio: A Critical Guide to the Complete Works.* Chicago, IL: University of Chicago Press, 2014.

Madden, Thomas F. *Venice: A New History.* New York, NY: Penguin Books, 2013.

Manion, Jen. *Female Husbands: A Trans History.* Cambridge, UK: Cambridge University Press, 2020.

Marrone, Gaetana, and Paolo Puppa, eds. *Encyclopedia of Italian Literary Studies.* New York, NY: Routledge, 2006.

McCormick, John, Alfonso Cipolla, and Alessandro Napoli. *The Italian Puppet Theater: A History.* Jefferson, NC: McFarland Publishing, 2010.

Sources

McCormick, John, and Bennie Pratasik. *Popular Puppet Theatre in Europe, 1800–1914*. Cambridge, UK: Cambridge University Press, 2005.

Mello, Alissa, Claudia Orenstein, and Cariad Astles. *Women and Puppetry: Critical and Historical Investigations*. London, UK: Routledge, 2019.

Nelson, Victoria. *The Secret Life of Puppets*. Cambridge, MA: Harvard University Press, 2002.

Norwich, John Julius. *Paradise of Cities: Venice in the 19th Century*. New York, NY: Vintage Books, 2004.

Pacchioni, Federico. *The Image of the Puppet in Italian Theater, Literature and Film*. New York, NY: Palgrave Macmillan, 2022.

Pistone, Danièle. *Nineteenth-Century Italian Opera: From Rossini to Puccini*. Translated E. Thomas Glasow. Portland, OR: Amadeus Press, 1995.

Plant, Margaret. *Venice, Fragile City, 1797–1997*. New Haven, CT: Yale University Press, 2002.

Posner, Dassia N., John Bell, and Claudia Orenstein, eds. *The Routledge Companion to Puppetry and Material Performance*. New York, NY: Routledge, 2015.

Riall, Lucy. *Risorgimento: The History of Italy from Napoleon to Nation-state*. Basingstoke, UK: Palgrave Macmillan, 2009.

Ritter, Dorothea. *Venice in Old Photographs: 1870–1920*. Toronto, ON: Bulfinch, 1994.

Schechter, Joel, ed. *Popular Theatre: A Sourcebook*. London, UK: Routledge, 2003.

Segel, Harold B. *Pinocchio's Progeny: Puppets, Marionettes, Automatons, and Robots in Modernist and Avant-garde Drama*. Baltimore, MD: Johns Hopkins University Press, 1995.

Shemek, Deanna. *Ladies Errant: Wayward Women and Social Order in Early Modern Italy*. Durham, NC: Duke University Press, 1998.

Shakespeare, William. *The Tragedy of Romeo and Juliet*. Edited by J. A. Bryant, Jr. New York, NY: Signet Classics, 1964.

Sherberg, Michael, ed. *Approaches to Teaching Collodi's* Pinocchio *and*

Adaptations. New York, NY: Modern Language Association of
America, 2006.

Smarr, Janet Levarie, and Daria Valentini, eds. *Italian Women and the City: Essays*. Madison, NJ: Fairleigh Dickinson University Press, 2003.

Stewart-Steinberg, Suzanne. *The Pinocchio Effect: On Making Italians, 1860–1920*. Chicago, IL: University of Chicago Press, 2007.

Waters, Sarah. *Tipping the Velvet*. London, UK: Virago, 2006.

Winterson, Jeanette. *The Passion*. New York, NY: Vintage, 1987.

ARTICLES

"The Decameron Project." *New York Times Magazine,* July 7, 2020, https://www.nytimes.com/interactive/2020/07/07/magazine/decameron-project-short-story-collection.html.

Edwards, Geoffrey. "Strangeness and Fantasy: Notes on Nineteenth-Century Venetian Glass at the National Gallery of Victoria." *Art Journal 37*, June 12, 2014, https://www.ngv.vic.gov.au/essay/strangeness-and-fantasy-notes-on-nineteenth-century-venetian-glass-at-the-national-gallery-of-victori.

"History of Murano Glass." The Glass of Venice, accessed March 13, 2022, https://www.glassofvenice.com/murano_glass_history.php.

"Venice and Its Lagoons." Venice the Future, accessed August 14, 2022, http://www.venicethefuture.com/uk/home.htm.

Webb, Sam. "Sinking City." *The Sun*, March 15, 2017, https://www.thesun.co.uk/news/3095970/venice-19th-century-colour-pictures.

Worrall, Simon. "The Centuries-Old History of Venice's Jewish Ghetto." *The Smithsonian Journeys Travel Quarterly*, November 6, 2015, https://www.smithsonianmag.com/travel/venice-ghetto-jews-italy-anniversary-shaul-bassi-180956867.

ACKNOWLEDGMENTS

This novel would not be in the world without a wide network of support. I'm especially grateful that crucial early stages of it were made possible by the Ontario Arts Council Writers' Works in Progress Grant and the Toronto Arts Council's Literary Grants for Mid-Career Writers. I greatly value living in a place that offers writers this financial support to dream up new work.

Eight Strings began when I worked with the talented writer and editor Marnie Woodrow. By that one short story prompt, she inspired so much more. The novel also owes a special debt to the generous Andrew David MacDonald. I set it aside for years to take care of my mother, who had Alzheimer's and Parkinson's diseases. After she died, Andrew suggested—well, demanded—that I pull *Eight Strings* out of the drawer. I'm so grateful that I did.

My two agents, first Grace Ross and now Markus Hoffmann, both went to bat for this book, and me, in many ways. Grace, a gifted editor, prompted exploratory conversations that made me invest in my own capacity to write and revise. Many of the ideas from those conversations are woven into this book, and the book was made better for it. When she left agenting, Grace gave me another gift—an introduction to Markus Hoffmann, who has been a stellar agent, editor, conversationalist, and all-around Renaissance man whose wise advice I always trust. I thank the team at my agency, Regal Hoffmann & Associates, for how they champion writers so meaningfully. I'm thrilled they're in my corner.

Simon & Schuster is a writer's dream to publish with, most of all because of my profoundly gifted editor, Sarah St. Pierre. At every step, her dedication and vision enriched this novel, from our first phone call on. Her insights opened this book up while sustaining its essence and voice—no small editorial feat. If I could, I'd shower her with many curtain calls and giant, colorful bouquets in thanks.

Also at Simon & Schuster, a big thank-you to my dedicated marketing and promotion team of Cayley Pimentel, Melanie Pedersen, and Cindy Ly. Special thanks to Arden Hagedorn, whose in-house "sneak peek" event generated such a warm and engaging conversation. On the production side, I'm grateful to Jasmine Elliott, Zoe Kaplan, Morgan Hart, Kristin Nappier, and Andrea Monagle, as well as Paul Barker, who designed the atmospheric map. Thank you, Jessica Boudreau, for creating the gorgeous cover of my dreams. It evoked the feeling of the novel so beautifully, and without a single gondola. Brava.

I have been fortunate to have an abundance of great readers and writers who have contributed to this book. My original writing group of now fourteen years are simply the best: Linda Rui Feng, Meghan Davidson Ladly, Franca Pelaccia, Keith Rombough, and Diane Terrana. I've also shared work, check-ins, writing sprints, and pet photos with a wonderful circle of writers who, in addition to Andrew above, includes Mel Carroll, Seth Dresbold, Julia Kramer, Adam Marston, JoAnna Novak, Erin Pienaar, and Ryan Shea. Additional dear friends who provided insights and valuable moral support at various stages include James Beaton, Camila Bonifaz, Geraldine Cahill, Lily Cho, Dianne Davis, Lisa Dey, Lisa Fitzgibbons, Emily Gagne, Michelle Johnson, Melinda Mainland, Mary Newberry, Justin

Paulson, Michelle Ramsay, Arielle Ricketts, Patti Ristich, Kaavya Roddick, Aviva Rubin, Sonya Suraci, Glyn Taylor, and Jill Tinmouth. *Mille grazie* to my brilliant Italian editor and historical accuracy consultant, Michelle Tarnopolsky.

I wouldn't be writing at all if not for the lifelong love and steadfast encouragement of my late mother, Carol DeRosia, who gave me books in the crib because I seemed to like them. Thank you also to my big, geographically scattered family. Arthur and Margaret DeRosia, my musical grandparents, gifted me with creativity, courage, and humor. Margarete Raab and Jerry Willing, my mother's closest friends and my surrogate parents, have been inspiring me for decades on how to live life well. My cousins in Michigan have always known how to make me laugh, even when things get hard. In Toronto, my family of in-laws root for me and make every party more fun. Finally, as a queer person, my friends *are* my family, too. Thank you all for gracing my history with an abundance of love.

Finally, this book is dedicated to my wife, Tracey Dey. An astute reader, you're so patient with all the imaginary people and dilemmas that invade my head and our home. You're kind and smart, creative and funny, romantic and practical, and, in sum, a perpetual delight whom I'm grateful beyond measure to know and love. Thank you.